Elisha Kent Kane

Arctic Explorations in Search of Sir John Franklin

Elisha Kent Kane

Arctic Explorations in Search of Sir John Franklin

ISBN/EAN: 9783337327729

Printed in Europe, USA, Canada, Australia, Japan

Cover: Foto ©Andreas Hilbeck / pixelio.de

More available books at **www.hansebooks.com**

ARCTIC EXPLORATIONS

IN SEARCH OF

SIR JOHN FRANKLIN.

BY

ELISHA KENT KANE, M.D.,
U. S. N.

LONDON:

T. NELSON AND SONS, PATERNOSTER ROW;

EDINBURGH; AND NEW YORK.

1877.

PREFACE.

HIS book is not a record of scientific investigations. While engaged, under the orders of the Navy Department, in arranging and elaborating the results of the late Expedition to the Arctic Seas, I have availed myself of the permission of the Secretary to connect together the passages of my journal that could have interest for the general reader, and to publish them as a narrative of the adventures of my party. I have attempted very little else.

The Engravings with which the work is illustrated will add greatly to any value the text may possess. Although largely, and in some instances exclusively, indebted for their interest to the skill of the artist, they are, with scarcely an exception, from sketches made on the spot.

E. K. K.

CONTENTS.

CHAPTER I.

Organization—Equipment—St. John's—Baffin's Bay—Sounding........................... 11

CHAPTER II.

Fiskernaes—The Fishery—Mr. Lassen—Hans Cristian—Lichtenfels—Sukkertoppen ... 15

CHAPTER III.

Coast of Greenland—Swarte-huk—Last Danish Outposts—Melville Bay—In the Ice—
Bears—Bergs—Anchor to a berg—Midnight Sunshine 20

CHAPTER IV.

Boring the Floes—Successful Passage through Melville Bay—Ice-navigation—Passage
of the Middle Pack—The North Water.. 25

CHAPTER V.

Crimson Cliffs of Beverley—Hakluyt and Northumberland—Red Snow—The Gates of
Smith's Straits—Cape Alexander—Cape Hatherton—Farewell Cairn—Life-boat
Depôt—Esquimaux Ruins found—Graves—Flagstaff Point............................... 28

CHAPTER VI.

Closing with the Ice—Refuge Harbour—Dogs—Walrus—Narwhal—Ice-hills—Beacon-
cairn—Anchored to a Berg—Esquimaux Huts—Peter Force Bay—Cape Cornelius
Grinnell—Shallows—A Gale—The Recreant Dogs....................................... 33

CHAPTER VII.

The *Eric* on a Berg—Godsend Ledge—Holding on—Adrift—Scudding—Towed by a
Berg—Under the Cliffs—Nippings—Aground—Ice-pressure—At Rest................. 40

CHAPTER VIII.

Tracking—Inspecting a Harbour—The Musk-ox—Still Tracking—Consultation—
Warping Again—Aground near the Ice-foot—A Breathing-spell—The Boat-expe-
dition—Departure 46

CHAPTER IX.

The Depôt journey—The Ice-belt—Crossing Minturn River—Skeleton Musk-ox—
Crossing the Glacier—Portage of Instruments—Excessive Burden—Mary Minturn
River—Fording the River—Thackeray Headland—Cape George Russell—Return to
the Brig—The Winter Harbour 54

CHAPTER X.

Approaching Winter—Storing Provisions—Butler Storehouse—Sunday at Rest—
Building Observatory—Training the Dogs—The *Little Willie*—The *Road*—The *Faith*
—Sledging—Reconnoissance—Depôt-party 61

CHAPTER XI.

The Observatory—Thermometers—The Rats—The Brig on Fire—Ancient Sledge-tracks—Esquimaux Huts—Hydrophobia—Sledge-driving—Musk-ox Tracks — A Sledge-party.. 69

CHAPTER XII.

Leaping a Chasm—The Ice-belt—Cape William Wood—Camp on the Floes—Return of Depôt-party—Bonsall's Adventure—Results—An Escape—The Third Cache—M'Gary Island.. 75

CHAPTER XIII.

Walrus-holes—Advance of Darkness—Darkness—The Cold—" The Ice-blink "—Fox-chase—Esquimaux Huts—Occultation of Saturn—Portrait of Old Grim............... 82

CHAPTER XIV.

Magnetic Observatory—Temperatures—Returning Light—Darkness and the Dogs—Hydrophobia—Ice-changes—The Ice-foot—The Ice-belt—The Sunlight—March... 89

CHAPTER XV.

Arctic Observations—Travel to Observatory—Its Hazards—Arctic Life—The Day—The Diet—The Amusements—The Labours—The Temperature—The " Eis-fod "—The Ice-belt—The Ice-belt encroaching—Expedition preparing—Good-bye—A Surprise—A Second Good-bye.. 97

CHAPTER XVI.

Preparation—Temperatures—Adventure—An Alarm—Party on the Floes—Rescue-party—Lost on the Floes—Party found—Return—Freezing—Returning Camp—A Bivouac—Exhausted—Escape—Consequences 107

CHAPTER XVII.

Baker's Death—A Visit—The Esquimaux—A Negotiation—Their Equipment—Their Deportment—A Treaty—The Farewell—The Sequel—Myouk—His Escape—Schubert's Illness... 118

CHAPTER XVIII.

An Exploration — Equipment — Outfit — Departure—Results—Features of Coast—Architectural Rocks—Three Brother Turrets—Tennyson's Monument—The Great Glacier of Humboldt.. 127

CHAPTER XIX.

Progress of the Party—Prostration—Dallas Bay—Death of Schubert—The Brig in May—Progress of Spring—M'Gary's Return—Dr. Hayes's Party—Equipment—Schubert's Funeral... 135

CHAPTER XX.

Seal-hunting — Sir John Franklin — Resources — Acclimatization—The *Hope*— Dr. Hayes's Return—His Journey—Snow-blindness—Cape Hayes—The Dogs Tangled—Mending the Harness—Capes Leidy and Frazer—Dobbin Bay—Fletcher Webster Headland—Peter Force Bay—New Parties—Their Orders—Progress of Season—The Seal—The Netsik and Usuk—A Bear—Our Encounter—Change in the Floe.......... 142

CHAPTER XXI.

Progress of Season—Plants in Winter—Birds Returning—Cochlearia—The Plants...... 157

CHAPTER XXII.

Mr. Bonsall's Return—His Story—The Bear in Camp—His Fate—Bears at Sport—The Thaws 162

CHAPTER XXIII.

Morton's Return—His Narrative—Peabody Bay -Through the Bergs—Bridging the Chasms—The West Land—The Dogs in Fright—Open Water—The Ice-foot—The Polar Tides—Capes Jackson and Morris—The Channel—Free of Ice—Birds and Plants—Bear and Cub—The Hunt—The Death—Franklin and Lafayette—The Antarctic Flag—Course of Tides—Mount Parry—Victoria and Albert Mountains—Resumé—The Birds Appear—The Vegetation—The Petrel--Cape Constitution—Theories of an Open Sea—Illusory Discoveries—Changes of Climate—A Suggestion 167

CHAPTER XXIV.

Prospects—Speculations—The Argument—The Conclusion—The Reconnoissance—The Scheme—Equipment of Boat-party—Eider Island—Hans Island—The Cormorant Gull—Sentiment—Our Charts—Captain Inglefield—Discrepancies—A Gale—Fast to a Floe.. 185

CHAPTER XXV.

Working on—A Boat-nip—Ice-barrier—The Barrier Pack—Progress Hopeless—Northumberland Glacier—Ice-cascades—Neve.. 194

CHAPTER XXVI.

The Ice-foot in August—The Pack in August—Ice-blasting—Fox-trap Point—Warping—The Prospect—Approaching Climax—Signal-cairn—The Record—Projected Withdrawal—The Question—The Determination—The Result........................ 201

CHAPTER XXVII.

Discipline—Building Igloë—Tossut—Mossing—After Seal—On the Young Ice—Going too far—Seals at Home—In the Water—In Safety—Death of Tiger................. 211

CHAPTER XXVIII.

The Esquimaux—Larceny—The Arrest—The Punishment—The Treaty—" Unbroken Faith"—My Brother—Return from a Hunt—Our Life—Anoatok—A Welcome—Treaty Confirmed.. 217

CHAPTER XXIX.

Walrus-grounds—Lost on the Ice—A Break-up—Igloë of Anoatok—Its Garniture—Creature Comforts—Esquimaux Music—Usages of the Table—New London Avenue—Scant Diet-list—Bear and Cub—A Hunt—Close Quarters—Bear-fighting—Bear-habits—Bear's Liver—Rats—The Terrier Fox—The Arctic Hare—The Ice-foot Canopy—A Wolf—Dogs and Wolves—Bear and Fox—The Natives and Ourselves—Winter Quarters—Morton's Return—The Light.. 225

CHAPTER XXX.

Journey of Morton and Hans—Reception—The Hut—The Walrus—Walrus-hunt—The Contest—Habits of Walrus—Ferocity of the Walrus—The Victory—The Jubilee—A Sipak.. 242

CHAPTER XXXI.

An Aurora—Wood-cutting--Fuel-estimate—The Stove-pipes—The Arctic Firmament—Esquimaux Astronomy—Heating-apparatus—Meteoric Shower—A Bear—Hasty Retreat—The Cabin by Night—Sickness Increasing—Cutting into the Brig—The Night-watch.. 250

CHAPTER XXXII.

Esquimaux Sledges—Bonsall's Return—Results of the Hunt—Return of Withdrawing Party—Their Reception—The Esquimaux Escort Conference—Conciliation—On Fire—Casualty—Christmas—Ole Ben—A Journey Ahead—Setting Out—A Dreary Night—Striking a Light—End of 1854.. 260

CHAPTER XXXIII.

Modes of Life—The Inside Dog—Projected Journey—Dog-habits—The Darkness—Raw Meat—Plans for Sledging—The South-east Winds—Plan of Journey—A Relishing Lunch—Itinerary—Outfit—Cargo and Clothing—Kapetah and Nessak—Foot-gear —The Fox-tail—Carpet-knights—Burning Cables... 271

CHAPTER XXXIV.

A Break-down—The Hut in a Storm—Two Nights in the Hut—Frost Again—The Back Track—Health-roll—Medical Treatment—Health Failing—Unsuccessful Hunt— The Last Bottles... 282

CHAPTER XXXV.

The Fire-clothed Bag—The Wraith—Cookery—A Respite—The Coming Dawn—The Trust—Prospects—Argument—Coloured Skies—Stove-fitting................................ 288

CHAPTER XXXVI.

The Bennesoak—A Dilemma—The Sun—End of February—Our Condition—The Warm South-easter—Moonlight—The Landscape... 295

CHAPTER XXXVII.

Our Condition—The Resorts—The Sick—The Rat in the Insect-box—Anticipations— Hans's Return—Famine at Etah—Myouk on Board—Walrus-tackle—The Meat-diet 301

CHAPTER XXXVIII

Line of Open Water—Awahtok—His First-born—Insubordination—The Plot—The Development—The Desertion.. 308

CHAPTER XXXIX.

Colloquy in the Bunks—Winter Travel—Preparations—Reindeer Feeding-grounds— Terraced Beaches—A Walk—Occupations.. 313

CHAPTER XL.

The Delectable Mountains—Review of March—The Deserter again—His Escape—God-frey's Meat—Convalescent.. 318

CHAPTER XLI.

Routine—Getting up—Breakfast—Work—Turning in—Hans still missing—The Determination.. 322

CHAPTER XLII.

Journey after Hans—Esquimaux Sledging—Hans found—Recepto Amico—Explanation—Further Search—Maturing Plans—Chances of Escape—Food plenty—Paulik —Famine among the Esquimaux—Extinction—Light Hearts—Deserter Recovered 326

CHAPTER XLIII.

Hartstene Bay—Esquimaux Dwellings—A crowded Interior—The Night's Lodging— A Morning Repast—Mourning for the Dead—Funeral Rites—Penance.................. 334

CONTENTS.   ix

CHAPTER XLIV.

The Esquimaux of Greenland—Change of Character—Labours of the Missionaries--
Nöluk—The Ominaks—Pingeiak and Jens—The Angekoks—Issiutok—The Imna-
pok—The Decree.. 339

CHAPTER XLV.

Walrus-hunting—Esquimaux Habits—Return from Etah—Preparing for Escape—
Making Sledges—Dr. Hayes.. 345

CHAPTER XLVI.

Kalutunah—The Hunting-party—Setting out—My Tallow-ball—A Wild Chase—Hunt-
ing still—The Great Glacier—The Escaladed Structure—Formation of Bergs—The
Viscous Flow—Crevices—The Frozen Water-tunnel—Cape Forbes—Face of
Glacier 351

CHAPTER XLVII.

Cape James Kent—Marshall Bay—Ice-rafts—Striated Boulders—Antiquities—The
Bear-chase—The Bear at Bay—The Single Hunt—Teeth-wounds—The Last Effort
—Close of the Search.. 359

CHAPTER XLVIII.

Preparations for Escape—Provisions—Boats—The Sledges—Instruments and Arms—
Cooking Apparatus—Table Furniture—Cradling the Boats—The Sledges moving
—The Recreation... 366

CHAPTER XLIX.

The Pledges—The Argument—Farewell to the Brig—The Muster—The Routine—The
Messes... 371

CHAPTER L.

The Sick-hut—To First Ravine—Moving the Sick—The Health-station—Convalescence 375

CHAPTER LI.

To the Brig again—Welcome at the Hut—Log of the Sledges—Educated Faith—
Good-bye to the Brig—Metek's Prayer.. 379

CHAPTER LII.

New Stations—The Ice-Marshes—Point Security—Oopegsoak—Catching Auks—
Aningnah—Nessark.. 385

CHAPTER LIII.

The Game of Ball—My Brother's Lake—The Polar Seasons—Fate of the Esquimaux—
The Esquimaux Limits—Esquimaux Endurance—Awahtok's Hunt—His Escape—
The Guardian Walrus.. 390

CHAPTER LIV.

The Bakery—The Guitar Ghost—The Boat Camp—Nessark's Wife—Out in a Gale—
Cape Misery—The Burrow—the Retreat.. 396

CHAPTER LV

Fresh Dogs—The Slides—Rocking-Stones—Ohlsen's Accident—Ice-Sailing—Mounting
the Belt—The Ice Marshes—Pekiutlik—Hans the Benedick 401

CHAPTER LVI.

The *Red Boat* Sinking—The Life-Boat Cache—The Open Water—Ohlsen's Death—His Funeral—Barentz, our Precursor—Accomodah—The Prescription—Cape Welcome—The Resolve.. 408

CHAPTER LVII.

The Farewell--Attempt to Embark 414

CHAPTER LVIII.

Sutherland Island—Hakluyt Island—Northumberland Island—Fitz-Clarence Rock—Dalrymple Rock--Giving Out—Break-up of the Floe—Broken Down—Weary Man's Rest--The Fourth—Short Commons........... 419

CHAPTER LIX.

A Look-Out—Providence Halt—The Glacier—Providence Diet......... 426

CHAPTER LX.

The Crimson Cliffs—The Esquimaux Eden—Depression of the Coast—Inventory—Imalik—Losing our Way—At the Rue-raddies—The Open Sea—Effects of Hunger—Rescue of the *Faith* 430

CHAPTER LXI.

The Seal! the Seal!—The Festival—Terra Firma—Paul Zacharias—The Fraulein Flaischer—The News—At the Settlements—The Welcome............................... 437

CONCLUSION.. 442

GLOSSARY.................................. 445

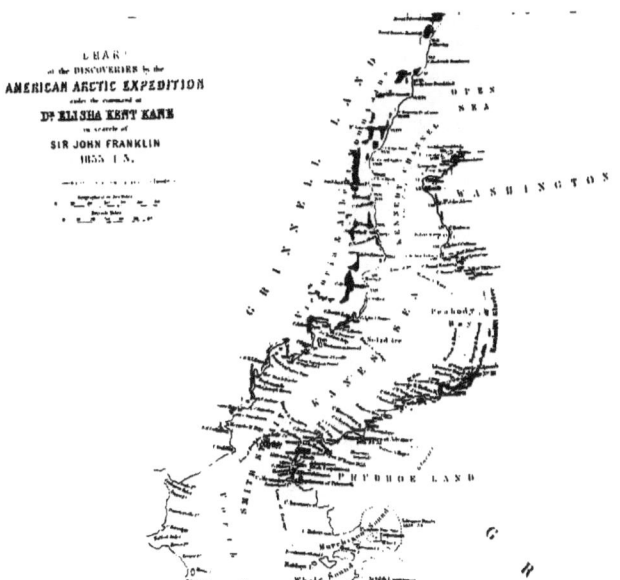

KANE'S ARCTIC EXPLORATIONS.

———◆———

CHAPTER I.

ORGANIZATION—PLAN OF OPERATIONS—COMPLEMENT—EQUIPMENT—
ST. JOHN'S.

IN the month of December 1852, I had the honour of receiving CHAPTER 1.
special orders from the Secretary of the Navy, to "conduct an
expedition to the Arctic Seas in search of Sir John Franklin."

I had been engaged, under Lieutenant De Haven, in the Grinnell Expedition, which sailed from the United States in 1850 on
the same errand; and I had occupied myself for some months
after our return in maturing the scheme of a renewed effort to A new
rescue the missing party, or at least to resolve the mystery of its resolved
fate. Mr. Grinnell, with a liberality altogether characteristic, had on.
placed the *Advance*, in which I sailed before, at my disposal for
the cruise; and Mr. Peabody of London, the generous representative of many American sympathies, had proffered his aid largely
toward her outfit. The Geographical Society of New York, the
Smithsonian Institution, the American Philosophical Society,—I
name them in the order in which they announced their contributions,—and a number of scientific associations and friends of
science besides, had come forward to help me; and by their aid I
managed to secure a better outfit for purposes of observation than
would otherwise have been possible to a party so limited in numbers and absorbed in other objects.

Ten of our little party belonged to the United States Navy, and
were attached to my command by orders from the Department;

CHAPTER
I.

Rules and
regula-
tions of
the expo-
dition. the others were shipped by me for the cruise, and at salaries entirely disproportioned to their services: all were volunteers. We did not sail under the rules that govern our national ships; but we had our own regulations, well considered and announced beforehand, and rigidly adhered to afterward through all the vicissitudes of the expedition. These included—first, absolute subordination to the officer in command or his delegate; second, abstinence from all intoxicating liquors, except when dispensed by special order; third, the habitual disuse of profane language. We had no other laws.

I had developed our plan of search in a paper read before the Geographical Society. It was based upon the probable extension of the land-masses of Greenland to the Far North,—a fact at that time not verified by travel, but sustained by the analogies of physical geography. Greenland, though looked upon as a congeries of islands connected by interior glaciers, was still to be regarded as a peninsula, whose formation recognised the same general laws as other peninsulas having a southern trend.

From the alternating altitudes of its mountain ranges, continued without depression throughout a meridional line of nearly eleven hundred miles, I inferred that this chain must extend very far to the north, and that Greenland might not improbably approach nearer the Pole than any other known land.

Proposed
route easy
from
Greenland
to far
north. Believing, then, in such an extension of this peninsula, and feeling that the search for Sir John Franklin would be best promoted by a course that might lead most directly to the open sea of which I had inferred the existence, and that the approximation of the meridians would make access to the West as easy from Northern Greenland as from Wellington Channel, and access to the East far more easy,—feeling, too, that the highest protruding headland would be most likely to afford some traces of the lost party,—I named, as the inducements in favour of my scheme,—

1. Terra firma as the basis of our operations, obviating the capricious character of ice-travel.

2. A due northern line, which, throwing aside the influences of terrestrial radiation, would lead soonest to the open sea, should such exist.

3. The benefit of the fan-like abutment of land, on the north face of Greenland, to check the ice in the course of its southern or

equatorial drift, thus obviating the great drawback of Parry in his CHAPTER
attempts to reach the Pole by the Spitzbergen Sea. I.

4. Animal life to sustain travelling parties.

5. The co-operation of the Esquimaux; settlements of these
people having been found as high as Whale Sound, and probably
extending still further along the coast.

We were to pass up Baffin's Bay, therefore, to its most northern Line of
attainable point; and thence, pressing on toward the Pole as far route.
as boats or sledges could carry us, examine the coast-lines for
vestiges of the lost party.

All hands counted, we were seventeen at the time of sailing. Names of
Another joined us a few days afterward; so that the party under the party
my command, as it reached the coast of Greenland, consisted of—

HENRY BROOKS, First Officer.	ISAAC I. HAYES, M.D., Surgeon.
JOHN WALL WILSON,	AUGUST SONTAG, Astronomer.
JAMES M'GARY,	AMOS BONSALL,
GEORGE RILEY,	GEORGE STEPHENSON,
WILLIAM MORTON,	GEORGE WHIPPLE,
CHRISTIAN OHLSEN.	WILLIAM GODFREY,
HENRY GOODFELLOW,	JOHN BLAKE,

JEFFERSON BAKER,
PETER SCHUBERT,
THOMAS HICKEY.

Two of these, Brooks and Morton, had been my associates in the
first expedition; gallant and trustworthy men, both of them, as
ever shared the fortunes or claimed the gratitude of a commander.

The *Advance* had been thoroughly tried in many encounters with The Ad-
the Arctic ice. She was carefully inspected, and needed very *vance.*
little to make her all a seaman could wish. She was a herma-
phrodite brig of one hundred and forty-four tons, intended origi-
nally for carrying heavy castings from an iron-foundry, but
strengthened afterward with great skill and at large expense. She
was a good sailer, and easily managed. We had five boats; one
of them a metallic life-boat, the gift of the maker, Mr. Francis.

Our equipment was simple. It consisted of little else than a The equip-
quantity of rough boards, to serve for housing over the vessel in ment.
winter, some tents of India-rubber and canvas, of the simplest
description, and several carefully-built sledges, some of them on a
model furnished me by the kindness of the British Admiralty,
others of my own devising.

Our store of provisions was chosen with little regard to luxury. We took with us some two thousand pounds of well-made pemmican, a parcel of Borden's meat-biscuit, some packages of an exsiccated potato, resembling Edwards's, some pickled cabbage, and a liberal quantity of American dried fruits and vegetables; besides these, we had the salt beef and pork of the navy ration, hard biscuit, and flour. A very moderate supply of liquors, with the ordinary *et ceteras* of an Arctic cruiser, made up the diet-list. I hoped to procure some fresh provisions in addition before reaching the upper coast of Greenland; and I carried some barrels of malt, with a compact apparatus for brewing.

We had a moderate wardrobe of woollens, a full supply of knives, needles, and other articles for barter, a large, well-chosen library, and a valuable set of instruments for scientific observations.

We left New York on the 30th of May 1853, escorted by several noble steamers; and, passing slowly on to the Narrows amid salutes and cheers of farewell, cast our brig off from the steam-tug and put to sea.

It took us eighteen days to reach St. John's, Newfoundland. The Governor, Mr. Hamilton, a brother of the Secretary of the Admiralty, received us with a hearty English welcome; and all the officials, indeed all the inhabitants, vied with each other in efforts to advance our views. I purchased here a stock of fresh beef, which, after removing the bones and tendons, we compressed into rolls by wrapping it closely with twine, according to the nautical process of *marling*, and hung it up in the rigging.

After two days we left this thriving and hospitable city; and, with a noble team of Newfoundland dogs on board, the gift of Governor Hamilton, headed our brig for the coast of Greenland.

We reached Baffin's Bay without incident. We took deep-sea-soundings as we approached its axis, and found a reliable depth of nineteen hundred fathoms: an interesting result, as it shows that the ridge which is known to extend between Ireland and New-foundland in the bed of the Atlantic is depressed as it passes further to the north. A few days more found us off the coast of Greenland, making our way toward Fiskernaes.

CHAPTER II.

FISKERNAES—THE FISHERY—MR. LASSEN—HANS CRISTIAN— LICHTENFELS
—SUKKERTOPPEN.

WE entered the harbour of Fiskernaes on the 1st of July, amid CHAPTER
the clamour of its entire population, assembled on the rocks to II.
greet us. This place has an enviable reputation for climate and Fisker-
health. Except perhaps Holsteinberg, it is the driest station upon naes.
the coast; and the springs, which well through the mosses, frequently remain unfrozen throughout the year.

The sites of the different Greenland colonies seem to have been Sites of the
chosen with reference to their trading resources. The southern Greenland
colonies.
posts around Julianshaab and Fredericstahl supply the Danish
market with the valued furs of the saddle-back seal ; Sukkertoppen
and Holsteinberg with reindeer skins ; Disco and the northern dis-
tricts with the seal and other oils. The little settlement of Fiskernaes rejoices in its codfish, as well as the other staples of the upper
coast. It is situated on Fisher's Fiord, some eight miles from the
open bay, and is approached by an island-studded channel of
moderate draught.

We saw the codfish here in all the stages of preparation for the Prepara-
table and the market ; the stockfish, dried in the open air, without tion of fish
for the
salt ; crapefish, salted and pressed ; fresh fish, a *lucus a non* market.
lucendo, as salt as a Mediterranean anchovy : we laid in supplies
of all of them. The exemption of Fiskernaes from the continued
fogs, and its free exposure to the winds as they draw up the fiord,
make it a very favourable place for drying cod. The backbone is
cut out, with the exception of about four inches near the tail ; the
body expanded and simply hung upon a frame : the head, a luxury
neglected with us, is carefully dried in a separate piece.

Seal and shark oils are the next in importance among the staples Seal and
shark oils
of Fiskernaes. The *spec* or blubber is purchased from the natives
with the usual articles of exchange, generally coffee and tobacco,
and rudely *tried out* by exposure in vats or hot expression in iron
boilers. None of the nicer processes which economy and despatch

have introduced at St. John's seem to have reached this out of-the-way coast. Even the cod-livers are given to the dogs, or thrown into the general vat.

We found Mr. Lassen, the superintending official of the Danish Company, a hearty, single-minded man, fond of his wife, his children, and his pipe. The visit of our brig was, of course, an incident to be marked in the simple annals of his colony; and, even before I had shown him my official letter from the Court of Denmark, he had most hospitably proffered everything for our accommodation. We became his guests, and interchanged presents with him before our departure; this last transaction enabling me to say, with confidence, that the inner fiords produce noble salmon-trout, and that the reindeer-tongue, a recognised delicacy in the old and new Arctic continents, is justly appreciated at Fiskernaes.

Feeling that our dogs would require fresh provisions, which could hardly be spared from our supplies on shipboard, I availed myself
of Mr. Lassen's influence to obtain an Esquimaux hunter for our party. He recommended to me one Hans Cristian, a boy of nineteen, as an expert with the kayak and javelin; and after Hans had given me a touch of his quality by spearing a bird on the wing, I engaged him. He was fat, good-natured, and, except under the excitements of the hunt, as stolid and unimpressible as one of our own Indians. He stipulated that, in addition to his very moderate wages, I should leave a couple of barrels of bread and fifty-two pounds of pork with his mother; and I became munificent in his eyes when I added the gift of a rifle and a new kayak. We found him very useful; our dogs required his services as a caterer, and our own table was more than once dependent on his energies.

No one can know so well as an Arctic voyager the value of foresight. My conscience has often called for the exercise of it, but my habits make it an effort. I can hardly claim to be provident, either by impulse or education. Yet, for some of the deficiencies of our outfit, I ought not, perhaps, to hold myself responsible. Our stock of fresh meats was too small, and we had no preserved vegetables; but my personal means were limited; and I could not press more severely than a strict necessity exacted upon the unquestioning liberality of my friends.

While we were beating out of the fiord of Fiskernaes, I had an

opportunity of visiting Lichtenfels, the ancient seat of the Green- CHAPTER.
land congregations, and one of the three Moravian settlements. I II.
had read much of the history of its founders ; and it was with Lichten-
feelings almost of devotion, that I drew near the scene their labours fels.
had consecrated.

MORAVIAN SETTLEMENT OF LICHTENFELS.

As we rowed into the shadow of its rock-embayed cove, every- Moravian
thing was so desolate and still, that we might have fancied brethren
ourselves outside the world of life ; even the dogs—those querulous,
never-sleeping sentinels of the rest of the coast—gave no signal of
our approach.   Presently, a sudden turn around a projecting cliff
brought into view a quaint old Silesian mansion, bristling with
irregularly-disposed chimneys, its black, overhanging roof studded
with dormer windows, and crowned with an antique belfry.
We were met, as we landed, by a couple of grave, ancient men
in sable jackets and close velvet skull-caps, such as Vandyke or
Rembrandt himself might have painted, who gave us a quiet, but

2

CHAPTER II.

kindly welcome. All inside of the mansion-house—the furniture, the matron, even the children—had the same time-sobered look. The sanded floor was dried by one of those huge, white-tiled stoves, which have been known for generations in the north of Europe; and the stiff-backed chairs were evidently coeval with the first days of the settlement. The heavy-built table in the middle of the room was soon covered with its simple offerings of hospitality; and we sat around to talk of the lands we had come from, and the changing wonders of the times.

The old mansion-house.

We learned that the house dated back as far as the days of Matthew Stach; built, no doubt, with the beams that floated so providentially to the shore some twenty-five years after the first landing of Egedé; and that it had been the home of the brethren who now greeted us, one for twenty-nine, and the other twenty-seven years. The "Congregation Hall" was within the building, cheerless now with its empty benches; a couple of French horns, —all that I could associate with the gladsome piety of the Moravians,—hung on each side the altar. Two dwelling-rooms, three chambers, and a kitchen, all under the same roof, made up the one structure of Lichtenfels.

Liberal spirit of the Moravians.

Its kind-hearted inmates were not without intelligence and education. In spite of the formal cut of their dress, and something of the stiffness that belongs to a protracted solitary life, it was impossible not to recognise, in their demeanour and course of thought, the liberal spirit that has always characterized their Church. Two of their "children," they said, had "gone to God" last year with the scurvy; yet they hesitated at receiving a scanty supply of potatoes as a present from our store.

We lingered along the coast for the next nine days, baffled by calms and light, adverse winds; and it was only on the 10th of July that we reached the settlement of Sukkertoppen.

The "Sukkertop."

The Sukkertop, or Sugar-loaf, a noted landmark, is a wild, isolated peak, rising some 3000 feet from the sea. The little colony which nestles at its base occupies a rocky gorge, so narrow and broken that a stairway connects the detached groups of huts, and the tide, as it rises, converts a part of the groundplot into a temporary island.

Of all the Danish settlements on this coast, it struck me as the most picturesque. The rugged cliffs seemed to blend with the

grotesque structures about their base. The trim red and white CHAPTER II.
painted frame mansion, which, in virtue of its green blinds and
flagstaff, asserted the gubernatorial dignity at Fiskernaes, was here
a lowly, dingy compound of tarred roof and heavy gables. The
dwellings of the natives, the natives themselves, and the wild
packs of dogs that crowded the beach, were all in keeping. It
was after twelve at night when we came into port; and the Light at midnight
peculiar light of the Arctic summer at this hour—which reminds
one of the effect of an eclipse, so unlike our orthodox twilight—
bathed everything in grey but the northern background—an
Alpine chain standing out against a blazing crimson sky.

Sukkertoppen is a principal depôt for reindeer-skins; and the Sukker-toppen.
natives were at this season engaged in their summer hunt, collecting them. Four thousand had already been sent to Denmark, and
more were on hand. I bought a stock of superior quality for fifty
cents a piece. These furs are valuable for their lightness and
warmth. They form the ordinary upper clothing of both sexes;
the seal being used only for pantaloons and for waterproof dresses.
I purchased also all that I could get of the crimped seal-skin boots
or moccasins, an admirable article of walking gear, much more
secure against the wet than any made by sewing. I would have
added to my stock of fish, but the cod had not yet reached this
part of the coast, and would not for some weeks.

Bidding good-bye to the governor, whose hospitality we had
shared liberally, we put to sea on Saturday, the 10th, beating to
the northward and westward in the teeth of a heavy gale.

OOMIAK, OR WOMEN'S BOAT.

CHAPTER III.

COAST OF GREENLAND—SWARTE-HUK—LAST DANISH OUTPOSTS—MELVILLE
BAY—IN THE ICE—BEARS—BERGS—ANCHOR TO A BERG—MIDNIGHT
SUNSHINE.

CHAPTER III. THE lower and middle coast of Greenland has been visited by so many voyagers, and its points of interest have been so often described, that I need not dwell upon them. From the time we left Sukkertoppen, we had the usual delays from fogs and adverse currents, and did not reach the neighbourhood of Wilcox Point, which defines Melville Bay, until the 27th of July.

Old friends at Proven. On the 16th we passed the promontory of Swarte-huk, and were welcomed the next day at Proven by my old friend Christiansen, the superintendent, and found his family much as I left them three years before. Frederick, his son, had married a native woman, and added a summer tent, a half-breed boy, and a Danish rifle to his stock of valuables. My former patient, Anna, had united fortunes with a fat-faced Esquimaux, and was the mother of a chubby little girl. Madame Christiansen, who counted all these and so many others as her happy progeny, was hearty and warm-hearted as ever. She led the household in sewing up my skins into various serviceable garments ; and I had the satisfaction, before I left, of completing my stock of furs for our sledge parties.

While our brig passed, half sailing, half drifting, up the coast, I left her under the charge of Mr. Brooks, and set out in the whale-boat to make my purchases of dogs among the natives. Gathering them as we went along from the different settlements, Reach Upernavik. we reached Upernavik, the resting-place of the Grinnell Expedition in 1851 after its winter drift, and for a couple of days shared, as we were sure to do, the generous hospitality of Governor Flaischer.

Last Danish outposts. Still coasting along, we passed in succession the Esquimaux settlement of Kingatok, the Kettle—a mountain-top so named from the resemblances of its profile—and finally Yotlik, the furthest point of colonization ; beyond which, save the sparse headlands of the charts, the coast may be regarded as unknown.

Then, inclining more directly toward the north, we ran close to the chapter III. Baffin Islands,—clogged with ice when I saw them three years before, now entirely clear,—sighted the landmark which is known as the Horse's Head, and, passing the Duck Islands, where the *Advance* grounded in 1851, bore away for Wilcox Point.

We stood lazily along the coast, with alternations of perfect calm and off-shore breezes, generally from the south or east; but on the morning of the 27th of July, as we neared the entrance of Melville Bay, one of those heavy ice-fogs, which I have described Melville Bay. in my former narrative as characteristic of this region, settled around us. We could hardly see across the decks, and yet were sensible of the action of currents carrying us we knew not where. By the time the sun had scattered the mist, Wilcox Point was to the south of us; and our little brig, now fairly in the bay, stood a fair chance of drifting over toward the Devil's Thumb, which then bore east of north. The bergs which infest this region, and Among the bergs which have earned for it among the whalers the title of the " Bergy Hole," showed themselves all around us : we had come in among them in the fog.

It was a whole day's work, towing with both boats; but toward evening we had succeeded in crawling off shore, and were doubly rewarded for our labour with a wind. I had observed with surprise, while we were floating near the coast, that the land ice was already broken and decayed ; and I was aware, from what I had read, as well as what I had learned from whalers and observed myself of the peculiarities of this navigation, that the in-shore track was in consequence beset with difficulty and delays. I made up my mind at once. I would stand to the westward until arrested by the pack, and endeavour to *double* Melville Bay by an Doubling Melville Bay. outside passage. A chronicle of this transit, condensed from my log-book, will have interest for navigators :—

" *July* 28, *Thursday*, 6 A.M.—Made the offsetting streams of the pack, and bore up to the northward and eastward ; heading for Cape York in tolerably free water.

" *July* 29, *Friday*, 9½ A.M.—Made loose ice, and very rotten ; the tables nearly destroyed, and much broken by wave action : water-sky to the northward. Entered this ice, intending to work to the northward and eastward, above or about Sabine Islands, in search of the north-eastern land-ice. The breeze freshened off

CHAPTER
III.
shore, breaking up and sending out the floes, the leads rapidly
closing.   Fearing a besetment, I determined to fasten to an iceberg; and after eight hours of very heavy labour, warping, heaving,
and planting ice-anchors, succeeded in effecting it.

Breaking
of an ice-
berg.
"We had hardly a breathing spell, before we were startled by a
set of loud, crackling sounds above us; and small fragments of
ice, not larger than a walnut, began to dot the water like the first
drops of a summer shower.   The indications were too plain; we
had barely time to cast off before the face of the berg fell in ruins,
crashing like near artillery.

FASTENED TO AN ICEBERG.

A critical
position.
"Our position, in the mean time, had been critical, a gale
blowing off the shore, and the floes closing and scudding rapidly.
We lost some three hundred and sixty fathoms of whale line,
which were caught in the floes, and had to be cut away to release

us from the drift. It was a hard night for boat-work, particularly
with those of the party who were taking their first lessons in floe
navigation.

" *July* 30, *Saturday.*—Again moored alongside of an iceberg.
The wind off shore, but hauling to the southward, with much free
water.

" 12 M.—The fog too dense to see more than a quarter of a
mile a head ; occasional glimpses through it show no practicable
leads. Land to the north-east very rugged; I do not recognise
its marks. Two lively bears seen about 2 A.M. The ' Red Boat,'
with Petersen and Hayes, got one ; I took one of the quarter-boats,
and shot the other.

" Holding on for clearer weather.

" *July* 31, *Sunday.*—Our open water beginning to fill up very
fast with loose ice from the south, went around the edges of the
lake in my gig, to hunt for a more favourable spot for the brig;
and, after five hours' hard heaving, we succeeded in changing our
fasts to another berg, quite near the free water. In our present
position, the first change must, I think, liberate us. In one hour
after we reached it, the place we left was consolidated into pack.
We now lie attached to a low and safe iceberg, only two miles
from the open sea, which is rapidly widening toward us under the
influence of the southerly winds.

" We had a rough time in working to our present quarters, in
what the whalers term an open hole. We drove into a couple of
bergs, carried away our jib-boom and shrouds, and destroyed one
of our quarter-boats.

" *August* 1, *Monday.*—Beset thoroughly with drifting ice, small
rotten floe-pieces. But for our berg, we would now be carried to
the south; as it is, we drift with it to the north and east.

" 2 A.M.—The continued pressure against our berg has begun
to affect it; and, like the great floe all around us, it has taken up
its line of march toward the south. At the risk of being entangled,
I ordered a light line to be carried out to a much larger berg, and,
after four hours' labour, made fast to it securely. This berg is a
moving breakwater, and of gigantic proportions ; it keeps its course
steadily toward the north, while the loose ice drifts by on each
side, leaving a wake of black water for a mile behind us.

" Our position last night, by midnight altitude of the sun, gave

CHAPTER III.

us 75° 27′; to day at noon, with a more reliable horizon, we made 75° 37′; showing that, in spite of all embarrassments, we still move to the north. We are, however, nearer than I could wish to the land,—a blank wall of glacier.

"About 10 P.M. the immediate danger was past; and, espying a lead to the north-east, we got under weigh, and pushed over in spite of the drifting trash. The men worked with a will, and we bored through the floes in excellent style."

On our road we were favoured with a gorgeous spectacle, which hardly any excitement of peril could have made us overlook. The Midnight sunshine. midnight sun came out over the northern crest of the great berg, our late "fast friend," kindling variously-coloured fires on every part of its surface, and making the ice around us one great resplendency of gemwork, blazing carbuncles, and rubies and molten gold.

ESQUIMAUX BOY ON DOG.

CHAPTER IV.

BORING THE FLOES—SUCCESSFUL PASSAGE THROUGH MELVILLE BAY—ICE
NAVIGATION—PASSAGE OF THE MIDDLE PACK—THE NORTH WATER.

OUR brig went crunching through all this jewellery; and, after a CHAPTER
IV.
tortuous progress of five miles, arrested here and there by tongues
which required the saw and ice-chisels, fitted herself neatly between Boring the
floes.
two floes. Here she rested till toward morning, when the leads
opened again, and I was able, from the crow's-nest, to pick our
way to a larger pool some distance ahead. In this we beat backward and forward, like China fish seeking an outlet from a glass
jar, till the fog caught us again; and so the day ended.

" *August 3, Wednesday.*—The day did not promise well; but
as the wind was blowing in feeble airs from the N.N.W., I
thought it might move the ice, and sent out the boats for a tow.
But, after they had had a couple of hours of unprofitable work,
the breeze freshened, and the floes opened enough to allow us to
beat through them. Everything now depended upon practical ice
knowledge; and, as I was not willing to trust any one else in
selecting the leads for our course, I have spent the whole day with
M'Gary at mast-head,—a somewhat confined and unfavourable
preparation for a journal entry.

" I am much encouraged, however; this off-shore wind is favour- Prospect
of escape
ing our escape. The icebergs, too, have assisted us to hold our own
against the rapid passage of the broken ice to the south; and since
the larger floes have opened into leads, we have nothing to do but
to follow them carefully and boldly. As for the ice-necks, and
prongs, and rafts, and tongues, the capstan and windlass have
done a great deal to work us through them; but a great deal
more, a brave headway and our little brig's hard head of oak.

" *Midnight.*—We are clear of the bay and its myriads of dis- Clear of
the bay.
couragements. The North Water, our highway to Smith's Sound,
is fairly ahead.

" It is only eight days ago that we made Wilcox Point, and
seven since we fairly left the inside track of the whalers, and made

our push for the west. I did so, not without full consideration of the chances. Let me set down what my views were and are."

The indentation known as Melville Bay is protected by its northern and north-eastern coast from the great ice and current drifts which follow the axis of Baffin's Bay. The interior of the country which bounds upon it is the seat of extensive glaciers, which are constantly shedding off icebergs of the largest dimensions. The greater bulk of these is below the water-line, and the depth to which they sink when floating subjects them to the action of the deeper sea currents, while their broad surface above the water is of course acted on by the wind. It happens, therefore, that they are found not unfrequently moving in different directions from the floes around them, and preventing them for a time from freezing into a united mass. Still, in the late winter, when the cold has thoroughly set in, Melville Bay becomes a continuous field of ice, from Cape York to the Devil's Thumb.

On the return of milder weather, the same causes renew their action ; and that portion of the ice which is protected from the outside drift, and entangled among the icebergs that crowd the bay, remains permanent long after that which is outside is in motion. Step by step, as the year advances, its outer edge breaks off ; yet its inner curve frequently remains unbroken through the entire summer. This is the " fast ice " of the whalers, so important to their progress in the earlier portions of the season ; for, however it may be encroached upon by storms or currents, they can generally find room to *track* their vessels along its solid margin ; or if the outside ice, yielding to off-shore winds, happens to recede, the interval of water between the fast and the drift allows them not unfrequently to use their sails.

It is therefore one of the whalers' canons of navigation, which they hold to most rigidly, to follow the shore. But it is obvious that this applies only to the early periods of the Arctic season, when the land ice of the inner bay is comparatively unbroken, as in May or June, or part of July, varying of course with the circumstances. Indeed, the bay is seldom traversed except in these months, the north-west fisheries of Pond's Bay, and the rest, ceasing to be of value afterward. Later in the summer, the inner ice breaks up into large floes, moving with wind and tide, that embarrass the navigator, misleading him into the notion that he is attached to his "fast," when in reality he is accompanying the movements of an immense floating ice-field.

I have been surprised sometimes that our national ships of discovery and search have not been more generally impressed by these views. Whether the season has been mild or severe, the ice fast and solid, or broken and in drift, they have followed in August the same course which the whalers do in June, running their vessels into the curve of the bay in search of the fast ice which had disappeared a month before, and involving themselves in a labyrinth of floes. It was thus the *Advance* was caught in her second season, under Captain de Haven; while the *Prince Albert*, leaving us, worked a successful passage to the west. So too the *North Star* in 1849 was carried to the northward, and hopelessly entangled there. Indeed, it is the common story of the disasters and delays that we read of in the navigation of these regions.

Now I felt sure, from the known openness of the season of 1852 and the probable mildness of the following winter, that we could scarcely hope to make use of the land ice for tracking, or to avail ourselves of leads along its margin by canvas. And this opinion was confirmed by the broken and rotten appearance of the floes during our coastwise drift at the Duck Islands. I therefore deserted the inside track of the whalers, and stood to the westward, until we made the first streams of the middle pack; and then, skirting the pack to the northward, headed in slowly for the middle portion of the bay above Sabine Islands. My object was to double, as it were, the loose and drifting ice that had stood in my way, and, reaching Cape York, as nearly as might be, trust for the remainder of my passage to warping and tracking by the heavy floes. We succeeded, not without some laborious boring and serious risks of entanglement among the broken icefields. But we managed, in every instance, to combat this last form of difficulty by attaching our vessel to large icebergs, which enabled us to hold our own, however swiftly the surface floes were pressing by us to the south. Four days of this scarcely varied yet exciting navigation brought us to the extended fields of the pack, and a fortunate north-wester opened a passage for us through them. We are now in the North Water.

CHAPTER V.

CRIMSON CLIFFS OF BEVERLEY—HAKLUYT AND NORTHUMBERLAND—RED
SNOW—THE GATES OF SMITH'S STRAITS—CAPE ALEXANDER—CAPE
HATHERTON—FAREWELL CAIRN—LIFE-BOAT DEPÔT—ESQUIMAUX RUINS
FOUND—GRAVES—FLAGSTAFF POINT.

CHAPTER
V.

The Crim-
son Cliffs.

My diary continues :—

"We passed the 'Crimson Cliffs' of Sir John Ross in the forenoon of August 5th. The patches of red snow, from which they
derive their name, could be seen clearly at the distance of ten
miles from the coast. It had a fine deep rose hue, not at all like
the brown stain which I noticed when I was here before. All the
gorges and ravines in which the snows had lodged were deeply
tinted with it. I had no difficulty now in justifying the somewhat poetical nomenclature which Sir John Franklin applied to
this locality; for if the snowy surface were more diffused, as it is
no doubt earlier in the season, crimson would be the prevailing
colour.

Pass Coni-
cal Rock.

"Late at night we passed Conical Rock, the most insulated and
conspicuous landmark of this coast; and, still later, Wolstenholme
and Saunder's Islands, and Oomenak, the place of the *North Star's*
winter-quarters—an admirable day's run; and so ends the 5th of
August. We are standing along, with studding-sails set, and open
water before us, fast nearing our scene of labour. We have
already got to work, sewing up blanket bags and preparing sledges
for our campaignings on the ice."

Reach
Hakluyt
Island.

We reached Hakluyt Island in the course of the next day. A
tall spire on it, probably of gneiss, rises 600 feet above the
water-level, and is a valuable landmark for very many miles around.
We were destined to become familiar with it before leaving this
region. Both it and Northumberland, to the south-east of it,
afforded studies of colour that would have rewarded an artist.

Red snow.

The red snow was diversified with large surfaces of beautifully-
green mosses and alopecurus, and where the sandstone was bare,
it threw in a rich shade of brown.

The coast to the north of Cape Atholl is of broken greenstone, CHAPTER
V.
in terraces. Nearing Hakluyt Island, the truncated and pyramidal
shapes of these rocks may still be recognised in the interior; but Geology of
the coast presents a coarse red sandstone, which continues well the coast.
characterized as far as Cape Saumarez. The nearly horizontal
strata of the sandstone thus exhibited contrast conspicuously with
the snow which gathers upon their exposed ledges. In fact, the
parallelism and distinctness of the lines of white and black would
have dissatisfied a lover of the picturesque. Porphyritic rocks,
however, occasionally broke their too great uniformity; occasionally, too, the red snow showed its colours; and at intervals of very
few miles—indeed, wherever the disrupted masses offered a pass-
age-way—glaciers were seen descending toward the water's edge.
All the back country appeared one great rolling distance of
glacier.

"*August 6, Saturday.*—Cape Alexander and Cape Isabella, the The gates
headlands of Smith's Sound, are now in sight; and, in addition Sound.
to these indications of our progress toward the field of search, a
marked swell has set in after a short blow from the northward,
just such as might be looked for from the action of the wind upon
an open water-space beyond.

"Whatever it may have been when Captain Inglefield saw it a Aspect of
year ago, the aspect of this coast is now most uninviting. As we the coast.
look far off to the west, the snow comes down with heavy uniformity to the water's edge, and the patches of land seem as rare as the
summer's snow on the hills about Sukkertoppen and Fiskernaes.
On the right we have an array of cliffs, whose frowning grandeur
might dignify the entrance to the proudest of southern seas. I
should say they would average from 400 to 500 yards in
height, with some of their precipices 800 feet at a single
steep. They have been until now the Arctic pillars of Hercules;
and they look down on us as if they challenged our right to pass.
Even the sailors are impressed as we move under their dark shadow. One of the officers said to our look-out, that the gulls and
eider that dot the water about us were as enlivening as the white
sails of the Mediterranean. 'Yes, sir,' he rejoined with sincere
gravity; 'yes, sir, in proportion to their size.'"

"*August 7, Sunday.*—We have left Cape Alexander to the south;
and Littleton Island is before us, hiding Cape Hatherton, the latest

of Captain Inglefield's positively-determined headlands. We are fairly inside of Smith's Sound.

"On our left is a capacious bay; and deep in its north-eastern recesses we can see a glacier issuing from a fiord."

We knew this bay familiarly afterwards as the residence of a body of Esquimaux with whom we had many associations; but we little dreamt then that it would bear the name of a gallant friend, who found there the first traces of our escape. A small cluster of rocks, hidden at times by the sea, gave evidence of the violent tidal action about them.

"As we neared the west end of Littleton Island, after breakfast this morning, I ascended to the crow's-nest, and saw to my sorrow the ominous blink of ice ahead. The wind has been freshening for a couple of days from the northward, and if it continues, it will bring down the floes on us.

"My mind has been made up from the first that we are to force our way to the north, as far as the elements will let us; and I feel the importance, therefore, of securing a place of retreat, that in case of disaster we may not be altogether at large. Besides, we have now reached one of the points at which, if any one is to follow us, he might look for some trace to guide him."

I determined to leave a cairn on Littleton Island, and to deposit a boat with a supply of stores in some convenient place near it. One of our whale-boats had been crushed in Melville Bay, and Francis's metallic life-boat was the only one I could spare. Its length did not exceed twenty feet, and our crew of twenty could hardly stow themselves in it with even a few days' rations; but it was air-chambered and buoyant.

Selecting from our stock of provisions and field equipage such portions as we might by good luck be able to dispense with, and adding with reluctant liberality some blankets and a few yards of india-rubber cloth, we set out in search of a spot for our first depôt. It was essential that it should be upon the mainland, for the rapid tides might so wear away the ice as to make an island inaccessible to a foot-party; and yet it was desirable that, while secure against the action of sea and ice, it should be approachable by boats. We found such a place after some pretty cold rowing. It was off the north-east cape of Littleton, and bore S.S.E. from Cape Hatherton, which loomed in the distance above the fog.

Here we buried our life-boat with her little cargo. We placed CHAPTER V. along her gunwale the heaviest rocks we could handle, and, filling up the interstices with smaller stones and sods of andromeda and Life-boat and cargo buried. moss, poured sand and water among the layers. This, frozen at once into a solid mass, might be hard enough, we hoped, to resist the claws of the polar bear.

We found to our surprise that we were not the first human beings who had sought a shelter in this desolate spot. A few ruined walls here and there showed that it had once been the seat of a rude settlement; and in the little knoll which we cleared away to cover in our storehouse of valuables, we found the mortal remains of their former inhabitants.

Nothing can be imagined more sad and homeless than these Ruins of a rude settlement. memorials of extinct life. Hardly a vestige of growth was traceable on the bare ice-rubbed rocks; and the huts resembled so much the broken fragments that surrounded them, that at first sight it was hard to distinguish one from the other. Walrus bones lay about in all directions, showing that this animal had furnished the staple of subsistence. There were some remains, too, of the fox and the narwhal; but I found no signs of the seal or reindeer.

These Esquimaux have no mother earth to receive their dead, Esquimaux cairns. but they seat them in the attitude of repose, the knees drawn close to the body, and enclose them in a sack of skins. The implements of the living man are then grouped around him; they are covered with a rude dome of stones, and a cairn is piled above. This simple cenotaph will remain intact for generation after generation. The Esquimaux never disturb a grave.

From one of the graves I took several perforated and rudely-fashioned pieces of walrus ivory, evidently part of sledge and lance gear. But wood must have been even more scarce with them than with the natives of Baffin's Bay north of the Melville glacier. We found, for instance, a child's toy spear, which, though elaborately tipped with ivory, had its wooden handle pieced out of four separate bits, all carefully patched and bound with skin. No piece was more than six inches in length or half an inch in thickness.

We found other traces of Esquimaux, both on Littleton Island Traces of Esquimaux. and in Shoal-Water Cove, near it. They consisted of huts, graves, places of deposit for meat, and rocks arranged as foxtraps. These

CHAPTER were evidently very ancient; but they were so well preserved that
  V.   it was impossible to say how long they had been abandoned there,
       whether for fifty or a hundred years before.

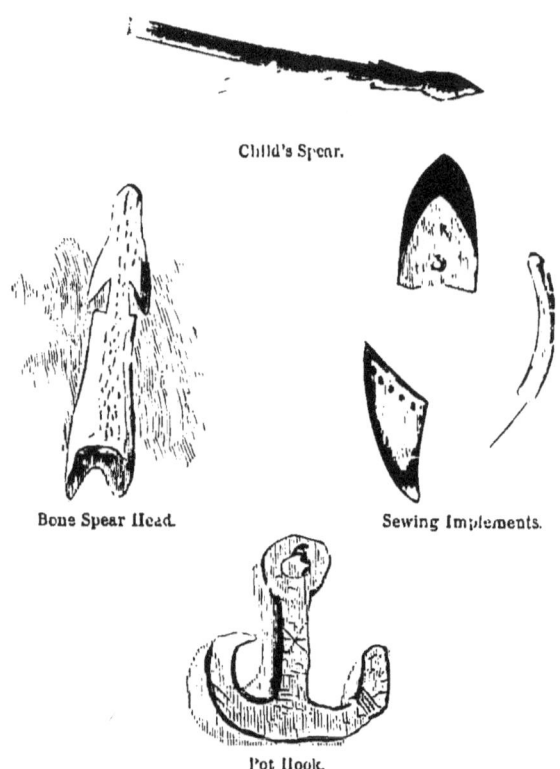

Child's Spear.

Bone Spear Head.   Sewing Implements.

Pot Hook.

ESQUIMAUX IMPLEMENTS, FROM GRAVES.

Erection of   Our stores deposited, it was our next office to erect a beacon,
a beacon   and intrust to it our tidings. We chose for this purpose the
over the
cairn   Western Cape of Littleton Island, as more conspicuous than Cape
         Hatherton; built our cairn; wedged a staff into the crevices of
         the rocks; and, spreading the American flag, hailed its folds with
         three cheers as they expanded in the cold midnight breeze. These
         important duties performed—the more lightly, let me say, for this
         little flicker of enthusiasm—we rejoined the brig early on the
         morning of the 7th, and forced on again towards the north, beating
         against wind and tide.

CHAPTER. VI.

CLOSING WITH THE ICE—REFUGE HARBOUR—DOGS—WALRUS--NARWHAL—
ICE-HILLS—BEACON CAIRN—ANCHORED TO A BERG—ESQUIMAUX HUTS
—PETER FORCE BAY—CAPE CORNELIUS GRINNELL—SHALLOWS—A GALE
—THE RECREANT DOGS.

" *August* 8, *Monday.*—I had seen the ominous blink ahead of us CHAPTER
from the Flagstaff Point of Littleton Island; and before two hours VI.
were over we closed with ice to the westward. It was in the Ice and
form of a pack, very heavy, and several seasons old; but we fog.
stood on, boring the loose stream-ice, until we had passed some
forty miles beyond Cape Life-Boat Cove. Here it became impossible to force our way further; and a dense fog gathering round
us, we were carried helplessly to the eastward. We should have
been forced upon the Greenland coast, but an eddy close in shore
released us for a few moments from the direct pressure, and we
were fortunate enough to get out a whale-line to the rocks, and
warp into a protecting niche.

" In the evening I ventured out again with the change of tide,
but it was only to renew a profitless conflict. The flood, encountering the southward movement of the floes, drove them in upon
the shore, and with such rapidity and force as to carry the
smaller bergs along with them. We were too happy, when, after Escape
a manful struggle of some hours, we found ourselves once more from the
out of their range.

" Our new position was rather nearer to the south than the one
we had left. It was in a beautiful cove, landlocked from east to
west, and accessible only from the north. Here we moored our vessel
securely by hawsers to the rocks and a whale-line carried out to
the narrow entrance. At M'Gary's suggestion, I called it ' Fog
Inlet ;' but we afterwards remembered it more thankfully as Refuge
REFUGE HARBOUR. Harbour

" *August* 9, *Tuesday.*—It may be noted among our little
miseries that we have more than fifty dogs on board, the majority
of whom might rather be characterized as ' ravening wolves.' To

3

feed this family, upon whose strength our progress and success
depend, is really a difficult matter.   The absence of shore or land
ice to the south in Baffin's Bay has prevented our rifles from contributing any material aid to our commissariat. Our two bears lasted
the cormorants but eight days; and to feed them upon the meagre
allowance of two pounds of raw flesh every other day is an
almost impossible necessity.   Only yesterday they were ready to
eat the caboose up, for I would not give them pemmican.   Corn
meal or beans, which Penny's dogs fed on, they disdain to touch,
and salt junk would kill them.

ESQUIMAUX DOGS.

"Accordingly I started out this morning to hunt walrus, with
which the Sound is teeming. We saw at least fifty of these dusky
monsters, and approached many groups within twenty paces; but
our rifle balls reverberated from their hides like cork pellets from
a pop gun target, and we could not get within harpoon-distance
of one.   Later in the day, however, Ohlsen, climbing a neighbouring hill to scan the horizon, and see if the ice had slackened,
found the dead carcase of a narwhal or sea-unicorn—a happy
discovery, which has secured for us at least six hundred pounds

of good fœtid wholesome flesh.   The length of the narwhal was
fourteen feet, and his process, or 'horn,' from the tip to its bony
encasement, four feet—hardly half the size of the noble specimen
I presented, to the Academy of Natural Sciences after my last
cruise.   We built a fire on the rocks, and melted down his
blubber; he will yield readily two barrels of oil.

"While we were engaged getting our narwhal on board, the
wind hauled round to the south-west, and the ice began to travel
back rapidly to the north.   This looks as if the resistance to the
northward was not very permanent.   There must be either great
areas of relaxed ice or open water leads along the shore.   But the
choking up of the floes on our eastern side still prevents an
attempt at progress.   This ice is the heaviest I have seen; and
its accumulation on the coast produces barricades more like bergs
than hummocks.   One of those rose perpendicularly more than
sixty feet.   Except the 'ice-hills' of Admiral Wrangell, on the
coast of Arctic Asia, nothing of ice-upheaval has ever been described equal to this.

"Still anxious beyond measure to get the vessel released, I
forced a boat through the drift to a point about a mile north of
us, from which I could overlook the Sound.   There was nothing
to be seen but a melancholy extent of impacted drift, stretching
northward as far as the eye could reach.   I erected a small
beacon-cairn on the point; and, as I had neither paper, pencil,
nor pennant, I burnt a K with powder on the rock, and scratching O. K. with a pointed bullet on my cap-lining, hoisted it as the
representative of a flag." *

With the small hours of Wednesday morning came a breeze from
the south-west, which was followed by such an apparent relaxation
of the floes at the slack-water of flood-tide, that I resolved to attempt
an escape from our little basin.   We soon warped to a narrow cul-
de-sac between the main pack on one side and the rocks on the other,
and after a little trouble made ourselves fast to a berg.

There was a small indentation ahead, which I had noticed on my
boat reconnoissance; and, as the breeze seemed to be freshening, I

* It was our custom, in obedience to a general order, to build cairns and leave notices
at every eligible point. One of these, rudely marked, much as I have described this one,
was found by Captain Hartstene, and, strange to say, was the only direct memorial of my
whereabouts communicated from some hundreds of beacons.

thought we might venture for it. But the floes were too strong for us; our eight-inch hawser parted like a whip-cord. There was no time for hesitation. I crowded sail, and bored into the drift, leaving Mr. Sontag and three men upon the ice. We did not reclaim them till, after some hours of adventure, we brought up under the lee of a grounded berg.

Working through the floes. I pass without notice our successive efforts to work the vessel to seaward through the floes. Each had its somewhat varied incidents, but all ended in failure to make progress. We found ourselves at the end of the day's struggles close to the same imperfectly-defined headland which I have marked on the chart as Cape Cornelius Grinnell, yet separated from it by a barrier of ice, and with our anchors planted in a berg.

In one of the attempts which I made with my boat to detect some pathway or outlet for the brig, I came upon a long rocky ledge, with a sloping terrace on its southern face, strangely green with sedges and poppies. I had learned to refer these unusual traces of vegetation to the fertilizing action of the refuse which gathers about the habitations of men. Yet I was startled, as I Esquimaux hut. walked round its narrow and dreary limits, to find an Esquimaux hut, so perfect in its preservation that a few hours' labour would have rendered it habitable. There were bones of the walrus, fox, and seal, scattered round it in small quantities; a dead dog was found close by, with the flesh still on his bones, and, a little further off, a bear-skin garment that retained its fur. In fact, for a deserted homestead, the scene had so little of the air of desolation about it, that it cheered my good fellows perceptibly.

Scenery on shore. The scenery beyond, upon the main shore, might have impressed men whose thoughts were not otherwise absorbed. An opening through the cliffs of trap rock disclosed a valley slope and distant rolling hills,—in fine contrast with the black precipices in front,— and a stream that came tumbling through the gorge ; we could hear its pastoral music even on board the brig, when the ice clamour intermitted.

The water around was so shoal that at three hundred yards from the shore we had but twelve-feet soundings at low tide. Great rocks, well worn and rounded, that must have been floated out by the ice at some former period, rose above the water at a half mile's distance, and the inner drift had fastened itself about them in

fantastic shapes. The bergs, too, were aground well out to sea- CHAPTER VI.
ward; and the cape ahead was completely packed with the ice
which they hemmed in. Tied up as we were to our own berg, we
were for the time in safety, though making no progress; but to
cast loose and tear out into the pack was to risk progress in the
wrong direction.

"*August* 12, *Friday.*—After careful consideration, I have deter- Sailing along the coast line.
mined to try for a further northing, by following the coast-line.
At certain stages of the tides—generally from three-quarters flood
to the commencement of the ebb—the ice evidently relaxes enough
to give a partial opening close along the land. The strength of
our vessel we have tested pretty thoroughly; if she will bear the
frequent groundings that we must look for, I am persuaded we may
seek these openings, and warp along them from one lump of
grounded ice to another. The water is too shoal for ice masses to
float in that are heavy enough to make a nip very dangerous. I
am preparing the little brig for this novel navigation, clearing her
decks, securing things below with extra lashings, and getting out
spars, to serve in case of necessity as shores to keep her on an even
keel.

"*August* 13, *Saturday.*—As long as we remain entangled in the Entangled in the shallows.
wretched shallows of this bight, the long, precipitous cape ahead
may prevent the north wind from clearing us; and the nearness of
the cliffs will probably give us squalls and flaws. Careful angular
distances taken between the shore and the chain of bergs to seaward show that these latter do not budge with either wind or tide.
It looks as if we were to have a change of weather. Is it worth
another attempt to warp out and see if we cannot double these
bergs to seaward? I have no great time to spare; the young ice
forms rapidly in quiet spots during the entire twenty-four hours.

August 14, *Sunday.*—The change of weather yesterday tempted Another tussle with the ice.
us to forsake our shelter and try another tussle with the ice. We
met it as soon as we ventured out; and the day closed with a
northerly progress, by hard warping, of about three-quarters of a
mile. The men were well tired; but the weather looked so
threatening, that I had them up again at three o'clock this morning. My immediate aim is to attain a low rocky island which we
see close into the shore, about a mile ahead of us.

"These low shallows are evidently caused by the rocks and

foreign materials discharged from the great valley. It is impossible to pass inside of them, for the huge boulders run close to the
shore.   Yet there is no such thing as doubling them outside,
without leaving the holding-ground of the coast and thrusting ourselves into the drifting chaos of the pack. If we can only reach
the little islet ahead of us, make a lee of its rocky crests, and hold
on there until the winds give us fairer prospects !

"*Midnight.*—We did reach it; and just in time. At 11-30
P.M. our first whale-line was made fast to the rocks. Ten minutes
later, the breeze freshened, and so directly in our teeth that we
could not have gained our mooring ground. It is blowing a gale
now, and the ice driving to the northward before it; but we can
rely upon our hawsers. All behind us is now solid pack.

August 15, Monday.—We are still fast, and, from the grinding
of the ice against the southern cape, the wind is doubtlessly blowing a strong gale from the southward. Once, early this morning,
the wind shifted by a momentary flaw, and came from the northward, throwing our brig with slack hawser upon the rocks. Though
she bumped heavily she started nothing, till we got out a stern-
line to a grounded iceberg.

"*August 16, Tuesday.*—Fast still ; the wind dying out, and the
ice outside closing steadily. And here, for all I can see, we must
hang on for the winter, unless Providence shall send a smart, ice-
shattering breeze, to open a road for us to the northward.

"More bother with these wretched dogs ! worse than a street of
Constantinople emptied upon our decks ; the unruly, thieving,
wild-beast pack ! Not a bear's paw, nor an Esquimaux cranium,
or basket of mosses, or any specimen whatever, can leave your
hands for a moment, without their making a rush at it, and, after
a yelping scramble, swallowing it at a gulp. I have seen them attempt a whole feather bed ; and here, this very morning, one of my
Karsuk brutes has eaten up two entire birds'-nests which I had
just before gathered from the rocks ; feathers, filth, pebbles, and
moss,—a peckful at the least. One was a perfect specimen of the
nest of the tridactyl, the other of the big burgomaster.

"When we reach a floe, or berg, or temporary harbour, they
start out in a body, neither voice nor lash restraining them, and
scamper off like a drove of hogs in an Illinois oak-opening. Two
of our largest left themselves behind at Fog Inlet, and we had to

send off a boat party to-day to their rescue. It cost a pull through
ice and water of about eight miles before they found the recreants,
fat and saucy, beside the carcass of the dead narwhal. After more
than an hour spent in attempts to catch them, one was tied and
brought on board; but the other suicidal scamp had to be left to
his fate."

CHAPTER VII.

THE ERIC ON A BERG—GODSEND LEDGE—HOLDING ON—ADRIFT—SCUDDING
—TOWED BY A BERG—UNDER THE CLIFFS—NIPPINGS—AGROUND—ICE
PRESSURE—AT REST.

CHAPTER
VII.

Prospect
of escape.

"*August* 16, *Tuesday.*—The formation of the young ice seems to
be retarded by the clouds ; its greatest nightly freezing has been
three-quarters of an inch. But I have no doubt, if we had continued
till now in our little Refuge Harbour, the winter would have closed
around us, without a single resource or chance for escape. Where
we are now I cannot help thinking our embargo must be temporary. Ahead of us, to the north-east, is the projecting headland
which terminates the long, shallow curve of Bedevilled Reach. This
serves as a lee to the northerly drift, and forms a bight into which
the south winds force the ice. The heavy floes and bergs that are
aground outside of us have encroached upon the lighter ice of the
reach, and choke its outlet to the sea. But a wind off shore would
start this whole pack, and leave us free. Meanwhile, for our comfort, a strong breeze is setting in from the southward, and the probabilities are that it will freshen to a gale.

"Eric the
Red."

"*August* 17, *Wednesday.*—This morning I pushed out into the
drift, with the useful little specimen of naval architecture, which I
call *Eric the Red*, but which the crew have named, less poetically, the *Red Boat.* We succeeded in forcing her on to one of
the largest bergs of the chain ahead, and I climbed it, in the hope
of seeing something like a lead outside, which might be reached
by boring. But there was nothing of the sort. The ice looked as
if perhaps an off-shore wind might spread it ; but, save a few

View from
an iceberg.

meagre pools, which from our lofty eminence looked like the
merest ink-spots on a table-cloth, not a mark of water could be
seen. I could see our eastern or Greenland coast extending on,
headland after headland, no less than five of them in number,
until they faded into the mysterious North. Everything else,
Ice !

"Up to this time we have had but two reliable observations to

PARTING HAWSERS OFF GODSEND LEDGE

determine our geographical position since entering Smith's Sound. These, however, were carefully made on shore by theodolite and artificial horizons; and, if our five chronometers, rated but two weeks ago at Upernavik, are to be depended upon, there can be no correspondence between my own and the Admiralty charts north of latitude 78° 18'. Not only do I remove the general coast-line some two degrees in longitude to the eastward, but its trend is altered sixty degrees of angular measurement. No landmarks of my predecessor, Captain Inglefield, are recognisable.

"In the afternoon came a gale from the southward. We had some rough rubbing from the floe-pieces, with three heavy hawsers out to the rocks of our little ice-breaker; but we held on. Toward midnight, our six-inch line, the smallest of the three, parted, but the other two held bravely. Feeling what good service this island has done us, what a Godsend it was to reach her, and how gallantly her broken rocks have protected us from the rolling masses of ice that grind by her, we have agreed to remember this anchorage as 'Godsend Ledge.'

"The walrus are very numerous, approaching within twenty feet of us, shaking their grim wet fronts, and mowing with their tusks the sea-ripples.

"*August* 19, *Friday*.—The sky looks sinister; a sort of scowl overhangs the blink under the great brow of clouds to the southward. The dovekies seem to distrust the weather, for they have forsaken the channel; but the walrus curvet around us in crowds. I have always heard that the close approach to land of these sphinx-faced monsters portends a storm. I was anxious to find a better shelter, and warped yesterday well down to the south end of the ledge; but I could not venture into the floes outside, without risking the loss of my dearly-earned ground. It may prove a hard gale; but we must wait it out patiently.

"*August* 20, *Saturday*, 3½ P.M.—By Saturday morning it blew a perfect hurricane. We had seen it coming, and were ready with three good hawsers out ahead, and all things snug on board.

"Still it came on heavier and heavier, and the ice began to drive more wildly than I thought I had ever seen it. I had just turned in to warm and dry myself during a momentary lull, and was stretching myself out in my bunk, when I heard the sharp twanging snap of a cord. Our six-inch hawser had parted, and we were swinging by the two others; the gale roaring like a lion to the southward.

"Half a minute more, and 'twang, twang!' came a second report. I knew it was the whale-line by the shrillness of the ring. Our noble ten-inch manilla still held on. I was hurrying my last sock into its seal-skin boot, when M'Gary came waddling down the companion-ladders:—'Captain Kane, she won't hold much longer: it's blowing the devil himself, and I am afraid to surge.'

"The manilla cable was proving its excellence when I reached the deck; and the crew, as they gathered round me, were loud in its praises. We could hear its deep Eolian chant, swelling through all the rattle of the running-gear and moaning of the shrouds. It was the death-song! The strands gave way with the noise of a shotted gun; and, in the smoke that followed their recoil, we were dragged out by the wild ice at its mercy.

"We steadied and did some petty warping, and got the brig a good bed in the rushing drift; but it all came to nothing. We then tried to beat back through the narrow ice-clogged water-way, that was driving, a quarter of a mile wide, between the shore and the pack. It cost us two hours of hard labour, I thought skilfully bestowed; but at the end of that time we were at least four miles off, opposite the great valley in the centre of Bedevilled Reach. Ahead of us, further to the north, we could see the strait growing still narrower, and the heavy ice-tables grinding up, and clogging it between the shore-cliffs on one side, and the ledge on the other. There was but one thing left for us --to keep in some sort the command of the helm, by going freely where we must otherwise be driven. We allowed her to scud under a reefed fore-top-sail, all hands watching the enemy, as we closed, in silence.

"At seven in the morning we were close upon the piling masses. We dropped our heaviest anchor with the desperate hope of winding the brig; but there was no withstanding the ice-torrent that followed us. We had only time to fasten a spar as a buoy to the chain, and let her slip. So went our best bower!

"Down we went upon the gale again, helplessly scraping along a lee of ice seldom less than thirty feet thick; one floe, measured

by a line as we tried to fasten to it, more than forty. I had seen CHAPTER VII.
such ice only once before, and never in such rapid motion. One
upturned mass rose above our gunwale, smashing in our bulwarks,
and depositing half a ton of ice in a lump upon our decks. Our
stanch little brig bore herself through all this wild adventure as
if she had a charmed life.

"But a new enemy came in sight ahead. Directly in our way, A group of
just beyond the line of floe-ice against which we were alternately bergs.
sliding and thumping, was a group of bergs. We had no power
to avoid them; and the only question was, whether we were to be
dashed in pieces against them, or whether they might not offer
us some providential nook of refuge from the storm. But, as we
neared them, we perceived that they were at some distance from
the floe-edge, and separated from it by an interval of open water.
Our hopes rose as the gale drove us toward this passage and into
it; and we were ready to exult, when, from some unexplained
cause,—probably an eddy of the wind against the lofty ice-walls,
—we lost our headway. Almost at the same moment we saw
that the bergs were not at rest; that with a momentum of their
own they were bearing down upon the other ice, and that it must
be our fate to be crushed between the two.

"Just then a broad sconce-piece or low water-washed berg
came driving up from the southward. The thought flashed upon
me of one of our escapes in Melville Bay; and as the sconce
moved rapidly close alongside us, M'Gary managed to plant an
anchor on its slope and hold on to it by a whale line. It was an
anxious moment. Our noble tow-horse, whiter than the pale Towed by
horse that seemed to be pursuing us, hauled us bravely on; the a berg.
spray dashing over his windward flanks, and his forehead ploughing
up the lesser ice as if in scorn. The bergs encroached upon us as
we advanced; our channel narrowed to a width of perhaps forty
feet; we braced the yards to clear the impending ice-walls.

". . . . We passed clear; but it was a close shave,—so close
that our port quarter-boat would have been crushed if we had not
taken it in from the davits,—and found ourselves under the lee
of a berg, in a comparatively open lead. Never did heart-tried
men acknowledge with more gratitude their merciful deliverance
from a wretched death. . . .

"The day had already its full share of trials; but there were

CHAPTER
VII.

more to come. A flaw drove us from our shelter, and the gale soon carried us beyond the end of the lead. We were again in the ice, sometimes escaping its onset by warping, sometimes forced to rely on the strength and buoyancy of the brig to stand its pressure, sometimes scudding wildly through the half-open drift. Our jib-boom was snapped off in the cap; we carried away our barricade stanchions, and were forced to leave our little *Eric*, with three brave fellows and their warps, out upon the floes behind us.

"A little pool of open water received us at last. It was just beyond a lofty cape that rose up like a wall, and under an iceberg that anchored itself between us and the gale. And here, close

Under the cliffs.

under the frowning shore of Greenland, ten miles nearer the Pole than our holding-ground of the morning, the men have turned in to rest.

"I was afraid to join them, for the gale was unbroken, and the floes kept pressing heavily upon our berg,—at one time so heavily as to sway it on its vertical axis toward the shore, and make its pinnacle overhang our vessel. My poor fellows had but a precarious sleep before our little harbour was broken up. They hardly reached the deck when we were driven astern, our rudder splintered, and the pintles torn from their boltings.

Nippings.

"Now began the nippings. The first shock took us on our port-quarter; the brig bearing it well, and, after a moment of the old-fashioned suspense, rising by jerks handsomely. The next was from a veteran floe, tongued and honeycombed, but floating in a single table over twenty feet in thickness. Of course, no wood or iron could stand this; but the shoreward face of our iceberg happened to present an inclined plane, descending deep into the water; and up this the brig was driven, as if some great steam screw-power was forcing her into a dry dock.

"At one time I expected to see her carried bodily up its face and tumbled over on her side. But one of those mysterious relaxations, which I have elsewhere called the pulses of the ice, lowered us quite gradually down again into the rubbish, and we were forced out of the line of pressure toward the shore. Here we succeeded in carrying out a warp, and making fast. We grounded as the tide fell; and would have heeled over to seaward, but for a mass of detached land-ice that grounded alongside of

THE NIP OFF CAPE CORNELIUS GRINNELL—FORGE BAY

us, and, although it stove our bulwarks as we rolled over it,
shored us up."

I could hardly get to my bunk, as I went down into our littered cabin on the Sunday morning after our hard-working vigil of thirty-six hours. Bags of clothing, food, tents, India - rubber blankets, and the hundred little personal matters which every man likes to save in a time of trouble, were scattered around in places where the owners thought they might have them at hand. The pemmican had been on deck, the boats equipped, and everything of real importance ready for a march, many hours before.

During the whole of the scenes I have been trying to describe, I could not help being struck by the composed and manly demeanour of my comrades. The turmoil of ice under a heavy sea often conveys the impression of danger when the reality is absent; but in this fearful passage, the parting of our hawsers, the loss of our anchors, the abrupt crushing of our stoven bulwarks, and the actual deposit of ice upon our decks, would have tried the nerves of the most experienced ice-men. All—officers and men—worked alike. Upon each occasion of collision with the ice which formed our lee-coast, efforts were made to carry out lines; and some narrow escapes were incurred by the zeal of the parties leading them into positions of danger. Mr. Bonsall avoided being crushed by leaping to a floating fragment; and no less than four of our men at one time were carried down by the drift, and could only be recovered by a relief party after the gale had subsided.

As our brig, borne on by the ice, commenced her ascent of the berg, the suspense was oppressive. The immense blocks piled against her, range upon range, pressing themselves under her keel and throwing her over upon her side, till, urged by the successive accumulations, she rose slowly and as if with convulsive efforts along the sloping wall. Still there was no relaxation of the impelling force. Shock after shock, jarring her to her very centre, she continued to mount steadily on her precarious cradle. But for the groaning of her timbers and the heavy sough of the floes, we might have heard a pin drop. And then, as she settled down into her old position, quietly taking her place among the broken rubbish, there was a deep-breathing silence, as though all were waiting for some signal before the clamour of congratulation and comment could burst forth.

CHAPTER VIII.

TRACKING INSPECTING A HARBOUR—THE MUSK OX—STILL TRACKING -
CONSULTATION—WARPING AGAIN—AGROUND NEAR THE ICE-FOOT—A
BREATHING SPELL—THE BOAT EXPEDITION—DEPARTURE.

CHAPTER
VIII.

IT was not until the 22d that the storm abated, and our absent
men were once more gathered back into their mess. During the
interval of forced inaction, the little brig was fast to the ice-belt
which lined the bottom of the cliffs, and all hands rested ; but as
soon as it was over, we took advantage of the flood-tide to pass
our tow-lines to the ice-beach, and, harnessing ourselves in like

Tracking. mules on a canal, made a good three miles by tracking along the
coast.

"*August 22, Monday.*—Under this coast, at the base of a
frowning precipice, we are now working toward a large bay which
runs well in, facing at its opening to the north and west. I should
save time if I could cross from headland to headland; but I am
obliged to follow the tortuous land-belt, without whose aid we
would go adrift in the pack again.

"The trend of our line of operations to-day is almost due
east. We are already protected from the south, but fearfully
exposed to a northerly gale. Of this there are fortunately no
indications.

The brig
grounds
again.

"*August 23, Tuesday.*—We tracked along the ice-belt for about
one mile, when the tide fell, and the brig grounded, heeling over
until she reached her bearings. She rose again at 10 P.M., and the
crew turned out upon the ice-belt.

Inclina-
tion of the
shore to
the east.

"The decided inclination to the eastward which the shore shows
here is important as a geographical feature ; but it has made our
progress to the actual north much less than our wearily-earned
miles should count for us. Our latitude, determined by the sun's
lower culmination, if such a term can be applied to his midnight
depression, gives 78° 41'. We are further north, therefore, than
any of our predecessors, except Parry on his Spitzbergen foot-
tramp. There are those with whom, no matter how insuperable

the obstacle, failure involves disgrace; we are safe at least from their censure.

"Last night I sent out Messrs. Wilson, Petersen, and Bonsall, to inspect a harbour which seems to lie between a small island and a

TRACKING ALONG THE ICE-BELT.

valley that forms the inner slope of our bay. They report recent traces of deer, and bring back the skull of a musk ox.

"Hitherto this animal has never been seen east of Melville Island. But his being here does not surprise me. The migratory passages of the reindeer, who is even less Arctic in his range than the musk ox, led me to expect it. The fact points to some pro-bable land connection between Greenland and America, or an approach sufficiently close to allow these animals to migrate between the two.

"The head is that of a male, well marked, but old; the teeth deficient, but the horns very perfect. These last measure 2 feet 3 inches across from tip to tip, and are each 1 foot 10 inches in length measured to the medium line of the forehead, up to which they are continued in the characteristic boss or protuberance. Our winter may be greatly cheered by their beef, should they revisit this solitude.

CHAPTER VIII.

Flora of the shore.

"We have collected thus far no less than twenty-two species of flowering plants on the shores of this bay. Scanty as this starved flora may seem to the botanists of more favoured zones, it was not without surprise and interest that I recognised among its thoroughly Arctic types many plants which had before been considered as indigenous only to more southern latitudes.

"The thermometer gave 25° last night, and the young ice formed without intermission; it is nearly two inches alongside the brig. I am loth to recognise these signs of the advancing cold. Our latitude to-day gives us 78° 37', taken from a station some three miles inside the indentation to the south.

Still tracking.

"*August 24, Wednesday.*—We have kept at it, tracking along, grounding at low water, but working like horses when the tides allowed us to move. We are now almost at the bottom of this indentation. Opposite us, on the shore, is a remarkable terrace, which rises in a succession of steps until it is lost in the low rocks of the back country. The ice around us is broken, but heavy, and so compacted that we can barely penetrate it. It has snowed hard since 10 P.M. of yesterday, and the sludge fills up the interstices of the floes. Nothing but a strong south wind can give us further progress to the north.

The young ice.

"*August 25, Thursday.*—The snow of yesterday has surrounded us with a pasty sludge; but the young ice continues to be our most formidable opponent. The mean temperatures of the 22d and 23d were 27° and 30° Fahrenheit. I do not like being caught by winter before attaining a higher northern latitude than this, but it appears almost inevitable. Favoured as we have been by the mildness of the summer and by the abraiding action of the tides, there are indications around us which point to an early winter.

"We are sufficiently surrounded by ice to make our chances of escape next year uncertain, and yet not as far as I could wish for our spring journeys by the sledge.

Proposal to return.

"*August 26, Friday.*—My officers and crew are stanch and firm men; but the depressing influences of want of rest, the rapid advance of winter, and, above all, our slow progress, make them sympathize but little with this continued effort to force a way to the north. One of them, an excellent member of the party, volunteered an expression of opinion this morning in favour of returning to the south and giving up the attempt to winter."

It is unjust for a commander to measure his subordinates in CHAPTER VIII. such exigencies by his own standard. The interest which they feel in an undertaking is of a different nature from his own. With him there are always personal motives, apart from official duty, to stimulate effort. He receives, if successful, too large a share of the credit, and he justly bears all the odium of failure.

An apprehension—I hope a charitable one—of this fact leads me to consider the opinions of my officers with much respect. I called them together at once, in a formal council, and listened to A council their views in full. With but one exception, Mr. Henry held. Brooks, they were convinced that a further progress to the north was impossible, and were in favour of returning southward to winter.

Not being able conscientiously to take the same view, I explained to them the importance of securing a position which might expedite our sledge journeys in the future; and, after assuring them that such a position could only be attained by continuing our efforts, announced my intention of warping toward the northern headland of the bay. " Once there, I shall be able to determine The decision. from actual inspection the best point for setting out on the operations of the spring; and at the nearest possible shelter to that point I will put the brig into winter harbour." My comrades received this decision in a manner that was most gratifying, and entered zealously upon the hard and cheerless duty it involved.

The warping began again, each man, myself included, taking his Warping through turn at the capstan. The ice seemed less heavy as we penetrated the ice. into the recess of the bay; our track-lines and shoulder-belts replaced the warps. Hot coffee was served out; and, in the midst of cheering songs, our little brig moved off briskly.

Our success, however, was not complete. At the very period of high-water she took the ground while close under the walls of the ice-foot. It would have been madness to attempt shoring her up. I could only fasten heavy tackle to the rocks which lined the base of the cliffs, and trust to the noble little craft's unassisted strength.

" *August* 27, *Saturday.*—We failed, in spite of our efforts, to get the brig off with last night's tide; and, as our night-tides are generally the highest, I have some apprehensions as to her liberation.

4

CHAPTER
VIII.

"We have landed everything we could get up on the rocks, put out all our boats and filled them with ponderables alongside, sunk our rudder astern, and lowered our remaining heavy anchor into one of our quarter-boats. Heavy hawsers are out to a grounded lump of berg-ice, ready for instant heaving.

"Last night she heeled over again so abruptly that we were all tumbled out of our berths. At the same time the cabin stove with a full charge of glowing anthracite was thrown down. The

The ship
on fire.

deck blazed smartly for a while; but, by sacrificing Mr. Sontag's heavy pilot-cloth coat to the public good, I choked it down till water could be passed from above to extinguish it. It was fortunate we had water near at hand, for the powder was not far off.

"3 P.M.—The ground-ice is forced in upon our stern, splintering our rudder, and drawing again the bolts of the pintle-casings.

AGROUND NEAR THE ICE-FOOT.

A float and
aground
again.

5 P.M.—She floats again, and our track-lines are manned. The men work with a will, and the brig moves along bravely.

"10 P.M.—Aground again; and the men, after a hot supper,

have turned in to take a spell of sleep. The brig has a hard time of it with the rocks. She has been high and dry for each of the two last tides, and within three days has grounded no less than five times. I feel that this is hazardous navigation, but am convinced it is my duty to keep on. Except the loss of a portion of our false keel, we have sustained no real injury. The brig is still water-tight; and her broken rudder and one shattered spar can be easily repaired. CHAPTER VIII.

Hazardous navigation.

"*August* 28, *Sunday.*— By a complication of purchases, jumpers, and shores, we started the brig at 4.10; and, Mr. Ohlsen having temporarily secured the rudder, I determined to enter the floe and trust to the calm of the morning for a chance of penetrating to the northern land-ice ahead.

"This land-ice is very old, and my hope is to get through the loose trash that surrounds it by springing, and then find a fast that may serve our tracking-lines. I am already well on my way, and, in spite of the ominous nods of my officers, have a fair prospect of reaching it. Here it is that splicing the main-brace is of service!

"I took the boat this morning with Mr. M'Gary, and sounded along outside the land-floe. I am satisfied the passage is practicable, and, by the aid of tide, wind, and springs, have advanced into the trash some two hundred yards.

"We have reached the floe, and find it as I hoped; the only drawback to tracking being the excessive tides, which expose us to grounding at low-water."

We had now a breathing spell, and I could find time to look out again upon the future. The broken and distorted area around us gave little promise of successful sledge-travel. But all this might change its aspect under the action of a single gale, and it was by no means certain that the ice-fields further north would have the same rugged and dispiriting character. Besides, the ice-belt was still before us, broken sometimes and difficult to traverse, but practicable for a party on foot, apparently for miles ahead; and I felt sure that a resolute boat's crew might push and track their way for some distance along it. I resolved to make the trial, and to judge what ought to be our wintering ground from a personal inspection of the coast. A short rest.

Plans for the future.

I had been quietly preparing for such an expedition for some

CHAPTER
VIII.
time. Our best and lightest whale boat had been fitted with a
canvass cover, that gave it all the comfort of a tent. We had a

THE FORLORN HOPE.

supply of pemmican ready packed in small cases, and a sledge
taken to pieces was stowed away under the thwarts. In the
morning of the 29th, Mr. Brooks, M'Gary, and myself, walked
fourteen miles along the marginal ice ; it was heavy and complicated with drift, but there was nothing about it to make me change
my purpose.

The boat
crew and
their
equipment
My boat crew consisted of seven, all of them volunteers and
reliable :—Brooks, Bonsall, M'Gary, Sontag, Riley, Blake, and
Morton. We had buffalo-robes for our sleeping-gear, and a single
extra day suit was put on board as common property. Each man
carried his girdle full of woollen socks, so as to dry them by the
warmth of his body, and a tin-cup, with a sheath-knife, at the belt;
a soup-pot and lamp for the mess completed our outfit.

Departure
of the For-
lorn Hope.
In less than three hours from my first order, the *Forlorn Hope*
was ready for her work, covered with tin to prevent her being cut
through by the bay-ice ; and at half-past three in the afternoon
she was freighted, launched, and on her way.

I placed Mr. Ohlsen in command of the *Advance*, and Dr. Hayes

charge of her log; Mr. Ohlsen with orders to haul the brig to ᴄʜᴀᴘᴛᴇʀ
ᵉ southward and eastward into a safe berth, and there to await ᴠ́ɪɪɪ.
y return.

Many a warm shake of the hand from the crew we left showed ᴀ ғʀɪᴇɴᴅʟʏ
c that our good-bye was not a mere formality.   Three hearty ᵖᵃʳᵗⁱⁿᵍ
ieers from all hands followed us,—a God-speed as we pushed off

CHAPTER IX.

THE DEPÔT JOURNEY—THE ICE-BELT—CROSSING MINTURN RIVER—SKELE
TON MUSK OX—CROSSING THE GLACIER—PORTAGE OF INSTRUMENTS—
EXCESSIVE BURDEN—MARY MINTURN RIVER—FORDING THE RIVER—
THACKERAY HEADLAND—CAPE GEORGE RUSSELL—RETURN TO THE BRIG
—THE WINTER HARBOUR.

CHAPTER IX. In the first portions of our journey, we found a narrow but obstructed passage between the ice-belt and the outside pack. It
was but a few yards in width, and the young ice upon it was
nearly thick enough to bear our weight. By breaking it up we
were able with effort to make about seven miles a day.

The night encampment. After such work, wet, cold, and hungry, the night's rest was
very welcome. A couple of stanchions were rigged fore and aft, a
sail tightly spread over the canvas cover of our boat, the cooking-
lamp lit, and the buffalo-robes spread out. Dry socks replaced
the wet; hot tea and pemmican followed; and very soon we forgot
the discomforts of the day,—the smokers musing over their pipes,
and the sleepers snoring in dreamless forgetfulness.

We had been out something less than twenty-four hours when
we came to the end of our boating. In front and on one side was
the pack, and on the other a wall some ten feet above our heads,
the impracticable ice-belt. By waiting for high tide, and taking
advantage of a chasm which a water-stream had worn in the ice,
we managed to haul up our boat on its surface ; but it was appa-
The boat left on the ice. rent that we must leave her there. She was stowed away snugly
under the shelter of a large hummock ; and we pushed forward in
our sledge, laden with a few articles of absolute necessity.

Here, for the first time, we were made aware of a remarkable
feature of our travel. We were on a table or shelf of ice, which
clung to the base of the rocks overlooking the sea, but itself over-
A highway of ice. hung by steep and lofty cliffs. Pure and beautiful as this icy
highway was, huge angular blocks, some many tons in weight,
were scattered over its surface ; and long tongues of worn-down
rock occasionally issued from the sides of the cliffs, and extended

across our course. The cliffs measured 1010 feet to the crest of the plateau above them.*

We pushed forward on this ice-table shelf as rapidly as the obstacles would permit, though embarrassed a good deal by the frequent watercourses, which created large gorges in our path, winding occasionally, and generally steep-sided. We had to pass our sledge carefully down such interruptions, and bear it ⸢.⸣pon our shoulders, wading, of course, through water of an extremely low temperature. Our night halts were upon knolls of snow under the rocks. At one of these the tide overflowed our tent, and forced us to save our buffalo sleeping-gear by holding it up until the water subsided. This exercise, as it turned out, was more of a trial to our patience than to our health. The circulation was assisted perhaps by a perception of the ludicrous. Eight Yankee Caryatides, up to their knees in water, and an entablature sustaining such of their household gods as could not bear immersion!

On the 1st of September, still following the ice-belt, we found that we were entering the recesses of another bay but little smaller than that in which we had left our brig. The limestone walls ceased to overhang us ; we reached a low fiord, and a glacier blocked our way across it. A succession of terraces, rising with symmetrical regularity, lost themselves in long parallel lines in the distance. They were of limestone shingle, and wet with the percolation of the melted ice of the glacier. Where the last of these terraced faces abutted upon the sea, it blended with the ice-foot, so as to make a frozen compound of rock and ice. Here, lying in a pasty slit, I found the skeleton of a musk ox. The head was united to the atlas ; but the bones of the spine were separated about two inches apart, and conveyed the idea of a displacement produced rather by the sliding of the bed beneath, than by a force from without. The paste, frozen so as to resemble limestone rock, had filled the costal cavity, and the ribs were beautifully polished. It was to the eye an embedded fossil, ready for the museum of the collector.

I am minute in detailing these appearances, for they connect

Marginal notes:
CHAP. IX.

Travelling on the ice-belt.

Limestone terraces.

Cliffs of rock and ice.

Skeleton of a musk ox.

---

* The cliffs were of tabular magnesian limestone, with interlaid and inferior sandstones. Their height, measured to the crest of the plateau, was 950 feet—a fair mean of the profile of the coast. The height of the talus of debris, where it united with the face of the cliff, was 590 feet, and its angle of inclination between 38° and 45°.

themselves in my mind with the fossils of the Eischoltz cliffs, and
the Siberian alluvions. I was startled at the facility with which
the silicious limestone, under the alternate energies of frost and
thaw, had been incorporated with the organic remains. It had
already begun to alter the structure of the bones, and in several
instances the vertebræ were entirely enveloped in travertin.

The table-lands and ravines round about this coast abound in
such remains. Their numbers and the manner in which they are
scattered imply that the animals made their migrations in droves,
as is the case with the reindeer now. Within the area of a few
acres we found seven skeletons and numerous skulls ; these all
occupied the snow streams or gullies that led to a gorge opening
on the ice-belt, and might thus be gathered in time to one spot by
the simple action of the watershed.

To cross this glacier gave us much trouble. Its sides were
steep, and a slip at any time might have sent us into the water
below. Our shoes were smooth, unfortunately ; but, by using
cords, and lying at full length upon the ice, we got over without
accident. On the other side of the glacier we had a portage of
about three miles ; the sledge being unladen and the baggage
carried on our backs. To Mr. Brooks, admitted with unanimity
to be the strongest man of our party, was voted our theodolite,
about sixty pounds of well-polished mechanism, in an angular
mahogany box. Our dip-circle, equally far from being an honorary
tribute, fell to the lot of a party of volunteers, who bore it by
turns.

During this inland crossing, I had fine opportunities of making
sections of the terraces. We ascertained the mean elevation of
the face of the coast to be 1300 feet. On regaining the seaboard
the same frowning cliffs and rock-covered ice-belt that we had left
greeted us.

After an absence of five days, we found by observation that we
were but forty miles from the brig. Besides our small daily progress, we had lost much by the tortuous windings of the coast.
The ice outside did not invite a change of plan in that direction ;
but I determined to leave the sledge and proceed overland on foot.
With the exception of our instruments, we carried no weight but
pemmican and one buffalo-robe. The weather, as yet not far below
the freezing-point, did not make a tent essential to the bivouac ; and,

with this light equipment, we could travel readily two miles to one CHAPTER IX.
with our entire outfit. On the 4th of September we made twenty-
four miles with comparative ease, and were refreshed by a comfortable sleep after the toils of the day.*

The only drawback to this new method of advance was the Load of
inability to carry a sufficient quantity of food. Each man at each man
starting had a fixed allowance of pemmican, which, with his
other load, made an average weight of thirty-five pounds. It
proved excessive ; the Canadian voyageurs will carry much more,
and for an almost indefinite period ; but we found—and we had
good walkers in our party—that a very few pounds overweight
broke us down.

Our progress on the 5th was arrested by another bay much Discovery
larger than any we had seen since entering Smith's Straits. It of a bay.
was a noble sheet of water, perfectly open, and thus in strange contrast to the ice outside. The cause of this at the time inexplicable
phenomenon was found in a roaring and tumultuous river, which,
issuing from a fiord at the inner sweep of the bay, rolled with the
violence of a snow-torrent over a broken bed of rocks. This river, Mary Min-
the largest probably yet known in North Greenland, was about three- turn river
quarters of a mile wide at its mouth, and admitted the tides for
about three miles, when its bed rapidly ascended, and could be
traced by the configuration of the hills as far as a large inner fiord,
I called it Mary Minturn River, after the sister of Mrs. Henry
Grinnell. Its course was afterwards pursued to an interior glacier,
from the base of which it was found to issue in numerous streams,
that united into a single trunk about forty miles above its mouth.
By the banks of this stream we encamped, lulled by the unusual
music of running waters.

Here, protected from the frost by the infiltration of the melted Flowers on
snows, and fostered by the reverberation of solar heat from the the banks
of the
rocks, we met a flower-growth, which, though drearily Arctic in stream.
its type, was 'rich in variety and colouring. Amid festuca and
other tufted grasses, twinkled the purple lychnis and the white
star of the chickweed ; and not without its pleasing associations

---

* This halt was under the lee of a large boulder of greenstone, measuring 14 feet in its
long diameter. It had the rude blocking out of a cube, but was rounded at the edges. The
country for fourteen miles around was of the low-bottom series; the nearest greenstone
must have been many miles remote. Boulders of syenite were numerous; their line of
deposit nearly due north and south.

CHAPTER IX.

I recognised a solitary hesperis,—the Arctic representative of the wallflowers of home.

Fording the river.

We forded our way across this river in the morning, carrying our pemmican as well as we could out of water, but submitting ourselves to a succession of plunge baths as often as we trusted our weight on the ice-capped stones above the surface. The average depth was not over our hips; but the crossing cost us so much labour that we were willing to halt half a day to rest.

Some seven miles further on a large cape projects into this bay and divides it into two indentations, each of them the seat of minor watercourses, fed by the glaciers. From the numerous tracks found in the moss-beds, they would seem to be the resort of deer. Our meridian observations by theodolite gave the latitude of but 78° 52': the magnetic dip was 84° 49'.

Direction of the coast.

It was plain that the coast of Greenland here faced toward the north. The axis of both these bays and the general direction of the watercourses pointed to the same conclusion. Our longitude was 78° 41' W.

Leaving four of my party to recruit at this station, I started the next morning, with three volunteers, to cross the ice to the north-eastern headland, and thus save the almost impossible circuit by the shores of the bay. This ice was new, and far from safe: its margin along the open water made by Minturn River required both care and tact in passing over it. We left the heavy theodolite behind us, and carried nothing except a pocket-sextant, my Fraunhöfer, a walking-pole, and three days' allowance of raw pemmican.

We reached the headland after sixteen miles of walk, and found the ice-foot in good condition, evidently better fitted for sledge-travel than it was to the south. This point I named Cape William Makepeace Thackeray. Our party knew it as Chimney Rock. It was the last station on the coast of Greenland, determined by intersecting bearings of theodolite, from known positions to the south. About eight miles beyond it is a large headland, the highest visible from the late position of our brig, shutting out all points further north. It is indicated on my chart as Cape Francis Hawks. We found the tablelands were 1200 feet high by actual measurement, and interior plateaus were seen of an estimated height of 1800.

Cape William Makepeace Thackeray

Height of the tablelands and plateaus.

I determined to seek some high headland beyond the cape, and make it my final point of reconnoissance.

I shall never forget the sight, when, after a hard day's walk, I looked out from an altitude of 1100 feet upon an expanse extending beyond the eightieth parallel of latitude. Far off on my left was the western shore of the Sound, losing itself in distance toward the north. To my right a rolling primary country led on to a low dusky wall-like ridge, which I afterwards recognised as the Great Glacier of Humboldt; and still beyond this, reaching northward from the N.N.E., was the land which now bears the name of Washington; its most projecting headland, Cape Andrew Jackson, bore 14° by sextant from the furthest hill, Cape John Barrow, on the opposite side. The great area between was a solid sea of ice. Close along its shore, almost looking down upon it from the crest of our lofty station, we could see the long lines of hummocks dividing the floes like the trenches of a beleaguered city. Further out, a stream of icebergs, increasing in numbers as they receded, showed an almost impenetrable barrier, since I could not doubt that among their recesses the ice was so crushed as to be impassable by the sledge.

Nevertheless, beyond these again the ice seemed less obstructed. Distance is very deceptive upon the ice, subduing its salient features, and reducing even lofty bergs to the appearance of a smooth and attractive plain. But, aided by my Fraunhöfer telescope, I could see that traversable areas were still attainable. Slowly, and almost with a sigh, I laid the glass down and made up my mind for a winter search.

I had seen no place combining so many of the requisites of a good winter harbour as the bay in which we left the *Advance*. Near its south-western corner the wide streams and the watercourses on the shore promised the earliest chances of liberation in the coming summer. It was secure against the moving ice : lofty headlands walled it in beautifully to seaward, enclosing an anchorage with a moderate depth of water ; yet it was open to the meridian sunlight, and guarded from winds, eddies, and drift. The space enclosed was only occupied by a few rocky islets and our brig. We soon came in sight of her on our return march, as she lay at anchor in its southern sweep, with her masts cutting sharply against the white glacier ; and, hurrying on through a gale, were taken on board without accident.

My comrades gathered anxiously around me, waiting for the

Marginal notes: CHAPTER IX. — The Great Glacier of Humboldt — A winter harbour — Return to the brig.

CHAPTER
IX.

news. I told them in a few words of the results of our journey, and why I had determined upon remaining, and gave at once the order to warp in between the islands. We found seven-fathom soundings and a perfect shelter from the outside ice; and thus laid our little brig in the harbour, which we were fated never to leave together,—a long resting-place to her indeed, for the same ice is around her still.

CHAPTER X.

APPROACHING WINTER—STORING PROVISIONS—BUTLER STOREHOUSE—SUN-
DAY AT REST—BUILDING OBSERVATORY—TRAINING THE DOGS—THE
LITTLE WILLIE—THE ROAD—THE FAITH—SLEDGING—RECONNOISSANCE
—DEPÔT PARTY.

THE winter was now approaching rapidly. The thermometer had
fallen by the 10th of September to 14°, and the young ice had
cemented the floes so that we could walk and sledge round the
brig. About sixty paces north of us an iceberg had been caught,
and was frozen in; it was our neighbour while we remained in
Rensselaer Harbour. The rocky islets around us were fringed

RENSSELAER HARBOUR.

with hummocks; and, as the tide fell, their sides were coated with
opaque crystals of bright white. The birds had gone. The sea

CHAPTER
X.

Migration
of the
birds.
swallows, which abounded when we first reached here, and even the young burgomasters that lingered after them, had all taken their departure for the south. Except the snow-birds, these are the last to migrate of all the Arctic birds.

"*September* 10, *Saturday.*—We have plenty of responsible work before us. The long 'night in which no man can work' is close at hand : in another month we shall lose the sun. Astronomically.

Probable
time of
the sun's
disappear-
ance.
he should disappear on the 24th of October, if our horizon were free ; but it is obstructed by a mountain ridge, and, making all allowance for refraction, we cannot count on seeing him after the 10th.

"First and foremost, we have to unstow the hold, and deposit its contents in the storehouse on Butler Island. Brooks and a

BUTLER'S ISLAND STOREHOUSE.

party are now briskly engaged in this double labour, running loaded boats along a canal that has to be recut every morning.

Catering
for winter
diet.
"Next comes the catering for winter diet. We have little or no game as yet in Smith's Sound ; and, though the traces of deer that we have observed may be followed by the animals themselves, I cannot calculate upon them as a resource. I am without the her-metically-sealed meats of our last voyage ; and the use of salt meat

in circumstances like ours is never safe. A fresh-water pond, which fortunately remains open at Medary, gives me a chance for some further experiments in freshening this portion of our stock. Steaks of salt junk, artistically cut, are strung on lines like a country-woman's dried apples, and soaked in festoons under the ice. The salmon-trout and salt codfish which we bought at Fiskernaes are placed in barrels, perforated to permit a constant circulation of fresh water through them. Our pickled cabbage is similarly treated, after a little potash has been used to neutralize the acid. All these are submitted to twelve hours of alternate soaking and freezing, the crust of ice being removed from them before each immersion. This is the steward's province, and a most important one it is.

" Every one else is well employed,—M'Gary arranging and Bonsall making the inventory of our stores ; Ohlsen and Petersen building our deck-house ; while I am devising the plan of an architectural interior, which is to combine, of course, the utmost ventilation, room, dryness, warmth, general accommodation, comfort,—in a word, all the appliances of health.

" We have made a comfortable dog-house on Butler Island ; but though our Esquimaux *canaille* are within scent of our cheeses there, one of which they ate yesterday for lunch, they cannot be persuaded to sleep away from the vessel. They prefer the bare snow, where they can couch within the sound of our voices, to a warm kennel upon the rocks. Strange that this dog-distinguish- ing trait of affection for man should show itself in an animal so imperfectly reclaimed from a savage state that he can hardly be caught when wanted !

" *September* 11, *Sunday.*—To-day came to us the first quiet Sunday of harbour life. We changed our log registration from sea-time to the familiar home series that begins at midnight. It is not only that the season has given us once more a local habitation ; but there is something in the return of varying day and night that makes it grateful to reinstate this domestic observance. The long staring day, which has clung to us for more than two months, to the exclusion of the stars, has begun to intermit its brightness. Even Aldebaran, the red eye of the Bull, flared out into familiar recollection as early as ten o'clock ; and the heavens, though still somewhat reddened by the gaudy tints of midnight,

CHAPTER
X.
The Polar
Star.
gave us Capella and Arcturus, and even that lesser light of home
memories, the Polar Star. Stretching my neck to look uncomfortably at this indication of our extreme northernness, it was hard to
realize that he was not directly overhead; and it made me sigh, as
I measured the few degrees of distance that separated our zenith
from the Pole over which he hung.

"We had our accustomed morning and evening prayers;
and the day went by, full of sober thought, and, I trust, wise
resolve.

"*September* 12, *Monday.*—Still going on with Saturday's operations, amid the thousand discomforts of house-cleaning and moving combined. I dodged them for an hour this morning, to fix
Site of the
observa-
tory.
with Mr. Sontag upon a site for our observatory; and the men are
already at work hauling the stone for it over the ice on sledges.
It is to occupy a rocky islet, about a hundred yards off, that I
"Fern
Rock."
have named after a little spot that I long to see again, 'FERN
ROCK.' This is to be for me the centre of familiar localities. As
the classic Mivins breakfasted lightly on a cigar and took it out in
sleep, so I have dined on salt pork and made my dessert of home
dreams.

Provision
depôts.
"*September* 13, *Tuesday.*—Besides preparing our winter quarters, I am engaged in the preliminary arrangements for my provision depôts along the Greenland coast. Mr. Kennedy is, I
believe, the only one of my predecessors who has used October and
November for Arctic field-work; but I deem it important to our
movements during the winter and spring, that the depôts in
advance should be made before the darkness sets in. I purpose
arranging three of them at intervals,—pushing them as far forward
as I can,—to contain in all some twelve hundred pounds of provision, of which eight hundred will be pemmican."

Plans of
future
search.
My plans of future search were directly dependent upon the success of these operations of the fall. With a chain of provision-
depôts along the coast of Greenland, I could readily extend my
travel by dogs. These noble animals formed the basis of my future
plans : the only drawback to their efficiency as a means of travel
was their inability to carry the heavy loads of provender essential
for their support. A badly-fed or heavily-loaded dog is useless for
a long journey ; but with relays of provision I could start empty,
and fill up at our final station.

My dogs were both Esquimaux and Newfoundlanders. Of these CHAPTER X.
last I had ten : they were to be carefully broken, to travel by voice
without the whip, and were expected to be very useful for heavy Training the dogs
draught, as their tractability would allow the driver to regulate their pace. I was already training them in a light sledge,
to drive, unlike the Esquimaux, two abreast, with a regular harness,
a breast-collar of flat leather, and a pair of traces. Six of them
made a powerful travelling-team ; and four could carry me and
my instruments, for short journeys around the brig, with great
ease.

The sledge I used for them was built, with the care of cabinet- The *Little Willie.*
work, of American hickory, thoroughly seasoned. The curvature
of the runners was determined experimentally; they were shod
with annealed steel, and fastened by copper rivets, which could
be renewed at pleasure. Except this, no metal entered into its
construction. All its parts were held together by seal-skin lashings, so that it yielded to inequalities of surface and to sudden
shock. The three paramount considerations of lightness, strength,
and diminished friction, were well combined in it. This beautiful
and, as we afterwards found, efficient and enduring sledge was
named the *Little Willie.*

The Esquimaux dogs were reserved for the great tug of the The Esquimaux dogs
actual journeys of search. They were now in the semi-savage
condition which marks their close approach to the wolf; and,
according to Mr. Petersen, under whose care they were placed,
were totally useless for journeys over such ice as was now
before us. A hard experience had not then opened my eyes to
the inestimable value of these dogs : I had yet to learn their
power and speed, their patient, enduring fortitude, their sagacity
in tracking these icy morasses, among which they had been born
and bred.

I determined to hold back my more distant provision parties as The road
long as the continued daylight would permit ; making the Newfoundland dogs establish the depôts within sixty miles of the brig.
My previous journey had shown me that the ice-belt, clogged with
the foreign matters dislodged from the cliffs, would not at this
season of the year answer for operations with the sledge, and that
the ice of the great pack outside was even more unfit, on account
of its want of continuity. It was now so consolidated by advanc-

ing cold as to have stopped its drift to the south ; but the large
floes or fields which formed it were imperfectly cemented together,
and would break into hummocks under the action of winds, or even
of the tides. It was made still more impassable by the numerous
bergs* which kept ploughing with irresistible momentum through
the ice-tables, and rearing up barricades that defied the passage of
a sledge.

It was desirable, therefore, that our depôt parties should not
enter upon their work until they could avail themselves of the
young ice. This now occupied a belt about 100 yards in mean
breadth, close to the shore, and, but for the fluctuations of the tides,
would already be a practicable road. For the present, however, a
gale of wind or a spring tide might easily drive the outer floes upon
it, and thus destroy its integrity.

Descrip-
tion of the
Faith. a
model
sledge.
The party appointed to establish this depôt was furnished with
a sledge, the admirable model of which I obtained through the
British Admiralty. The only liberty that I ventured to take with
this model—which had been previously tested by the adventurous
journeys of M'Clintock in Lancaster Sound—was to lessen the
height, and somewhat increase the breadth of the runner ; both of
which, I think, were improvements, giving increased strength.
and preventing too deep a descent into the snow. I named

her the *Faith*. Her length was thirteen
feet, and breadth four. She could readily
carry fourteen hundred pounds of mixed
stores.

This noble old sledge, which is now en-
deared to me by every pleasant association,
bore the brunt of the heaviest parties, and
came back, after the descent of the coast,
comparatively sound. The men were attached in her in such a way as to make the
line of draught or traction as near as possible in the axis of the weight. Each man

THE RUE-RADDY.

had his own shoulder-belt, or "rue-raddy," as we used to call it,
and his own track-line, which, for want of horse-hair, was made of

* The general drift of these great masses was to the south,—a plain indication of deep
sea-currents in that direction. and a convincing proof, to me, of a discharge from some
northern water.

Manilla rope ; it traversed freely by a ring on a loop or bridle, CHAPTER
that extended from runner to runner in front of the sledge.   X.
These track-ropes varied in length, so as to keep the members of
the party from interfering with each other by walking abreast.
The longest was three fathoms, eighteen feet, in length ; the
shortest, directly fastened to the sledge runner, as a means of
guiding or suddenly arresting and turning the vehicle.

The cargo for this journey, without including the provisions of the Cargo.
party, was almost exclusively pemmican. Some of this was put
up in cylinders of tinned iron with conical terminations, so as to
resist the assaults of the white bear ; but the larger quantity was
in strong wooden cases or kegs, well hooped with iron, holding about
seventy pounds each. Surmounting this load was a light india-
rubber boat, made quite portable by a frame of basket willow,
which I hoped to launch on reaching open water.

The personal equipment of the men was a buffalo-robe for the Outfit.
party to lie upon, and a bag of Mackinaw blanket for each man to
crawl into at night. India-rubber cloth was to be the protection
from the snow beneath. The tent was of canvas, made after the
plan of our English predecessors. We afterward learned to modify
and reduce our travelling gear, and found that in direct proportion
to its simplicity and our apparent privation of articles of supposed
necessity were our actual comfort and practical efficiency. Step
by step, as long as our Arctic service continued, we went on reducing our sledging outfit, until at last we came to the Esquimaux
ultimatum of simplicity—raw meat and a fur bag.

While our arrangements for the winter were still in progress, I Reconnais
sent out Mr. Wilson and Dr. Hayes, accompanied by our Esqui- sance.
maux, Hans, to learn something of the interior features of the
country, and the promise it afforded of resources from the
hunt. They returned on the 16th of September, after a hard
travel, made with excellent judgment and abundant zeal.
They penetrated into the interior about ninety miles, when
their progress was arrested by a glacier, 400 feet high, and extending to the north and west as far as the eye could reach. This
magnificent body of interior ice formed on its summit a complete
plateau,—a *mer de glace*, abutting upon a broken plain of syenite.
They found no large lakes. They saw a few reindeer at a distance,
and numerous hares and rabbits, but no ptarmigan.

"*September* 20, *Tuesday.*—I was unwilling to delay my depôt party any longer. They left the brig, M'Gary, and Bonsall, with five men, at half-past one to-day. We gave them three cheers, and I accompanied them with my dogs as a farewell escort for some miles.

"Our crew proper is now reduced to three men; but all the officers, the doctor among the rest, are hard at work upon the observatory and its arrangements."

CHAPTER XI.

HE OBSERVATORY—THERMOMETERS—THE RATS—THE BRIG ON FIRE—
ANCIENT SLEDGE-TRACKS—ESQUIMAUX HUTS—HYDROPHOBIA—SLEDGE-
DRIVING—MUSK OX TRACKS—A SLEDGE PARTY.

HE island on which we placed our observatory was some fifty ʜᴇ island on which we placed our observatory was some fifty
aces long by perhaps forty broad, and about thirty feet above the
rater-line. Here we raised four walls of granite blocks, cementing
hem together with moss and water, and the never-failing aid of
rost. On these was laid a substantial wooden roof, perforated at
he meridian and prime vertical. For pedestals we had a conglo-
nerate of gravel and ice, well rammed down while liquid in our
on-hooped pemmican-casks, and as free from all vibration as the
ock they rested on. Here we mounted our transit and theodolite.

The magnetic observatory adjoining had rather more of the
ffectation of comfort. It was of stone, ten feet square, with a
rooden floor as well as roof, a copper fire-grate, and stands of the
ame Arctic breccia as those in its neighbour. No iron was used
a its construction. Here were our magnetometer and dip instruments.

Our tide-register was on board the vessel, a simple pulley-gauge,
rranged with a wheel and index, and dependent on her rise and
all for its rotation.

Our meterological observatory was upon the open ice-field, one
undred and forty yards from the ship. It was a wooden struc-
ure, latticed and pierced with augur-holes on all sides, so as to
llow the air to pass freely, and firmly luted to its frozen base.
'o guard against the fine and almost impalpable drift, which in-
inuates itself everywhere, and which would interfere with the ob-
ervation of minute and sudden changes of temperature, I placed
, series of screens at right angles to each other, so as to surround
he inner chamber.

The thermometers were suspended within the central chamber;
, pane of glass permitted the light of our lanterns to reach them
rom a distance, and a lens and eye-glass were so fixed as to allow

CHAPTER
XI.

Building
for the
observa-
tory.

Magnetic
observa-
tory.

Tide regi-
ster.

Meteoro-
logical
observa-
tory.

Thermo-
meters.

us to observe the instruments without coming inside the screens. Their sensibility was such, that, when standing at 40° and 50° below zero, the mere approach of the observer caused a perceptible rise of the column. One of them, a three-feet spirit standard by Taliabue, graduated to 70° minus, was of sufficiently extended register to be read by rapid inspection to tenths of a degree. The influence of winds I did not wish absolutely to neutralize; but I endeavoured to make the exposure to them so uniform as to give a relative result for every quarter of the compass. We were well supplied with thermometers of all varieties.

Wind-gauge.

I had devised a wind-gauge to be observed by a tell-tale below deck; but we found that the condensing moisture so froze around it as to clog its motion.

Rats.

"*September* 30, *Friday.*—We have been terribly annoyed by rats. Some days ago we made a brave effort to smoke them out with the vilest imaginable compound of vapours,—brimstone, burnt leather, and arsenic,—and spent a cold night in a deck-bivouac, to give the experiment fair play. But they survived the fumigation. We now determined to dose them with carbonic acid gas. Dr. Hayes burnt a quantity of charcoal; and we shut down the hatches, after pasting up every fissure that communicated aft and starting three stoves on the skin of the forepeak.

The cook's misadventure.

"As the gas was generated with extreme rapidity in the confined area below, great caution had to be exercised. Our French cook, good Pierre Schubert,—who to a considerable share of bull-headed intrepidity unites a commendable portion of professional zeal,—stole below, without my knowledge or consent, to season a soup. Morton fortunately saw him staggering in the dark, and, reaching him with great difficulty as he fell, both were hauled up in the end,—Morton, his strength almost gone, and the cook perfectly insensible.

A serious disaster.

"The next disaster was of a graver sort. I record it with emotions of mingled awe and thankfulness. We have narrowly escaped being burnt out of house and home. I had given orders that the fires, lit under my own eye, should be regularly inspected; but I learned that Pierre's misadventure had made the watch pretermit for a time opening the hatches. As I lowered a lantern, which was extinguished instantly, a suspicious odour reached me, as of burning wood. I descended at once. Reaching the deck of the forecastle, my first glance toward the fires showed me that all was safe there ; and, though the quantity of smoke still surprised me, I was disposed to attribute it to the recent kindling. But at this moment, while passing on my return near the door of the bulkhead, which leads to the carpenter's room, the gas began to affect me. My lantern went out as if quenched by water ; and, as I ran by the bulkhead door, I saw the deck near it a mass of glowing fire for some three feet in diameter. I could not tell how much further it extended, for I became quite insensible at the foot of the ladder, and would have sunk had not Mr. Brooks seen my condition and hauled me out.

"When I came to myself, which happily was very soon, I confided my fearful secret to the four men around me, Brooks, Ohlsen, Blake, and Stevenson. It was all-important to avoid confusion : we shut the doors of the galley, so as to confine the rest of the crew and officers aft, and then passed up water from the fire-hole alongside. It was done very noiselessly. Ohlsen and myself went down to the burning deck ; Brooks handed us in the buckets ; and in less than ten minutes we were in safety. It was interesting to observe the effect of steam upon the noxious gas. Both Ohlsen and myself were greatly oppressed until the first bucket was poured on ; but as I did this, directly over the burning coal, raising clouds of steam, we at once experienced relief : the fine aqueous particles seemed to absorb the carbonic acid instantly. We found the fire had originated in the remains of a barrel of charcoal, which had been left in the carpenter's room, ten feet from the stoves, and with a bulkhead separating it from them. How it had been ignited it was impossible to know. Our safety was due to the dense charge of carbonic acid gas which surrounded the fire, and the exclusion of atmospheric air. When the hatches were opened the flame burst out with energy. Our fire-hole was invaluable ; and I rejoiced that, in the midst of our heavy duties, this essential of an Arctic winter harbour had not been neglected. The ice around the brig was already fourteen inches thick.

"*October* 1, *Saturday*.—Upon inspecting the scene of yesterday's operations, we found twenty-eight well-fed rats of all varieties of age. The cook, though unable to do duty, is better ; I can hear him chanting his Béranger through the blankets in his bunk, happy over his holiday, happy to be happy at everything. I had

CHAPTER XI.

The deck on fire.

Measures taken to extinguish it.

Effect of steam on gas.

Origin of the fire.

Means of safety.

CHAPTER XI. a larger dose of carbonic acid even than he, and am suffering considerably with palpitations and vertigo. If the sentimental asphyxia of Parisian charcoal resembles in its advent that of the Arctic zone, it must be, I think, a poor way of dying.

Old sledge tracks. "*October* 3, *Monday.*—On shore to the south-east, above the first terrace, Mr Petersen found unmistakable signs of a sledge-passage. The tracks were deeply impressed, but certainly more than one season old. This adds to our hope that the natives, whose ancient traces we saw on the point south of Godsend Ledge, may return this winter.

Esquimaux huts. "*October* 5, *Wednesday.*—I walked this afternoon to another group of Esquimaux huts, about three miles from the brig. They are four in number, long deserted, but, to an eye unpractised in Arctic antiquarian inductions, in as good preservation as a last year's tenement at home. The most astonishing feature is the presence of some little out-huts, or, as I first thought them, dog-kennels. These are about four feet by three in ground plan, and some three feet high; no larger than the pologs of the Tchuschi. In shape they resemble a rude dome, and the stones of which they are composed are of excessive size, and evidently selected for smoothness. They were, without exception, of water-washed limestone. They are heavily sodded with turf, and a narrow slab of clay-slate serves as a door. No doubt they are human habitations,—retiring chambers, into which, away from the crowded families of the hut, one or even two Esquimaux have burrowed for sleep,—chilly dormitories in the winter of this high latitude.

"A circumstance that happened to-day is of serious concern to us. Our sluts have been adding to our stock. We have now on hand four reserved puppies of peculiar promise; six have been ignominiously drowned, two devoted to a pair of mittens for Dr.

A dog attacked by hydrophobia. Kane, and seven eaten by their mammas. Yesterday the mother of one batch, a pair of fine white pups, showed peculiar symptoms. We recalled the fact that for days past she had avoided water, or had drunk with spasm and evident aversion; but hydrophobia, which is unknown north of 70°, never occurred to us. The animal was noticed this morning walking up and down the deck with a staggering gait, her head depressed, and her mouth frothing and tumid. Finally she snapped at Petersen, and fell foaming and biting at his feet. He reluctantly pronounced it hydrophobia, and

advised me to shoot her. The advice was well-timed: I had hardly CHAPTER XI.
cleared the deck before she snapped at Hans, the Esquimaux, and
recommenced her walking trot. It was quite an anxious moment
to me; for my Newfoundlanders were around the housing, and the
hatches open. We shot her, of course.

" *October* 6, *Thursday.*—The hares are less numerous than they Hares.
were. They seek the coast when the snows fall in the interior,
and the late south-east wind has probably favoured their going
back. These animals are not equal in size either to the European
hare or their brethren of the North American continent. The latter,
according to Seamann, weigh upon an average fourteen pounds. A
large male, the largest seen by us in Smith's Sound, weighed but
nine; and our average so far does not exceed seven and a half.
They measure generally less by some inches in length than those
noticed by Dr. Richardson. Mr. Petersen is quite successful in
shooting these hares: we have a stock of fourteen now on hand.

" We have been building stone traps on the hills for the foxes,
whose traces we see there in abundance, and have determined to
organize a regular hunt as soon as they give us the chance.

" *October* 8, *Saturday.*—I have been practising with my dog- The dog-
sledge and an Esquimaux team till my arms ache. To drive such sledge.
an equipage a certain proficiency with the whip is indispensable;
which, like all proficiency, must be worked for. In fact the weapon
has an exercise of its own, quite peculiar, and as hard to learn as
single-stick or broadsword.

" The whip is 6 yards long, and the handle but 16 inches,—
a short lever, of course, to throw out such a length of seal-hide.
Learn to do it, however, with a masterly sweep, or else make up
your mind to forego driving sledge; for the dogs are guided solely
by the lash, and you must be able not only to hit any particular
dog out of a team of twelve, but to accompany the feat also with
a resounding crack. After this you find that to get your lash back
involves another difficulty; for it is apt to entangle itself among
the dogs and lines, or to fasten itself cunningly round bits of ice,
so as to drag you head over heels into the snow.

" The secret by which this complicated set of requirements is
fulfilled consists in properly describing an arc from the shoulder,
with a stiff elbow, giving the jerk to the whip handle from the
hand and wrist alone. The lash trails behind as you travel, and

when thrown forward is allowed to extend itself without an effort to bring it back. You wait patiently after giving the projectile impulse until it unwinds its slow length, reaches the end of its tether, and cracks to tell you that it is at its journey's end. Such a crack on the ear or forefoot of an unfortunate dog is signalized by a howl quite unmistakable in its import.

"The mere labour of using this whip is such that the Esquimaux travel in couples, one sledge after the other. The hinder dogs follow mechanically, and thus require no whip ; and the drivers change about so as to rest each other.

"I have amused myself, if not my dogs, for some days past with this formidable accessory of Arctic travel. I have not quite got the knack of it yet, though I might venture a trial of cracking against the postilion college of Lonjumeau.

"*October* 9, *Sunday.*—Mr. Petersen shot a hare yesterday. They are very scarce now, for he travelled some five hours without seeing another. He makes the important report of musk ox tracks on the recent snow. Dr. Richardson says that these are scarcely distinguishable from the reindeer's except by the practised eye : he characterizes them as larger, but not wider. The tracks that Petersen saw had an interesting confirmation of their being those of the musk ox, for they were accompanied by a second set of footprints, evidently belonging to a young one of the same species, and about as large as a middle-sized reindeer's. Both impressions also were marked as if by hair growing from the pastern joint, for behind the hoof was a line brushed in the snow.

"To-day Hans brought in another hare he had shot. He saw seven reindeer in a large valley off Bedevilled Reach, and wounded one of them. This looks promising for our winter commissariat.

"*October* 10, *Monday.*—Our depôt party has been out twenty days, and it is time they were back : their provisions must have run very low, for I enjoined them to leave every pound at the depôt they could spare. I am going out with supplies to look after them. I take four of our best Newfoundlanders, now well broken, in our lightest sledge ; and Blake will accompany me with his skates. We have not hands enough to equip a sledge party, and the ice is too unsound for us to attempt to ride with a large team. The thermometer is still 4° above zero."

CHAPTER XII.

LEAPING A CHASM—THE ICE-BELT—CAPE WILLIAM WOOD—CAMP ON THE
FLOES—RETURN OF DEPÔT PARTY—BONSALL'S ADVENTURE—RESULTS—
AN ESCAPE—THE THIRD CACHE—M'GARY ISLAND.

I FOUND little or no trouble in crossing the ice until we passed be- CHAPTER
yond the north-east headland, which I have named Cape William XII.
Wood. But, on emerging into the channel, we found that the Travelling
spring tides had broken up the great area around us, and that the on the ice
passage of the sledge was interrupted by fissures, which were beginning to break in every direction through the young ice.

My first effort was of course to reach the land ; but it was unfortunately low tide, and the ice-belt rose up before me like a wall.
The pack was becoming more and more unsafe, and I was extremely
anxious to gain an asylum on shore ; for, though it was easy to find
a temporary refuge by retreating to the old floes which studded
the more recent ice, I knew that in doing so we should risk being
carried down by the drift.

The dogs began to flag ; but we had to press them ;—we were
only two men ; and, in the event of the animals failing to leap
any of the rapidly-multiplying fissures, we could hardly expect to
extricate our laden sledge. Three times in less than three hours
my shaft or hinder dogs went in ; and John and myself, who had
been trotting alongside the sledge for sixteen miles were nearly as
tired as they were. This state of things could not last ; and I
therefore made for the old ice to seaward.

We were nearing it rapidly, when the dogs failed in leaping a A plunge
chasm that was somewhat wider than the others, and the whole in the
water.
concern came down in the water. I cut the lines instantly, and,
with the aid of my companion, hauled the poor animals out. We
owed the preservation of the sledge to their admirable docility and
perseverance. The tin-cooking apparatus and the air confined in
the India-rubber coverings kept it afloat till we could succeed in
fastening a couple of seal-skin cords to the cross-pieces at the front
and back. By these John and myself were able to give it an un-

certain support from the two edges of the opening, till the dogs, after many fruitless struggles, carried it forward at last upon the ice.

Although the thermometer was below zero, and in our wet state we ran a considerable risk of freezing, the urgency of our position left no room for thoughts of cold. We started at a run, men and dogs, for the solid ice; and by the time we had gained it we were steaming in the cold atmosphere like a couple of Nootka Sound vapour-baths.

We rested on the floe. We could not raise our tent, for it had frozen as hard as a shingle. But our buffalo-robe bags gave us protection; and, though we were too wet inside to be absolutely comfortable, we managed to get something like sleep before it was light enough for us to move on again.

The journey was continued in the same way; but we found, to our great gratification, that the cracks closed with the change of the tide, and at high-water we succeeded in gaining the ice-belt under the cliffs. This belt had changed very much since my journey in September. The tides and frosts together had coated it with ice as smooth as satin, and this glossy covering made it an excellent road. The cliffs discharged fewer fragments in our path, and the rocks of our last journey's experience were now fringed with icicles. I saw with great pleasure that this ice-belt would serve as a highway for our future operations.

The nights which followed were not so bad as one would suppose from the saturated condition of our equipment. Evaporation is not so inappreciable in this Arctic region as some theorists imagine. By alternately exposing the tent and furs to the air, and beating the ice out of them we dried them enough to permit sleep. The dogs slept in the tent with us, giving it warmth as well as fragrance. What perfumes of nature are lost at home upon our ungrateful senses! How we relished the companionship!

We had averaged twenty miles a day since leaving the brig, and were within a short march of the cape which I have named William Wood, when a broad chasm brought us to a halt. It was in vain that we worked out to seaward, or dived into the shoreward recesses of the bay: the ice everywhere presented the same impassable fissures. We had no alternative but to retrace our steps and seek among the bergs some place of security. We found a camp

for the night on the old floe-ices to the westward, gaining them CHAPTER XII.
some time after the darkness had closed in.

On the morning of the 15th, about two hours before the late
sunrise, as I was preparing to climb a berg from which I might
have a sight of the road ahead, I perceived far off upon the white
snow a dark object, which not only moved, but altered its shape
strangely,—now expanding into a long black line, now waving, now
gathering itself up into compact mass. It was the returning sledge
party. They had seen our black tent of Kedar, and ferried across
to seek it.

They were most welcome; for their absence, in the fearfully Return of the depôt party.
open state of the ice, had filled me with apprehensions. We could
not distinguish each other as we drew near in the twilight; and
my first good news of them was when I heard that they were singing. On they came, and at last I was able to count their voices,
one by one. Thank God, seven! Poor John Blake was so breathless with gratulation, that I could not get him to blow his signal-
horn. We gave them, instead, the good old Anglo-Saxon greeting, "three cheers!" and in a few minutes were among them.

They had made a creditable journey, and were, on the whole, in Sufferings from the frost.
good condition. They had no injuries worth talking about, al-
though not a man had escaped some touches of the frost. Bonsall was minus a big toe-nail, and plus a scar upon the nose.
M'Gary had attempted, as Tom Hickey told us, to *pluck* a fox, it
being so frozen as to defy skinning by his knife; and his fingers
had been tolerably frost-bitten in the operation. "They're very
horny, sir, are my fingers," said M'Gary, who was worn down to a
mere shadow of his former rotundity; "very horny, and they water
up like bladders." The rest had suffered in their feet; but like
good fellows, postponed limping until they reached the ship.

Within the last three days they had marched fifty-four miles, or Rate of travelling over the ice.
eighteen a day. Their sledge being empty, and the young ice north
of Cape Bancroft smooth as a mirror, they had travelled, the day
before we met them, nearly twenty-five miles. A very remarkable
pace for men who had been twenty-eight days in the field.

My supplies of hot food, coffee, and marled beef soup, which I
had brought with me, were very opportune. They had almost exhausted their bread; and, being unwilling to encroach on the depôt stores, had gone without fuel in order to save alcohol. Leaving

CHAPTER XII.

orders to place my own sledge stores in *cache*, I returned to the brig, ahead of the party, with my dog-sledge, carrying Mr. Bonsall with me.

Leaping ice cracks.

On this return I had much less difficulty with the ice cracks ; my team of Newfoundlanders leaping them in almost every instance, and the impulse of our sledge carrying it across. On one occasion, while we were making these flying leaps, poor Bonsall was tossed out, and came very near being carried under by the rapid tide. He fortunately caught the runner of the sledge as he fell; and I

NEWFOUNDLAND DOG TEAM.

succeeded, by whipping up the dogs, in hauling him out. He was, of course, wet to the skin ; but we were only twenty miles from the brig, and he sustained no serious injury from his immersion.

I return to my journal.

The spar-deck.

"The spar-deck—or, as we call it from its wooden covering, the 'house'—is steaming with the buffalo-robes, tents, boots, socks, and heterogeneous costumings of our returned parties. We have ample work in repairing these and restoring the disturbed order of our domestic life. The men feel the effects of their journey, but are very content in their comfortable quarters. A pack of cards, grog at dinner, and the promise of a three days' holiday, have made the decks happy with idleness and laughter."

I give the general results of the party; referring to the Appendix CHAPTER XII. for the detailed account of Messrs. M'Gary and Bonsall.

They left the brig, as may be remembered, on the 20th of Sep- Cache near Cape Russell. tember, and they reached Cape Russell on the 25th. Near this spot I had, in my former journey of reconnoissance, established a cairn; and here, as by previously concerted arrangement, they left their first cache of pemmican, together with some bread, and alcohol for fuel.

On the 28th, after crossing a large bay, they met a low cape about thirty miles to the north-east of the first depôt. Here they made a second cache of a hundred and ten pounds of beef and pemmican, and about thirty of a mixture of pemmican and Indian meal, with a bag of bread.

The day being too foggy for sextant observations for position, or even for a reliable view of the landmarks, they built a substantial cairn, and buried the provision at a distance of ten paces from its A cairn built over provisions. centre, bearing by compass, E. by N. $\frac{1}{2}$ N. The point on which this cache stood I subsequently named after Mr. Bonsall, one of the indefatigable leaders of the party.

I will give the geographical outline of the track of this party in a subsequent part of this narrative, when I have spoken of the after-travel and surveys which confirmed and defined it. But I should do injustice both to their exertions and to the results of them, were I to omit mention of the difficulties which they encountered.

On the twenty-fifth day of their outward journey they met a Stopped by a glacier. great glacier, which I shall describe hereafter. It checked their course along the Greenland coast abruptly; but they still endeavoured to make their way outside its edge to seaward, with the commendable object of seeking a more northern point for the provision depôt. This journey was along the base of an icy wall, which constantly threw off its discharging bergs, breaking up the ice for miles around, and compelling the party to ferry themselves and their sledge over the cracks by rafts of ice.

One of these incidents I give nearly in the language of Mr. Bonsall.

They had camped, on the night of 5th October, under the lee of some large icebergs, and within hearing of the grand artillery of the glacier. The floe on which their tent was pitched was of re-

cent and transparent ice; and the party, too tired to seek a safer
asylum, had turned in to rest; when, with a crack like the snap of
a gigantic whip, the ice opened directly beneath them. This was,
as nearly as they could estimate the time, at about one o'clock in
the morning. The darkness was intense; and the cold, about 10°
below zero, was increased by a wind which blew from the north-
east over the glacier. They gathered together their tent and sleeping furs, and lashed them, according to the best of their ability,
upon the sledge. Repeated intonations warned them that the ice
was breaking up; a swell, evidently produced by the avalanches
from the glacier, caused the platform on which they stood to rock
to and fro.

Mr. M'Gary derived a hope from the stable character of the
bergs near them: they were evidently not adrift. He determined
to select a flat piece of ice, place the sledge upon it, and, by aid of
tent-poles and cooking-utensils, paddle to the old and firm fields
which clung to the bases of the bergs. The party waited in
anxious expectation until the returning daylight permitted this
attempt; and, after a most adventurous passage, succeeded in
reaching the desired position.

My main object in sending them out was the deposit of provisions, and I had not deemed it advisable to complicate their duties
by any organization for a survey. They reached their highest
latitude on the 6th of October; and this, as determined by dead
reckoning, was in latitude 79° 50', and longitude 76° 20'. From
this point they sighted and took sextant bearings of land to the
north,* having a trend or inclination west by north and east by
south, at an estimated distance of thirty miles. They were at this
time entangled in the icebergs; and it was from the lofty summit
of one of these, in the midst of a scene of surpassing desolation,
that they made their observations.

They began the third or final cache, which was the main object
of the journey, on the 10th of October; placing it on a low island
at the base of the large glacier which checked their further march
along the coast.

Before adopting this site, they had perseveringly skirted the base

The high-
est lati-
tude
reached
by the
party.

* I may mention that the results of their observations were not used in the construction
of our charts, except their interesting sextant bearings. These were both numerous and
valuable, but not sustained at the time by satisfactory astronomical observations for position.

of the glacier, in a fruitless effort to cross it to the north. In spite
of distressing cold, and the nearly constant winds from the ice-
clothed shore, they carried out all my instructions for securing this
important depôt. The stores were carefully buried in a natural
excavation among the cliffs; and heavy rocks, brought with great
labour, were piled above them. Smaller stones were placed over
these, and incorporated into one solid mass by a mixture of sand
and water. The power of the bear in breaking up a provision
cache is extraordinary; but the Esquimaux to the south had assured
me that frozen sand and water, which would wear away the animal's claws, were more effective against him than the largest rocks.
Still, knowing how much trouble the officers of Commodore
Austin's Expedition experienced from the destruction of their
caches, I had ordered the party to resort to a combination of these
expedients.

They buried here six hundred and seventy pounds of pemmican,
forty of Borden's meat biscuit, and some articles of general diet;
making a total of about eight hundred pounds. They indicated
the site by a large cairn, bearing E. ½ S. from the cache, and at
the distance of thirty paces. The landmarks of the cairn itself
were sufficiently evident, but were afterwards fixed by bearings,
for additional certainty.

The island which was so judiciously selected as the seat of this
cache was named after my faithful friend and excellent second
officer, Mr. James M'Gary of New London.

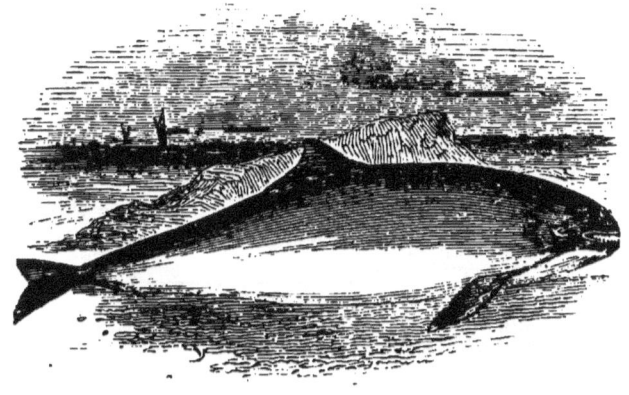

CHAPTER XIII.

WALRUS HOLES—ADVANCE OF DARKNESS—DARKNESS—THE COLD—"THE
ICE BLINK"—FOX-CHASE—ESQUIMAUX HUTS—OCCULTATION OF SAT-
URN—PORTRAIT OF OLD GRIM.

CHAPTER XIII.

The moon.

"*October* 28, *Friday.*—The moon has reached her greatest northern declination of about 25° 35'. She is a glorious object: sweeping around the heavens, at the lowest part of her curve, she is still 14° above the horizon. For eight days she has been making her circuit with nearly unvarying brightness. It is one of those sparkling nights that bring back the memory of sleigh-bells and songs and glad communings of hearts in lands that are far away.

"Our fires and ventilation fixtures are so arranged that we are able to keep a mean temperature below of 65°; and on deck, under our housing, above the freezing-point. This is admirable success; for the weather outside is at 25° below zero, and there is quite a little breeze blowing.

The temperature.

Walrus holes.

"The last remnant of walrus did not leave us until the second week of last month, when the temperature had sunk below zero. Till then they found open water enough to sport and even sleep in, between the fields of drift, as they opened with the tide; but they had worked numerous breathing-holes besides, in the solid ice nearer shore.* Many of these were inside the capes of Rensselaer Harbour. They had the same circular, cleanly-finished margin as the seals', but they were in much thicker ice, and the radiating lines of fracture round them much more marked. The animal evidently used his own buoyancy as a means of starting the ice.

"Around these holes the ice was much discoloured: numbers of broken clam-shells were found near them, and, in one instance, some gravel, mingled with about half a peck of the coarse shingle of the beach. The use of the stones which the walrus swallows is still

---

* The walrus often sleeps on the surface of the water while his fellows are playing around him. In this condition I frequently surprised the young ones, whose mothers were asleep by their side.

an interesting question. The ussuk or bearded seal has the same habit.

WALRUS SPORTING.

"*November* 7, *Monday.*—The darkness is coming on with in- Darkness sidious steadiness, and its advances can only be perceived by com- increas-ing. paring one day with its fellow of some time back. We still read the thermometer at noonday without a light, and the black masses of the hills are plain for about five hours with their glaring patches of snow; but all the rest is darkness. Lanterns are always on the spar-deck, and the lard-lamps never extinguished below. The stars of the sixth magnitude shine out at noonday.

"Except upon the island of Spitzbergen, which has the advantages of an insular climate and tempered by ocean currents, no Christians have wintered in so high a latitude as this. They are Russian sailors who make the encounter there, men inured to hardships and cold. I cannot help thinking of the sad chronicles of the early Dutch, who perished year after year, without leaving a comrade to record their fate.

"Our darkness has ninety days to run before we shall get back Duration again even to the contested twilight of to-day. Altogether, our of winter winter will have been sunless for one hundred and forty days.

It requires neither the 'Ice-foot' with its growing ramparts, nor the rapid encroachments of the night, nor the record of our thermometers, to portend for us a winter of unusual severity. The mean temperatures of October and September are lower than those of Parry for the same months at Melville Island. Thus far we have no indications of that deferred fall cold which marks the insular climate.

"*November* 9, *Wednesday.*—Wishing to get the altitude of the cliffs on the south-west cape of our bay before the darkness set in thoroughly, I started in time to reach them with my Newfoundlanders at noonday. Although it was but a short journey, the rough shore-ice and a slight wind rendered the cold severe. I had been housed for a week with my wretched rheumatism, and felt that daily exposure was necessary to enable me to bear up against the cold. The thermometer indicated 23° below zero.

The cold.   "Fireside astronomers can hardly realize the difficulties in the way of observations at such low temperatures. The mere burning of the hands is obviated by covering the metal with chamois-skin; but the breath, and even the warmth of the face and body, cloud the sextant-arc and glasses with a fine hoar-frost. Though I had much clear weather, we barely succeeded by magnifiers in reading the verniers. It is, moreover, an unusual feat to measure a baseline in the snow at 55° below freezing.

"*November* 16, *Wednesday.*—The great difficulty is to keep up
Poor Hans a cheery tone among the men. Poor Hans has been sorely home-
the Esqui- sick. Three days ago he bundled up his clothes and took his rifle,
maux.   to bid us all good-bye. It turns out that besides his mother there is another one of the softer sex at Fiskernaes that the boy's heart is dreaming of. He looked as wretched as any lover of a milder clime. I hope I have treated his nostalgia successfully, by giving him first a dose of salts, and secondly, promotion. He has now all the dignity of a henchman. He harnesses my dogs, builds my traps, and walks with me on my ice tramps; and, except hunting, is excused from all other duty. He is really attached to me, and as happy as a fat man ought to be.

"*November* 21, *Monday.*—We have schemes innumerable to cheat the monotonous solitude of our winter. We are getting up a fancy ball; and to-day the first number of our Arctic newspaper,
The "Ice- 'The Ice-Blink,' came out, with the motto, ' IN TENEBRIS SERVARE
Blink."   FIDEM.' The articles are by authors of every nautical grade : some

of the best from the forecastle. I transfer a few of them to my CHAPTER XIII.
Appendix.

"*November* 22, *Tuesday.*—I offered a prize to-day of a Guernsey A fox chase.
shirt to the man who held out longest in a 'fox-chase' round the
decks. The rule of the sport was, that 'Fox' was to run a given
circuit between galley and capstan, all hands following on his track ;
every four minutes a halt to be called to blow, and the fox making
the longest run to take the prize ; each of the crew to run as fox
in turn. William Godfrey sustained the chase for fourteen minutes,
and *wore* off the shirt.

"*November* 27, *Sunday.*—I sent out a volunteer party some days A volunteer party
ago with Mr. Bonsall, to see whether the Esquimaux have returned
to the huts we saw empty at the cape. The thermometer was in
the neighbourhood of 40° below zero, and the day was too dark to
read at noon. I was hardly surprised when they returned after
camping one night upon the snow. Their sledge broke down, and
they were obliged to leave tents and everything else behind them.
It must have been very cold, for a bottle of Monongahela whisky
of good stiff proof froze under Mr. Bonsall's head.

"Morton went out on Friday to reclaim the things they had A long journey.
left ; and to day at 1 P.M. he returned successful. He reached the
wreck of the former party, making nine miles in three hours,—
pushed on six miles further on the ice-foot,—then camped for the
night ; and, making a sturdy march the next day without luggage,
reached the huts, and got back to his camp to sleep. This journey of his was, we then thought, really an achievement,—sixty-two
miles in three marches, with a mean temperature of 40° below
zero, and a noonday so dark that you could hardly see a hummock
of ice fifty paces ahead.

" Under more favouring circumstances, Bonsall, Morton, and my- Forced marches
self made eighty-four miles in three consecutive marches. I go for
the system of forced marches on journeys that are not over a
hundred and fifty miles. A practised walker unencumbered by
weight does twenty miles a day nearly as easily as ten : it is the
uncomfortable sleeping that wears a party out.

" Morton found no natives ; but he saw enough to satisfy me
that the huts could not have been deserted long before we came to
this region. The foxes had been at work upon the animal remains
that we found there, and the appearances which we noted of recent

CHAPTER XIII
—
Deserted huts.
habitation had in a great degree disappeared. Where these Esqui maux have travelled to is matter for conjecture. The dilapidated character of the huts we have seen further to the north seems to imply that they cannot have gone in that direction. They have more probably migrated southward, and, as the spring opens, may return, with the walrus and seal, to their former haunts. We shall see them, I think, before we leave our icy moorings.

Occulta-
tion of
Saturn.
" *December* 12, *Monday.*—A grand incident in our great mono tony of life ! We had an occultation of Saturn at 2 A.M., and got a most satisfactory observation. The emersion was obtained with greater accuracy than could have been expected from the exces sive atmospheric undulation of these low temperatures. My little Fraunhöfer sustained its reputation well. We can now fix our position without a cavil.

Total
darkness.
" *December* 15, *Thursday.*—We have lost the last vestige of our mid-day twilight. We cannot see print, and hardly paper : the fingers cannot be counted a foot from the eyes. Noonday and midnight are alike, and, except a vague glimmer on the sky that seems to define the hill outlines to the south, we have nothing to tell us that this Arctic world of ours has a sun. In one week more we shall reach the midnight of the year.

" *December* 22, *Thursday.*—There is an excitement in our little community that dispenses with reflections upon the solstitial night. ' Old Grim ' is missing, and has been for more than a day. Since the lamented demise of Cerberus, my leading Newfoundlander, he has been patriarch of our scanty kennel.

' A cha-
racter."
" Old Grim was ' a character' such as peradventure may at some time be found among beings of a higher order and under a more temperate sky. A profound hypocrite and time-server, he so wriggled his adulatory tail as to secure every one's good graces and nobody's respect. All the spare morsels, the cast-off delicacies of the mess, passed through the winnowing jaws of ' Old Grim,'—an illustration not so much of his eclecticism as his universality of taste. He was never known to refuse anything offered or ap proachable, and never known to be satisfied, however prolonged and abundant the bounty or the spoil.

" Grim was an ancient dog : his teeth indicated many winters ; and his limbs, once splendid tractors for the sledge, were now covered with warts and ringbones. Somehow or other, when the

dogs were harnessing for a journey, 'Old Grim' was sure not to be
found ; and upon one occasion, when he was detected hiding away
in a cast-off barrel, he incontinently became lame.   Strange to say
he has been lame ever since, except when the team is away without
him.

"Cold disagrees with Grim ; but by a system of patient watch-
ings at the door of our deck-house, accompanied by a discrimi-
nating use of his tail, he became at last the one privileged intruder.
My seal-skin coat has been his favourite bed for weeks together.
Whatever love for an individual Grim expressed by his tail, he
could never be induced to follow him on the ice after the cold
darkness of the winter set in ; yet the dear good old sinner would
wriggle after you to the very threshold of the gangway, and bid
you good-bye with a deprecatory wag of the tail which disarmed
resentment.

"His appearance was quite characteristic :—his muzzle roofed
like the old-fashioned gable of a Dutch garret-window ; his forehead indicating the most meagre capacity of brains that could consist with his sanity as a dog ; his eyes small, his mouth curtained
by long black dewlaps, and his hide a mangy russet studded with
chestnut-burrs ; if he has gone indeed, we 'ne'er shall look upon
his like again.'   So much for old Grim !

"When yesterday's party started to take soundings, I thought
the exercise would benefit Grim, whose time-serving sojourn on our
warm deck had begun to render him over-corpulent.   A rope was
fastened round him ; for at such critical periods he was obstinate,
and even ferocious ; and, thus fastened to the sledge, he commenced his reluctant journey.   Reaching a stopping-place after a
while, he jerked upon his line, parted it a foot or two from its
knot, and, dragging the remnant behind him, started off through
the darkness in the direction of our brig.   He has not been seen
since.

"Parties are out with lanterns seeking him ; for it is feared that
his long cord may have caught upon some of the rude pinnacles of
ice which stud our floe, and thus made him a helpless prisoner.
The thermometer is at 44° 6' below zero, and old Grim's teeth could
not gnaw away the cord.

"*December* 23, *Friday*.—Our anxieties for old Grim might have
interfered with almost anything else ; but they could not arrest our

CHAPTER XIII.

celebration of yesterday. Dr. Hayes made us a well-studied oration, and Morton a capital punch ; add to these a dinner of marled beef,—we have two pieces left, for the sun's return and the 4th of July,—and a bumper of champagne all round ; and the elements of our frolic are all registered.

Traces of "Grim."

"We tracked old Grim to-day through the snow to within six hundred yards of the brig, and thence to that mass of snow-packed sterility which we call the shore. His not rejoining the ship is a mystery quite in keeping with his character."

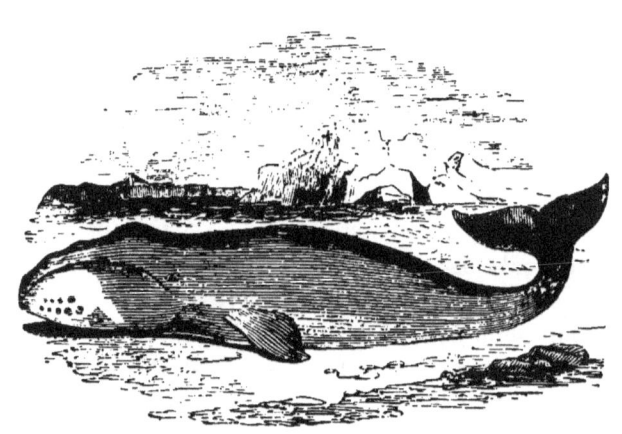

CHAPTER XIV.

MAGNETIC OBSERVATORY — TEMPERATURES — RETURNING LIGHT — DARK-
NESS AND THE DOGS—HYDROPHOBIA—ICE-CHANGES—THE ICE-FOOT—
THE ICE-BELT—THE SUNLIGHT—MARCH.

My journal for the first two months of 1854 is so devoid of in- CHAPTER XIV.
terest, that I spare the reader the task of following me through it.
In the darkness and consequent inaction, it was almost in vain
that we sought to create topics of thought, and by a forced excitement to ward off the encroachments of disease. Our observatory and the dogs gave us our only regular occupations.

On the 9th of January we had again an occultation of Saturn. Occulta-
The emersion occurred during a short interval of clear sky, and our tion of Saturn.
observation of it was quite satisfactory; the limit of the moon's
disc and that of the planet being well defined: the mist prevented
our seeing the immersion. We had a recurrence of the same
phenomenon on the 5th of February, and an occultation of Mars
on the 14th; both of them observed under favourable circumstances, the latter especially.

Our magnetic observations went on; but the cold made it al- Magnetic
most impossible to adhere to them with regularity. Our obser- Observa-
vatory was, in fact, an ice-house of the coldest imaginable descrip- tory.
tion. The absence of snow prevented our backing the walls with
that important non-conductor. Fires, buffalo-robes, and an arras
of investing sail-cloth, were unavailing to bring up the mean temperature to the freezing-point at the level of the magnetometer;*
and it was quite common to find the platform on which the
observer stood full 50° lower, (—20°.) Our astronomical observations were less protracted, but the apartment in which they

* We had a good unifilar, that had been loaned to us by Professor Bache, of the Coast
Survey; and a dip instrument, a Barrow's circle, obtained from the Smithsonian Institution,
through the kindness of Col. Sabine. I owe much to Mr. Sontag, Dr. Hayes, and Mr. Bonsall, who bore the brunt of the term-day observations; it was only toward the close of the
season that I was enabled to take my share of them. In addition to these, we had weekly
determinations of variation of declination, extending through the twenty-four hours, besides observations of intensity, deflection, inclination, and total force, with careful nota-
tions of temperature.

CHAPTER
XIV.

were made was of the same temperature with the outer air. The cold, was of course, intense; and some of our instruments, the dip-circle particularly, became difficult to manage, in consequence of the unequal contraction of the brass and steel.

THE OBSERVATORY.

Excessive cold.

On the 17th of January, our thermometers stood at 49° below zero : and on the 20th, the range of those at the observatory was at —64° to —67°. The temperature on the floes was always somewhat higher than at the island ; the difference being due, as I suppose, to the heat conducted from the sea-water, which was at a temperature of + 29°; the suspended instruments being affected by radiation.

On the 5th of February, our thermometers began to show un-exampled temperature. They ranged from 60° to 75° below zero, and one very reliable instrument stood upon the taffrail of our brig at —65°. The reduced mean of our best spirit-standards gave —67°, or 99° below the freezing-point of water.

Ether and chloroform freeze.

At these temperatures chloric ether became solid, and carefully-prepared chloroform exhibited a granular pellicle on its surface. Spirit of naphtha froze at —54°, and oil of sassafras at —49°. The oil of winter-green was in a flocculent state at —56°, and solid at —63° and —65°.*

---

* I repeated my observations on the effects of these low temperatures with great care

The exhalations from the surface of the body invested the ex- posed or partially-clad parts with a wreath of vapour. The air had a perceptible pungency upon inspiration, but I could not perceive the painful sensation which has been spoken of by some Siberian travellers. When breathed for any length of time it imparted a sensation of dryness to the air-passages. I noticed that, as it were involuntarily, we all breathed guardedly, with compressed lips.

The first traces of returning light were observed at noon on the 21st of January, when the southern horizon had for a short time a distinct orange tint. Though the sun had perhaps given us a band of illumination before, it was not distinguishable from the cold light of the planets. We had been nearing the sunshine for thirty-two days, and had just reached that degree of mitigated darkness which made the extreme midnight of Sir Edward Parry in latitude 74° 47'. Even as late as the 31st, two very sensitive daguerreotype plates, treated with iodine and bromine, failed to indicate any solar influence when exposed to the southern horizon at noon; the camera being used in-doors, to escape the effects of cold.

The influence of this long, intense darkness was most depress- ing. Even our dogs, although the greater part of them were natives of the Arctic Circle, were unable to withstand it. Most of them died from an anomalous form of disease, to which, I am satisfied, the absence of light contributed as much as the extreme cold. I give a little extract from my journal of January 20.

"This morning at five o'clock—for I am so afflicted with the insomnium of this eternal night, that I rise at any time between midnight and noon—I went upon deck. It was absolutely dark ; the cold not permitting a swinging lamp. There was not a glimmer came to me through the ice-crusted window-panes of the cabin. While I was feeling my way, half puzzled as to the best method of steering clear of whatever might be before me, two of my Newfoundland dogs put their cold noses against my hand, and instantly commenced the most exuberant antics of satisfaction. It then occurred to me how very dreary and forlorn must these poor animals be, at atmospheres + 10° in-doors and —50° without,—living in darkness, howling at an accidental light, as if it reminded them of the moon,—and with nothing, either of instinct or sensation, to tell them of the passing hours, or to explain the long-lost daylight. They shall see the lanterns more frequently."

I may recur to the influence which our long winter night exerted on the health of these much-valued animals. The subject has some interesting bearings ; but I content myself for the present with transcribing another passage from my journal, of a few days later.

"*January 25, Wednesday.*—The mouse-coloured dogs, the leaders of my Newfoundland team, have for the past fortnight been

THE DECKS BY LAMPLIGHT.

nursed like babies. No one can tell how anxiously I watch them. They are kept below, tended, fed, cleansed, caressed, and *doctored*, to the infinite discomfort of all hands. To-day I give up the last hope of saving them. Their disease is as clearly mental as in the case of any human being. The more material functions of the poor. brutes go on without interruption : they eat voraciously, retain their strength, and sleep well. But all the indications beyond this go to prove that the original epilepsy, which was the first

manifestation of brain disease among them, has been followed by
a true lunacy. They bark frenziedly at nothing, and walk in
straight and curved lines with anxious and unwearying perseverance.

"They fawn on you, but without seeming to appreciate the
notice you give them in return; pushing their head against your
person, or oscillating with a strange pantomime of fear. Their
most intelligent actions seem automatic: sometimes they claw you,
as if trying to burrow into your seal-skins; sometimes they remain
for hours in moody silence, and then start off howling as if pursued, and run up and down for hours.

"So it was with poor Flora, our 'wise dog.' She was seized
with the endemic spasms and, after a few wild, violent paroxysms,
lapsed into a lethargic condition, eating voraciously, but gaining
no strength. This passing off, the same crazy wildness took possession of her, and she died of brain disease (*arachnoidal effusion*)
in about six weeks. Generally, they perish with symptoms resembling locked-jaw in less than thirty-six hours after the first
attack."

On the 22d, I took my first walk on the great floe, which had
been for so long a time a crude, black labyrinth. I give the appearance of things in the words of my journal:—

"The floe has changed wonderfully. I remember it sixty-four
days ago, when our twilight was as it now is, a partially snow-
patched plain, chequered with ridges of sharp hummocks, or a
series of long icy levels, over which I coursed with my Newfoundlanders. All this has gone. A lead-coloured expanse stretches its
'rounding gray' in every direction, and the old angular hummocks
are so softened down as to blend in rolling dunes with the distant
obscurity. The snow upon the levels shows the same remarkable
evaporation. It is now in crisp layers, hardly six inches thick,
quite undisturbed by drift. I could hardly recognise any of the
old localities.

We can trace the outline of the shore again, and even some of
the long horizontal bands of its stratification. The cliffs of Sylvia
Mountain, which open toward the east, are, if anything, more
covered with snow than the ridges fronting west across the bay.

"But the feature which had changed most was the ice-belt. When
I saw it last, it was an investing zone of ice, coping the margin of

the floe. The constant accumulation by overflow of tides and freezing has turned this into a bristling wall, 20 feet high, (20 ft. 8 in.) No language can depict the chaos at its base. It has been rising and falling throughout the long winter, with a tidal wave of 13 perpendicular feet. The fragments have been tossed into every possible confusion, rearing up into fantastic equilibrium, surging in long inclined planes, dipping into dark valleys, and piling in contorted hills, often high above the ice-foot.

"The frozen rubbish has raised the floe itself, for a width of 50 yards, into a broken level of crags. To pass over this to our rocky island, with its storehouse, is a work of ingenious pilotage and clambering, only practicable at favouring periods of the tide, and often impossible for many days together. Fortunately for our observatory, a long table of heavy ice has been so nicely poised on the crest of the ice-foot, that it swings like a seesaw with the changing water-level, and has formed a moving beach to the island, on which the floes could not pile themselves. Shoreward between Medary and the ' terrace,' the shoal-water has reared up the ice-fields, so as to make them almost as impass- able as the floes ; and between Fern Rock and the gravestone, where I used to pass with my sledges, there is built a sort of garden-wall of crystal 20 feet high. It needs no iron spikes or broken bottles to defend its crest from trespassers.

"Mr. Sontag amuses me quite as much as he does himself with his daily efforts to scale it."

My next extract is of a few days later.

"*February* 1, *Wednesday.*—The ice-foot is the most wonderful and unique characteristic of our high northern position. The spring-tides have acted on it very powerfully, and the coming day enables us now to observe their stupendous effects. This ice-belt, as I have sometimes called it, is now 24 feet in solid thickness by 65 in mean width; the second, or appended ice, is 38 feet wide; and the third 34 feet. All three are ridges of immense ice-tables, serried like the granite blocks of a rampart, and invest- ing the rocks with a triple circumvallation. We know them as the belt-ices.

"The separation of the true ice-foot from our floe was at first a simple interval, which by the recession and advance of the tides gave a movement of about six feet to our brig. Now, however, the compressed ice grinds closely against the ice-foot, rising into inclined planes, and freezing so as actually to push our floe further and further from the shore. The brig has already moved 28 feet, without the slightest perceptible change in the cradle which imbeds her."

I close my notice of these dreary months with a single extract more. It is of the date of February the 21st.

" We have had the sun, for some days, silvering the ice between the headlands of the bay; and to-day, toward noon, I started out to be the first of my party to welcome him back. It was the longest walk and toughest climb that I have had since our imprisonment; and scurvy and general debility have made me 'short o' wind.' But I managed to attain my object. I saw him once more; and upon a projecting crag nestled in the sunshine. It was like bathing in perfumed water." Welcoming back the sun.

The month of March brought back to us the perpetual day. The sunshine had reached our deck on the last day of February; we needed it to cheer us. We were not as pale as my experience in Lancaster Sound had foretold; but the scurvy-spots that mottled our faces gave sore proof of the trials we had undergone. It was plain that we were all of us unfit for arduous travel on foot at the intense temperatures of the nominal spring; and the return of the sun, by increasing the evaporation from the floes, threatened us with a recurrence of still severer weather. Return of perpetual day.

But I felt that our work was unfinished. The great object of the expedition challenged us to a more northward exploration. My dogs, that I had counted on so largely, the nine splendid Newfoundlanders and thirty-five Esquimaux of six months before, had perished; there were only six survivors of the whole pack, and one of these was unfit for draught. Still, they formed my principal reliance, and I busied myself from the very beginning of the month in training them to run together. The carpenter was set to work upon a small sledge, on an improved model, and adapted to the reduced force of our team; and, as we had exhausted our stock of small cord to lash its parts together, Mr. Brooks rigged up a miniature rope-walk, and was preparing a new supply from part of the material of our deep-sea lines. The operations of shipboard, however, went on regularly; Hans, and Preparations for a further search.

occasionally Petersen, going out on the hunt, though rarely returning successful.

Meanwhile we talked encouragingly of spring hopes and summer prospects, and managed sometimes to force an occasion for mirth out of the very discomforts of our unyielding winter life.

This may explain the tone of my diary.

CHAPTER XV.

ARCTIC OBSERVATIONS—TRAVEL TO OBSERVATORY—ITS HAZARDS—ARCTIC
LIFE—THE DAY—THE DIET—THE AMUSEMENTS—THE LABOURS—THE
TEMPERATURE—THE "EIS-FOD"—THE ICE-BELT—THE ICE-BELT EN-
CROACHING — EXPEDITION PREPARING — GOOD-BYE — A SURPISE — A
SECOND GOOD-BYE.

"*March* 7, *Tuesday.* —I have said very little in this business journal CHAPTER
about our daily Arctic life. I have had no time to draw pictures. XV.

"But we have some trials which might make up a day's adven- Daily
trials.

THE MAGNETIC OBSERVATORY.

tures. Our Arctic observatory is cold beyond any of its class,
Kesan, Pulkowa, Toronto, or even its shifting predecessors, Bossetop

and Melville Island. Imagine it a term-day, a magnetic term day.

"The observer, if he were only at home, would be the 'observed of all observers.' He is clad in a pair of seal-skin pants, a dog skin cap, a reindeer jumper, and walrus boots. He sits upon a box that once held a transit instrument. A stove, glowing with at least a bucketful of anthracite, represents pictorially a heating apparatus, and reduces the thermometer as near as may be to 10° below zero. One hand holds a chronometer, and is left bare to warm it; the other luxuriates in a fox-skin mitten. The right hand and the left take it 'watch and watch about.' As one burns with cold, the chronometer shifts to the other, and the mitten takes its place.

"Perched on a pedestal of frozen gravel is a magnetometer; stretching out from it, a telescope; and, bending down to this, an abject human eye. Every six minutes said eye takes cognizance of a finely-divided arc, and notes the result in a cold memorandum-book. This process continues for twenty-four hours, two sets of eyes taking it by turns; and, when twenty-four hours are over, term-day is over too.

Labours
and suffer-
ings from
cold in the
observa-
tory. "We have such frolics every week. I have just been relieved from one, and after a few hours am to be called out of bed in the night to watch and dot again. I have been engaged in this way when the thermometer gave 20° above zero at the instrument, 20° below at two feet above the floor, and 43° below at the floor itself; on my person, facing the little lobster-red fury of a stove, 94° above; on my person, away from the stove, 10° below zero. 'A grateful country' will of course appreciate the value of these labours, and, as it cons over hereafter the four hundred and eighty results which go to make up our record for each week, will never think of asking, 'Cui bono all this?'

"But this is no adventure. The adventure is the travel to and fro. We have night now only half the time; and half the time can go and come with eyes to help us. It was not so a little while since.

"Taking an ice-pole in one hand, and a dark lantern in the other, you steer through the blackness for a lump of greater blackness, the Fern Rock knob. Stumbling over some fifty yards, you come to a wall; your black knob has disappeared, and nothing

but grey indefinable ice is before you. Turn to the right; plant
your pole against that inclined plane of slippery smoothness, and
jump to the hummock opposite; it is the same hummock you
skinned your shins upon the last night you were here. Now wind
along, half serpentine, half zigzag, and you cannot mistake that
twenty feet wall just beyond, creaking and groaning, and even
nodding its crest with a grave cold welcome; it is the 'seam
of the second ice.' Tumble over it at the first gap, and
you are upon the first ice; tumble over that and you are at
the ice-foot; and there is nothing else now between you and
the rocks, and nothing after them between you and the observatory.

"But be a little careful as you come near this ice-foot. It is
munching all the time at the first ice, and you have to pick your
way over the masticated fragments. Don't trust yourself to the
half-balanced, half-fixed, half-floating ice-lumps, unless you relish
a bath like Marshal Suwarrow's—it might be more pleasant if you
were sure of getting out—but feel your way gingerly, with your
pole held crosswise, not disdaining lowly attitudes—hands and
knees, or even full length. That long wedge-like hole just before
you, sending up its puffs of steam into the cold air, is the 'seam
of the ice-foot;' you have only to jump it and you are on the
smooth, level icefoot itself. Scramble up the rocks now, get on
your wooden shoes, and go to work observing an oscillating needle
for some hours to come.

"Astronomy, as it draws close under the pole-star, cannot lavish
all its powers of observation on things above. It was the mistake
of Mr. Sontag some months ago, when he wandered about for an
hour on his way to the observatory, and was afraid after finding
it to try and wander back. I myself had a slide down an inclined
plane, whose well-graded talus gave me ample time to contemplate the contingencies at its base; a chasm peradventure, for my
ice-pole was travelling ahead of me and stopped short with a
clang; or it might be a pointed hummock—there used to be one
just below; or by good luck it was only a water-pool, in which my
lantern made the glitter. I exulted to find myself in a cushion
of snow.

"*March* 9, *Thursday.*—How do we spend the day when it
is not term-day, or rather the twenty-four hours? for it is either

CHAPTER XV.

all day here, or all night, or a twilight mixture of both. How do we spend the twenty-four hours?

Morning.

"At six in the morning M'Gary is called, with all hands who have *slept in*. The decks are cleaned, the ice-hole opened, the refreshing beef-nets examined, the ice-tables measured, and things aboard put to rights. At half-past seven all hands rise, wash on deck. open the doors for ventilation, and come below for breakfast. We are short of fuel, and therefore cook in the cabin. Our

Breakfast.

breakfast, for all fare alike, is hard tack, pork, stewed apples frozen like molasses-candy, tea and coffee, with a delicate portion of raw potato. After breakfast the smokers take their pipe till nine; then all hands turn to, idlers to idle and workers to work; Ohlsen to his bench, Brooks to his 'preparations' in canvas, M'Gary to play tailor, Whipple to make shoes, Bonsall to tinker, Baker to skin birds, and the rest to the 'Office!' Take a look into the Arctic Bureau! One table, one salt-pork lamp with rusty chlorinated flame, three stools, and as many waxen-faced men with their legs drawn up under them, the deck at zero being too cold for the feet. Each has his department: Kane is writing, sketching, and

Employments.

projecting maps; Hayes copying logs and meteorologicals; Sontag reducing his work at Fern Rock. A fourth, as one of the working members of the hive, has long been defunct; you will find him in bed, or studying 'Littell's Living Age.' At twelve a business round of inspection, and orders enough to fill up the day with work. Next, the drill of the Esquimaux dogs—my own peculiar recreation—a dog-trot specially refreshing to legs that creak with every kick, and rheumatic shoulders that chronicle every descent of the whip. And so we get on to dinner-time—the occasion of another gathering, which misses the tea and coffeee of breakfast, but rejoices in pickled cabbage and dried peaches instead.

Dinner.

"At dinner as at breakfast the raw potato comes in, our hygienic luxury. Like doctor-stuff generally, it is not as appetizing as desirable. Grating it down nicely, leaving out the ugly red spots liberally, and adding the utmost oil as a lubricant, it is as much as I can do to persuade the mess to shut their eyes and bolt it, like Mrs. Squeers's molasses and brimstone at Dotheboys Hall. Two absolutely refuse to taste it. I tell them of the Silesians using its leaves as spinach, of the whalers in the South Seas

getting drunk on the molasses which had preserved the large
potatoes of the Azores—·I point to this gum, so fungoid and angry
the day before yesterday, and so flat and amiable to-day—all by a
potato poultice; my eloquence is wasted; they persevere in rejecting the admirable compound.

"Sleep, exercise, amusement, and work at will, carry on the day Supper.
till our six o'clock supper, a meal something like breakfast and
something like dinner, only a little more scant; and the officers
come in with the reports of the day. Dr. Hayes shows me the
log, I sign it; Sontag the weather, I sign the weather; Mr. Bonsall the tides and thermometers. Thereupon comes in mine ancient,

WINTER LIFE ON BOARD SHIP.

Brooks; and I enter in his journal No. 3 all the work done under
his charge, and discuss his labours for the morrow.

"M'Gary comes next, with the cleaning-up arrangement, inside, Close of
outside, and on decks; and Mr. Wilson follows with ice-measure- the day
ments. And last of all comes my own record of the day gone by;

CHAPTER
XV.
every line, as I look back upon its pages, giving evidence of a weakened body and harassed mind.

Amusements.
"We have cards sometimes, and chess sometimes,—and a few magazines, Mr. Littell's thoughtful present to cheer away the evening.

" *March* 11, *Saturday.*—All this seems tolerable for commonplace routine; but there is a lack of comfort which it does not tell of. Our fuel is limited to three bucketfuls of coal a-day, and our mean temperature outside is 40° below zero; 46° below as I write. London Brown Stout, and somebody's Old Brown Sherry, freeze in the cabin lockers; and the carlines overhead are hung with tubs of chopped ice, to make water for our daily drink. Our Privations. lamps cannot be persuaded to burn salt lard; our oil is exhausted; and we work by muddy tapers of cork and cotton floated in saucers. We have not a pound of fresh meat, and only a barrel of potatoes left.

Disease.
"Not a man now, except Pierre and Morton, is exempt from scurvy; and, as I look around upon the pale faces and haggard looks of my comrades, I feel that we are fighting the battle of life at disadvantage, and that an Arctic night and an Arctic day age a man more rapidly and harshly than a year anywhere else in all this weary world.

Preparations for travel
" *March* 13, *Monday.*—Since January, we have been working at the sledges and other preparations for travel. The death of my dogs, the rugged obstacles of the ice, and the intense cold, have obliged me to re-organize our whole equipment. We have had to discard all our India-rubber fancy-work; canvas shoe-making, fur-socking, sewing, carpentering, are all going on; and the cabin, our only fire-warmed apartment, is the workshop, kitchen, parlour, and hall. Pemmican cases are thawing on the lockers; buffalo robes are drying around the stove; camp equipments occupy the corners; and our woe-begone French cook, with an infinitude of useless saucepans, insists on monopolizing the stove.

Mean temperature.
" *March* 15, *Wednesday.*—The mean temperature of the last five days has been,—

March 10	—46°.03
11	—45°.60
12	—46°.64
13	—46°.56
14	—46°.65

giving an average of —46° 30′, with a variation between the CHAPTER XV. extremes of less than three-quarters of a degree.

"These records are remarkable. The coldest month of the Polar year has heretofore been February; but we are evidently about to experience for March a mean temperature not only the lowest of our own series, but lower than that of any other recorded observations.

"This anomalous temperature seems to disprove the idea of a diminished cold as we approach the Pole. It will extend the isotherm of the solstitial month higher than ever before projected.

"The mean temperature of Parry for March (in lat. 74° 30′) Mean temperature was —29°; our own will be at least 41° below zero.

"At such temperatures the ice or snow covering offers a great resistance to the sledge-runners. I have noticed this in training my dogs. The dry snow in its finely-divided state resembles sand, and the runners creak as they pass over it. Baron Wrangell notes the same fact in Siberia at —40°.

"The difficulties of draught, however, must not interfere with my parties. I am only waiting until the sun, now 13° high at noon, brings back a little warmth to the men in sleeping. The Slight re mean difference between bright clear sunshine and shade is now turn of warmth 5°. But on the 10th, at noon, the shade gave —42° 2′, and the sun —28° ; a difference of more than 14°. This must make an impression before long.

"*March* 17, *Friday.*—It is nine o'clock, P.M., and the thermometer outside at —46°. I am anxious to have this depôt party off ; but I must wait until there is a promise of milder weather. It must come soon. The sun is almost at the equator. On deck, I can see to the northward all the bright glare of sunset, streaming out in long bands of orange through the vapours of the ice-foot, and the frost-smoke exhaling in wreaths like those from the house-chimneys a man sees in the valleys as he comes down a mountain-side."

I must reserve for my official report the detailed story of this ice-foot and its changes.

The name is adopted on board ship from the Danish "Eis-fod," The "Eis to designate a zone of ice which extends along the shore from the fod." untried north beyond us almost to the Arctic circle. To the south it breaks up during the summer months, and disappears as high as

Upernavik or even Cape Alexander; but in this our high northern winter harbour, it is a perennial growth, clinging to the bold faces of the cliffs, following the sweeps of the bays and the indentations of rivers.

This broad platform, although changing with the seasons, never

disappears. It served as our highway of travel, a secure and level sledge-road, perched high above the grinding ice of the sea, and adapting itself to the tortuosities of the land. As such I shall call it the "ice-belt."

I was familiar with the Arctic shore-ices of the Asiatic and American explorers, and had personally studied the same formations in Wellington Channel, where, previous to the present voyage, they might have been supposed to reach their greatest development. But this wonderful structure has here assumed a form which none of its lesser growths to the south had exhibited. As a physical feature, it may be regarded as hardly second, either in importance or prominence, to the glacier; and as an agent of geological change, it is in the highest degree interesting and instructive.

Although subject to occasional disruption, and to loss of volume

from evaporation and thaws, it measures the severity of the year by its rates of increase. Rising with the first freezings of the late summer, it crusts the sea-line with curious fretwork and arabesques; a little later, and it receives the rude shock of the drifts, and the collision of falling rocks from the cliffs which margin it; before the early winter has darkened, it is a wall, resisting the grinding floes; and it goes on gathering increase and strength from the successive freezing of the tides, until the melted snows and water-torrents of summer for a time check its progress. During our first winter at Rensselaer Harbour, the ice-belt grew to three times the size which it had upon our arrival; and, by the middle of March, the islands and adjacent shores were hemmed in by an investing plane of nearly 30 feet high (27 feet) and 120 wide.

The ice-foot at this season was not, however, an unbroken level. It had, like the floes, its barricades, serried and irregular—which it was a work of great labour and some difficulty to traverse. Our stores were in consequence nearly inaccessible; and, as the ice-foot still continued to extend itself, piling ice-table upon ice-table, it threatened to encroach upon our anchorage and peril the safety

of the vessel.   The ridges were already within twenty feet of her, CHAPTER
and her stern was sensibly lifted up by their pressure.   We had, XV.
indeed, been puzzled for six weeks before, by remarking that the Ice-floe
receding
floe we were imbedded in was gradually receding from the shore;
and had recalled the observation of the Danes of Upernavik, that
their nets were sometimes forced away strangely from the land.
The explanation is, perhaps, to be found in the alternate action of
the tides and frost ; but it would be out of place to enter upon the
discussion here.

"*March* 18, *Saturday.*—To-day our spring-tides gave to the
massive ice which sustains our little vessel a rise and fall of seventeen feet.   The crunching and grinding, the dashing of the water,
the gurgling of the eddies, and the toppling over of the nicely-
poised ice-tables, were unlike the more brisk dynamics of hummock action, but conveyed a more striking expression of power
and dimension.

"The thermometer at four o'clock in the morning was minus
49°; too cold still, I fear, for our sledgemen to set out.   But we
packed the sledge and strapped on the boat, and determined to see Preparations for
how she would drag.   Eight men attached themselves to the lines, travel.
but were scarcely able to move her.   This may be due in part to
an increase of friction produced by the excessive cold, according to
the experience of the Siberian travellers ; but I have no doubt it
is principally caused by the very thin runners of our Esquimaux
sledge cutting through the snow-crust.

"The excessive refraction this evening, which entirely lifted up
the northern coast as well as the icebergs, seems to give the promise of milder weather.   In the hope that it may be so, I have
fixed on to-morrow for the departure of the sledge, after very
reluctantly dispensing with more than two hundred pounds of her
cargo, besides the boat.   The party think they can get along with
it now.

"*March* 20, *Monday.*—I saw the depôt party off yesterday.   They The depar
ture.
gave the usual three cheers, with three for myself.   I gave them
the whole of my brother's great wedding-cake and my last two
bottles of Port, and they pulled the sledge they were harnessed to
famously.   But I was not satisfied.   I could see it was hard work ;
and, besides, they were without the boat, or enough extra pemmican to make their deposit of importance.   I followed them, there-

CHAPTER
XV.
fore, and found that they encamped at 8 P.M. only five miles from the brig.

"When I overtook them I said nothing to discourage them, and gave no new orders for the morning ; but after laughing at good Ohlsen's rueful face, and listening to all Petersen's assurances that the cold and nothing but the cold retarded his Greenland sledge, and that no sledge of any other construction could have been moved at all through —40° snow, I quietly bade them good-night, leaving all hands under their buffaloes.

A sled
prepared.
"Once returned to the brig, all my tired remainder-men were summoned ; a large sled with broad runners, which I had built somewhat after the neat Admiralty model sent me by Sir Francis Beaufort, was taken down, scraped, polished, lashed, and fitted with trackropes and *rue-raddies*—the lines arranged to draw as near as possible in a line with the centre of gravity. We made an entire cover of canvas, with snugly-adjusted fastenings ; and by one in the morning we had our discarded excess of pemmican and the boat once more in stowage.

"Off we went for the camp of the sleepers. It was very cold, but a thoroughly Arctic night—the snow just tinged with the crimson stratus above the sun, which, equinoctial as it was, glared beneath the northern horizon like a smelting-furnace. We found the tent of the party by the bearings of the stranded bergs. Quietly and stealthily we hauled away their Esquimaux sledge, and placed her cargo upon the *Faith*. Five men were then rue-raddied to the track-lines ; and with the whispered word, 'Now, boys, when Mr. Brooks gives his third snore, off with you !' off they went, and the *Faith* after them, as free and nimble as a
A night
surprise.
volunteer. The trial was a triumph. We awakened the sleepers with three cheers ; and, giving them a second good-bye, returned to the brig, carrying the dishonoured vehicle along with us. And now, bating mishaps past anticipation, I shall have a depôt for my long trip.

Last sight
of the
party.
"The party were seen by M'Gary from aloft, at noon to-day, moving easily, and about twelve miles from the brig. The temperature too is rising, or rather unmistakably about to rise. Our lowest was —43°, but our highest reached —22° ; this extreme range, with the excessive refraction and a gentle misty air from about the south-east, makes me hope that we are going to have a warm spell. The party is well off. Now for my own to follow them."

CHAPTER XVI.

REPARATION—TEMPERATURES—ADVENTURE—AN ALARM—PARTY ON THE
FLOES—RESCUE PARTY—LOST ON THE FLOES—PARTY FOUND—RETURN
—FREEZING—RETURNING CAMP—A BIVOUAC—EXHAUSTED—ESCAPE—
CONSEQUENCES.

March 21, *Tuesday.*—All hands at work house cleaning. Ther- CHAPTER XVI.
ometer —48°. Visited the fox-traps with Hans in the afternoon, Fox frozen in a trap.
id found one poor animal frozen dead. He was coiled up, with
s nose buried in his bushy tail, like a fancy foot-muff, or the
-ie-dieu of a royal sinner. A hard thing about his fate was that
? had succeeded in effecting his escape from the trap, but, while
orking his way underneath, had been frozen fast to a smooth stone
y the moisture of his own breath. He was not probably aware
' it before the moment when he sought to avail himself of his
ırd-gained liberty. These saddening thoughts did not impair my
ιpetite at supper, where the little creature looked handsomer
ıan ever.

" *March* 22, *Wednesday.*—We took down the forward bulkhead
ı-day, and moved the men aft, to save fuel. All hands are still
; work clearing up the decks, the scrapers sounding overhead,
ıd the hickory brooms crackling against the frozen woodwork.
fternoon comes, and M'Gary brings from the traps two foxes, a
lue and a white. Afternoon passes, and we skin them. Evening Welcome visitors.
ısses, and we eat them. Never were foxes more welcome visitors,
r treated more like domestic animals.

" *March* 23, *Thursday.*—The accumulated ice upon our housing
ıows what the condensed and frozen moisture of the winter has
een. The average thickness of this curious deposit is five inches,
ery hard and well crystallized. Six cart loads have been already
ıopped out, and about four more remain.

" It is very far from a hardship to sleep under such an ice-roof An ice roof
; this. In a climate where the intense cold approximates all ice
) granite, its thick air-tight coating contributes to our warmth,
ives a beautiful and cheerful lustre to our walls, and condenses

any vapours which our cooks allow to escape the funnels. I only remove it now because I fear the effects of damp in the season of sunshine.

"*March* 27, *Monday.*—We have been for some days in all the flurry of preparation for our exploration trip : buffalo-hides, leather, and tailoring utensils everywhere. Every particle of fur comes in play for mits, and muffs, and wrappers. Poor Flora is turned into a pair of socks, and looks almost as pretty as when she was heading the team.

"The wind to-day made it intensely cold. In riding but four miles to inspect a fox-trap, the movement froze my cheeks twice. We avoid masks with great care, reserving them for the severer weather ; the jaw when protected recovers very soon the sensibility which exposure has subdued.

"Our party is now out in its ninth day. It has had some trying weather :—

On the 19th	—42°.3
20th	—35°.4
21st	—19°.37
22d	— 7°.47
23d	— 9°.07
24th	—18°.32
25th	—34°.80
26th	—42°.8
27th	—34°.38

of mean daily temperature ; making an average of 27°.13 below zero.

"*March* 29, *Wednesday.*—I have been out with my dog-sledge inspecting the ice to-day from the north-western headland. There seems a marked difference between this sound and other estuaries, in the number of icebergs. Unlike Prince Regent's, or Wellington, or Lancaster Sounds, the shores here are lined with glaciers, and the water is everywhere choked and harassed by their discharges This was never so apparent to me as this afternoon. The low sun lit up line after line of lofty bergs, and the excessive refraction elevated them so much, that I thought I could see a chain of continuous ice running on toward the north until it was lost in illimitable distance.

"*March* 31, *Friday.*—I was within an ace to-day of losing my dogs, every one of them. When I reached the ice-foot, they

lked;—who would not?—the tide was low, the ice rampant,
d a jump of four feet necessary to reach the crest. The howling
the wind and the whirl of the snow-drift confused the poor
:atures; but it was valuable training for them, and I strove to
:ce them over. Of course I was on foot, and they had a light
ld behind them. 'Now, Stumpy! Now, Whitey!' 'Good
gs!' 'Tu-lee-ĕĕ-ĕĕ! Tuh!' They went at it like good stanch
utes, and the next minute the whole team was rolling in a lump,
me sixteen feet below me, in the chasm of the ice-foot. The
ift was such that at first I could not see them. The roaring of
e tide, and the subdued wail of the dogs, made me fear for the
)rst. I had to walk through the broken ice, which rose in
ppling spires over my head, for nearly fifty yards, before I found
opening to the ice face, by which I was able to climb down to
em. A few cuts of a sheath-knife released them, although the
resses of the dear brutes had like to have been fatal to me, for
had to straddle with one foot on the fast ice and the other on
ose piled rubbish. But I got a line attached to the cross-pieces
the sledge-runners, flung it up on the ice-foot, and then piloted
y dogs out of their slough. In about ten minutes we were
veating along at eight miles an hour."

Everything looked promising, and we were only waiting for
telligence that our advance party had deposited its provisions in
fety to begin our transit of the bay. Except a few sledge-
shings and some trifling accoutrements to finish, all was ready.
We were at work cheerfully, sewing away at the skins of some
occasins by the blaze of our lamps, when, toward midnight, we
:ard the noise of steps above, and the next minute Sontag, Ohlsen,
ld Petersen, came down into the cabin. Their manner startled
e even more than their unexpected appearance on board. They
ere swollen and haggard, and hardly able to speak.
Their story was a fearful one. They had left their companions
the ice, risking their own lives to bring us the news; Brooks,
aker, Wilson, and Pierre, were all lying frozen and disabled.
There? They could not tell; somewhere in among the hummocks
the north and east; it was drifting heavily round them when
ley parted. Irish Tom had stayed by to feed and care for the
:hers: but the chances were sorely against them. It was in vain

CHAPTER XVI.

to question them further. They had evidently travelled a great distance, for they were sinking with fatigue and hunger, and could hardly be rallied enough to tell us the direction in which they had come.

My first impulse was to move on the instant with an unencumbered party; a rescue, to be effective or even hopeful, could not be too prompt. What pressed on my mind most was where the sufferers were to be looked for among the drifts. Ohlsen seemed to have his faculties rather more at command than his associates, and I thought that he might assist us as a guide; but he was sinking with exhaustion, and if he went with us we must carry him.

A hasty departure.

There was not a moment to be lost. While some were still busy with the new-comers and getting ready a hasty meal, others were rigging out the *Little Willie* with a buffalo cover, a small tent, and a package of pemmican; and, as soon as we could hurry through our arrangements, Ohlsen was strapped on in a fur bag, his legs wrapped in dog-skins and eider down, and we were off upon the ice. Our party consisted of nine men and myself. We carried only the clothes on our backs. The thermometer stood at —46°, seventy-eight below the freezing point.

THE RESCUE PARTY.

. A well-known peculiar tower of ice, called by the men the " Pinnacly Berg," served as our first landmark; other icebergs of

:olossal size, which stretched in long beaded lines across the bay,
lelped to guide us afterward; and it was not until we had travelled
'or sixteen hours that we began to lose our way.

We knew that our lost companions must be somewhere in the
.rea before us, within a radius of forty miles. Mr. Ohlsen, who
iad been for fifty hours without rest, fell asleep as soon as we
)egan to move, and awoke now with unequivocal signs of mental
listurbance. It became evident that he had lost the bearing of
he icebergs, which in form and colour endlessly repeated them-
elves; and the uniformity of the vast field of snow utterly forbade
he hope of local landmarks.

Pushing ahead of the party, and clambering over some rugged
ce-piles, I came to a long level floe, which I thought might pro-
,ably have attracted the eyes of weary men in circumstances like
·ur own. It was a light conjecture; but it was enough to turn
he scale, for there was no other to balance it. I gave orders to
bandon the sledge, and disperse in search of footmarks. We
aised our tent, placed our pemmican in *cache*, except a small
llowance for each man to carry on his person; and poor Ohlsen,
ow just able to keep his legs, was liberated from his bag. The
hermometer had fallen by this time to —49°.3, and the wind
·as setting in sharply from the north-west. It was out of the
uestion to halt; it required brisk exercise to keep us from freez-
1g. I· could not even melt ice for water; and, at these tempe-
atures, any resort to snow for the purpose of allaying thirst was
llowed by bloody lips and tongue; it burnt like caustic.

It was indispensable, then, that we should move on, looking out
·r traces as we went. Yet when the men were ordered to spread
1emselves, so as to multiply the chances, though they all obeyed
eartily, some painful impress of solitary danger, or perhaps it
1ay have been the varying configuration of the ice-field, kept them
losing up continually into a single group. The strange manner
1 which some of us were affected I now attribute as much to
hattered nerves as to the direct influence of the cold. Men like
l·Gary and Bonsall, who had stood out our severest marches,
·ere seized with trembling fits and short breath; and, in spite of
ll my efforts to keep up an example of sound bearing, I fainted
·vice on the snow.

We had been nearly eighteen hours out without water or food, when a new hope cheered us. I think it was Hans, our Esquimaux hunter, who thought he saw a broad sledge-track. The drift had nearly effaced it, and we were some of us doubtful at first whether it was not one of those accidental rifts which the gales make in the surface-snow. But, as we traced it on to the deep snow among the hummocks, we were led to footsteps; and, following these with religious care, we at last came in sight of a small American flag fluttering from a hummock, and lower down a little Masonic banner hanging from a tent-pole hardly above the drift. It was the camp of our disabled comrades; we reached it after an unbroken march of twenty-one hours.

The little tent was nearly covered. I was not among the first to come up; but, when I reached the tent-curtain, the men were standing in silent file on each side of it. With more kindness and delicacy of feeling than is often supposed to belong to sailors, but
which is almost characteristic, they intimated their wish that I should go in alone. As I crawled in, and, coming upon the darkness, heard before me the burst of welcome gladness that came from the four poor fellows stretched on their backs, and then for the first time the cheer outside, my weakness and my gratitude together almost overcame me. "They had expected me: they were sure I would come!"

We were now fifteen souls; the thermometer 75° below the freezing point; and our sole accommodation a tent barely able to contain eight persons: more than half our party were obliged to keep from freezing by walking outside while the others slept. We could not halt long. Each of us took a turn of two hours' sleep; and we prepared for our homeward march.

We took with us nothing but the tent, furs to protect the rescued party, and food for a journey of fifty hours. Everything else was abandoned. Two large buffalo-bags, each made of four skins, were doubled up, so as to form a sort of sack, lined on each side by fur, closed at the bottom, but opened at the top. This was laid on the sledge; the tent, smoothly folded, serving as a floor. The sick, with their limbs sewed up carefully in reindeer-skins, were placed upon the bed of buffalo-robes, in a half-reclining posture; other skins and blanket-bags were thrown above them; and the whole litter was lashed together so as to allow but a single opening opposite the mouth for breathing.

This necessary work cost us a great deal of time and effort ; but it was essential to the lives of the sufferers. It took us no less than four hours to strip and refresh them, and then to embale them in the manner I have described. Few of us escaped without frost-bitten fingers : the thermometer was at 55°.6 below zero, and a slight wind added to the severity of the cold.

It was completed at last, however ; all hands stood round, and, after repeating a short prayer, we set out on our retreat. It was fortunate indeed that we were not inexperienced in sledging over the ice. A great part of our track lay among a succession of hummocks, some of them extending in long lines, fifteen or twenty feet high, and so uniformly steep that we had to turn them by a considerable deviation from our direct course ; others that we forced our way through, far above our heads in height, lying in parallel ridges, with the space between too narrow for the sledge to be lowered into it safely, and yet not wide enough for the runners to cross without the aid of ropes to stay them. These spaces, too, were generally choked with light snow, hiding the openings between the ice-fragments. They were fearful traps to disengage a limb from, for every man knew that a fracture or a sprain even would cost him his life. Besides all this, the sledge was top-heavy with its load : the maimed men could not bear to be lashed down tight enough to secure them against falling off. Notwithstanding our caution in rejecting every superfluous bur-den, the weight, including bags and tent, was eleven hundred pounds.

And yet our march for the first six hours was very cheering. We made, by vigorous pulls and lifts, nearly a mile an hour, and reached the new floes before we were absolutely weary. Our sledge sustained the trial admirably. Ohlsen, restored by hope, walked steadily at the leading belt of the sledge lines ; and I began to feel certain of reaching our half-way station of the day before, where we had left our tent. But we were still nine miles from it, when, almost without premonition, we all became aware of an alarming failure of our energies.

I was, of course, familiar with the benumbed and almost lethargic sensation of extreme cold ; and once, when exposed for some hours in the midwinter of Baffin's Bay, I had experienced symptoms which I compared to the diffused paralysis of the electro-galvanic shock. But I had treated the *sleepy comfort* of freezing as something like the embellishment of romance. I had evidence now to the contrary.

Bonsall and Morton, two of our stoutest men, came to me, begging permission to sleep : "they were not cold : the wind did not enter them now : a little sleep was all they wanted." Presently Hans was found nearly stiff under a drift; and Thomas, bolt upright, had his eyes closed, and could hardly articulate. At last John Blake threw himself on the snow, and refused to rise. They did not complain of feeling cold; but it was in vain that I wrestled, boxed, ran, argued, jeered, or reprimanded : an immediate halt could not be avoided.

We pitched our tent with much difficulty. Our hands were too powerless to strike a fire : we were obliged to do without water or food. Even the spirits (whisky) had frozen at the men's feet,

INSIDE OF TENT.

under all the coverings. We put Bonsall, Ohlsen, Thomas, and Hans, with the other sick men, well inside the tent, and crowded in as many others as we could. Then, leaving the party in charge of Mr. M'Gary, with orders to come on after four hours' rest, I pushed ahead with William Godfrey, who volunteered to be my companion. My aim was to reach the half-way tent, and thaw some ice and pemmican before the others arrived.

The floe was of level ice, and the walking excellent. I cannot tell how long it took us to make the nine miles, for we were in a strange sort of stupor, and had little apprehension of time. It was probably about four hours. We kept ourselves awake by imposing on each other a continued articulation of words ; they must have been incoherent enough. I recall these hours as among the most wretched I have ever gone through : we were neither of us in our right senses, and retained a very confused recollection of what preceded our arrival at the tent. We both of us, however, remember a bear, who walked leisurely before us, and tore up as he went a jumper that Mr. M'Gary had improvidently thrown off the day before. He tore it into shreds and rolled it into a ball, but never offered to interfere with our progress. I remember this, and with it a confused sentiment that our tent and buffalo-robes might probably share the same fate. Godfrey, with whom the memory of this day's work may atone for many faults of a later time, had a better eye than myself ; and, looking some miles ahead, he could see that our tent was undergoing the same unceremonious treatment. I thought I saw it too, but we were so drunken with cold that we strode on steadily, and, for aught I know, without quickening our pace.

Probably our approach saved the contents of the tent; for when we reached it the tent was uninjured, though the bear had overturned it, tossing the buffalo-robes and pemmican into the snow ; we missed only a couple of blanket-bags. What we recollect, however, and perhaps all we recollect, is, that we had great difficulty in raising it. We crawled into our reindeer sleeping-bags without speaking, and for the next three hours slept on in a dreamy but intense slumber. When I awoke my long beard was a mass of ice, frozen fast to the buffalo-skin : Godfrey had to cut me out with his jack-knife. Four days after our escape I found my woollen comfortable with a goodly share of my beard still adhering to it.

We were able to melt water and get some soup cooked before the rest of our party arrived : it took them but five hours to walk the nine miles. They were doing well, and, considering the circumstances, in wonderful spirits. The day was almost providentially windless, with a clear sun. All enjoyed the refreshment we had got ready : the crippled were repacked in their robes ; and

we sped briskly toward the hummock-ridges which lay between us
and the Pinnacly Berg.

"The hummocks we had now to meet came properly under the
designation of squeezed ice. A great chain of bergs stretching
from north-west to south-east, moving with the tides, had compressed the surface floes; and rearing them upon their edges, produced an area more like the volcanic pedragal of the basin of
Mexico than anything else I can compare it to.

Desperate
efforts.
It required desperate efforts to work our way over it—literally
desperate, for our strength failed us anew, and we began to lose
our self-control. We could not abstain any longer from eating
snow; our mouths swelled, and some of us became speechless.
Happily the day was warmed by a clear sunshine, and the thermo-
mometer rose to —4° in the shade; otherwise we must have
frozen.

Sleeping
on the
snow.
Our halts multiplied, and we fell half-sleeping on the snow. I
could not prevent it. Strange to say, it refreshed us. I ventured upon the experiment myself, making Riley wake me at the
end of three minutes; and I felt so much benefited by it that I
timed the men in the same way. They sat on the runners of the
sledge, fell asleep instantly, and were forced to wakefulness when
their three minutes were out.

By eight in the evening we emerged from the floes. The sight
of the Pinnacly Berg revived us. Brandy, an invaluable resource
in emergency, had already been served out in table-spoonful doses.
We now took a longer rest, and a last but stouter dram, and reached
the brig at 1 P.M., we believe without a halt.

Delirious-
ness from
suffering.
I say we believe; and here perhaps is the most decided proof of
our sufferings; we were quite delirious, and had ceased to entertain a sane apprehension of the circumstances about us. We
moved on like men in a dream. Our footmarks seen afterward
showed that we had steered a bee-line for the brig. It must have
been by a sort of instinct, for it left no impress on the memory.
Bonsall was sent staggering ahead, and reached the brig, God
knows how, for he had fallen repeatedly at the track-lines; but he
delivered with punctilious accuracy the messages I had sent by
him to Dr. Hayes. I thought myself the soundest of all, for I
went through all the formula of sanity, and can recall the mutter-
ing delirium of my comrades when we got back into the cabin of

our brig. Yet I have been told since of some speeches and some orders too of mine, which I should have remembered for their absurdity if my mind had retained its balance.

Petersen and Whipple came out to meet us about two miles from the brig. They brought my dog-team, with the restoratives I had sent for by Bonsall. I do not remember their coming. Dr. Hayes entered with judicious energy upon the treatment our condition called for, administering morphine freely, after the usual frictions. He reported none of our brain-symptoms as serious, referring them properly to the class of those indications of ex- hausted power which yield to generous diet and rest. Mr. Ohlsen suffered some time from strabismus and blindness; two others underwent amputation of parts of the foot, without unpleasant consequences; and two died in spite of all our efforts. This rescue party had been out for seventy-two hours. We had halted in all eight hours, half of our number sleeping at a time. We travelled between eighty and ninety miles, most of the way dragging a heavy sledge. The mean temperature of the whole time, including the warmest hours of three days, was at minus 41°.2. We had no water except at our two halts, and were at no time able to intermit vigorous exercise without freezing.

"*April* 4, *Tuesday.*—Four days have passed, and I am again at my record of failures, sound but aching still in every joint. The rescued men are not out of danger, but their gratitude is very touching. Pray God that they may live!"

CHAPTER XVII.

BAKER'S DEATH — A VISIT—THE ESQUIMAUX — A NEGOTIATION — THEIR
EQUIPMENT—THEIR DEPORTMENT—A TREATY—THE FAREWELL—THE
SEQUEL—MYOUK—HIS ESCAPE—SCHUBERT'S ILLNESS.

CHAPTER XVII. THE week that followed has left me nothing to remember but anxieties and sorrow. Nearly all our party, as well the rescuers as the rescued, were tossing in their sick-bunks, some frozen, others undergoing amputations, several with dreadful premonitions of tetanus. I was myself among the first to be about; the necessities of the others claimed it of me.

Baker's illness and death. Early in the morning of the 7th I was awakened by a sound from Baker's throat, one of those the most frightful and ominous that ever startle a physician's ear. The lock-jaw had seized him; that dark visitant whose foreshadowings were on so many of us. His symptoms marched rapidly to their result; he died on the 8th of April. We placed him the next day in his coffin, and, forming a rude, but heart-full procession, bore him over the broken ice and up the steep side of the ice-foot to Butler Island; then, passing along the snow-level to Fern-Rock, and, climbing the slope of the Observatory, we deposited his corpse upon the pedestals which had served to support our transit-instrument and theodolite. We His funeral. read the service for the burial of the dead, sprinkling over him snow for dust, and repeated the Lord's Prayer; and then icing up again the opening in the walls we had made to admit the coffin, left him in his narrow house.

Jefferson Baker was a man of kind heart and true principles. I knew him when we were both younger. I passed two happy seasons at a little cottage adjoining his father's farm. He thought it a privilege to join this expedition, as in those green summer days when I had allowed him to take a gun with me on some shooting-party. He relied on me with the affectionate confidence of boyhood, and I never gave him a harsh word or a hard thought.

We were watching in the morning at Baker's death-bed, when

one of our deck-watch, who had been cutting ice for the melter, came hurrying down into the cabin with the report, "People hollaing ashore!" I went up, followed by as many as could mount the gangway; and there they were, on all sides of our rocky harbour, dotting the snow-shores and emerging from the blackness of the cliffs,—wild and uncouth, but evidently human beings.

As we gathered on the deck they rose upon the more elevated fragments of the land-ice, standing singly and conspicuously like the figures in a tableau of the opera, and distributing themselves around almost in a half-circle. They were vociferating as if to attract our attention, or perhaps only to give vent to their sur-

MEETING THE ESQUIMAUX.

prise; but I could make nothing out of their cries, except "Hoah, ha, ha!" and "Ka, kääh! ka, kääh!" repeated over and over again.

There was light enough for me to see that they brandished no

CHAPTER
XVII.

weapons, and were only tossing their heads and arms about in violent gesticulations. A more unexcited inspection showed us, too, that their numbers were not as great nor their size as Patagonian as some of us had been disposed to fancy at first. In a word, I was satisfied that they were natives of the country; and, calling Petersen from his bunk to be my interpreter, I proceeded, unarmed, and waving my open hands, toward a stout figure who made himself conspicuous and seemed to have a greater number near him than the rest. He evidently understood the movement, for he at once, like a brave fellow, leaped down upon the floe and advanced to meet me fully half way.

Dress of the Esquimaux.

He was nearly a head taller than myself, extremely powerful and well-built, with swarthy complexion and piercing black eyes. His dress was a hooded *capôte* or jumper of mixed white and blue fox-pelts, arranged with something of fancy, and booted trousers of white bear-skin, which at the end of the foot were made to terminate with the claws of the animal.

I soon came to an understanding with this gallant diplomatist. Almost as soon as we commenced our parley, his companions, probably receiving signals from him, flocked in and surrounded us; but we had no difficulty in making them know positively that they must remain where they were, while Metek went with me on board the ship. This gave me the advantage of negotiating, with an important hostage.

A negotiation.

Fearlessness of the Esquimaux.

Although this was the first time he had ever seen a white man, he went with me fearlessly; his companions staying behind on the ice. Hickey took them out what he esteemed our greatest delicacies,—slices of good-wheat bread, and corned pork, with exhorbitant lumps of white sugar; but they refused to touch them. They had evidently no apprehension of open violence from us. I found afterward that several among them were singly a match for the white bear and the walrus, and that they thought us a very pale-faced crew.

Being satisfied with my interview in the cabin, I sent out word that the rest might be admitted to the ship; and, although they, of course, could not know how their chief had been dealt with, some nine or ten of them followed with boisterous readiness upon the bidding. Others in the mean time, as if disposed to give us their company for the full time of a visit, brought up from behind he land-ice as many as fifty-six fine dogs, with their sledges, and CHAPTER XVII. ecured them within two hundred feet of the brig, driving their lances into the ice, and picketing the dogs to them by the seal-kin traces. The animals understood the operation perfectly, and ay down as soon as it commenced. The sledges were made up *Sledges* if small fragments of porous bone, admirably knit together by longs of hide; the runners, which glistened like burnished steel, vere of highly-polished ivory, obtained from the tusks of the valrus.

The only arms they carried were knives, concealed in their *Arms* loots; but their lances, which were lashed to the sledges, were quite a formidable weapon. The staff was of the horn of the narwhal, or else of the thigh-bones of the bear, two lashed together, or sometimes the mirabilis of the walrus, three or four f them united. This last was a favourite material also for the ross-bars of their sledges. They had no wood. A single rusty loop from a current-drifted cask might have furnished all the nives of the party; but the fleam-shaped tips of their lances vere of unmistakable steel, and were rivetted to the tapering bony loint with no mean skill. I learned afterward that the metal was obtained in traffic from the more southern tribes.

They were clad much as I have described Metek, in jumpers, *Dress.* loots, and white bear-skin breeches, with their feet decorated like is, *en griffe.* A strip of knotted leather worn round the neck, very greasy and dirty-looking, which no one could be persuaded o part with for an instant, was mistaken at first for an ornament y the crew: it was not until mutual hardships had made us better acquainted that we learned its mysterious uses.

When they were first allowed to come on board, they were very *Behaviour* ude and difficult to manage. They spoke three or four at a ime, to each other and to us, laughing heartily at our ignorance n not understanding them, and then talking away as before. They were incessantly in motion, going everywhere, trying doors, nd squeezing themselves through dark passages, round casks and loxes, and out into the light again, anxious to touch and handle verything they saw, and asking for, or else endeavouring to teal, everything they touched. It was the more difficult to estrain them, as I did not wish them to suppose that we were at ll intimidated. But there were some signs of our disabled con-

dition which it was important they should not see; it was especially necessary to keep them out of the forecastle, where the dead
body of poor Baker was lying; and, as it was in vain to reason or
persuade, we had at last to employ the "gentle laying-on of
hands," which, I believe, the laws of all countries tolerate, to keep
them in order.

Our whole force was mustered and kept constantly on the
alert; but though there may have been something of discourtesy
in the occasional shoulderings and hustlings that enforced the
police of the ship, things went on good-humouredly. Our guests
continued running in and out and about the vessel, bringing in
provisions, and carrying them out again to their dogs on the ice,
—in fact, stealing all the time, until the afternoon; when, like
tired children, they threw themselves down to sleep. I ordered
them to be made comfortable in the hold; and Morton spread a
large buffalo-robe for them, not far from a coal-fire in the galley-
stove.

Esqui-
maux
cooking
and eat-
ing.
They were lost in barbarous amaze at the new fuel,—too hard
for blubber, too soft for firestone,—but they were content to
believe it might cook as well as seals' fat. They borrowed from
us an iron pot and some melted water, and parboiled a couple of
pieces of walrus-meat; but the real *pièce de resistance*, some five
pounds a head, they preferred to eat raw. Yet there was something of the *gourmet* in their mode of assorting their mouthfuls of
beef and blubber. Slices of each, or rather strips, passed between
the lips, either together or in strict alternation, and with a
regularity of sequence that kept the molars well to their work.

They did not eat all at once, but each man when and as often
as the impulse prompted. Each slept after eating, his raw chunk
lying beside him on the buffalo skin; and as he woke, the first
act was to eat, and the next to sleep again. They did not lie
down, but slumbered away in a sitting-posture, with the head
declined upon the breast, some of them snoring famously.

A treaty.
In the morning they were anxious to go; but I had given
orders to detain them for a parting interview with myself. It
resulted in a treaty, brief in its terms, that it might be certainly
remembered, and mutually beneficial, that it might possibly be
kept. I tried to make them understand what a powerful Prospero
they had had for a host, and how beneficent he would prove him-

self so long as they did his bidding. And, as an earnest of my
favour, I bought all the walrus-meat they had to spare, and four

WILD DOG TEAM.

of their dogs, enriching them in return with needles and beads,
and a treasure of old cask staves.

In the fulness of their gratitude, they pledged themselves emphatically to return in a few days with more meat, and to allow me to use their dogs and sledges for my excursions to the north. I then gave them leave to go. They yoked in their dogs in less than two minutes, got on their sledges, cracked their two-fathom-and-a-half-long seal-skin whips, and were off down the ice to the south-west at a rate of seven knots an hour.

They did not return. I had read enough of treaty-makings not to expect them too confidently. But the next day came a party of five, on foot—two old men, one of middle age, and a couple of gawky boys. We had missed a number of articles soon after the first party left us, an axe, a saw, and some knives. We found afterward that our storehouse at Butler Island had been entered; we were too short-handed to guard it by a special watch. Besides all this, reconnoitring stealthily beyond Sylvia Head, we discovered a train of sledges drawn up behind the hummocks.

There was cause for apprehension in all this; but I felt that I could not afford to break with the rogues. They had it in their power to molest us seriously in our sledge-travel; they could make our hunts around the harbour dangerous; and my best chance of obtaining an abundant supply of fresh meat, our great desideratum, was by their agency. I treated the new party with marked kindness, and gave them many presents; but took care to make them aware that, until all the missing articles were restored, no member of the tribe would be admitted again as a guest on board the brig. They went off with many pantomimic protestations of innocence; but M'Gary, nevertheless, caught the incor-

rigible scamps stealing a coal-barrel as they passed Butler Island, and expedited their journey homeward by firing among them a charge of small shot.

Still, one peculiar worthy—we thought it must have been the venerable of the party, whom I knew afterwards as a stanch friend, old Shang-huh—managed to work round in a westerly direction, and to cut to pieces my India-rubber boat, which had been left on the floe since Mr. Brooks's disaster, and to carry off every particle of the wood.

A few days after this, an agile, elfin youth drove up to our floe in open day. He was sprightly and good-looking, and had quite a neat turn-out of sledge and dogs. He told his name with frankness, " *Myouk*, I am,"—and where he lived. We asked him about the boat; but he denied all knowledge of it, and refused either to confess or repent. He was surprised when I ordered him to be confined to the hold. At first he refused to eat, and sat down in the deepest grief; but after a while he began to sing, and then to talk and cry, and then to sing again; and so he kept on rehearsing his limited *solfeggio*,—

and crying and talking by turns, till a late hour of the night. When I turned in, he was still noisily disconsolate.

There was a simplicity and *bonhommie* about this boy that interested me much; and I confess that when I made my appearance next morning—I could hardly conceal it from the gentleman on duty, whom I affected to censure—I was glad my bird had flown. Some time during the morning-watch he had succeeded in throwing off the hatch and escaping. We suspected that he had confederates ashore, for his dogs had escaped with as much address as himself. I was convinced, however, that I had the truth from him, where he lived, and how many lived with him— my cross-examination on these points having been very complete and satisfactory.

It was a sad business for some time after these Esquimaux left us, to go on making and registering our observations at Fern Rock. Baker's corpse still lay in the vestibule, and it was not long before another was placed by the side of it. We had to pass the bodies as often as we went in or out; but the men, grown feeble and nervous, disliked going near them in the night-time. When the summer thaw came, and we could gather stones enough, we built up a grave on a depression of the rocks, and raised a substantial cairn above it.

" *April* 19, *Wednesday.*—I have been out on the floe again, breaking in my dogs. My re-inforcement from the Esquimaux makes a noble team for me. For the last five days I have been striving with them, just as often and as long as my strength allowed me; and to-day I have my victory. The Society for Preventing Cruelty to Animals would have put me in custody if they had been near enough; but, thanks to a merciless whip freely

CHAPTER XVII.

administered, I have been dashing along twelve miles in the last hour, and am back again ; harness, sledge, and bones all unbroken. I am ready for another journey.

"*April* 22, *Saturday.*—Schubert has increasing symptoms of erysipelas around his amputated stump ; and every one on board is depressed and silent except himself. He is singing in his bunk, as joyously as ever, 'Aux gens atrabilaires,' &c. Poor fellow! I am alarmed about him : it is a hard duty which compels me to take the field, while my presence might cheer his last moments."

CHAPTER XVIII.

AN EXPLORATION — EQUIPMENT — OUTFIT — DEPARTURE — RESULTS — FEA-
TURES OF COAST—ARCHITECTURAL ROCKS—THREE BROTHER TURRETS—
TENNYSON'S MONUMENT—THE GREAT GLACIER OF HUMBOLDT.

THE month of April was about to close, and the short season CHAPTER
available for Arctic search was upon us. The condition of things XVIII.
on board the brig was not such as I could have wished for ; but
there was nothing to exact my presence, and it seemed to me clear
that the time had come for pressing on the work of the expedition.
The arrangements for our renewed exploration had not been Prepara-
intermitted, and were soon complete. I leave to my journal its tions.
own story.

"*April 25, Tuesday.*—A journey on the carpet ; and the crew
busy with the little details of their outfit : the officers the same.

" I have made a log-line for sledge-travel, with a contrivance
for fastening it to the ice, and liberating it at pleasure. It will
give me my dead reckoning quite as well as on the water. I have
a team now of seven dogs—four that I bought of the Esquimaux,
and three of my old stock. They go together quite respectably.
Godfrey and myself will go with them on foot, following the first
sledge on Thursday.

"*April 26, Wednesday.*—M'Gary went yesterday with the
leading sledge ; and, as Brooks is still on his back in consequence
of the amputation, I leave Ohlsen in charge of the brig. He has
my instructions in full ; among them I have dwelt largely upon
the treatment of the natives.

" These Esquimaux must be watched carefully, at the same Rules for
time they are to be dealt with kindly, though with a strict en- treatment
forcement of our police regulations, and some caution as to the of the
freedom with which they may come on board. No punishments natives.
must be permitted, either of them or in their presence, and no
resort to fire-arms unless to repel a serious attack. I have given
orders, however, that if the contingency does occur, there shall be
no firing over head. The *prestige* of the gun with a savage is in

his notion of its infallibility. You may spare bloodshed by killing a dog, or even wounding him ; but in no event should you throw away your ball. It is neither politic nor humane.

"Our stowage precautions are all arranged, to meet the chance of the ice breaking up while I am away; and a boat is placed ashore with stores, as the brig may be forced from her moorings.

"The worst thought I have now in setting out is, that of the entire crew I can leave but two behind in able condition, and the doctor and Bonsall are the only two officers who can help Ohlsen. This is our force, four able-bodied, and six disabled, to keep the brig ; the commander and seven men, scarcely better upon the average, out upon the ice. Eighteen souls, thank God ! certainly not eighteen bodies !

"I am going this time to follow the ice-belt (Eis-fod) to the Great Glacier of Humboldt, and there load up with pemmican from our cache of last October. From this point I expect to stretch along the face of the glacier inclining to the west of north, and make an attempt to cross the ice to the American side. Once on smooth ice, near this shore, I may pass to the west, and enter the large indentation whose existence I can infer with nearly positive certainty. In this I may find an outlet, and determine the state of things beyond the ice-clogged area of this bay.

"I take with me pemmican, and bread, and tea, a canvas tent, five feet by six, and two sleeping-bags of reindeer-skin. The sledge has been built on board by Mr. Ohlsen. It is very light, of hickory, and but nine feet long. Our kitchen is a soup-kettle for melting snow and making tea, arranged so as to boil with either lard or spirits."

The pattern of the tent was suggested by our experience during the fall journeys. The greatest discomfort of the Arctic traveller when camping out is from the congealed moisture of the breath forming long feathers of frost against the low shelving roof of the tent within a few inches of his face. The remedy which I adopted was to run the tent-poles through grummet-holes in the canvas about eighteen inches above the floor, and allow the lower part of the sides to hang down vertically like a valance, before forming the floor-cloth. This arrangement gave ample room for breathing; it prevented the ice forming above the sleeper's head, and the melted rime from trickling down upon it.

"For instruments, I have a fine Gambey sextant, in addition to my ordinary pocket-instrument, an artificial horizon, and a Barrow's dip-circle. These occupy little room upon the sledge. My telescope and chronometer I carry on my person.

"M'Gary has taken the *Faith*. He carries few stores, intending to replenish at the cache of Bonsall Point, and to lay in pemmican at M'Gary Island. Most of his cargo consists of bread, which we find it hard to dispense with in eating cooked food. It has a good effect in absorbing the fat of the pemmican, which is apt to disagree with the stomach."

THE FAITH.

Godfrey and myself followed on the 27th, as I had intended. The journey was an arduous one to be undertaken, even under the most favouring circumstances, and by unbroken men. It was to be the crowning expedition of the campaign, to attain the Ultima Thule of the Greenland shore, measure the waste that lay between it and the unknown West, and seek round the furthest circle of the ice for an outlet to the mysterious channels beyond. The scheme could not be carried out in its details; yet it was prosecuted far enough to indicate what must be our future fields of labour, and to determine many points of geographical interest. Our observations were in general confirmatory of those which had

CHAPTER XVIII. been made by Mr. Bonsall ; and they accorded so well with our subsequent surveys as to trace for us the outline of the coast with great certainty.

The outline of the coast. If the reader has had the patience to follow the pathway of our little brig, he has perceived that at Refuge Harbour, our first asylum, a marked change takes place in the line of direction of the coast. From Cape Alexander, which may be regarded as the westernmost cape of Greenland, the shore runs nearly north and south, like the broad channel of which it is the boundary ; but on reaching Refuge Inlet it bends nearly at a right angle, and follows on from west to east till it has passed the 65th degree of longitude. Between Cape Alexander and the inlet it is broken by two indentations, the first of them near the Etah settlement, which was visited in 1855 by the Rescue Expedition under Lieutenant Hartstene, and which bears on my charts the name of that noble-spirited commander ; the other remembered by us as Lifeboat Cove. In both of these the glaciers descend to the water-line, from an interior of lofty, rock-clad hills.

Headlands. The coast-line is diversified, however, by numerous water-worn headlands, which, on reaching Cape Hatherton, decline into rolling hills, their margins studded with islands, which are the favourite breeding-places of the eider, the glaucous gull, and the tern. Cape Hatherton rises boldly above these, a mass of porphyritic rock.

After leaving Refuge Harbour, the features of the coast undergo a change. There are no deep bays or discharging glaciers ; and it is only as we approach Rensselaer Harbour, where the shore-line begins to incline once more to the north, that the deep recesses and ice-lined fiords make their appearance again.

Geological structure. The geological structure changes also, and the cliffs begin to assume a series of varied and picturesque outlines along the coast, that scarcely require the aid of imagination to trace in them the ruins of architectural structure. They come down boldly to the shore-line, their summits rising sometimes more than a thousand feet above the eye, and the long cones of rubbish at their base mingling themselves with the ice-foot.

The coast retains the same character as far as the Great Glacier. It is indented by four great bays, all of them communicating with deep gorges, which are watered by streams from the interior ice-fields; yet none of them exhibit glaciers of any magni- CHAPTER tude at the water-line. Dallas Bay shows a similar formation, XVIII. and the archipelago beyond Cape Hunter retains it almost without change.

The mean height of the table-land, till it reaches the bed of Mean the Great Glacier, may be stated, in round numbers, at 900 height of the table-feet, its tallest summit near the water at 1300 and the land. rise of the background above the general level at 600 more. The face of this stupendous ice-mass, as it defined the coast, was everywhere an abrupt and threatening precipice, only broken by clefts and deep ravines, giving breadth and interest to its wild expression.

The most picturesque portion of the North Greenland coast is to be found after leaving Cape George Russell and approaching

THREE BROTHER TURRETS.

Dallas Bay. The red sandstones contrast most favourably with Contrast of the blank whiteness, associating the cold tints of the dreary Arctic colours landscape with the warm colouring of more southern lands. The seasons have acted on the different layers of the cliff so as to give

CHAPTER XVIII.

them the appearance of jointed masonry, and the narrow line of greenstone at the top caps them with well-simulated battlements.

Three Brother Turrets.

One of these interesting freaks of nature became known to us as the "Three Brother Turrets."

The sloping rubbish at the foot of the coast-wall led up, like an artificial causeway, to a gorge that was streaming at noon-day with the southern sun, while everywhere else the rock stood out in the blackest shadow. Just at the edge of this bright opening rose the dreamy semblance of a castle, flanked with triple towers, completely isolated and defined. These were the "Three Brother Turrets."

I was still more struck with another of the same sort, in the immediate neighbourhood of my halting-ground beyond Sunny Gorge, to the north of latitude 79°. A single cliff of greenstone, marked by the slaty limestone that once encased it, rears itself from a crumbled base of sandstones, like the boldly chiselled rampart of an ancient city. At its northern extremity, on the brink of a deep ravine which has worn its way among the ruins, there

A natural minaret tower.

stands a solitary column, or minaret-tower, as sharply finished as if it had been cast for the Place Vendôme. Yet the length of the shaft alone is 480 feet, and it rises on a plinth or pedestal itself 280 feet high.

I remember well the emotions of my party as it first broke upon our view. Cold and sick as I was, I brought back a sketch of it, which may have interest for the reader, though it scarcely suggests the imposing dignity of this magnificent landmark. Those who are happily familiar with the writings of Tennyson, and have communed with his spirit in the solitudes of a wilderness, will apprehend the impulse that inscribed the scene with his name.

The archipelago.

Still beyond this comes the archipelago which bears the name of our brig, studded with the names of those on board of her who adhered to all the fortunes of the expedition; and at its eastern cape spreads out the Great Glacier of Humboldt. My recollections of this glacier are very distinct. The day was beautifully clear on which I first saw it, and I have a number of sketches made as we drove along in view of its magnificent face. They disappoint me, giving too much white surface and badly-fading distances, the grandeur of the few bold and simple lines of nature being almost entirely lost.

TENNYSON'S MONUMENT.

I will not attempt to do better by florid description. Men only rhapsodize about Niagara and the ocean. My notes speak simply of the " long, ever-shining line of cliff diminished to a well-pointed wedge in the perspective ; " and again, of " the face of glistening ice, sweeping in a long curve from the low interior, the facets in front intensely illuminated by the sun." But this line of cliff rose in solid glassy wall 300 feet above the water-level, with an unknown, unfathomable depth below it ; and its curved face, 60 miles in length from Cape Agassiz to Cape Forbes, vanished into unknown space at not more than a single day's railroad-travel from the Pole. The interior with which it communicated, and from which it issued, was an unsurveyed *mer de glace*, an ice-ocean, to the eye of boundless dimensions.

It was in full sight—the mighty crystal bridge which connects the two continents of America and Greenland. I say continents ; for Greenland, however insulated it may ultimately prove to be, is in mass strictly continental. Its least possible axis, measured from Cape Farewell to the line of this glacier, in the neighbourhood of the 80th parallel gives a length of more than 1200 miles, not materially less than that of Australia, from its northern to its southern cape.

Imagine, now, the centre of such a continent, occupied through nearly its whole extent by a deep, unbroken sea of ice, that gathers perennial increase from the water-shed of vast snow-covered moun- tains and all the precipitations of the atmosphere upon its own surface. Imagine this, moving onward like a great glacial river, seeking outlets at every fiord and valley, rolling icy cataracts into the Atlantic and Greenland seas ; and, having at last reached the northern limit of the land that has borne it up, pouring out a mighty frozen torrent into unknown Arctic space.

It is thus, and only thus, that we must form a just conception of a phenomenon like this Great Glacier. I had looked in my own mind for such an appearance, should I ever be fortunate enough to reach the northern coast of Greenland. But now that it was before me, I could hardly realize it. I had recognised, in my quiet library at home, the beautiful analogies which Forbes and Studer have developed between the glacier and the river ; but I could not comprehend at first this complete substitution of ice for water.

It was slowly that the conviction dawned on me that I was

looking upon the counterpart of the great river-system of Arctic Asia and America. Yet here were no water-feeders from the south. Every particle of moisture had its origin within the Polar circle, and had been converted into ice. There were no vast alluvions, no forest or animal traces borne down by liquid torrents. Here was a plastic, moving, semi-solid mass, obliterating life, swallowing rocks and islands, and ploughing its way with irresistible march through the crust of an investing sea.

CHAPTER XIX.

PROGRESS OF THE PARTY—PROSTRATION—DALLAS BAY—DEATH OF SCHU-
BERT—THE BRIG IN MAY—PROGRESS OF SPRING—M'GARY'S RETURN—
DR. HAYES'S PARTY—EQUIPMENT—SCHUBERT'S FUNERAL.

"It is now the 20th of May, and for the first time, I am CHAPTER
XIX.
able, propped up by pillows and surrounded by sick messmates,
to note the fact that we have failed again to force the passage to
the north.

"Godfrey and myself overtook the advance party under M'Gary
two days after leaving the brig. Our dogs were in fair travelling
condition, and, except snow-blindness, there seemed to be no drawback to our efficiency. In crossing Marshall Bay we found the Involved
in snow.
snow so accumulated in drifts that, with all our efforts to pick
out a track, we became involved ; we could not force our sledges
through. We were forced to unload, and carry forward the cargo
on our backs, beating a path for the dogs to follow in. In this
way we plodded on to the opposite headland, Cape William Wood,
where the waters of Mary Minturn River, which had delayed the
freezing of the ice, gave us a long reach of level travel. We then
made a better rate ; and our days' marches were such as to carry
us by the 4th of May nearly to the glacier.

"This progress, however, was dearly earned. As early as the Reappear
ance of
disease
3d of May the winter's scurvy reappeared painfully among our
party. As we struggled through the snow along the Greenland
coast we sank up to our middle ; and the dogs, floundering about,
were so buried as to preclude any attempts at hauling. This excessive snow-deposit seemed to be due to the precipitation of cold
condensing wind suddenly wafted from the neighbouring glacier ;
for at Rensselaer Harbour we had only four inches of general
snow depth. It obliged us to unload our sledges again, and carry
their cargo,—a labour which resulted in dropsical swellings, with
painful prostration. Here three of the party were taken with
snow-blindness, and George Stephenson had to be condemned as
unfit for travel altogether, on account of chest-symptoms accom-

CHAPTER
XIX.
panying his scorbutic troubles. On the 4th Thomas Hickey also gave in, although not quite disabled for labour at the track-lines.

"Perhaps we would still have got on; but, to crown all, we found that the bears had effected an entrance into our pemmican casks, and destroyed our chances of reinforcing our provisions at

The caches
robbed by
the bears.
the several caches. This great calamity was certainly inevitable; for it is simple justice to the officers under whose charge the provision depôts were constructed, to say that no means in their power could have prevented the result. The pemmican was covered with blocks of stone which it had required the labour of three men to adjust; but the extraordinary strength of the bear had enabled him to force aside the heaviest rocks, and his pawing had broken the iron casks which held our pemmican literally into chips. Our alcohol cask, which it had cost me a separate and special journey in the late fall to deposit, was so completely destroyed that we could not find a stave of it.

"Off Cape James Kent, about eight miles from 'Sunny Gorge,' while taking an observation for latitude, I was myself seized with a

Illness
from fa-
tigue and
cold.
sudden pain, and fainted. My limbs became rigid, and certain obscure tetanoid symptoms of our late winter's enemy disclosed themselves. In this condition I was unable to make more than nine miles a-day. I was strapped upon the sledge, and the march continued as usual; but my powers diminished so rapidly that I could not resist even the otherwise comfortable temperament of 5° below zero. My left foot becoming frozen up to the metatarsal joint, caused a vexatious delay; and the same night it became evident that the immovability of my limbs was due to dropsical effusion.

Entire
prostra-
tion.
"On the 5th, becoming delirious, and fainting every time that I was taken from the tent to the sledge, I succumbed entirely. I append the report of our surgeon, made upon my return. This will best exhibit the diseased condition of myself and party, and explain, in stronger terms than I can allow myself to use, the extent of my efforts to contend against it.

"My comrades would kindly persuade me that, even had I continued sound, we could not have proceeded on our journey. The snows were very heavy, and increasing as we went; some of the drifts perfectly impassable, and the level floes often four feet deep in yielding snow. The scurvy had already broken out among the men, with symptoms like my own; and Morton, our strongest

man, was beginning to give way.　It is the reverse of comfort to
me that they shared my weakness.　All that I should remember
with pleasurable feeling is, that to five brave men, Morton, Riley,
Hickey, Stephenson, and Hans, themselves scarcely able to travel,
I owe my preservation.　They carried me back by forced marches,
after cacheing our stores and India-rubber boat near Dallas Bay,
in lat. 79°.5, lon. 66°.

APPROACHING DALLAS BAY.

"I was taken into the brig on the 14th.　Since then, fluctuat-
ing between life and death, I have by the blessing of God reached
the present date, and see feebly in prospect my recovery.　Dr.
Hayes regards my attack as one of scurvy, complicated by typhoid
fever.　George Stephenson is similarly affected.　Our worst
symptoms are dropsical effusion and night-sweats.

"*May 22, Monday.*—Let me, if I can, make up my record for
the time I have been away or on my back.

"Poor Schubert is gone.　Our gallant, merry-hearted companion
left us some ten days ago, for, I trust, a more genial world.　It is
sad, in this dreary little homestead of ours, to miss his contented
face and the joyous troll of his ballads.

"The health of the rest has, if anything, improved.　Their
complexions show the influence of sunlight, and I think several

have a firmer and more elastic step. Stephenson and Thomas are the only two beside myself who are likely to suffer permanently from the effects of our break-down. Bad scurvy both : symptoms still serious.

"Before setting out, a month ago, on a journey that should have extended into the middle of June, I had broken up the establishment of Butler Island, and placed all the stores around the brig, upon the heavy ice. My object in this was a double one. First, to remove from the Esquimaux the temptation and ability to pilfer. Second, to deposit our cargo where it could be re-stowed by very few men, if any unforeseen change in the ice made it necessary. Mr. Ohlsen, to whose charge the brig was committed, had orders to stow the hold slowly, remove the forward housing, and fit up the forecastle for the men to inhabit it again.

All these he carried out with judgment and energy. I find, upon my return, the brig so stowed and refitted that four days would prepare us for sea. The quarter-deck alone is now boarded in ; and here all the officers and sick are sojourning. The wind makes this wooden shanty a somewhat airy retreat ; but, for the health of our maimed, scorbutic men, it is infinitely preferable to the less-ventilated quarters below. Some of the crew, with one stove, are still in the forecastle, but the old cabin is deserted.

"I left Hans as hunter. I gave him a regular exemption from all other labour, and a promised present to his lady-love on reaching Fiskernaes. He signalized his promotion by shooting two deer, *Tukkuk*, the first yet shot. We have now on hand one hundred and forty-five pounds of venison, a very gift of grace to our diseased crew. But, indeed, we are not likely to want for wholesome food, now that the night is gone, which made our need of it so pressing. On the first of May those charming little migrants the snow-birds, *ultima cœlicolum*, which only left us on the 4th of November, returned to our ice-crusted rocks, whence they seem to 'fill the sea and air with their sweet jargoning.' Seal literally abound, too. I have learned to prefer this flesh to the reindeer's, at least that of the female seal, which has not the fetor of her mate's.

"By the 12th, the sides of the *Advance* were free from snow, and her rigging clean and dry. The floe is rapidly undergoing its wonderful processes of decay, and the level ice measures but six feet in thickness. To-day they report a burgomaster gull

seen, one of the earliest but surest indications of returning open
water. It is not strange, ice-leaguered exiles as we are, that we
observe and exult in these things. They are the pledges of renewed life, the olive-branch of this dreary waste : we feel the
spring in all our pulses.

"The first thing I did after my return was to send M'Gary to the
Life-boat Cove, to see that our boat and its buried provisions were
secure. He made the journey by dog-sledge in four days, and has
returned reporting that all is safe : an important help for us, should
this heavy ice of our more northern prison refuse to release us.

"But the pleasantest feature of his journey was the disclosure
of open water, extending up in a sort of tongue, with a trend of
north by east to within two miles of Refuge Harbour, and there
widening as it expanded to the south and west.

"Indeed, some circumstances which he reports seem to point to
the existence of a north water all the year round ; and the frequent
water-skies, fogs, &c., that we have seen to the south-west during
the winter, go to confirm the fact. The breaking up of the Smith
Strait's ice commences much earlier than this ; but as yet it has
not extended further than Littleton Island, where I should have
wintered if my fall journey had not pointed to the policy of remaining here. The open water undoubtedly has been the cause
of the retreat of the Esquimaux. Their sledge-tracks have been
seen all along the land-foot ; but, except a snow-house at Esquimaux Point, we have met nothing which to the uninitiated traveller would indicate that they had rested upon this desert coast.

"As soon as I had recovered enough to be aware of my failure,
I began to devise means for remedying it. But I found the resources of the party shattered. Pierre had died but a week before, and his death exerted an unfavourable influence. There were
only three men able to do duty. Of the officers, Wilson, Brooks,
Sontag, and Petersen, were knocked up. There was no one except
Sontag, Hayes, or myself who was qualified to conduct a survey ;
and, of us three, Dr. Hayes was the only one on his feet.

"The quarter to which our remaining observations were to be
directed lay to the north and east of the Cape Sabine of Captain
Inglefield. The interruption our progress along the coast of
Greenland had met from the Great Glacier, and the destruction of
our provision-caches by the bears, left a blank for us of the entire

northern coast-line. It was necessary to ascertain whether the
furthermost expansion of Smith's Strait did not find an outlet in
still more remote channels; and this became our duty the more
plainly, since our theodolite had shown us that the northern coast
trended off to the eastward, and not toward the west, as our
predecessor had supposed. The angular difference of 60°
between its bearings on his charts and our own left me completely
in the dark as to what might be the condition of this unknown area.

"I determined to trust almost entirely to the dogs for our
travel in the future, and to send our parties of exploration, one
after the other, as rapidly as the strength and refreshing of our
team would permit.

"Dr. Hayes was selected for that purpose; and I satisfied myself that, with a little assistance from my comrades, I could be
carried round to the cots of the sick, and so avail myself of his
services in the field.

"He was a perfectly fresh man, not having yet undertaken a
journey. I gave him a team and my best driver, William Godfrey. He is to cross Smith's Straits above the inlet, and make
as near as may be a straight course for Cape Sabine. My opinion
is, that by keeping well south he will find the ice less clogged and
easier sledging. Our experience proves, I think, that the transit
of this broken area must be most impeded as we approach the
glacier. The immense discharge of icebergs cannot fail to break
it up seriously for travel.

"I gave him the small sledge which was built by Mr. Ohlsen.
The snow was sufficiently thawed to make it almost unnecessary
to use fire as a means of obtaining water: they could therefore
dispense with tallow or alcohol, and were able to carry pemmican
in larger quantities. Their sleeping-bags were a very neat article
of a light reindeer-skin. The dogs were in excellent condition
too, no longer foot-sore, but well rested and completely broken,
including the four from the Esquimaux, animals of great power
and size. Two of these, the stylish leaders of the team, a span
of thoroughly wolfish iron-grays, have the most powerful and
wild-beast-like bound that I have seen in animals of their kind.

"I made up the orders of the party on the 19th, the first day
that I was able to mature a plan; and with commendable zeal
they left the brig on the 20th.

" *May 23, Tuesday.*—They have had superb weather, thank
Heaven !—a profusion of the most genial sunshine, bringing out
he seals in crowds to bask around their breathing-holes. A
ptarmigan was killed to-day, a male, with but two brown feathers
in the back of his little neck to indicate the return of his summer
plumage.

" The winter is gone ! The Andromeda has been found on
hore under the snow, with tops vegetating and green ! I have a
hoot of it in my hand.

" *May 25, Thursday.*—Bands of soft mist hide the tops of the
hills : the unbroken transparency of last month's atmosphere has
disappeared, and the sky has all the ashen or pearly obscurity of
he Arctic summer.

" *May 26, Friday.*—I get little done; but I have too much to
attend to in my weak state to journalize. Thermometer above
freezing-point, without the sun to-day.

" *May 27, Saturday.*—Everything showing that the summer
changes have commenced. The ice is rapidly losing its integrity,
and a melting snow has fallen for the last two days,—one of
hose comforting home-snows that we have not seen for so long.

" *May 28, Sunday.*—Our day of rest and devotion. It was a
fortnight ago last Friday since our poor friend Pierre died. For
nearly two months he had been struggling against the enemy with
a resolute will and mirthful spirit, that seemed sure of victory.
But he sunk in spite of them.

" The last offices were rendered to him with the same careful
ceremonial that we observed at Baker's funeral. There were fewer
to walk in the procession ; but the body was encased in a decent
pine coffin and carried to Observatory Island, where it was placed
side by side with that of his messmate. Neither could yet be
buried; but it is hardly necessary to say that the frost has em-
balmed their remains. Dr. Hayes read the chapter from Job
which has consigned so many to their last resting-place, and a
little snow was sprinkled upon the face of the coffin. Pierre was
a volunteer not only of our general expedition, but of the party
with which he met his death-blow. He was a gallant man, a
universal favourite on board, always singing some Béranger ballad
or other, and so elastic in his merriment, that even in his last
sickness he cheered all that were about him."

CHAPTER XX.

SEAL-HUNTING — SIR JOHN FRANKLIN—RESOURCES—ACCLIMATIZATION—
THE "HOPE"—DR. HAYES'S RETURN—HIS JOURNEY—SNOW-BLINDNESS
—CAPE HAYES—THE DOGS TANGLED—MENDING THE HARNESS—CAPES
LEIDY AND FRAZER—DOBBIN BAY—FLETCHER WEBSTER HEADLAND—
PETER FORCE BAY — NEW PARTIES — THEIR ORDERS — PROGRESS OF
SEASON—THE SEAL—THE NETSIK AND USUK—A BEAR—OUR ENCOUNTER
—CHANGE IN THE FLOE.

CHAPTER
XX.

Ice and
snow
melting.

"*May* 30, *Tuesday.*—We are gleaning fresh water from the rocks,
and the icebergs begin to show commencing streamlets. The
great floe is no longer a Sahara, if still a desert. The floes are
wet, and their snow dissolve readily under the warmth of the
foot, and the old floe begins to shed fresh water into its hollows.
Puddles of salt water collect around the ice-foot. It is now
hardly recognisable,—rounded, sunken, broken up with water-
pools overflowing its base. Its diminished crusts are so percolated
by the saline tides, that neither tables nor broken fragments unite
any longer by freezing. It is lessening so rapidly that we do not
fear it any longer as an enemy to the brig. The berg indeed
vanished long before the sun-thermometers indicated a noon-tem-
perature above 32°.

Limited
influence
of thaw

"The changes of this ice at temperatures far below the freezing-
point confirm the views I formed upon my last cruise as to the
limited influence of direct thaw. I am convinced that the expansion of the ice after the contraction of low temperatures, and the
infiltrative or endosmometric changes thus induced,—the differing
temperatures of sea-water and ice, and their chemical relations,—
the mechanical action of pressure, collapse, fracture, and disruption,—the effects of sun-heated snow-surfaces, falls of warm snow,
currents, wind, drifts, and wave-action,—all these leave the great
mass of the Polar ice-surfaces so broken, disintegrated, and reduced,
when the extreme cold abates, and so changed in structure and
molecular character, that the few weeks of summer thaw have but
a subsidiary office to perform in completing their destruction.

" Seal of the Hispid variety, the Netsik of the Esquimaux and
Danes, grow still more numerous on the level floes, lying

SHOOTING SEAL.

cautiously in the sun beside their *atluks*.   By means of the
Esquimaux stratagem of a white screen pushed forward on a

sledge until the concealed hunter comes within range, Hans has shot four of them. We have more fresh meat than we can eat. For the past three weeks we have been living on ptarmigan, rabbits, two reindeer, and seal.

"They are fast curing our scurvy. With all these resources,— coming to our relief so suddenly too,—how can my thoughts turn despairingly to poor Franklin and his crew?

" . . . . Can they have survived? No man can answer with certainty; but no man without presumption can answer in the negative.

"If, four months ago,—surrounded by darkness and bowed down by disease,—I had been asked the question, I would have turned toward the black hills and the frozen sea, and responded in sympathy with them, 'No.' But with the return of light a savage people come down upon us, destitute of any but the rudest appliances of the chase, who were fattening on the most wholesome diet of the region, only forty miles from our anchorage, while I was denouncing its scarcity.

"For Franklin everything depends upon locality; but, from what I can see of Arctic exploration thus far, it would be hard to find a circle of fifty miles' diameter entirely destitute of animal
resources. The most solid winter-ice is open here and there in pools and patches worn by currents and tides. Such were the open spaces that Parry found in Wellington Channel; such are the stream-holes (stromhols) of the Greenland coast, the polynia of the Russians; and such we have ourselves found in the most rigorous cold of all.

"To these spots the seal, the walrus, and the early birds crowd in numbers. One which kept open, as we find from the Esquimaux, at Littleton Island, only forty miles from us, sustained three families last winter until the opening of the north water. Now, if we have been entirely supported for the past three weeks by the hunting of a single man,—seal-meat alone being plentiful enough to subsist us till we turn homeward,—certainly a party of tolerably skilful hunters might lay up an abundant stock for the winter. As it is, we are making caches of meat under the snow, to prevent it spoiling on our hands, in the very spot which a few days ago I described as a Sahara. And, indeed, it was so for nine whole months, when this flood of animal life burst upon us like fountains of water and pastures and date-trees in a southern desert.

" I have undergone one change in opinion.   It is of the ability
of Europeans or Americans to inure themselves to an ultra-Arctic
climate.   God forbid, indeed, that civilized man should be exposed
for successive years to this blighting darkness ! but around the
Arctic circle, even as high as $72°$, where cold and cold only is to
be encountered, men may be acclimatized, for there is light enough
for out-door labour.

" Of the one hundred and thirty-six picked men of Sir John
Franklin in 1846, Northern Orkney men, Greenland whalers, so
many young and hardy constitutions, with so much intelligent
experience to guide them, I cannot realize that some may not yet
be alive ; that some small squad or squads, aided or not aided by
the Esquimaux of the expedition, may not have found a hunting-
ground, and laid up from summer to summer enough of fuel and
food and seal-skins to brave three or even four more winters in
succession.

" I speak of the miracle of this bountiful fair season.   I could
hardly have been much more surprised if these black rocks, instead
of sending out upon our solitude the late inroad of yelling Esquimaux, had sent us naturalized Saxons.   Two of our party at first
fancied they were such.

" The mysterious compensations by which we adapt ourselves
to climate are more striking here than in the tropics.   In the
Polar zone the assault is immediate and sudden, and, unlike the
insidious fatality of hot countries, produces its results rapidly.   It
requires hardly a single winter to tell who are to be the heat-
making and acclimatized men.   Petersen, for instance, who has
resided for two years at Upernavik, seldom enters a room with a
fire.   Another of our party, George Riley, with a vigorous constitution, established habits of free exposure, and active, cheerful temperament, has so inured himself to the cold that he sleeps on our
sledge-journeys without a blanket or any other covering than his
walking-suit, while the outside temperature is $30°$ below zero.
The half-breeds of the coast rival the Esquimaux in their powers of
endurance.

" There must be many such men with Franklin.   The North
British sailors of the Greenland seal and whale fisheries I look
upon as inferior to none in capacity to resist the Arctic climates.

" My mind never realizes the complete catastrophe, the destruc-

CHAPTER
XX.

Hopes of
finding
Franklin's
party.

tion of all Franklin's crews. I picture them to myself broken into detachments, and my mind fixes itself on one little group of some thirty, who have found the open spot of some tidal eddy, and, under the teachings of an Esquimaux, or perhaps one of their own Greenland whalers, have set bravely to work, and trapped the fox, speared the bear, and killed the seal and walrus and whale. I think of them ever with hope. I sicken not to be able to reach them.

"It is a year ago to-day since we left New York. I am not as sanguine as I was then: time and experience have chastened me. There is everything about me to check enthusiasm and moderate hope. I am here in forced inaction, a broken-down man, oppressed by cares, with many dangers before me, and still under the shadow of a hard wearing winter, which has crushed two of my best associates. Here, on the spot, after two unavailing expeditions of search, I hold my opinions unchanged; and I record them as a matter of duty upon a manuscript which may speak the truth when I can do so no longer.

Return of
Dr. Hayes.

"*June* 1, *Thursday.*—At ten o'clock this morning the wail of the dogs outside announced the return of Dr. Hayes and William Godfrey. Both of them were completely snow-blind, and the doctor had to be led to my bedside to make his report. In fact, so exhausted was he, that in spite of my anxiety I forbore to question him until he had rested. I venture to say, that both he and his companion well remember their astonishing performance over stewed apples and seal-meat.

"The dogs were not so foot-sore as might have been expected; but two of them, including poor little Jenny, were completely knocked up. All attention was bestowed upon these indispensable essentials of Arctic search, and soon they were more happy than their masters."

DR. HAYES'S JOURNEY.

Dr.
Hayes's
route.

Dr. Hayes made a due north line on leaving the brig; but, encountering the "squeezed ices" of my own party in March, he wisely worked to the eastward. I had advised him to descend to Smith's Sound, under a conviction that the icebergs there would be less numerous, and that the diminished distance from land to land would make his transit more easy. But he managed to effect the object by a less circuitous route than I had anticipated; for, although he made but fifteen miles on the 20th, he emerged the next day from the heavy ice, and made at least fifty. On this day his meridian observation gave the latitude of 79° 8' 6", and from a large berg he sighted many points of the coast.

On the 22d he encountered a wall of hummocks, exceeding 20 feet in height, and extending in a long line to the north-east.

After vain attempts to force them, becoming embarrassed in fragmentary ice, worn, to use his own words, into "deep pits and valleys," he was obliged to camp, surrounded by masses of the wildest character, some of them 30 feet in height.

The next three days were spent in struggles through this broken plain; fogs sometimes embarrassed them, but at intervals land could be seen to the north-west. On the 27th they reached the north side of the bay, passing over but few miles of new and unbroken floe.

The excessively broken and rugged character of this ice they had encountered must be due to the discharges from the Great Glacier of Humboldt, which arrest the floes, and make them liable to excessive disruption under the influence of winds and currents.

DOGS AMONG BERGS.

Dr. Hayes told me, that in many places they could not have advanced a step but for the dogs. Deep cavities filled with snow intervened between lines of ice-barricades, making their travel as slow and tedious as the same obstructions had done to the party of poor Brooks before their eventful rescue last March.

Their course was now extremely tortuous; for although from from the headlands of Rensselaer Harbour to the point which they first reached on the northern coast was not more than ninety miles as the crow flies, yet by the dead reckoning of the party they must have had an actual travel of two hundred and seventy.

For the details of this passage I refer the reader to the appended report of Dr. Hayes. His gravest and most insurmountable diffi-
culty was snow-blindness, which so affected him that for some time he was not able to use the sextant. His journal-entry, referring to the 23d, while tangled in the ice, says, " I was so snow-blind that I could not see ; and as riding, owing to the jaded condition of the dogs, was seldom possible, we were obliged to lay-to."

It was not until the 25th that their eyesight was sufficiently restored to enable them to push on. In these devious and un-trodden ice-fields even the instinct of the dogs would have been of little avail to direct their course. It was well for the party that during this compulsory halt the temperatures were mild and endur-able. From their station of the 25th they obtained reliable sights of the coast, trending to the northward and eastward, and a reliable determination of latitude, in 79° 24′ 4″. A fine headland, bearing
nearly due north-west, I named Cape Hayes, in commemoration of the gentleman who discovered it.

Instead, however, of making for the land, which could not have aided their survey, they followed the outer ice, at the same time edging in toward a lofty bluff whose position they had determined by intersection. They hoped here to effect a landing, but encoun-tered a fresh zone of broken ice in the attempt. The hummocks could not be turned. The sledge had to be lifted over them by main strength, and it required the most painful efforts of the whole party to liberate it from the snow between them.
On the 26th, disasters accumulated. William Godfrey, one of the sturdiest travellers, broke down ; and the dogs, the indispen-sable reliance of the party, were in bad working trim. The rude harness, always apt to become tangled and broken, had been mended so often and with such imperfect means as to be scarcely serviceable.

This evil would seem the annoyance of an hour to the travellers CHAPTER XX. in a stage-coach, but to a sledge-party on the ice-waste it is the gravest that can be conceived. The Esquimaux dog, as I before Harness of a dog team. mentioned, is driven by a single trace, a long thin thong of seal or walrus hide, which passes from his chest over his haunches to the sledge. The team is always driven abreast, and the traces are of course tangling and twisting themselves up incessantly, as the half-wild or terrified brutes bound right or left from their prescribed positions. The consequence is, that the seven or nine or fourteen lines have a marvellous aptitude at knotting themselves up beyond the reach of skill and patience. If the weather is warm enough to thaw the snow, they become utterly soft and flaccid, and the naked hand, if applied ingeniously, may dispense with a resort to the Gordian process; but in the severe cold, such as I experienced in my winter journeys of 1854, the knife is often the only appliance,—an unsafe one if invoked too often, for every new attachment shortens your harness, and you may end by drawing your dogs so close that they cannot pull. I have been Trial of patience obliged to halt and camp on the open floe, till I could renew enough of warmth and energy and patience to disentangle the knots of my harness. Oh, how charitably have I remembered Doctor Slop !

It was only after appropriating an undue share of his seal-skin Mending the harness. breeches that the leader of the party succeeded in patching up his mutilated dog-lines. He was rewarded, however, for he shortly after found an old floe, over which his sledge passed happily to the north coast. It was the first time that any of our parties had succeeded in penetrating the area to the north. The ice had baffled three organized foot-parties. It could certainly never have been traversed without the aid of dogs ; but it is equally certain that the effort must again have failed, even with their aid, but for the energy and determination of Dr. Hayes, and the endurance of his partner, William Godfrey. The latitude by observation was 79° 45′ N., the longitude 69° 12′ W. The coast here trended more to the westward than it had done. It was sighted for thirty miles to the northward and eastward. This was the culminating point of his survey, beyond which his observations did not extend. Two large headlands, Capes Joseph Leidy and John Frazer, indi- Capes Leidy and Frazer. cate it.

CHAPTER
XX.
The cliffs were of mingled limestone and sandstone, corresponding to those on the southern side of Peabody Bay. To the north they exceeded 2000 feet in height, while to the southward they dimished to 1200. The ice-foot varied from 50 to 150 feet in width, and stood out against the dark debris thrown down by the cliffs in a clean naked shelf of dazzling white.

Mending
the sledge.
The party spent the 28th in mending the sledge, which was completely broken, and feeding up their dogs for a renewal of the journey. But, their provisions being limited, Dr. Hayes did not deem himself justified in continuing to the north. He determined to follow and survey the coast toward Cape Sabine.

His pemmican was reduced to eighteen pounds; there was apparently no hope of deriving resources from the hunt; and the coasts were even more covered with snow than those he had left on Forced to
return. the southern side. His return was a thing of necessity.

The course of the party to the westward along the land-ice was interrupted by a large indentation, which they had seen and charted while approaching the coast. It is the same which I surveyed in April 1855, and which now bears the name of the Dobbin
Bay. Secretary of the Navy, Mr. Dobbin. Dr. Hayes discovered two islands near its entrance. He saw also on its south-western side a lofty pyramid, truncated at its summit, which corresponded both in its bearings and position with the survey of my April journey.

The latter portion of Dr. Hayes's journey was full of incident. The land-ice was travelled for a while at the rate of five or six miles an hour ; but, after crossing Dobbin Bay, the snows were an unexpected impediment, and the ice-foot was so clogged that they made but fifteen miles from camp to camp on the floes. After Cape
Sabine. fixing the position of Cape Sabine, and connecting it with the newly-discovered coast-line to the north and east, he prepared to cross the bay further to the south.

Most providentially they found this passage free from bergs ; but their provisions were nearly gone, and their dogs were exhausted. They threw away their sleeping-bags, which were of reindeer-skin and weighed about twelve pounds each, and abandoned, besides, clothing enough to make up a reduction in weight of nearly fifty pounds. With their load so lightened, they were enabled to make good the crossing of the bay. They landed at Peter Force Bay, and reached the brig on the 1st of June.

This journey connected the northern coast with the survey of my predecessor; but it disclosed no channel or any form of exit from this bay.

It convinced me, however, that such a channel must exist; for this great curve could be no cul-de-sac. Even were my observations since my first fall journey of September 1853, not decisive on this head, the general movement of the icebergs, the character of the tides, and the equally sure analogies of physical geography, would point unmistakably to such a conclusion.

To verify it, I at once commenced the organization of a double party. This, which is called in my Report the North-east Party, was to be assisted by dogs, but was to be subsisted as far as the Great Glacier by provisions carried by a foot-party in advance.

For the continuation of my plans I again refer to my journal.

"*June 2, Friday.*—There is still this hundred miles wanting to the north-west to complete our entire circuit of this frozen water. This is to be the field for our next party. I am at some loss how to organize it. For myself, I am down with scurvy. Dr. Hayes is just from the field, worn-out and snow-blind. His health-roll makes a sorry parade. It runs thus :—

Officers.

MR. BROOKS	Unhealed stump.
MR. WILSON	do.
MR. SONTAG	Down with scurvy.
MR. BONSALL	Scurvy knee, but mending.
MR. PETERSEN	General scurvy.
MR. GOODFELLOW	Scurvy.
MR. OHLSEN	Well.
MR. M'GARY	Well.

Crew.

WILLIAM MORTON	Nearly recovered.
THOMAS HICKEY	Well.
GEORGE WHIPPLE	Scurvy.
JOHN BLAKE	Scurvy.
HANS CRISTIAN	Well.
GEORGE RILEY	Sound.
GEORGE STEPHENSON	Scurvy from last journey.
WILLIAM GODFREY	Snow-blind.

"*June 3, Saturday.*—M'Gary, Bonsall, Hickey, and Riley were

detailed for the first section of the new parties : they will be
accompanied by Morton, who has orders to keep himself as fresh
as possible, so as to enter on his own line of search to the greatest
possible advantage.   I keep Hans a while to recruit the dogs, and
do the hunting and locomotion generally for the rest of us ; but I
shall soon let him follow, unless things grow so much worse on
board as to make it impossible.

" They start light, with a large thirteen-feet sledge, arranged
with broad runners on account of the snow, and are to pursue my
own last track, feeding at the caches which I deposited, and aiming
directly for the glacier barrier on the Greenland side.   Here, sustained as I hope by the remnants of the great cache of last fall,
they will survey and attempt to scale the ice, to look into the
interior of the great *mer de glace.*

" My notion is, that the drift to the southward both of berg and
floe, not being reinforced from the glacier, may leave an interval
of smooth frozen ice; but if this route should fail, there ought
still to be a chance by sheering to the southward and westward
and looking out for openings among the hummocks.

" I am intensely anxious that this party should succeed; it is
my last throw.   They have all my views, and I believe they will
carry them out unless overruled by a higher power.

" Their orders are, to carry the sledge forward as far as the base
of the Great Glacier, and fill up their provisions from the cache of
my own party of last May.   Hans will then join them with the
dogs; and, while M'Gary and three men attempt to scale and
survey the glacier, Morton and Hans will push to the north across
the bay with the dog-sledge, and advance along the more distant
coast.   Both divisions are provided with clampers, to steady
them and their sledges on the irregular ice-surfaces; but I am not
without apprehensions that, with all their eff rts, the glacier cannot be surmounted.

" In this event, the main reliance must be on Mr. Morton.   He
he takes with him a sextant, artificial horizon, and pocket chronometer, and has intelligence, courage, and the spirit of endurance,
in full measure.   He is withal a long-tried and trust-worthy follower.

" *June 5, Monday.*—The last party are off; they left yesterday
at 2 P.M.   I can do nothing more but await the ice-changes

that are to determine for us our liberation or continued impri- CHAPTER
sonment.   XX.

"The sun is shining bravely, and the temperature feels like a Sunshine.
home summer.

"A *sanderling*, the second migratory land-bird we have seen,
came to our brig to-day, and is now a specimen.

"*June 6, Tuesday.*—We are a parcel of sick men, affecting to
keep ship till our comrades get back. Except Mr. Ohlsen and
George Whipple, there is not a sound man among us. Thus
wearily in our Castle of Indolence, for 'labour dire it was, and
weary woe,' we have been watching the changing days, and noting bird and insect and vegetable, as it tells us of the coming
summer. One fly buzzed around William Godfrey's head to-
day,—he could not tell what the species was; and Mr. Petersen brought in a cocoon from which the grub had eaten its way Animals
to liberty. Hans gives us a seal almost daily, and for a pass- and birds
ing luxury we have ptarmigan and hare. The little snow-birds appear.
have crowded to Butler Island, and their songs penetrate the
cracks of our rude housing. Another snipe, too, was mercilessly
shot the very day of his arrival.

"The andromeda shows green under its rusty winter-dried Growth of
stems; the willows are sappy and puffing, their catskins of last vegeta-
year dropping off. Draba, lichens, and stellaria, can be detected tion.
by an eye accustomed to this dormant vegetation, and the stone-
crops are really green and juicy in their centres; all this under
the snow. So we have assurance that summer is coming; though
our tide-hole freezes every night alongside, and the ice-floe seems
to be as fast as ever.

"*June 8, Thursday.*—Hans brings us in to-day a couple of Seal
seal; all of them as yet are of the Rough or Hispid species. The
flesh of this seal is eaten universally by the Danes of Greenland,
and is almost the staple diet of the Esquimaux. When raw, it
has a flabby look, more like coagulated blood than muscular fibre;
cooking gives it a dark soot-colour. It is close-grained, but soft
and tender, with a flavour of lamp-oil—a mere *soupçon*, however, for the blubber, when fresh, is at this season sweet and delicious.

"The seal are shot lying by their *atluk* or breathing-holes. As
the season draws near midsummer, they are more approachable;

Seal
cooked in
the sun.

their eyes being so congested by the glare of the sun that they are sometimes nearly blind. Strange to say, a few hours' exposure of a recently-killed animal to the sun blisters and destroys the hide; or, as the sealers say, cooks it. We have lost several skins in this way. Each seal yields a liberal supply of oil, the average thus far being five gallons each."

Besides the Hispid seal, the only species which visited Rensselaer Harbour was the *Phoca barbata*, the large bearded seal, or *usuk* of the Esquimaux. I have measured these ten feet in length, and eight in circumference, of such unwieldy bulk as not unfrequently to be mistaken for the walrus.

The
netsik.

The netsik will not perforate ice of more than one season's growth, and are looked for, therefore, where there was open water the previous year. ·But the bearded seals have no *atluk*. ·They depend for respiration upon the accidental chasms in the ice, and are found wherever the bergs or floes have been in motion. They are thus more diffused in their range than their sun-basking little brethren, who crowd together in communities, and in some places absolutely throng the level ices.

The usuk.

The *usuk* appears a little later than the *netsik*, and his coming is looked for anxiously by the Esquimaux. The lines, *atlunak*, which are made from his skin, are the lightest and strongest and most durable of any in use. They are prized by the hunters in their contests with the walrus.

Atlunak
now made.

To obtain the atlunak in full perfection, the animal is skinned in a spiral, so as to give a continuous coil from head to tail, This is carefully chewed by the teeth of the matrons, and after being well greased with the burnt oil of their lamps, is hung up in their huts to season. At the time referred to in my journal, Anoatok was completely festooned with them.

On one occasion, while working my way toward the Esquimaux huts, I saw a large *usuk* basking asleep upon the ice. Taking off my shoes, I commenced a somewhat refrigerating process of stalking, lying upon my belly, and crawling along step by step behind the little knobs of floe. At last, when I was within long rifle shot, the animal gave a sluggish roll to one side, and suddenly lifted his head. The movement was evidently independent of me, for he strained his neck in nearly the opposite direction. Then, for the first time, I found that I had a

rival seal-hunter in a large bear, who was, on his belly like myself, waiting with commendable patience and cold feet for a
chance of nearer approach.

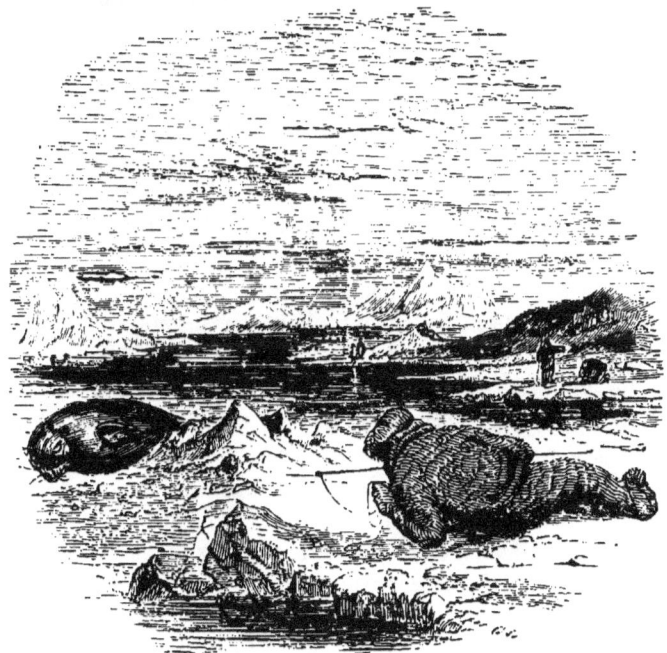

ESQUIMAUX APPROACHING A SEAL.

What should I do? the bear was doubtless worth more to
me than the seal; but the seal was now within shot, and the
bear "a bird in the bush." Besides, my bullet once invested in
the seal would leave me defenceless. I might be giving a dinner
to the bear and saving myself for his dessert. These medita-
tions were soon brought to a close; for a second movement of the
seal so aroused my hunter's instincts that I pulled the trigger.
My cap alone exploded. Instantly, with a floundering splash, the
seal descended into the deep, and the bear with three or four
rapid leaps, stood disconsolately by the place of his descent. For
a single moment we stared each other in the face, and then, with
that discretion which is the better part of valour, the bear ran off
in one direction, and I followed his example in the other.

The generally-received idea of the Polar bear battling with the
walrus meets little favour among the Esquimaux of Smith's Straits.

CHAPTER
XX.
My own experience is directly adverse to the truth of the story. The walrus is never out of reach of water, and, in his peculiar element, is without a rival. I have seen the bear follow the usuk by diving; but the tough hide and great power of the walrus forbid such an attack.

Observatory.
" *June* 9, *Friday.*—To-day I was able to walk out upon the floe for the first time. My steps were turned to the observatory, where, close beside the coffins of Baker and Schubert, Sontag was at work with the unifilar, correcting the winter disturbances. Our local deviation seems to have corrected itself; the iron in our comfortless little cell seems to have been so distributed that our results were not affected by it.

Change on
the floe-
ice.
" I was very much struck by the condition of the floe-ice. Hitherto I have been dependent upon the accounts of my messmates, and believed that the work of thaw was going on with extreme rapidity. They are mistaken; we have a late season. The ice-foot has not materially changed either in breadth or level, and its base has been hardly affected at all, except by the overflow of the tides. The floe, though undergoing the ordinary molecular changes which accompany elevation of temperature, shows less surface change than the Lancaster Sound ices in early May. All this, but especially the condition of the ice-foot, warns me to prepare for the contingency of not escaping. It is a momentous warning. We have no coal for a second winter here; our stock of fresh provisions is utterly exhausted; and our sick need change, as essential to their recovery.

Plants.
" The willows are tolerably forward on Butler Island. Poor, stunted crawlers, they show their expanded leaflets against the grey rocks. Among these was the Bear berry (*S. uva ursi*), knowing its reputation with the Esquimaux to the south as a remedy for scurvy, I gleaned leaves enough for a few scanty mouthfuls. The lichens are very conspicuous; but the mosses and grasses and heaths have not yet made their appearance in the little valley between the rocks."

CHAPTER XXI.

PROGRESS OF SEASON — PLANTS IN WINTER — BIRDS RETURNING — COCH-
LEARIA — THE PLANTS.

"*June* 10, *Saturday.*—Hans was ordered yesterday to hunt in the CHAPTER
XXI. direction of the Esquimaux huts, in the hope of determining the position of the open water. He did not return last night; but Hans out
hunting. Dr. Hayes and Mr. Ohlsen, who were sent after him this morning with the dog-sledge, found the hardy savage fast asleep not five

DRAGGING SEAL

miles from the brig. Along side of him was a large usuk or bearded seal (*P. barbata*), shot, as usual, in the head. He had dragged it for seven hours over the ice-foot. The dogs having now recruited, he started light to join Morton at the glacier.

"*June* 11, *Sunday.*—Another walk on shore showed me the Vegeta andromeda in flower, and the saxifrages and carices green under tion. the dried tufts of last year. This rapidly-maturing vegetation is of curious interest. The andromeda tetragona had advanced rapidly toward fructification without a corresponding development of either stalk or leaflet. In fact, all the heaths—and there were three species around our harbour—had a thoroughly moorland and stunted aspect. Instead of the graceful growth which should characterize them, they showed only a low, scrubby sod or turf, yet studded with flowers. The spots from which I gathered them were well infiltrated with melted snows, and the rocks enclosed them so as to aid the solar heat by reverberation. Here, too, silene and cerathium, as well as the characteristic flower-growths of the later summer, the poppy, and sorrel, and saxifrages, were already recognisable.

" Few of us at home can realize the protecting value of this warm coverlet of snow. No eider-down in the cradle of an infant is tucked in more kindly than the sleeping-dress of winter about this feeble flower-life. The first warm snows of August and September falling on a thickly-pleached carpet of grasses, heaths, and willows, enshrine the flowery growths which nestle round them in a non-conducting air-chamber; and, as each successive snow increases the thickness of the cover, we have, before the intense cold of winter sets in, a light cellular bed covered by drift, six, eight, or ten feet deep, in which the plant retains its vitality. The frozen subsoil does not encroach upon this narrow zone of vegetation. I have found in midwinter, in this high latitude of 78° 50', the surface so nearly moist as to be friable to the touch; and upon the ice-floes, commencing with a surface temperature of −30°, I found at two feet deep a temperature of −8°, at four feet +2°, and at eight feet +26°. This was on the largest of a range of east and west hummock-drifts in the open way of Cape Stafford. The glacier which we became so familiar with afterward at Etah yields an uninterrupted stream throughout the year.

" My experiments prove that the conducting power of the snow is proportioned to its compression by winds, rains, drifts, and congelation. The early spring and late fall and summer snows are more cellular and less condensed than the nearly impalpable powder of winter. The drifts, therefore, that accumulate during nine months of the year, are dispersed in well-defined layers of differing density. We have first the warm cellular snows of fall which surround the plant, next the fine impacted snow dust of winter, and above these the later humid deposits of the spring.

" It is interesting to observe the effects of this disposition of layers chapter xxi.
upon the safety of the vegetable growths below them. These, at
least in the earlier summer, occupy the inclined slopes that face Plants
the sun, and the several strata of snow take of course the same in- under snow
clination. The consequence is, that as the upper snow is dissipated
by the early thawings, and sinks upon the more compact layer below, it is to a great extent arrested, and runs off like rain from a
slope of clay. The plant reposes thus in its cellular bed, guarded
from the rush of waters, and protected too from the nightly frosts
by the icy roof above it.

"*June* 16, *Friday.*—Two long-tailed ducks (*Harelda glacialis*) Water
visited us, evidently seeking their breeding-grounds. They are fowl.
beautiful birds, either at rest or on the wing. We now have the
snow-birds, the snipe, the burgomaster gull, and the long-tailed
duck, enlivening our solitude ; but the snow-birds are the only ones
in numbers, crowding our rocky islands, and making our sunny
night-time musical with home-remembered songs. Of each of
the others we have but a solitary pair, who seem to have left
their fellows for this far northern mating-ground in order to
live unmolested. I long for specimens ; but they shall not be
fired at.

The ptarmigan show a singular backwardness in assuming the Ptar-
summer feathering. The male is still entirely white ; except, in migan.
some specimens, a few brown feathers on the crown of the head.
The female has made more progress, and is now well coated with
her new plumage, the coverts and quill-feathers still remain white.
At Upernavik, in lat. 73°, they are already in full summer costume.

" *June* 18, *Sunday.*—Another pair of long-tailed ducks passed Ducks and
over our bay, bound for further breeding-grounds ; we saw also an gulls.
ivory-gull and two great northern divers (*Colymbus glacialis*), the
most imposing birds of their tribe. These last flew very high,
emitting at regular intervals their reed-like 'kawk.'

" Mr. Ohlsen and Dr. Hayes are off on an overland tramp. I
sent them to inspect the open water to the southward. The immovable state of the ice-foot gives me anxiety : last year, a large
bay above us was closed all summer ; and the land-ice, as we find
it here, is as perennial as the glacier.

"*June* 20, *Tuesday.*—This morning, to my great surprise,

Petersen brought me quite a handful of scurvy-grass (*C. fenestrata*).
In my fall list of the stinted flora here, it had quite escaped my
notice. I felt grateful to him for his kindness, and, without the
affectation of offering it to any one else, ate it at once. Each plant
stood about one inch high, the miniature leaves expanding throughout a little radius of hardly one inch more. Yet, dwarfed as it was,
the fructifying process was nearly perfected ; the buds already expanding and nearly ready to burst. We found cochlearia afterward at Littleton Island, but never in any quantity north of Cape
Alexander. Although the melted snows distil freely over the
darker rocks (porphyries and greenstones), it is a rare exception to
note any vegetable discoloration of the surface beneath. There
are few signs of those confervaceous growths which are universal as
high as Upernavik. The nature of this narrative does not permit
me to indulge in matters unconnected with my story : I cite these
in passing, as among the indications of our high northern latitude.

"*June 21, Wednesday.*—A snow, moist and flaky, melting upon
our decks, and cleaning up the dingy surface of the great ice-plain
The sum-
mer sol-
stice. with a new garment. We are at the summer solstice, the day of
greatest solar light ! Would that the traditionally-verified but
meteorologically-disproved equinoctial storm could break upon us,
to destroy the tenacious floes !

"*June 22, Thursday.*—The ice changes slowly, but the progress
of vegetation is excessively rapid. The growth on the rocky group
near our brig is surprising.

Eider
ducks. "*June 23, Friday.*—The eiders have come back : a pair were
seen in the morning, soon followed by four ducks and drakes.
The poor things seemed to be seeking breeding-grounds, but the
ice must have scared them. They were flying southward.

"*June 25, Sunday.*—Walked on shore and watched the changes :
andromeda in flower, poppy and ranunculus the same : saw two snipe
and some tern.

"Mr. Ohlsen returned from a walk with Mr. Petersen. They
saw reindeer, and brought back a noble specimen of the king duck.
It was a solitary male, resplendent with the orange, black, and
green of his head and neck.

"Stephenson is better ; and I think that a marked improvement,
although a slow one, shows itself in all of us. I work the men

lightly, and allow plenty of basking in the sun.   In the afternoon
we walk on shore, to eat such succulent plants as we can find amid
the snow.   The pyrola I have not found, nor the cochlearia, save
in one spot, and then dwarfed.   But we have the lychnis, the
young sorrel, the andromeda, the draba, and the willow-bark ; this
last an excellent tonic, and, in common with all the Arctic vegetable astringents, I think, powerfully antiscorbutic."

CHAPTER
XXI.

Succulent
plants.

CHAPTER XXII.

MR. BONSALL'S RETURN—HIS STORY—THE BEAR IN CAMP—HIS FATE –
BEARS AT SPORT—THE THAWS.

CHAPTER XXII.

Return of M'Gary and Bonsall.

"*June* 27, *Tuesday.*—M'Gary and Bonsall are back with Hickey and Riley. They arrived last evening : all well, except that the snow has affected their eyesight badly, owing to the scorbutic condition of their systems. Mr. M'Gary is entirely blind, and I fear will be found slow to cure. They have done admirably. They bring back a continued series of observations, perfectly well kept up, for the further authentication of our survey. They had a good chronometer, artificial horizon, and sextant, and their results correspond entirely with those of Mr. Sontag and myself. They are connected, too, with the station at Chimney Rock, Cape Thackeray,

Satisfactory observations.

which we have established by theodolite. I may be satisfied now with our projection of the Greenland coast. The different localities to the south have been referred to the position of our winter harbour, and this has been definitely fixed by the labours of Mr. Sontag, our astronomer. We have, therefore, not only a reliable base, but a set of primary triangulations, which, though limited, may support the minor field-work of our sextants.

JOURNEY OF MESSRS. M'GARY AND BONSALL.

"They left the brig on the 3d, and reached the Great Glacier on the 15th, after only twelve days of travel. They showed great judgment in passing the bays ; and, although impeded by the heavy snows, would have been able to remain much longer in the field, but for the destruction of our provision-depôts by the bears.

"I am convinced, however, that no efforts of theirs could have scaled the Great Glacier ; so that the loss of our provisions, though certainly a very serious mishap, cannot be said to have caused their failure. They were well provided with pointed staves, foot-clampers, and other apparatus for climbing ice ; but, from all they tell me, any attempt to scale this stupendous glacial mass would have been madness; and I am truly glad that they desisted from it before fatal accident befell them.

"Mr Bonsall is making out his report of the daily operations of this party. It seems that the same heavy snow which had so much interfered with my travel in April and May still proved their greatest drawback. It was accumulated particularly between the headlands of the bays; and, as it was already affected by the warm sun, it called for great care in crossing it. They encountered drifts which were altogether impenetrable, and in such cases could only advance by long circuits, after reconnoitring from the top of ice-bergs.

"I have tried in vain to find out some good general rule, when traversing the ice near the coast, to avoid the accumulation of snows and hummock-ridges. It appears that the direct line between headland and headland or cape and cape is nearly always ob-structed by broken ice; while in the deep recesses the grounded ice is even worse. I prefer a track across the middle of the bay, outside of the grounded ices and inside of the hummock-ridges; unless, as sometimes happens, the late fall-ice is to be found extending in level flats outside.

"This is evidently the season when the bears are in most abun-dance. Their tracks were everywhere, both on shore and upon the floes. One of them had the audacity to attempt intruding itself upon the party during one of their halts upon the ice; and Bon-sall tells a good story of the manner in which they received and returned his salutations. It was about half an hour after midnight, and they were all sleeping away a long day's fatigue, when M'Gary either heard or felt, he could hardly tell which, something that was scratching at the snow immediately by his head. It waked him just enough to allow him to recognise a huge animal actively en-gaged in reconnoitring the circuit of the tent. His startled outcry aroused his companion-inmates, but without in any degree disturb-ing the unwelcome visitor; specially unwelcome at that time and place, for all the guns had been left on the sledge, a little distance off, and there was not so much as a walking pole inside. There was, of course, something of natural confusion in the little council of war. The first impulse was to make a rush for the arms; but this was soon decided to be very doubtfully practicable, if at all; for the bear, having satisfied himself with his observations of the

exterior, now presented himself at the tent-opening.   Sundry vol-
leys of lucifer matches and some impromptu torches of newspaper

THE BEAR IN CAMP.

were fired without alarming him, and, after a little while, he planted
himself at the doorway and began making his supper upon the
carcass of a seal which had been shot the day before.

A sortie
from the
postern.
"Tom Hickey was the first to bethink him of the military device
of a sortie from the postern, and, cutting a hole with his knife,
crawled out at the rear of the tent.   Here he extricated a boat-
hook, that formed one of the supporters of the ridge-pole, and
made it the instrument of a right valorous attack.   A blow well
administered on the nose caused the animal to retreat for the
moment a few paces beyond the sledge, and Tom, calculating his
distance nicely, sprang forward, seized a rifle, and fell back in
safety upon his comrades.   In a few seconds more, Mr. Bonsall
had sent a ball through and through the body of his enemy.   I
was assured that after this adventure the party adhered to the
custom I had enjoined, of keeping at all times a watch and fire-
arms inside the camping-tent.

The last
cache
destroyed.
"The final cache, which I relied so much upon, was entirely destroyed.   It had been built with extreme care, of rocks which had
been assembled by very heavy labour, and adjusted with much aid

often from capstan-bars as levers. The entire construction was, CHAPTER
so far as our means permitted, most effective and resisting. Yet XXII.
these tigers of the ice seemed to have scarcely encountered an ob- The de-
stacle. Not a morsel of pemmican remained except in the iron caused by
cases, which, being round with conical ends, defied both claw and the beais
teeth. They had rolled and pawed them in every direction, tossing them about like footballs, although over eighty pounds in
weight. An alcohol-case, strongly iron-bound, was dashed into
small fragments, and a tin can of liquor mashed and twisted almost
into a ball. The claws of the beast had perforated the metal, and
torn it up as with a cold chisel.

"They were too dainty for salt meats: ground coffee they had an
evident relish for: old canvas was a favourite for some reason or
other; even our flag, which had been reared 'to take possession' of
the waste, was gnawed down to the very staff. They had made a

THE CACHE DESTROYED.

regular frolic of it; rolling our bread-barrels over the ice-foot and
into the broken outside ice; and, unable to masticate our heavy
India-rubber cloth, they had tied it up in unimaginable hard
knots.

"M'Gary describes the whole area around the cache as marked
by the well-worn paths of these animals; and an adjacent slope of

ice-covered rock, with an angle of 45°, was so worn and covered with their hair, as to suggest the idea that they had been amusing themselves by sliding down it on their haunches. A performance, by the way, in which I afterward caught them myself.

"*June 28, Wednesday.*—Hans came up with the party on the 17th. Morton and he are still out. They took a day's rest; and then, 'following the old tracks,' as M'Gary reports, 'till they were clear of the cracks near the islands, pushed northward at double-quick time. When last seen, they were both of them walking, for the snow was too soft and deep for them to ride with their heavy load.' Fine weather, but the ice yields reluctantly."

While thus watching the indications of advancing summer, my mind turned anxiously to the continued absence of Morton and Hans. We were already beyond the season when travel upon the ice was considered practicable by our English predecessors in Wellington Channel, and, in spite of the continued solidity around us, it was unsafe to presume too much upon our high northern position.

The ice, although seemingly as unbroken as ever, was no longer fit for dog-travel; the floes were covered with water-pools, many of which could not be forded by our team; and, as these multiplied with the rapidly-advancing thaws, they united one with another, chequering the level waste with an interminable repetition of confluent lakes. These were both embarrassing and dangerous. Our little brig was already so thawed out where her sides came in contact with her icy cradle as to make it dangerous to descend without a gangway, and our hunting parties came back wet to the skin.

It was, therefore, with no slight joy that on the evening of the 10th, while walking with Mr. Bonsall, a distant sound of dogs caught my ear. These faithful servants generally bayed their full-mouthed welcome from afar off, but they always dashed in with a wild speed which made their outcry a direct precursor of their arrival. Not so these well-worn travellers. Hans and Morton staggered beside the limping dogs, and poor Jenny was riding as a passenger upon the sledge. It was many hours before they shared the rest and comfort of our ship.

CHAPTER XXIII.

MORTON'S RETURN—HIS NARRATIVE—PEABODY BAY—THROUGH THE BERGS
—BRIDGING THE CHASMS—THE WEST LAND—THE DOGS IN FRIGHT—
OPEN WATER—THE ICE-FOOT—THE POLAR TIDES—CAPES JACKSON AND
MORRIS—THE CHANNEL—FREE OF ICE—BIRDS AND PLANTS—BEAR AND
CUB—THE HUNT—THE DEATH—FRANKLIN AND LAFAYETTE—THE ANT-
ARCTIC FLAG—COURSE OF TIDES—MOUNT PARRY—VICTORIA AND ALBERT
MOUNTAINS—RESUMÉ—THE BIRDS APPEAR—THE VEGETATION—THE
PETREL—CAPE CONSTITUTION—THEORIES OF AN OPEN SEA—ILLUSORY
DISCOVERIES—CHANGES OF CLIMATE—A SUGGESTION.

MR. MORTON left the brig with the relief party of M'Gary on the 4th of June. He took his place at the track-lines like the others; but he was ordered to avoid all extra labour, so as to hus-band his strength for the final passage of the ice. *CHAPTER XXIII. Time of departure.*

On the 15th he reached the base of the Great Glacier, and on the 16th was joined by Hans with the dogs. A single day was given to feed and refresh the animals, and on the 18th the two companies parted. Morton's account I have not felt myself at liberty to alter. I give it as nearly as possible in his own words, without affecting any modification of his style.

MORTON'S JOURNEY.

The party left Cache Island at 12.35 A.M., crossing the land- *Route.* ices by portage, and going south for about a mile to avoid a couple of bad seams caused by the breakage of the glacier. Here Mor-ton and Hans separated from the land-party, and went northward, keeping parallel with the glacier, and from five to seven miles dis-tant. The ice was free from hummocks, but heavily covered with snow, through which they walked knee deep. They camped about *First encamp-ment.* eight miles from the glacier, at 7.45, travelling that night about twenty-eight miles. Here a crack allowed them to measure the thickness of the ice : it was seven feet five inches. The thermometer at 6 A.M. gave $+ 28°$ for the temperature of the air; 29.2 for the water.

They started again at half-past nine. The ice, at first, was very

CHAPTER
XXIII.
_____
Difficulties
of the
Journey.

heavy, and they were frequently over their knees in the dry snow; but, after crossing certain drifts, it became hard enough to bear the sledge, and the dogs made four miles an hour until twenty minutes past four, when they reached the middle of Peabody Bay. They then found themselves among the bergs which on former occasions had prevented other parties from getting through. These were generally very high, evidently newly separated from the glacier. Their surfaces were fresh and glassy, and not like those generally met with in Baffin's Bay,—less worn, and bluer, and looking in all respects like the face of the Grand Glacier. Many were rectangular, some of them regular squares, a quarter of a mile each way; others, more than a mile long.

They could not see more than a ship's-length ahead, the icebergs were so unusually close together. Old icebergs bulge and tongue out below, and are thus prevented from uniting; but these showed that they were lately launched, for they approached each other so nearly that the party were sometimes forced to squeeze through places less than four feet wide, through which the dogs could just

Narrow
passages
between
the bergs

draw the sledge. Sometimes they could find no passage between two bergs, the ice being so crunched up between them that they could not force their way. Under these circumstances, they would either haul the sledge over the low tongues of the berg, or retrace their steps, searching through the drift for a practicable road.

This they were not always fortunate in finding, and it was at best a tedious and in some cases a dangerous alternative, for oftentimes they could not cross them; and, when they tried to double, the compass, their only guide, confused them by its variation.

It took them a long while to get through into smoother ice. A tolerably wide passage would appear between two bergs, which they would gladly follow; then a narrower one; then no opening in front, but one to the side. Following that a little distance, a blank ice-cliff would close the way altogether, and they were forced

Persever-
ance.

to retrace their steps and begin again. Constantly baffled, but, like true fellows, determined to "go ahead," they at last found a lane some six miles to the west, which led upon their right course. But they were from eight o'clock at night till two or three the next morning, puzzling their way out of the maze, like a blind man in the streets of a strange city.

June 19, Monday.—At 8.45 A.M. they encamped. Morton then

climbed a berg, in order to select their best road. Beyond some CHAPTER XXIII.
bergs he caught glimpses of a great white plain, which proved to
be the glacier seen far into the interior ; for, on getting up another The glacier in the dis-tance.
berg further on, he saw its face as it fronted on the bay. This
was near its northern end. It looked full of stones and earth,
while large rocks projected out from it and rose above it here and
there.

They rested till half-past ten, having walked all the time to
spare the dogs. After starting, they went on for ten miles, but
were then arrested by wide seams in the ice, bergs, and much
broken ice. So they turned about, and reached their last camp
by twelve, midnight. They then went westward, and, after several
trials, made a way, the dogs running well. It took them but
two hours to reach the better ice, for the bergs were in a narrow
belt.

The chasms between them were sometimes four feet wide, with The chasms.
water at the bottom. These they bridged in our usual manner ;
that is to say, they attacked the nearest large hummocks with
their axes, and, chopping them down, rolled the heaviest pieces
they could move into the fissure, so that they wedged each other
in. They then filled up the spaces between the blocks with
smaller lumps of ice as well as they could, and so contrived a rough
sort of bridge to coax the dogs over. Such a seam would take
about an hour and a half to fill up well and cross.

On quiting the berg-field, they saw two dovekies in a crack, and Dovekies.
shot one. The other flew to the north-east. Here they sighted
the northern shore (" West Land "), mountainous, rolling, but very
distant, perhaps fifty or sixty miles off. They drove on over the
the best ice they had met due north. After passing about twelve
miles of glacier, and seeing thirty of opposite shore, they camped
at 7.20 A.M.

They were now nearly abreast of the termination of the Great The termi nation of the Great Glacier.
Glacier. It was mixed with earth and rocks. The snow sloped
from the land to the ice, and the two seemed to be mingled
together for eight or ten miles to the north, when the land became
solid, and the glacier was lost. The height of this land seemed
about 400 feet, and the glacier lower.

June 21, Wednesday.—They stood to the north at 11.30 P.M.,
and made for what Morton thought a cape, seeing a vacancy

CHAPTER XXIII.

Mist and cold.

between it and the West Land. The ice was good, even, and free from bergs, only two or three being in sight. The atmosphere became thick and misty, and the west shore, which they saw faintly on Tuesday, was not visible. They could only see the cape for which they steered. The cold was sensibly felt, a very cutting wind blowing north-east by north. They reached the opening seen to the westward of the cape by Thursday, 7 A.M. It proved to be a channel ; for, as they moved on in the misty weather, a sudden lifting of the fog showed them the cape and the western shore.

The dogs tremble.

The ice was weak and rotten, and the dogs began to tremble. Proceeding at a brisk rate, they had got upon unsafe ice before they were aware of it. Their course was at the time nearly up the middle of the channel ; but, as soon as possible, they turned, and, by a backward circuit, reached the shore. The dogs, as their fashion is, at first lay down and refused to proceed, trembling violently. The only way to induce the terrified, obstinate brutes to get on was for Hans to go to a white-looking spot where the ice was thicker, the soft stuff looking dark ; then, calling the dogs coaxingly by name, they would crawl to him on their bellies. So they retreated from place to place, until they reached the firm ice they had quitted. A half-mile brought them to comparatively safe ice, a mile more to good ice again.

Safe ice again.

In the midst of this danger they had during the liftings of the fog sighted open water, and they now saw it plainly. There was no wind stirring, and its face was perfectly smooth. It was two miles further up the channel than the firm ice to which they had retreated. Hans could hardly believe it. But for the birds that were seen in great numbers, Morton says he would not have believed it himself.

The ice covered the mouth of the channel like a horse-shoe. One end lapped into the west side a considerable distance up the channel, the other covered the cape for about a mile and a half, so that they could not land opposite their camp, which was about a mile and a half from the cape.

· That night they succeeded in climbing on to the level by the floe-pieces, and walked around the turn of the cape for some distance, leaving their dogs behind. They found a good ice-foot, very wide, which extended as far as the cape. They saw a good

many birds on the water, both eider-ducks and dovekies, and the
rocks on shore were full of sea-swallows.   There was no ice.   A
fog coming on, they turned back to where the dogs had been left.
    They started again at 11.30 A.M. of the 21st.   On reaching the
land-ice they unloaded, and threw each package of provision from
the floe up to the ice-foot, which was eight or nine feet above

MAKING THE LAND-ICE, (CLIMBING).

them.   Morton then climbed up with the aid of the sledge, which
they converted into a ladder for the occasion.   He then pulled the
dogs up by the lines fastened round their bodies, Hans lending a
helping hand and then climbing up himself.   They then drew up
the sledge.   The water was very deep, a stone the size of Morton's head taking twenty-eight seconds to reach the bottom, which
was seen very clearly.
    As they had noticed the night before, the ice-foot lost its good
character on reaching the cape, becoming a mere narrow ledge
hugging the cliffs, and looking as if it might crumble off altogether

into the water at any moment. Morton was greatly afraid there would be no land-ice there at all when they came back. Hans and he thought they might pass on by climbing along the face of the crag ; in fact they tried a path about 50 feet high, but it grew so narrow that they saw they could not get the dogs past with their sledge-load of provisions. He therefore thought it safest to

leave some food, that they might not starve on the return in case the ice-foot should disappear. He accordingly cached enough provision to last them back, with four days' dog-meat.

At the pitch of the cape the ice-ledge was hardly three feet wide ; and they were obliged to unloose the dogs and drive them forward alone. Hans and he then tilted the sledge up, and succeeded in carrying it past the narrowest place. The ice-foot was firm under their tread, though it crumbled on the verge.

The tide was running very fast. The pieces of heaviest draught floated by nearly as fast as the ordinary walk of a man, and the surface pieces passed them much faster, at least four knots. On their examination the night before, the tide was from the north, running southward, carrying very little ice. The ice which was now moving so fast to northward seemed to be the broken land-ice around the cape, and the loose edge of the south ice. The thermometer in the water gave + 36°, 7° above the freezing-point of sea-water at Rensselaer Harbour.

They now yoked in the dogs, and set forward over the worst sort of mashed ice for three-quarters of a mile. After passing the

cape, they looked ahead, and saw nothing but open water. The land to the westward seemed to overlap the land on which they stood, a long distance ahead : all the space between was open water. After turning the cape,—that which is marked on the chart as Cape Andrew Jackson,—they found a good smooth ice-foot in the entering curve of a bay, since named after the great financier of the American Revolution, Robert Morris. It was glassy ice, and the dogs ran on it full speed. Here the sledge made at least six miles an hour. It was the best day's travel they made on the journey.

After passing four bluffs at the bottom and sides of the bay, the land grew lower ; and presently a long low country opened on the land-ice, a wide plain between large headlands, with rolling hills through it. A flock of brent geese were coming down the valley

of this low land, and ducks were seen in crowds upon the open CHAPTER XXIII.
water.   When they saw the geese first, they were apparently
coming from the eastward; they made a curve out to seaward, and Flight of the wild geese, eiders, dovekies, gulls, &c
then, turning, flew far ahead over the plain, until they were lost to
view, showing that their destination was inland.   The general line
of flight of the flock was to the north-east.   Eiders and dovekies
were also seen ; and tern were very numerous, hundreds of them
squealing and screeching in flocks.   They were so tame that they
came within a few yards of the party.   Flying high overhead, their
notes echoing from the rocks, were large white birds, which they
took for burgomasters.   Ivory gulls and mollemokes were seen
further on.   They did not lose sight of the birds after this, as far
as they went.   The ivory gulls flew very high, but the mollemokes
alit, and fed on the water, flying over it well out to sea, as we had
seen them do in Baffin's Bay.   Separate from these flew a dingy
bird unknown to Morton.   Never had they seen the birds so
numerous : the water was actually black with dovekies, and the
rocks crowded.

The part of the channel they were now coasting was narrower, Form of the chan-nel.
but as they proceeded it seemed to widen again.   There was some
ice arrested by a bend of the channel on the eastern shore ; and,
on reaching a low gravel point, they saw that a projection of land
shut them in just ahead to the north.   Upon this ice numerous
seal were basking, both the netsik and ussuk.

To the left of this, toward the West Land, the great channel
(Kennedy Channel) of open water continued.   There was broken
ice floating in it, but with passages fifteen miles in width and perfectly clear.   The end of the point—"Gravel Point," as Morton
called it—was covered with hummocks and broken ice for about
two miles from the water.   This ice was worn and full of gravel.
Six miles inland the point was flanked by mountains.

A little higher up they noticed that the pieces of ice in the Movement of the ice.
middle of the channel were moving up, while the lumps near
shore were floating down.   The channel was completely broken
up, and there would have been no difficulty in a frigate standing
anywhere.   The little brig, or "a fleet of her like," could have
beat easily to the northward.

The wind blew strong from the north, and continued to do so
for three days, sometimes blowing a gale, and very damp, the tops

CHAPTER XXIII.

Fogs and mist.

of the hills becoming fixed with dark foggy clouds. The damp falling mist prevented their seeing any distance. Yet they saw no ice borne down from the northward during all this time ; and, what was more curious, they found, on their return south, that no ice had been sent down during the gale. On the contrary, they then found the channel perfectly clear from shore to shore.

Shores of the channel.

June 22, Thursday.—They camped at 8.30 A.M., on a ledge of low rock, having made in the day's journey forty-eight miles in a straight line. Morton thought they were at least forty miles up the channel. The ice was here moving to the southward with the tide. The channel runs northwardly, and is about thirty-five miles wide. The opposite coast appears straight, but still sloping, its head being a little to the west of north. This shore is high, with lofty mountains of sugar-loaf shape at the tops, which, set together in ranges, looked like piles of stacked cannon-balls. It was too cloudy for observations when they camped, but they obtained several higher up. The cider were in such numbers here that Hans fired into the flocks, and killed two birds with one shot.

Start at midnight.

June 23, Friday.—In consequence of the gale of wind they did not start till 12.30 midnight. They made about eight miles, and were arrested by the broken ice of the shore. Their utmost efforts could not pass the sledge over this ; so they tied the dogs to it, and went ahead to see how things looked. They found the land-ice growing worse and worse, until at last it ceased, and the water broke directly against the steep cliffs.

They continued their course overland until they came to the entrance of a bay, whence they could see a cape and an island to the northward. They then turned back, seeing numbers of birds on their way, and, leaving the dogs to await their return, prepared to proceed on foot.

Early flower-life.

This spot was the greenest that they had seen since leaving the headlands of the channel. Snow patched the valleys, and water was trickling from the rocks. Early as it was, Hans was able to recognise some of the flower-life. He ate of the young shoots of the lychnis, and brought home to me the dried pod (*siliqua*) of a hesperis, which had survived the wear and tear of winter. Morton was struck with the abundance of little stone-crops, "about the size of a pea."

June 23, 24, Friday, Saturday.—At 3 A.M. they started again, carrying eight pounds of pemmican and two of bread, besides the artificial horizon, sextant, and compass, a rifle, and the boat-hook. After two hours' walking the travel improved, and, on nearing a plain about nine miles from where they had left the sledge, they were rejoiced to see a she-bear and her cub. They had tied the dogs securely, as they thought; but Toodla and four others had broken loose and followed them, making their appearance within an hour. They were thus able to attack the bear at once.

Hans, who to the simplicity of an Esquimaux united the shrewd observation of a hunter, describes the contest which followed so graphically, that I try to engraft some of the quaintness of his description upon Mr. Morton's report. The bear fled; but the little one being unable either to keep ahead of the dogs or to keep pace with her, she turned back, and, putting her head under its haunches, threw it some distance ahead. The cub safe for the moment, she would wheel round and face the dogs, so as to give it a chance to run away; but it always stopped just as it alighted, till she came up and threw it ahead again: it seemed to expect her aid, and would not go on without it. Sometimes the mother would run a few yards ahead, as if to coax the young one up to her, and when the dogs came up she would turn on them and drive them back; then, as they dodged her blows, she would rejoin the cub and push it on, sometimes putting her head under it, sometimes catching it in her mouth by the nape of the neck.

For a time she managed her retreat with great celerity, leaving the two men far in the rear. They had engaged her on the land-ice; but she led the dogs in-shore, up a small stony valley which opened into the interior. But, after she had gone a mile and a half, her pace slackened, and, the little one being jaded, she soon came to a halt.

The men were then only half a mile behind; and, running at full speed, they soon came up to where the dogs were holding her at bay. The fight was now a desperate one. The mother never went more than two yards ahead, constantly looking at the cub. When the dogs came near her, she would sit upon her haunches and take the little one between her hind legs, fighting the dogs with her paws, and roaring so that she could have been heard a mile off. "Never," said Morton, "was an animal more distressed."

She would stretch her neck and snap at the nearest dog with her shining teeth, whirling her paws like the arms of a windmill. If she missed her aim, not daring to pursue one dog lest the others should harm the cub, she would give a great roar of baffled rage, and go on pawing, and snapping, and facing the ring, grinning at them with her mouth stretched wide.

When the men came up, the little one was perhaps rested, for it was able to turn round with her dam, no matter how quick she moved, so as to keep always in front of her belly. The five dogs were all the time frisking about her actively, tormenting her like so many gad-flies ;- indeed, they made it difficult to draw a bead on at her without killing them. But Hans, lying on his elbow, took a quiet aim and shot her through the head. She dropped and rolled over dead without moving a muscle.

The dogs sprang toward her at once ; but the cub jumped upon her body and reared up, for the first time growling hoarsely. They seemed quite afraid of the little creature, she fought so actively and made so much noise ; and, while tearing mouthfuls of hair from the dead mother, they would spring aside the minute the cub turned toward them. The men drove the dogs off for a time, but were obliged to shoot the cub at last, as she would not quit the body.

Hans fired into her head. It did not reach the brain, though it knocked her down ; but she was still able to climb on her mother's body and try to defend it still, "her mouth bleeding like a gutter-spout." They were obliged to despatch her with stones.

After skinning the old one they gashed its body, and the dogs fed upon it ravenously. The little one they cached for themselves on the return ; and, with difficulty taking the dogs off, pushed on, crossing a small bay which extended from the level ground and had still some broken ice upon it. Hans was tired out, and was sent on shore to follow the curve of the bay, where the road was easier.

The ice over the shallow bay which Morton crossed was hummocked, with rents through it, making very hard travel. He walked on over this, and saw an opening not quite eight miles across, separating the two islands, which I have named after Sir John Franklin and his comrade Captain Crozier. He had seen them before from the entrance of the larger bay,—Lafayette Bay,

— but had taken them for a single island, the channel between them not being then in sight. As he neared the northern land, at the east shore which led to the cape (Cape Constitution), which terminated his labours, he found only a very small ice-foot, under the lee of the headland and crushed up against the side of the rock. He went on ; but the strip of land-ice broke more and more, until about a mile from the cape it terminated altogether, the waves breaking with a cross sea directly against the cape. The wind had moderated, but was still from the north, and the current ran up very fast, four or five knots perhaps.

The cliffs were here very high : at a short distance they seemed about 2000 feet ; but the crags were so overhanging that Morton could not see the tops as he drew closer. The echoes were confusing, and the clamour of half a dozen ivory gulls, who were frightened from their sheltered nooks, was multiplied a hundred-fold. The mollemokes were still numerous ; but he now saw no ducks.

He tried to pass round the cape. It was in vain : there was no ice-foot ; and, trying his best to ascend the cliffs, he could get up but a few hundred feet. Here he fastened to his walking-pole the Grinnell flag of the *Antarctic*—a well-cherished little relic, which had now followed me on two Polar voyages. This flag had been saved from the wreck of the United States sloop-of-war *Peacock*, when she stranded off the Columbia River ; it had accompanied Commodore Wilkes in his far southern discovery of an Antarctic continent. It was now its strange destiny to float over the highest northern land, not only of America, but of our globe. Side by side with this were our Masonic emblems of the compass and the square. He let them fly for an hour and a half from the black cliff over the dark rock-shadowed waters, which rolled up and broke in white caps at its base.

He was bitterly disappointed that he could not get round the cape, to see whether there was any land beyond ; but it was impossible. Rejoining Hans, they supped off their bread and pemmican, and, after a good nap, started on their return on Sunday, the 25th, at 1. 30 P.M. From Thursday night, the 22d, up to Sunday at noon, the wind had been blowing steadily from the north, and for thirty-six hours of the time it blew a gale. But as he returned, he remarked that the more southern ice toward

Marginal notes: CHAPTER XXIII. — Cape Constitution — Height of the cliffs. — The *Antarctic* flag — A bitter disappointment

CHAPTER
XXIII.

Kennedy Channel was less than it had been when he passed up. At the mouth of the channel it was more broken than when he saw it before, but the passage above was clear. About halfway between the furthest point which he reached and the channel, the

Floating
Ice.

few small lumps of ice which he observed floating—they were not more than half a dozen—were standing with the wind to the southward, while the shore current or tide was driving north.

His journal of Monday, 26th, says, " As far as I could see, the open passages were fifteen miles or more wide, with sometimes mashed ice separating them. But it is all small ice, and I think it either drives out to the open space to the north, or rots and sinks,* as I could see none ahead to the far north."

Direction
of the
coast.

The coast after passing the cape, he thought must trend to the eastward, as he could at no time when below it see any land beyond. But the west coast still opened to the north : he traced it for about fifty miles. The day was very clear, and he was able to follow the range of mountains which crowns it much further. They were very high, rounded at their summits, not peaked like those immediately abreast of him ; though, as he remarked, this apparent change of their character might be referred to distance, for their undulations lost themselves like a wedge in the northern horizon.

Highest
station of
outlook.

His highest station of outlook at the point where his progress was arrested he supposed to be about 300 feet above the sea. From this point some 6° to the west of north, he remarked in the furthest distance a peak truncated at its top like the cliffs of Magdalena Bay. It was bare at its summit, but striated vertically with protruding ridges. Our united estimate assigned to it an elevation of from 2500 to 3000 feet. This peak, the most remote

Mount
Parry.

northern land known upon our globe, takes its name from the great pioneer of Arctic travel, Sir Edward Parry.

The range with which it was connected was much higher, Mr. Morton thought, than any we had seen on the southern or Greenland side of the bay. The summits were generally rounded, resembling, to use his own expression, a succession of sugar-loaves and stacked cannon-balls declining slowly in the perspective. I have named these mountains after the name of the lady sovereign

---

* As I quote his own words, I do not think it advisable to comment upon his view. Ice never sinks in a liquid of the same density as that in which it formed.

under whose orders Sir John Franklin sailed, and the prince her chapter xxiii.
consort. They are similar in their features to those of Spitzbergen; and, though I am aware how easy it is to be deceived in Victoria
and Albert
our judgment of distant heights, I am satisfied from the estimate moun-
of Mr. Morton, as well as from our measurements of the same tains.
range further to the south, that they equal them in elevation, 2500
feet.

Two large indentations broke in upon the uniform margin of the
coast. Everywhere else the spinal ridge seemed unbroken. Mr.
Morton saw no ice.

It will be seen by the abstract of our "field-notes" in the Appen- Resumé of
Morton's
dix, as well as by an analysis of the results which I have here journal
rendered nearly in the very words of Mr. Morton, that, after travelling due north over a solid area choked with bergs and frozen,
fields, he was startled by the growing weakness of the ice : its surface became rotten, and the snow wet and pulpy. His dogs, seized
with terror, refused to advance. Then for the first time the fact
broke upon him, that a long dark band seen to the north beyond
a portruding cape—Cape Andrew Jackson—was water. With
danger and difficulty he retraced his steps, and, reaching sound ice,
made good his landing on a new coast.

The journeys which I had made myself, and those of my different parties, had shown that an unbroken surface of ice covered
the entire sea to the east, west, and south. From the southernmost ·
ice, seen by Dr. Hayes only a few weeks before, to the region of
this mysterious water, was, as the crow flies, 106 miles. But for
the unusual sight of birds and the unmistakeable giving way of the
ice beneath them, they would not have believed in the evidence of
eyesight. Neither Hans nor Morton was prepared for it.

Landing on the cape, and continuing their exploration, new Exploration on the
phenomena broke upon them. They were on the shores of a channel, shores of
so open that a frigate, or a fleet of frigates, might have sailed up the channel of open
it. The ice, already broken and decayed, formed a sort of horse- water.
shoe shaped beach, against which the waves broke in surf. As
they travelled north, this channel expanded into an iceless area ;
"for four or five small pieces"—lumps—were all that could be seen
over the entire surface of its white-capped waters. Viewed from
the cliffs, and taking 36 miles as the mean radius open to reliable

survey, this sea had a justly-estimated extent of more than 4000 square miles.

Animal life, which had so long been a stranger to us to the south, now burst upon them. At Rensselaer Harbour, except the Netsik seal or a rarely encountered Harelda, we had no life available for the hunt. But here the Brent goose (*Anas bernicla*), the eider, and the king duck, were so crowded together that our Esquimaux killed two at a shot with a single rifle-ball.

The Brent goose had not been seen before since entering Smith's Straits. It is well known to the Polar traveller as a migratory bird of the American continent. Like the others of the same family, it feeds upon vegetable matter, generally on marine plants with their adherent molluscous life. It is rarely or never seen in the interior, and from its habits may be regarded as singularly indicative of open water. The flocks of this bird, easily distinguished by their wedge-shaped line of flight, now crossed the water obliquely, and disappeared over the land to the north and east. I had shot these birds on the coast of Wellington Channel in latitude 74° 50′, nearly six degrees to the south : they were then flying in the same direction.

The rocks on shore were crowded with sea-swallows (*Sterna Arctica*), birds whose habits require open water, and they were already breeding.

It may interest others besides the naturalist to state, that all of these occupied the southern limits of the channel for the first few miles after reaching open water, but, as the party continued their progress to the north, they disappeared, and marine birds took their place. The gulls were now represented by no less than four
species. The kittiwakes (*Larus tridactylis*)—reminding Morton of "old times in Baffin's Bay"—were again stealing fish from the water, probably the small whiting (*Merlangus Polaris*), and their grim cousins, the burgomasters, enjoying the dinner thus provided at so little cost to themselves. It was a picture of life all round.

Of the flora and its indications I can say but little ; still less can I feel justified in drawing from them any thermal inferences. The season was too early for a display of Arctic vegetation ; and, in the absence of specimens, I am unwilling to adopt the observations of Mr. Morton, who was no botanist. It seems clear, however, that many flowering plants, at least as developed as those of Rens-

THE OPEN WATER FROM CAPE JEFFERSON.

selaer Harbour, had already made themselves recognisable ; and, strange to say, the only specimen brought back was a crucifer (*Hesperis pygmœa*—Durand), the *siliquœ* of which, still containing seed, had thus survived the winter, to give evidence of its perfected growth. This plant I have traced to the Great Glacier, thus extending its range from the South Greenland zone. It has not, I believe, been described at Upernavik.

It is another remarkable fact, that as they continued their journey, the land-ice and snow, which had served as a sort of pathway for their dogs, crumbled and melted, and at last ceased altogether ; so that, during the final stages of their progress, the sledge was rendered useless, and Morton found himself at last toiling over rocks and along the beach of a sea, which like the familiar waters of the south, dashed in waves at his feet.

Here for the first time he noticed the Arctic Petrel (*Procellaria* *glacialis*), a fact which shows the accuracy of his observation, though he was then unaware of its importance. This bird had not been met with since we left the North Water of the English whalers, more than two hundred miles south of the position on which he stood. Its food is essentially marine, the acalephæ, &c. &c. ; and it is seldom seen in numbers, except in the highways of open water frequented by the whale and the larger representatives of ocean life. They were in numbers flitting and hovering over the crests of the waves, like their relatives of kinder climates, the Cape of Good Hope Pigeons, Mother Carey's Chickens, and the petrels everywhere else.

As Morton, leaving Hans and his dogs, passed between Sir John Franklin Island and the narrow beach-line, the coast became more wall-like, and dark masses of porphyritic rock abutted into the sea. With growing difficulty he managed to climb from rock to rock, in hopes of doubling the promontory and sighting the coasts beyond, but the water kept encroaching more and more on his track.

It must have been an imposing sight, as he stood at this termi- nation of his journey, looking out upon the great waste of waters before him. Not a " speck of ice," to use his own words, could be seen. There, from a height of 480 feet, which commanded a horizon of almost forty miles, his ears were gladdened with the novel music of dashing waves ; and a surf, breaking in among the rocks at his feet, stayed his further progress.

CHAPTER
XXIII.
———

Cape Constitution.

Conjectures about an open sea near the Pole.

Beyond this cape all is surmise. The high ridges to the northwest dwindled off into low blue knobs, which blended finally with the air. Morton called the cape, which baffled his labours, after his commander; but I have given it the more enduring name of Cape Constitution.

The homeward journey, as it was devoted to the completion of his survey and developed no new facts, I need not give. But I am reluctant to close my notice of this discovery of an open sea, without adding that the details of Mr. Morton's narrative harmonized with the observations of all our party. I do not propose to discuss here the causes or conditions of this phenomenon. How far it may extend,—whether it exists simply as a feature of the immediate region, or as part of a great and unexplored area communicating with a Polar basin,—and what may be the argument in favour of one or the other hypothesis, or the explanation which reconciles it with established laws,—may be questions for men skilled in scientific deductions. Mine has been the more humble duty of recording what we saw. Coming as it did, a mysterious fluidity in the midst of vast plains of solid ice, it was well calculated to arouse emotions of the highest order; and I do not believe there was a man among us who did not long for the means of embarking upon its bright and lonely waters. But he who may be content to follow our story for the next few months will feel, as we did, that a controlling necessity made the desire a fruitless one.

An open sea near the Pole, or even an open Polar basin, has been a topic of theory for a long time, and has been shadowed forth to some extent by actual or supposed discoveries. As far back as the days of Barentz, in 1596, without referring to the earlier and more uncertain chronicles, water was seen to the eastward of the northernmost cape of Novaia Zemlia; and, until its limited extent was defined by direct observation, it was assumed to be the sea itself. The Dutch fisherman above and around Spitzbergen pushed their adventurous cruises through the ice into open spaces varying in size and form with the season and the winds; and Dr. Scoresby, a venerated authority, alludes to such vacancies in the floe as pointing in argument to a freedom of movement from the north, inducing open water in the neighbourhood of the Pole. Baron Wrangell, when forty miles from the coast of Arctic Asia, saw, as he thought, a "vast, illimitable ocean," forgetting for the moment

how narrow are the limits of human vision on a sphere. So, still
more recently, Captain Penny proclaimed a sea in Wellington
Sound, on the very spot where Sir Edward Belcher has since left
his frozen ships ; and my predecessor, Captain Inglefield, from the
mast-head of his little vessel, announced an " open Polar basin,"
but fifteen miles off from the ice which arrested our progress the
next year.

All these illusory discoveries were no doubt chronicled with
perfect integrity ; and it may seem to others, as since I have left
the field it sometimes does to myself, that my own, though on a
larger scale, may one day pass within the same category. Unlike
the others, however, that which I have ventured to call an open
sea has been travelled for many miles along its coast, and was
viewed from an elevation of 580 feet, still without a limit, moved
by a heavy swell, free of ice, and dashing in surf against a rock-
bound shore.

It is impossible, in reviewing the facts which connect themselves
with this discovery,—the melted snow upon the rocks, the crowds
of marine birds, the limited, but still advancing vegetable life, the
rise of the thermometer in the water,—not to be struck with their
bearing on the question of a milder climate near the Pole. To
refer them all to the modification of temperature induced by the
proximity of open water is only to change the form of the question; for it leaves the inquiry unsatisfied—What is the cause of
the open water ?

This, however, is not the place to enter upon such a discussion.
There is no doubt on my mind, that at a time within historical and
even recent limits, the climate of this region was milder than it is
now. I might base this opinion on the fact, abundantly developed
by our expedition, of a secular elevation of the coast line. But,
independently of the ancient beaches and terraces, and other geological marks which show that the shore has risen, the stone huts
of the natives are found scattered along the line of the bay in spots
now so fenced in by ice as to preclude all possibility of the hunt,
and, of course, of habitation by men who rely on it for subsistence.

Tradition points to these as once favourite hunting-grounds near
open water. At Rensselaer Harbour, called by the natives *Aunatok*,
or the Thawing-Place, we met with huts in quite tolerable preservation, with the stone pedestals still standing which used to sustain

the carcases of the captured seals and walrus. Sunny Gorge, and
a large indentation in Dallas Bay, which bears the Esquimaux name
of the Inhabited Place, showed us the remains of a village, surrounded by the bones of seals, walrus, and whales—all now cased
in ice. In impressive connection with the same facts, showing not
only the former extension of the Esquimaux race to the higher
north, but the climatic changes which may perhaps be still in progress there, is the sledge-runner which Mr. Morton saw on the shores
of Morris Bay, in latitude 81°. It was made of the bone of a whale,
and worked out with skilful labour.

In this recapitulation of facts, I am not entering upon the question of a warmer climate impressed upon this region in virtue of a
physical law which extends the isotherms toward the Pole. Still
less am I disposed to express an opinion as to the influence which
ocean-currents may exert on the temperature of these far-northern
regions; there is at least one man, an officer in the same service
with myself, and whose scientific investigations do it honour, with
whom I am content to leave that discussion. But I would respect-
fully suggest to those whose opportunities facilitate the inquiry,
whether it may not be that the Gulf Stream, traced already to the
coast of Novaia Zemlia, is deflected by that peninsula into the
space around the Pole. It would require a change in the mean
summer temperature of only a few degrees to develop the periodical recurrence of open water. The conditions which define the line
of perpetual snow and the limits of the glacier formation may have
certainly a proximate application to the problem of such water-
spaces near the Pole.

CHAPTER XXIV.

PROSPECTS—SPECULATIONS—THE ARGUMENT—THE CONCLUSION—THE RE-
CONNOISSANCE — THE SCHEME—EQUIPMENT OF BOAT PARTY—EIDER
ISLAND — HANS ISLAND — THE CORMORANT GULL—SENTIMENT— OUR
CHARTS—CAPTAIN INGLEFIELD—DISCREPANCIES—A GALE—FAST TO A
FLOE.

ATTEMPT TO REACH BEECHY ISLAND.

ALL the sledge-parties were now once more aboard ship, and the season of Arctic travel had ended. For more than two months we had been imprisoned in ice, and throughout all that period, except during the enforced holiday of the midwinter darkness, or while repairing from actual disaster, had been constantly in the field. The summer was wearing on, but still the ice did not break up as it should. As far as we could see, it remained inflexibly solid between us and the North Water of Baffin's Bay. The questions and speculations of those around me began to show that they too had anxious thoughts for the coming year. There was reason for all our apprehensions, as some of my notes may show. *[margin: CHAPTER XXIV. Imprisoned again in the ice.]*

"*July* 8, *Saturday.*—Penny saw water to the southward in Barrow's Straits as early as June ; and by the first of July the leads were within a mile of his harbour in Wellington Channel. Dr. Sutherland says he could have cut his way out by the 15th. Austin was not liberated till the 10th of August ; but the water had worked up to within three miles and a half of him as early as the 1st, having advanced twenty miles in the preceding month. If, now, we might assume that the ice between us and the nearest water would give way as rapidly as it did in these two cases,—an assumption, by-the-way, which the difference of the localities is all against, the mouth of our harbour should be reached in fifty days, or by the last day of August ; and after that, several days, or perhaps weeks must go by before the inside ice yields around our brig. *[margin: Speculations about the breaking up of the ice.]*

"I know by experience how soon the ice breaks up after it once begins to go, and I hardly think that it can continue advancing so slowly much longer. Indeed, I look for it to open, if it opens at all, about the beginning of September at furthest, somewhere near the date of Sir James Ross's liberation at Leopold. But then, I have to remember that I am much further to the north than my predecessors, and that by the 28th of last August I had already, after twenty days of unremitting labour, forced the brig nearly forty miles through the pack, and that the pack began to close on us only six days later, and that on the 7th of September we were fairly frozen in. Yet last summer was a most favourable one for ice-melting. Putting all this together, it looks as if the winter must catch us before we can get halfway through the pack, even though we should begin warping to the south at the earliest moment that we can hope for water.

" It is not a pleasant conclusion of the argument ; for there never was, and I trust never will be, a party worse armed for the encounter of a second Arctic winter. We have neither health, fuel, nor provisions. Dr. Hayes, and indeed all I have consulted about

it indirectly, despond at the thought ; and when I look round upon our diseased and disabled men, and think of the fearful work of the last long night, I am tempted to feel as they do.

" The alternative of abandoning the vessel at this early stage of our absence, even were it possible, would, I feel, be dishonouring ; but, revolving the question as one of practicability alone, I would not undertake it. In the first place, how are we to get along with

our sick and newly-amputated men ? It is a dreary distance at the best to Upernavik or Beechy Island, our only seats of refuge, and a precarious traverse if we were all of us fit for moving ; but we are hardly one-half in efficiency of what we count in number. Besides, how can I desert the brig while there is still a chance of saving her ? There is no use of noting *pros* and *cons :* my mind is made up ; I will not do it.

" But I must examine this ice-field for myself. I have been maturing through the last fortnight a scheme of relief, based upon a communication with the English squadron to the south, and to-morrow I set out to reconnoitre. Hans will go with me. We will fit out our poor travel-worn dogs with canvas shoes, and cross the floes to the true water edge, or at least be satisfied that it is impossible. ' He sees best who uses his own eyes.' After that I have my course resolved on.

July 11, *Tuesday.*—We got back last night : a sixty miles' jour-rey,—comfortless enough, with only three hours' sleep on the ice. For thiry-five miles south the straits are absolutely tight. Off Refuge Inlet and Esquimaux Point we found driving leads ; but between these points and the brig not a crack. I pushed the dogs over the drift-ice, and, after a fair number of mischances, found the North Water. It was flowing and free ; but since M'Gary saw it last May it has not advanced more than four miles. It would be absurd at this season of the year to attempt escaping in open boats with this ice between us and water. All that can be done is to re-inforce our energies as we may, and look the worst in the face.

"In view of these contingencies, I have determined to attempt in person to communicate with Beechy Island, or at least make the effort. If I can reach Sir Edward Belcher's squadron, I am sure of all I want. I will take a light whaleboat, and pick my companions for a journey to the south and west. I may find perhaps the stores of the *North Star* at the Wostenholm Islands, or by great good luck come across some passing vessel of the squadron, and make known our whereabouts and wants ; or, failing these, we will try and coast it along to Wellington Channel.

"A depôt of provisions and a seaworthy craft large enough to carry us,—if I had these, everything would be right. Even Sir John Ross's launch, the *Little Mary*, that he left at Union Bay, would serve our purpose. If I had her I could make a southern passage after the fall tides. The great enemy of that season is the young shore-ice, that would cut through our frail boats like a saw. Or, if we can only renew our stock of provisions for the winter, we may await the chances of next year.

"I know it is a hazardous venture, but it is a necessary one, and under the circumstances an incumbent duty. I should have been glad, for some reasons, if the command of such an attempt could have been delegated to a subordinate ; but I feel that I have no right to devolve this risk upon another, and I am, besides, the only one possessed of the necessary local knowledge of Lancaster Sound and its ice-movements.

"As a prelude to this solemn undertaking, I met my officers in the evening, and showed them my ice-charts ; explaining, what I found needed little explanation, the prospect immediately before us. I then discussed the probable changes, and, giving them my personal opinion that the brig might after all be liberated at a

CHAPTER XXIV.

Results of the journey.

Resolution to attempt another expedition.

Prelude to the undertaking.

late date, I announced my project. I will not say how gratified I was with the manner in which they received it. It struck me
that there was a sense of personal relief experienced everywhere. I told them that I did not choose to call a council or connect any of them with the responsibilities of the measure, for it involved only the personal safety of those who chose to share the risk. Full instructions were then left for their guidance during my absence.

" It was the pleasantest interview I ever had with my associates. I believe every man on board would have volunteered, but I confined myself to five active men : James M'Gary, William Morton,
George Riley, Hans Christian, and Thomas Hickey, made up my party."

Our equipment had been getting ready for some time, though without its object being understood or announced. The boat was our old *Forlorn Hope*, mended up and revised for her new destinies. She was 23 feet long, had 6½ feet beam, and was 2 feet 6 inches deep. Her build was the characteristic one of the American whaleboats, too flat-bottomed for ordinary use, but much improved by a false keel, which Ohlsen had given her throughout her entire length. After all, she was a mere cockle-shell.

Her great fault was her knife-like bow, which cut into the short seas most cruelly. To remedy this in some degree, and to make up for her want of height, I devised a sort of half-deck of canvas and gum-elastic cloth, extending back beyond the fore-mast, and continued along the gunwale,—a sort of weather-cloth, which might possibly add to her safety, and would certainly make her more comfortable in heavy weather.

I left her rig altogether to M'Gary. She carried what any one but a New London whaler would call an inordinate spread of canvas, a light cotton fore-sail of 12 feet lift, a stouter main-sail of 14 feet lift with a spreet 18 feet long, and a snug little jib. Her masts were of course selected very carefully, for we could not carry extra sticks : and we trusted to the good old-fashioned steering-oar rather than a rudder.

Morton, who was in my confidence from the first, had all our stores ready. We had no game, and no meat but pork, of which we took some hundred and fifty pounds. I wanted pemmican, and sent the men out in search of the cases which were left on the floe by the frozen depôt-party during the rescue of last March; but they could not find a trace of them, or indeed of anything else we abandoned at that time—a proof, if we wanted one, how blurred all our faculties must have been by suffering, for we marked them, as we thought, with marvellous care.

We lifted our boat over the side in the afternoon, and floated her to the crack at the Observatory Island; mounted her there on our large sledge *The Faith*, by an arrangement of cradles of Mr. Ohlsen's devising; stowed in everything but the provisions, and carried her on to the bluff of Sylvia Headland—and the next morning a party consisting of all but the sick was detailed to transport her to open water; while M'Gary, Hans, and myself, followed with our *St. John's* sledge, carrying our stores.

The surface of the ice was very irregular and covered with water-pools. Our sledge broke down with repeated strainings, and we had a fatiguing walk of thirty-six miles to get another. We passed the first night wet and supperless on the rocks—a bad beginning, for the next day found us stiff and out of sorts.

The ice continued troublesome, the land-ices swaying hither and thither with the tide. The second day's progress, little as it was, cost us very hard labour. But another night of repose on the rocks refreshed us; so that, the day after, we were able to make about seven miles along the ice-belt. Two days more, and we had carried the boat across twenty miles of heavy ice-floe, and launched her in open water. It was not far from the hut on Esquimaux Point.

The straits were much clogged with drift, but I followed the coast southward without difficulty. We travelled at night, resting when the sun was hottest. I had every reason to be pleased with the performance of the whaleboat, and the men kept up their spirits well. We landed at the point where we left our life-boat a year ago, and to our great joy found it untouched: the cove and inlet were still fast in ice.

We now neared the Littleton Island of Captain Inglefield, where a piece of good fortune awaited us. We saw a number of ducks, both eiders and heraldas; and it occurred to me that by tracking their flight we should reach their breeding-grounds. There was no trouble in doing so, for they flew in a bee-line to a group of rocky islets, above which the whole horizen was studded with birds. A rugged little ledge, which I named Eider Island, was so

thickly colonized that we could hardly walk without treading on a
nest.   We killed with guns and stones over two hundred birds in
a few hours.

It was near the close of the breeding-season.   The nests were
still occupied by the mother-birds, but many of the young had
burst the shell, and were nestling under the wing, or taking their
first lessons in the water-pools.   Some, more advanced, were
already in the ice-sheltered channels, greedily waiting for the shell-
fish and sea-urchins, which the old bird busied herself in procuring
for them.

Near by was a low and isolated rock-ledge, which we called
Hans Island.   The glaucous gulls, those cormorants of the Arctic
seas, had made it their peculiar homestead.   Their progeny, already
full-fledged and voracious, crowded the guano-whitened rocks; and
the mothers, with long necks and gaping yellow bills, swooped
above the peaceful shallows of the eiders, carrying off the young
birds, seemingly just as their wants required.   A more domineer-
ing and insatiable rapacity I have never witnessed.   The gull
would gobble up and swallow a young eider in less time than it
takes me to describe the act.   For a moment you would see the
paddling feet of the poor little wretch protruding from the mouth;
then came a distension of the neck as it descended into the
stomach; a few moments more, and the young gulls were feeding
on the ejected morsel.

The mother-duck, of course nearly distracted, battles, and battles
well; but she cannot always re-assemble her brood; and in her
efforts to defend one, uncovering the others, I have seen her left
as destitute as Niobe.   Hans tells me that in such cases she
adopts a new progeny; and, as he is well versed in the habits of
the bird, I see no reason to doubt his assertion.

The glaucous is not the only predatory gull of Smith's Strait.
In fact, all the Arctic species, without including their cousins the
jagers, have the propensity strongly marked.   I have seen the
ivory gull, the most beautiful and snowy St. Agnes of the ice-fields,
seize our wounded awks, and, after a sharp battle, carry them off
in her talons.   A novel use of a palmated foot.

I could sentimentalize on these bereavements of the ducks and
their companions in diet: it would be only the everyday ser-
monizing of the world.   But while the gulls were fattening their

young on the eiders, the eiders were fattening theirs on the lesser
life of the sea, and we were as busily engaged upon both in true
predatory sympathy.   The squab-gull of Hans Island has a well-
earned reputation in South Greenland for its delicious juices, and
the eggs of Eider Island can well afford to suffer from the occasional visits of gulls and other bipeds; for a locust-swarm of
foragers might fatten without stint on their surplus abundance.

We camped at this nursery of wild-fowl, and laid in four large
India-rubber bags full, cleaned and rudely boned.   Our boat was
hauled up and refitted; and, the trial having shown us that she
was too heavily laden for safety, I made a general reduction of our
stores, and cached the surplus under the rocks.

On Wednesday, the 19th, we left Flagstaff Point, where we fixed
our beacon last year; and stood west 10° south under full canvas.
My aim was to take the channel obliquely at Littleton Island;
and, making the drift-ice or the land to the south-west in the
neighbourhood of Cape Combermere, push on for Kent Island and
leave a cairn there.

I had the good fortune to get satisfactory meridian observations,
as well as angular bearings between Cape Alexander and Flagstaff
Point, and found, as our operations by theodolite had already indicated, that the entire coast-line upon the Admiralty charts of my
predecessor would have to be altered.

Cape Isabella, the western headland of the strait, whose discovery, by-the-way, is due rather to old Baffin than his follower,
Sir John Ross, bears west 22° north (solar) from Cape Alexander;
its former location being some 20° to the south of west.   The
narrowest part of Smith's Straits is not, as has been considered,
between these two capes, but upon the parallel of 78° 24′, where
Cape Isabella bears due west of Littleton Island, and the diameter
of the channel is reduced to thirty-seven miles.

The difference between our projection of this coast and Captain
Inglefield's, refers itself naturally to the differing circumstances
under which the two were framed.   The sluggishness of the compass, and the eccentricities of refraction in the Arctic seas, are well
fitted to embarrass and mislead a navigator.   I might hesitate to
assert the greater certainty for our results, had not the position of
our observatory at Fern Rock, to which our survey is referred,
been determined by a careful series of astronomical observations.

CHAPTER XXIV.   Captain Inglefield gives the mean trend of the east coast about 20° too much to the north, in consequence of which the capes and indentations sighted by him are too high in latitude.

Cape Frederick VII.   Cape Frederick VII., his highest northern point, is placed in lat. 79° 30′, while no land—the glacier not being considered as such—is found on that coast beyond 79° 13′. The same cape, as laid down in the Admiralty Chart of 1852, is about eighty miles from the furthest position reached by Captain Inglefield. To see land upon the horizon at this distance, even from a mast-head 80 feet high, would require it to be a mountain whose altitude exceeded 3500 feet. An island similar in position to that designated by Captain Inglefield as Louis Napoleon does not exist. The land sighted in that direction may have been the top of a high mountain on the north side of Franklin Pierce Bay, though this supposition requires us to assume an error in the bearing; for, as given in the chart, no land could be within the range of sight. In deference to Captain Inglefield, I have continued for this promontory the name which he had impressed upon it as an island.

Boat navigation in the open sea.   Toward night the wind freshened from the northward, and we passed beyond the protection of the straits into the open sea-way. My journal gives no picture of the life we now entered on. The oldest sailor, who treads the deck of his ship with the familiar confidence of a man at home, has a distrust of open-boat navigation which a landsman hardly shares. The feeling grew upon us as we lost the land. M'Gary was an old Behring's Straits whaler, and there is no better boatman in the world than he; but I know that he shared my doubts, as the boat buried herself again and again in the trough of a short chopping sea, which it taxed all his dexterity in steering to meet.

Baffin passed around this gulf in 1616 with two small vessels; but they were giants beside ours. I thought of them as we crossed his track steering for Cape Combermere, then about sixty miles distant, with every prospect of a heavy gale.

We were in the centre of this large area of open water when the gale broke upon us from the north. We were near foundering. Our false bow of India-rubber cloth was beaten in, and our frail weather-boarding soon followed it. With the utmost exertion we could hardly keep our boat from broaching to: a broken oar or an

accidental twitch would have been fatal to us at any time.
But M'Gary handled that whaler's marvel, the long steering-oar,
with admirable skill.   None of us could pretend to take his place.
For twenty-two unbroken hours he stuck to his post without re-
laxing his attention or his efforts.

I was not prepared for such a storm.   I do not think I have
seen a worse sea raised by the northers of the Gulf of Mexico.
At last the wind hauled to the eastward, and we were glad to
drive before it for the in-shore floes.   We had passed several
bergs ; but the sea dashed against their sides so furiously as to
negative all hope of protection at their base ; the pack or floe, so
much feared before, was now looked to for a refuge.

I remember well our anxiety as we entered the loose streams of
drift after four hours' scudding, and our relief when we felt their
influence upon the sea.   We fastened to an old floe, not 50
yards in diameter, and, with the weather-surf breaking over our
heads, rode out the storm under a warp and grapnel.

WORKING ON—A BOAT NIP—ICE-BARRIER—THE BARRIER PACK—PROGRESS HOPELESS—NORTHUMBERLAND ISLAND—NORTHUMBERLAND GLACIER—ICE-CASCADES—NEVE.

CHAPTER XXV. THE obstacle we had now to encounter was the pack that stretched between us and the south.

Boring into the ice-pack. When the storm abated we commenced boring into it,—slow work at the best of times; but my companions encountered it with a persevering activity quite as admirable as their fortitude in danger. It had its own hazards too; and more than once it looked as if we were permanently beset. I myself knew that we might rely on the southerly wind to liberate us from such an imprisonment; but I saw that the men thought otherwise, as the ice-fields closed around us and the horizon showed an unchanging circle of ice.

We were still labouring on, hardly past the middle of the bay, when the floes began to relax. On Sunday, the 23d of July, the The sun appears. whole aspect around us changed. The sun came out cheeringly, the leads opened more and more, and, as we pulled through them to the south, each ice-tongue that we doubled brought us nearer to the Greenland shore. A slackening of the ice to the east enabled us after a while to lay our course for Hakluyt Island. We spread our canvas again, and reached the in-shore fields by one in the afternoon. We made our camp, dried our buffalo-skins, and sunned and slept away our fatigue.

Working on. We renewed our labours in the morning. Keeping inside the pack, we coasted along for the Cary Islands, encountering now and then a projecting floe, and either boring or passing around it, but making a satisfactory progress on the whole toward Lancaster Sound. But at the south point of Northumberland Island the pack arrested us once more. The seam by which we had come east lay between Whale Sound and Murchison Inlet, and the ice-drift from the southern of these had now piled itself in our way.

I was confident that I should find the "Eastern Water" if I could only reach Cape Parry, and that this would give me a free track to Cary Islands. I therefore looked anxiously for a fissure in the pack, and pressed our little craft into the first one that seemed at all practicable. CHAPTER XXV.

For the next three days we worked painfully through the half-open leads, making in all some fifteen miles to the south. We had very seldom room enough to row ; but, as we tracked along, it was not difficult to escape nippings, by hauling up the boat on the ice. Still she received some hard knocks, and a twist or two that did not help her sea-worthiness, for she began to leak ; and this, with the rain which fell heavily, forced us to bale her out every other hour. Of course we could not sleep, and one of our little party fell sick with the unmitigated fatigue. Painful work.

On the 29th it came on to blow, the wind still keeping from the south-west, but cold and almost rising to a gale. We had had another wet and sleepless night, for the floes still baffled us by their capricious movements. But at three in the afternoon we had the sun again, and the ice opened just enough to tempt us. It was uncomfortable toil. We pushed forward our little weather-worn craft, her gunwales touching on both sides, till the toppling ice began to break down on us, and sometimes, critically suspended, met above our heads. A gale.

One of these passages I am sure we all of us remember. We were in an alley of pounded ice-masses, such as the receding floes leave when they have crushed the tables that were between them, and had pushed our way far enough to make retreat impossible, when the fields began to close in. There was no escaping a nip, for everything was loose and rolling around us, and the floes broke into hummock ridges as they came together. They met just ahead of us, and gradually swayed in toward our boat. The fragments were already splitting off and spinning over us, when we found ourselves borne up by the accumulating rubbish, like the *Advance* in her winter drift ; and, after resting for twenty minutes high out of water, quietly lowered again as the fields relaxed their pressure. A boat nip.

Generally, however, the ice-fields came together directly, and so gradually as to enable us to anticipate their contact. In such cases, as we were short-handed and our boat heavily laden, we

CHAPTER
XXV.
———
Plan of
getting
through
the ice.
were glad to avail ourselves of the motion of the floes to assist in lifting her upon them. We threw her across the lead by a small pull of the steering-oar, and let her meet the approaching ice upon her bow. The effect, as we found in every instance, was to press her down forward as the floe advanced against her, and to raise her stern above the level of the other field. We held ourselves ready for the spring as she began to rise.

It was a time of almost unbroken excitement; yet I am not surprised, as I turn over the notes of my meagre diary, to find how little of stirring incident it records. The story of one day's strife with the ice-floes might almost serve for those which followed it; I remember that we were four times nipped before we succeeded in releasing ourselves, and that we were glad to haul upon the floes as often as a dozen times a day. We attempted to drag forward on the occasional fields; but we had to give it up, for it strained the boat so much that she was barely sea-worthy; it kept one man busy the last six days baling her out.

An ice
barrier.
On the 31st, at the distance of ten miles from Cape Parry, we came to a dead halt. A solid mass lay directly across our path, extending onward to our furthest horizon. There were bergs in sight to the westward, and by walking for some four miles over the moving floe in that direction, M'Gary and myself succeeded in reaching one. We climbed it to the height of a hundred and twenty feet, and, looking out from it with my excellent spy-glass to the south and west, we saw that all within a radius of thirty miles was a motionless, unbroken, and impenetrable sea.

I had not counted on this. Captain Inglefield found open water two years before at this very point. I myself met no ice here only seven days later in 1853. Yet it was plain, that from Cape Combermere on the west side, and an unnamed bay immediately to the north of it, across to Hackluyt Island, there extended a continuous barrier of ice. We had scarcely penetrated beyond its margin.

The divid-
ing pack
of Baffin's
Bay.
We had, in fact, reached the dividing pack of the two great open waters of Baffin's Bay. The experience of the whalers and of the expedition-ships that have traversed this region have made all of us familiar with that great expanse of open sea, to the north of Cape Dudley Diggs, which has received the name of the North Water. Combining the observations of Baffin, Ross, and Ingle-

field, we know that this sometimes extends as far north as Littleton CHAPTER Island, embracing an area of 90,000 square miles. The voyagers XXV. I have named could not, of course, be aware of the interesting fact The divi- that this water is divided, at least occasionally, into two distinct sion of the open bodies ; the one comprehended between Lancaster and Jones's water. Sounds, the other extending from the point we had now reached to the upper pack of Smith's Straits. But it was evident to all of our party that the barrier which now arrested us was made up of the ices which Jones's Sound on the west and Murchison's on the east had discharged and driven together.

I may mention, as bearing on the physical geography of the region, that south of Cape Isabella the western shore is invested by a zone of unbroken ice. We encountered it when we were about A zone of twenty miles from the land. It followed the curves of three great unbroken ice. indentations, whose bases were lined with glaciers rivalling those of Melville Bay. The bergs from them were numerous and large, entangling the floating floes, and contributing as much as the currents to the ice-clad character of this most dreary coast. The currents alone would not explain it. Yet when we recur to the observations of Graah, who describes a similar belt on the eastern coast of Greenland, and to the observations of the same character that have been made on the coasts of Arctic America to the southeast, it is not easy to escape the thought, that this accumulation of ice on the western shores must be due, in part at least, to the rotary movements of the earth, whose increasing radius as we recede from the Pole gives increased velocity to the southern ice-pack.

To return to our narrative. It was obvious that a further Further attempt to penetrate to the south must be hopeless till the ice- progress hopeless barrier before us should undergo a change. I had observed, when passing Northumberland Island, that some of its glacier-slopes were margined with verdure, an almost unfailing indication of animal life; and, as my men were much wasted with diarrhœa, and our supplies of food had become scanty, I resolved to work my way to the island, and recruit there for another effort.

Tracking and sometimes rowing through a heavy rain, we traversed the leads for two days, working eastward; and on the morning of the third gained the open water near the shore. Here a breeze came to our aid, and in a couple of hours more we passed with now unwonted facility to the southern face of the island. We met several flocks of little auks as we approached it, and found on landing that it was one enormous homestead of the auks, dovekies, and gulls.

Traces of
an Esqui-
maux
settle-
ment.
We encamped on the 31st, on a low beach at the foot of a moraine that came down between precipitous cliffs of surpassing wildness. It had evidently been selected by the Esquimaux for a winter settlement : five well-built huts of stone attested this. Three of them were still tolerably perfect, and bore marks of recent habitation. The droppings of the birds had fertilized the soil, and it abounded in grasses, sorrel, and cochlearia, to the water's edge.

GLACIER OF NORTHUMBERLAND ISLAND.

Foxes.
The foxes were about in great numbers, attracted, of course, by the abundance of birds. They were all of them of the lead-coloured variety, without a white one among them. The young ones, as

yet lean and seemingly unskilled in hospitable courtesies, barked
at us as we walked about.

I was greatly interested by a glacier that occupied the head of
the moraine. It came down abruptly from the central plateau of
the island, with an angle of descent of more than 70°. I have never
seen one that illustrated more beautifully the viscous or semi-solid
movement of these masses. Like a well-known glacier of the Alps,
it had two planes of descent; the upper nearly precipitous for about
400 feet from the summit, the lower of about the same height, but
with an angle of some 50°,—the two communicating by a slightly-
inclined platform perhaps half a mile long. This ice was unbroken
through its entire extent. It came down from the level of the
upper country, a vast icicle, with the folds or waves impressed
upon it by its onward motion, undisturbed by any apparent fracture or crevasse. Thus it rolled onward over the rugged and contracting platform below, and thence poured its semi-solid mass
down upon the plain. Where it encountered occasional knobs of
rock it passed round them, bearing still the distinctive marks of
an imperfect fluid obstructed in its descent; and its lower fall
described a dome, or, to use the more accurate simile of Forbes, a
great outspread clam-shell of ice.

It seemed as if an interior ice-lake was rising above the brink
of the cliffs that confined it. In many places it could be seen ex-
uding or forcing its way over the very crest of the rocks, and
hanging down in huge icy stalactites 70 and 100 feet long. These
were still lengthening out by the continuous overflow,—some of
them breaking off as their weight became too great for their
tenacity; others swelling by constant supplies from the interior,
but spitting off fragmentary masses with an unremitting clamour.
The plain below these cataractine glaciers was piling up with the
debris, while torrents of the melted rubbish found their way,
foaming and muddy, to the sea, carrying gravel and rocks along
with them.

These ice-cascades, as we called them, kept up their din the
whole night, sometimes startling us with a heavy booming sound,
as the larger masses fell, but more generally rattling away like the
random fires of a militia parade. On examining the ice of which
they were made up, I found grains of *neve* larger than a walnut,
so large, indeed, that it was hard to realize that they could be

CHAPTER
XXV.
—

formed by the ordinary granulating processes of the winter snows.
My impression is, that the surface of the plateau-ice, the *mer de glace* of the island, is made up of these agglomerated nodules, and that they are forced out and discarded by the advance of the more compact ice from higher levels.

CHAPTER XXVI.

THE ICE-FOOT IN AUGUST—THE PACK IN AUGUST—ICE-BLASTING—FOX-
TRAP POINT—WARPING—THE PROSPECT—APPROACHING CLIMAX—SIG-
NAL CAIRN— THE RECORD—PROJECTED WITHDRAWAL—THE QUESTION—
THE DETERMINATION—THE RESULT.

IT was with mingled feelings that we neared the brig. Our little party had grown fat and strong upon the auks and eiders and scurvy-grass; and surmises were rife among us as to the condition of our comrades and the prospects of our ice-bound little ship. *CHAPTER XXVI. Return to the brig.*

The tide-leads, which one year ago had afforded a precarious passage to the vessel, now barely admitted our whale-boat; and, as we forced her through the broken ice, she showed such signs of hard usage, that I had her hauled up upon the land-belt and noused under the cliffs at Six-mile Ravine. We crossed the rocks on foot, aided by our jumping-poles, and startled our shipmates by our sudden appearance.

In the midst of the greeting which always met our returning parties, and which gave to our little vessel the endearing associations of a homestead, our thoughts reverted to the feeble chances of our liberation, and the failure of our recent effort to secure the means of a retreat.

The brig had been imprisoned by closely-cementing ice for eleven months, during which period she had not budged an inch from her icy cradle. My journal will show the efforts and the hopes which engrossed our few remaining days of uncertainty and suspense :— *Time of imprisonment in the ice.*

"*August* 8, *Tuesday.*—This morning two saw-lines were passed from the open-water pools at the sides of our stern-post, and the ice was bored for blasting. In the course of our operations the brig surged and righted, rising two and a half feet. We are now trying to warp her a few yards toward Butler Island, where we again go to work with our powder-canisters. *Operations in August*

"*August* 11, *Friday.*—Returned yesterday from an inspection of the ice toward the Esquimaux settlements; but, absorbing as was my errand, I managed to take geognostical sections and pro-

files of the coast as far south as Peter Force Bay, beyond which
the ice was impenetrable.

"I have often referred to the massive character of the ice in
that neighbourhood. The ice-foot, by our winter measurement 27
feet in mean thickness by 40 yards in width, is now of dimensions
still more formidable. Large masses, released like land-slides by
the action of torrents from the coast, form here and there a belt or
reef, which clogs the shoal water near the shore and prevents a
passage. Such ice I have seen 36 feet in height; and when subjected, as it often is, to hummock-squeezing, 60 and 70 feet. It
requires experience to distinguish it from the true iceberg.

"When I passed up the sound on the 6th of August, after my
long southern journey, I found the ice-foot comparatively unbroken, and a fine interval of open water between it and the large
floes of the pack. Since then this pack has been broken up, and
the comminuted fragments, forming a great drift, move with tides
and currents in such a way as to obliterate the 'landwater' at high
tide, and under some circumstances at other times. This broken
rubbish occasionally expands enough to permit a boat to pass
through; but, as we found it, a passage could only be effected by
heavy labour, and at great expense to our boat, nearly unseaworthy
now from her former trials. We hauled her up near Bedevilled
Headland, and returned to the brig on foot.

"As I travelled back along the coast, I observed the wonderful
changes brought about by the disruption of the pack. It was my
hope to have extricated the brig, if she was ever to be liberated,
before the drift had choked the land-leads; but now they are
closely jammed with stupendous ice-fragments, records of incon-
ceivable pressures. The bergs, released from their winter cement,
have driven down in crowds, grounding on the shallows, and extending in roofs or chains out to seaward, where they have caught
and retained the floating ices. The prospect was really desolation
itself. One floe measured nine feet in mean elevation above the
water-level; thus implying a tabular thickness by direct congelation of 63 feet. It had so closed in with the shore, too, as to rear
up a barricade of crushed ice which it was futile to attempt to
pass. All prospect of forcing a passage ceased north of Six-mile
Ravine.

"On reaching the brig I found that the blasting had succeeded;

one canister cracked and uplifted 200 square yards of ice with but five pounds of powder. A prospect showed itself of getting inside the island at high water ; and I determined to attempt it at the highest spring-tide, which takes place on the 12th.

"*August* 12, *Saturday.*—The brig bore the strain of her new position very well. The tide fell 15 feet, leaving her high and dry ; but, as the water rose, everything was replaced, and the deck put in order for warping again. Every one in the little vessel turned to ; and after much excitement, at the very top of the tide, she passed ' by the skin of her teeth.' She was then warped into a bight of the floe, near Fox-Trap Point, and there she now lies.

"We congratulate ourselves upon effecting this crossing. Had we failed, we should have had to remain fast probably for the high tides a fortnight hence. The young ice is already making, and our hopes rest mainly upon the gales of late August and September.

"*August* 13, *Sunday.*—Still fast to the old floe near Fox-Trap Point, waiting a heavy wind as our only means of liberation. The land-trash is cemented by young ice, which is already an inch and a half thick. The thermometer has been as low as 29° ; but the fog and mist which prevail to-day are in our favour. The perfect clearness of the past five days hastened the growth of young ice, and it has been forming without intermission.

" I took a long walk to inspect the ice towards Six-mile Ravine. This ice has never been moved either by wind or water since its formation. I found that it lined the entire shore with long ridges of detached fragments—a discouraging obstacle, if it should remain, in the way of our future liberation. It is in direct contact with the big floe that we are now fast to, and is the remnant of the triple lines of ' land-ices' which I have described already. I attribute its permanency to the almost constant shadow of the mountains near it.

"*August* 15, *Tuesday.*—To-day I made another ice-inspection to the north-east. The floe on which I have trudged so often, the big bay-floe of our former mooring, is nearly the same as when we left it. I recognised the holes and cracks, through the fog, by a sort of instinct. M'Gary and myself had little difficulty in reaching the Fiord Water by our jumping-poles.

" I have my eye on this water ; for it may connect with the North-east Headland, and hereafter give us a passage.

CHAPTER XXVI.

"The season travels on : the young ice grows thicker, and my messmates' faces grow longer every day. I have again to play buffoon to keep up the spirits of the party.

Signs of approaching winter.

"A raven! The snow-birds begin to fly to the south in groups, coming at night to our brig to hover on the rigging. Winter is hurrying upon us. The poppies are quite wilted.

"Examined ice with Mr. Bonsall, and determined to enter the broken land-ices by warping ; not that there is the slightest probability of getting through, but it affords moral aid and comfort to the men and officers : it looks as if we were doing something.

Warping.

"*August* 17, *Thursday.*—Warped about 100 yards into the trash, and, after a long day of labour, have turned in, hoping to recommence at 5 A.M. to-morrow.

"In five days the spring-tides come back : should we fail in passing with them, I think our fortunes are fixed. The young ice bore a man this morning : it had a bad look, this man-supporting August ice ! The temperature never falls below 28° ; but it is cold o' nights with no fire.

Allowance of fuel reduced.

"*August* 18, *Friday.*—Reduced our allowance of wood to six pounds a meal. This, among eighteen mouths, is one-third of a pound of fuel for each. It allows us coffee twice a day, and soup once. Our fare besides this is cold pork boiled in quantity and eaten as required. This sort of thing works badly ; but I must save coal for other emergencies. I see ' darkness a-head.'

"I inspected the ice again to-day. Bad ! bad !—I must look another winter in the face. I do not shrink from the thought ; but, while we have a chance ahead, it is my first duty to have all

A horrible prospect.

things in readiness to meet it. It is *horrible*—yes, that is the word—to look forward to another year of disease and darkness to be met without fresh food and without fuel. I should meet it with a more tempered sadness if I had no comrades to think for and protect.

Sunday rest and daily prayer.

"*August* 20, *Sunday.*—Rest for all hands. The daily prayer is no longer, ' Lord, accept our gratitude and bless our undertaking,' but, ' Lord, accept our gratitude and restore us to our homes.' The ice shows no change : after a boat and foot journey around the entire south-eastern curve of the bay, no signs !

"I was out in the *Red Eric* with Bonsall, M'Gary, Hans, Riley and John. We tracked her over the ice to the Burgomaster Cove the flanking cape of Charlotte Wood Fiord and its river. Here we launched her, and went all round the long canal which the running waters have eaten into the otherwise unchanged ice. Charlotte Wood Fiord is a commanding sheet of water, nearly as wide as the Delaware : in the midst of the extreme solidity around us, it looked deceitfully gladdening. After getting to the other side, near Little Willie's Monument, we ascended a high bluff, and saw everything weary and discouraging beyond. Our party returned quite crestfallen."

My attempt to reach Beechy Island had disclosed, as I thought it would, the impossibility of reaching the settlements of Green- land. Between the American and the opposite side of the bay was one continuous pack of ice, which, after I had travelled on it for many miles to the south, was still of undefined extent before me. The birds had left their colonies. The water-streams from the bergs and of the shore were freezing up rapidly. The young ice made the water-surface impassable even to a whaleboat. It was clear to me that without an absolute change of circumstances, such as it was vain to look for any longer, to leave the ship would be to enter upon a wilderness destitute of resources, and from which it would be difficult, if not impracticable, to return.

Everything before us was involved in gloomy doubt. Hopeful as I had been, it was impossible not to feel that we were near the climax of the expedition.

I determined to place upon Observatory Island a large signal- beacon or cairn, and to bury under it documents which, in case of disaster to our party, would convey to any who might seek us in- telligence of our proceedings and our fate. The memory of the first winter quarters of Sir John Franklin, and the painful feelings with which, while standing by the graves of his dead, I had five years before sought for written signs pointing to the fate of the living, made me careful to avoid a similar neglect.

A conspicuous spot was selected upon a cliff looking out upon the icy desert, and on a broad face of rock the words :—

A D V A N C E,
A.D. 1853-54.

were painted in letters which could be read at a distance. A pyramid of heavy stones, perched above it, was marked with the

CHAPTER XXVI.

A beacon and a gravestone.

Christian symbol of the cross. It was not without a holier senti ment than that of mere utility that I placed under this the coffins of our two poor comrades. It was our beacon and their gravestone.

Near this a hole was worked into the rock, and a paper, enclosed in glass, sealed in with melted lead. It read as follows :—

BRIG ADVANCE, *August* 14, 1854.

Names of the members of the expedition.

" E. K. Kane, with his comrades, Henry Brooks, John Wall Wilson, James M'Gary, I. I. Hayes, Christian Ohlsen, Amos Bonsall, Henry Goodfellow, August Sontag, William Morton, J. Carl Petersen, George Stephenson, Jefferson Temple Baker, George Riley, Peter Schubert, George Whipple, John Blake, Thomas Hickey, William Godfrey, and Hans Cristian, members of the Second Grinnell Expedition in search of Sir John Franklin and the missing crews of the *Erebus* and *Terror*, were forced into this harbour while endeavouring to bore the ice to the north and east.

When frozen in.

" They were frozen in on the 8th of September, 1853, and liberated———

Labours of the expedition.

" During this period the labours of the expedition have delineated 960 miles of coast-line, without developing any traces of the missing ships or the slightest information bearing upon their fate. The amount of travel to effect this exploration exceeded 2000 miles, all of which was upon foot or by the aid of dogs.

" Greenland has been traced to its northern face, whence it is connected with the further north of the opposite coast by a great glacier. This coast has been charted as high as lat. 82° 27'. Smith's Sound expands into a capacious bay : it has been surveyed throughout its entire extent. From its northern and eastern corner, in lat. 80° 10', long. 66°, a channel has been discovered and followed until further progress was checked by water free from ice. This channel trended nearly due north, and expanded into an apparently open sea, which abounded with birds and bears and marine life.

" The death of the dogs during the winter threw the travel essential to the above discoveries upon the personal efforts of the officers and men. The summer finds them much broken in health and strength.

" Jefferson Temple Baker and Peter Schubert died from injuries CHAPTER
received from cold while in manly performance of their duty. XXVI.
Their remains are deposited under a cairn at the north point of Deaths
Observatory Island. from cold.

" The site of the observatory is 76 English feet from the Site of the
northernmost salient point of this island, in a direction south 14° observa-
east. Its position is in lat. 78° 37′ 10″, long. 70° 40′. The mean tory.
tidal level is 29 feet below the highest point upon this island.
Both of these sites are further designated by copper bolts sealed
with melted lead into holes upon the rocks.

" On the 12th of August, 1854, the brig warped from her posi- Position
tion, and, after passing inside the group of islands, fastened to the brig.
outer floe about a mile to the north-west, where she is now awaiting further changes in the ice.

(Signed) " E. K. KANE,
" Commanding Expedition.
" FOX-TRAP POINT, August 14, 1854."

Some hours later, the following note was added :—

" The young ice having formed between the brig and this island, Additional
and prospects of a gale showing themselves, the date of departure note.
is left unfilled. If possible, a second visit will be made to insert
our dates, our final escape being still dependent upon the course
of the season. E. K. KANE."

And now came the question of the second winter : how to look Prospect
our enemy in the face, and how to meet him. Anything was bet- winter.
ter than inaction; and, in spite of the uncertainty which yet
attended our plans, a host of expedients were to be resorted to,
and much Robinson Crusoe labour ahead. Moss was to be
gathered for eking out our winter fuel, and willow-stems, and
stonecrops, and sorrel, as antiscorbutics, collected and buried in the
snow. But while all these were in progress came other and
graver questions

Some of my party had entertained the idea that an escape to
the south was still practicable; and this opinion was supported by
Mr. Petersen, our Danish interpreter, who had accompanied the
Searching Expedition of Captain Penny, and had a matured experience in the changes of Arctic ice. They even thought that the
safety of all would be promoted by a withdrawal from the brig.

CHAPTER
XXVI.
"*August*, 21, *Monday*.—The question of detaching a party was
in my mind some time ago ; but the more I thought it over, the
The cap-
tain's
duty.
more I was convinced that it would be neither right in itself nor
practically safe.   For myself personally, it is a simple duty of
honour to remain by the brig : I could not think of leaving her
till I had proved the effect of the latter tides ; and after that, as I
have known all along, it would be too late.   Come what may, I
share her fortunes.

"But it is a different question with my associates.   I cannot
What
ought the
crew to
do ?
expect them to adopt my impulses ; and I am by no means sure
that I ought to hold them bound by my conclusions.   Have I the
moral right ? for, as to nautical rules, they do not fit the circumstances ; among the whalers, when a ship is hopelessly beset, the
master's authority gives way, and the crew take counsel for themselves whether to go or stay by her.   My party is subordinate and
well-disposed ; but if the restlessness of suffering makes some of
them anxious to brave the chances, they may certainly plead that
a second winter in the ice was no part of the cruise they bargained
for.

Bad pro-
spect for
winter.
"But what presses on me is of another character.   I cannot
disguise it from myself that we are wretchedly prepared for another winter on board.   We are a set of scurvy-riddled, broken-
down men ; our provisions are sorely reduced in quantity, and are
altogether unsuited to our condition.   My only hope of maintain-
ing or restoring such a degree of health among us as is indispensable to our escape in the spring has been and must be in a wholesome, elastic tone of feeling among the men : a reluctant, brooding,
disheartened spirit would sweep our decks like a pestilence.   I
fear the bane of depressing example.

"I know all this as a medical man and an officer ; and I feel
that we might be wearing away the hearts and energies, if not the
lives of all, by forcing those who were reluctant to remain.
With half a dozen confiding, resolute men, I have no fears of ulti-
mate safety.

"I will make a thorough inspection of the ice to-morrow, and
decide finally the prospects of our liberation.

Escape of
the brig
hopeless.
"*August* 23, *Wednesday*.—The brig cannot escape.   I got an
eligible position with my sledge to review the floes, and returned
this morning at two o'clock.   There is no possibility of our re-

lease, unless by some extreme intervention of the coming tides. CHAPTER
XXVI. I doubt whether a boat could be forced as far as the Southern Water. When I think of the extraordinary way in which the ice was impacted last winter, how very little it has yielded through the summer, and how early another winter is making its onset upon us, I am very doubtful, indeed, whether our brig can get away at all. It would be inexpedient to attempt leaving her now in boats ; the water-streams closing, the pack nearly fast again, and the young ice almost impenetrable.

"I shall call the officers and crew together, and make known to The captain's resolution. them very fully how things look, and what hazards must attend such an effort as has been proposed among them. They shall have my views unequivocally expressed. I will then give them twenty-four hours to deliberate ; and at the end of that time all who determine to go shall say so in writing, with a full exposition of the circumstances of the case. They shall have the best outfit I can give, an abundant share of our remaining stores, and my good-bye blessing.

"*August 24, Thursday.*—At noon to-day I had all hands called, A council called. and explained to them frankly the considerations which have determined me to remain where we are. I endeavoured to show them that an escape to open water could not succeed, and that the effort must be exceedingly hazardous : I alluded to our duties to the ship : in a word, I advised them strenuously to forego the project. I then told them that I should freely give my permission to such as were desirous of making the attempt, but that I should require them to place themselves under the command of officers selected by them before setting out, and to renounce in writing all claims upon myself and the rest who were resolved to stay by the vessel. Having done this, I directed the roll to be called, and each man to answer for himself."

In the result, eight out of the seventeen survivors of my party The decision of the crew resolved to stand by the brig. It is just that I should record their names. They were Henry Brooks, James M'Gary, J. W. Wilson, Henry ·Goodfellow, William Morton, Christian Ohlsen, Thomas Hickey, Hans Cristian.

I divided to the others their portion of our resources justly and even liberally ; and they left us on Monday, the 28th, with every appliance our narrow circumstances could furnish to speed and

14

guard them.　One of them, George Riley, returned a few days afterward; but weary months went by before we saw the rest again.　They carried with them a written assurance of a brother's welcome should they be driven back; and this assurance was redeemed when hard trials had prepared them to share again our fortunes.

CHAPTER XXVII.

DISCIPLINE—BUILDING IGLOE—TOSSUT—MOSSING—AFTER SEAL—ON THE
YOUNG ICE—GOING TOO FAR—SEALS AT HOME—IN THE WATER—IN
SAFETY—DEATH OF TIGER.

THE party moved off with the elastic step of men confident in their CHAPTER XXVII.
purpose, and were out of sight in a few hours. As we lost them
among the hummocks, the stern realities of our condition pressed Dreary forebod-
themselves upon us anew. The reduced numbers of our party, ings.
the helplessness of many, the waning efficiency of all, the impending winter, with its cold, dark night, our penury of resources, the
dreary sense of increased isolation,—these made the staple of our
thoughts. For a time Sir John Franklin and his party, our daily
topic through so many months, gave place to the question of our
own fortunes,—how we were to escape, how to live. The summer
had gone, the harvest was ended, and—— We did not care to
finish the sentence.

Following close on this gloomy train, and in fact blending with
it, came the more important discussion of our duties. We were
like men driven to the wall, quickened, not depressed. Our plans
were formed at once : there is nothing like emergency to speed, if
not to instruct, the energies.

It was my first definite resolve that, come what might, our Arrange-
organization and its routine of observances should be adhered to ment of duties.
strictly. It is the experience of every man who has either combated difficulties himself, or attempted to guide others through
them, that the controlling law shall be systematic action. Nothing depresses and demoralizes so much as a surrender of the
approved and habitual forms of life. I resolved that everything
should go on as it had done. The arrangement of hours, the distribution and details of duty, the religious exercises, the cere-
monials of the table, the fires, the lights, the watch, even the
labours of the observatory and the notation of the tides and the
sky,—nothing should be intermitted that had contributed to make
up the day.

CHAPTER
XXVII.

Lessons
learned
from
Esqui-
maux.

My next was to practise on the lessons we had learned from the Esquimaux. I had studied them carefully, and determined that their form of habitation and their peculiarities of diet, without their unthrift and filth, were the safest and best to which the necessity of our circumstances invited us.

My journal tells how these resolves were carried out :—

"*September 6, Wednesday.*—We are at it, all hands, sick and well, each man according to his measure, working at our winter's home. We are none of us in condition to brave the frost, and our fuel is nearly out. I have determined to borrow a lesson from our Esquimaux neighbours, and am turning the brig into an *igloë*.

"The sledge is to bring us moss and turf from wherever the men can scrape it. This is an excellent non-conductor ; and when

GATHERING MOSS.

we get the quarter-deck well padded with it we shall have a nearly cold-proof covering. Down below we will enclose a space some eighteen feet square, and pack it from floor to ceiling with inner walls of the same material. The floor itself we are calking carefully with plaster of Paris and common paste, and will cover it, when we have done, with Manilla oakum a couple of inches deep, and a canvas carpet. The entrance is to be from the hold, by a low, moss-lined tunnel, the *tossut* of the native huts, with as

many doors and curtains to close it up as our ingenuity can devise. This is to be our apartment of all uses,—not a very large
one ; but we are only ten to stow away, and the closer the
warmer.

"*September* 9, *Saturday*.—All hands but the carpenter and
Morton are out ' mossing.' This mossing, though it has a very
May-day sound, is a frightfully wintry operation. The mixed turf
of willows, heaths, grasses, and moss is frozen solid. We cannot cut it out from the beds of the snow-streams any longer, and
are obliged to seek for it on the ledges of the rocks, quarrying it
with crowbars, and carrying it to the ship like so much stone. I
would escape this labour if I could, for our party have all of them
more or less scurvy in their systems, and the thermometer is often
below zero. But there is no help for it. I have some eight
sledge-loads more to collect before our little home can be called
wind-proof ; and then, if we only have snow enough to bank up
against the brig's sides, I shall have no fear either for height or
uniformity of temperature.

"*September* 10, *Sunday*.—'The work goes bravely on.' We
have got moss enough for our roof, and something to spare for
below. To-morrow we begin to strip off the outer-deck planking
of the brig, and to stack it for firewood. It is cold work, hatches
open and no fires going ; but we saved time enough for our
Sunday's exercises, though we forego its rest.

"It is twelve months to-day since I returned from the weary
foot-tramp that determined me to try the winter search. Things
have changed since then, and the prospect ahead is less cheery.
But I close my pilgrim-experience of the year with devout gratitude for the blessings it has registered, and an earnest faith in the
support it pledges for the times to come.

"*September* 11, *Monday*.—Our stock of game is down to a mere
mouthful,—six long-tailed ducks not larger than a partridge, and
three ptarmigan. The rabbits have not yet come to us, and the
foxes seem tired of touching our trap-baits.

" I determined last Saturday to try a novel expedient for catching seal. Not more than ten miles to seaward the icebergs keep
up a rude stream of broken ice and water, and the seals resort there
in scanty numbers to breathe. I drove out with my dogs, taking
Hans along ; but we found the spot so hemmed in by loose and

fragile ice that there was no approaching it. The thermometer was 8°, and a light breeze increased my difficulties.

"*Deo volente*, I will be more lucky to-morrow. I am going to take my long Kentucky rifle, the kayack, an Esquimaux harpoon with its attached line and bladder, *naligeit* and *awahtok*, and a pair of large snow-shoes to boot. My plan this time is to kneel where the ice is unsafe, resting my weight on the broad surface of the snow-shoes, Hans following astride of his kayack, as a sort of life-preserver in case of breaking in. If I am fortunate enough to stalk within gun-range, Hans will take to the water and secure the game before it sinks. We will be gone for some days probably, tenting it in the open air; but our sick men—that is to say, all of us—are languishing for fresh meat."

I started with Hans and five dogs, all we could muster from our disabled pack, and reached the "Pinnacly Berg" in a single hour's run. But where was the water? where were the seal? The floes had closed, and the crushed ice was all that told of our intended hunting-ground.

Ascending a berg, however, we could see to the north and west the dark cloud-stratus which betokens water. It ran through our
old battle-ground, the "Bergy Belt,"—the labyrinth of our wanderings after the frozen party of last winter. I had not been over it since, and the feeling it gave me was anything but joyous.

But in a couple of hours we emerged upon a plain unlimited to the eye and smooth as a billiard-table. Feathers of young frosting gave a plush-like nap to its surface, and toward the horizon dark columns of frost-smoke pointed clearly to the open water. This ice was firm enough; our experience satisfied us that it was not a very recent freezing. We pushed on without hesitation, cheering ourselves with the expectation of coming every minute to the seals. We passed a second ice-growth; it was not so strong as the one we had just come over, but still safe for a party like ours. On we went at a brisker gallop, maybe for another mile, when Hans sang
out, at the top of his voice, "Pusey! puseymut! seal, seal!" At the same instant the dogs bounded forward, and, as I looked up, I saw crowds of grey netsik, the rough or hispid seal of the whalers, disporting in an open sea of water.

'I had hardly welcomed the spectacle when I saw that we had passed upon a new belt of ice that was obviously unsafe. To the

right and left and front was one great expanse of snow-flowered CHAPTER XXVII.
ice. The nearest solid floe was a mere lump, which stood like an
island in the white level. To turn was impossible; we had to keep Unsafe ice.
up our gait. We urged on the dogs with whip and voice, the ice
rolling like leather beneath the sledge-runners; it was more than
a mile to the lump of solid ice. Fear gave to the poor beasts their
utmost speed, and our voices were soon hushed to silence.

The suspense, unrelieved by action or effort, was intolerable; we
knew that there was no remedy but to reach the floe, and that
everything depended upon our dogs, and our dogs alone. A
moment's check would plunge the whole concern into the rapid
tideway; no presence of mind or resource, bodily or mental, could
avail us. The seals—for we were now near enough to see their The seals in safety.
expressive faces—were looking at us with that strange curiosity
which seems to be their characteristic expression: we must have
passed some fifty of them, breast-high out of water, mocking us by
their self-complacency.

This desperate race against fate could not last: the rolling of the
tough salt-water ice terrified our dogs; and when within fifty paces
from the floe they paused. The left-hand runner went through; The sledge and dogs in the water.
our leader "Toodlamick" followed, and in one second the entire
left of the sledge was submerged. My first thought was to liberate the dogs. I leaned forward to cut poor Tood's traces, and the
next minute was swimming in a little circle of pasty ice and water
alongside him. Hans, dear good fellow, drew near to help me,
uttering piteous expressions in broken English; but I ordered him
to throw himself on his belly, with his hands and legs extended,
and to make for the island by cogging himself forward with his
jack-knife. In the meantime—a mere instant—I was floundering
about with sledge, dogs, and lines, in confused puddle around
me.

I succeeded in cutting poor Tood's lines and letting him scramble
to the ice, for the poor fellow was drowning me with his piteous
caresses, and made my way for the sledge; but I found that it
would not buoy me, and that I had no resource but to try the
circumference of the hole. Around this I paddled faithfully, the
miserable ice always yielding when my hopes of a lodgment were
greatest. During this process I enlarged my circle of operations
to a very uncomfortable diameter, and was beginning to feel weaker

after every effort. Hans meanwhile had reached the firm ice, and was on his knees, like a good Moravian, praying incoherently in English and Esquimaux; at every fresh crushing-in of the ice he would ejaculate "God!" and when I recommenced my paddling he recommenced his prayers.

I was nearly gone. My knife had been lost in cutting out the dogs; and a spare one which I carried in my trousers-pocket was so enveloped in the wet skins that I could not reach it. I owed my extrication at last to a newly broken team dog, who was still fast to the sledge, and in struggling carried one of the runners chock against the edge of the circle. All my previous attempts to use the sledge as a bridge had failed, for it broke through, to the much greater injury of the ice. I felt that it was a last chance. I threw myself on my back, so as to lessen as much as possible my weight,

and placed the nape of my neck against the rim or edge of the ice; then with caution slowly bent my leg, and, placing the ball of my mocassined foot against the sledge, I pressed steadily against the runner, listening to the half-yielding crunch of the ice beneath.

Presently I felt that my head was pillowed by the ice, and that my wet fur jumper was sliding up the surface. Next came my shoulders; they were fairly on. One more decided push, and I was launched up on the ice and safe. I reached the ice-floe, and was frictioned by Hans with frightful zeal. We saved all the dogs; but the sledge, kayack, tent, gun, snow-shoes, and everything besides, were left behind. The thermometer at 8° will keep them frozen fast in the sledge till we can come and cut them out.

On reaching the ship, after a twelve mile trot, I found so much of comfort and warm welcome that I forgot my failure. The fire was lit up, and one of our few birds slaughtered forthwith. It is with real gratitude that I look back upon my escape, and bless the great presiding Goodness for the very many resources which remain to us.

"*September* 14, *Thursday.*—Tiger, our best remaining dog. the partner of poor Bruiser, was seized with a fit, ominously resembling the last winter's curse. In the delirium which followed his seizure, he ran into the water and drowned himself, like a sailor with the horrors. The other dogs are all doing well."

CHAPTER XXVIII.

THE ESQUIMAUX—LARCENY—THE ARREST—THE PUNISHMENT—THE TREATY
—" UNBROKEN FAITH "—MY BROTHER—RETURN FROM A HUNT—OUR
LIFE—ANOATOK—A WELCOME—TREATY CONFIRMED.

IT is, I suppose, the fortune of every one who affects to register **CHAPTER XXVIII.** the story of an active life, that his record becomes briefer and more imperfect in proportion as the incidents press upon each **Journal writing.** other more rapidly and with increasing excitement. The narrative is arrested as soon as the faculties are claimed for action, and the memory brings back reluctantly afterward those details which, though interesting at the moment, have not reflected themselves in the result. I find that my journal is exceedingly meagre for the period of our anxious preparations to meet the winter, and that I have omitted to mention the course of circumstances which led us step by step into familiar communication with the Esquimaux.

My last notice of this strange people, whose fortunes became afterward so closely connected with our own, was at the time of Myouk's escape from imprisonment on board the brig. Although during my absence on the attempted visit to Beechy Island, the men I had left behind had frequent and unrestrained intercourse with them, I myself saw no natives in Rensselaer Bay till immediately after the departure of Petersen and his companions. Just then, by a coincidence which convinced me how **Appearance of a party of Esquimaux.** closely we had been under surveillance, a party of three made their appearance, as if to note for themselves our condition and resources.

Times had indeed altered with us. We had parted with half our provisions, half our boats and sledges, and more than half our able-bodied·men. It looked very much as if we were to lie ensconced in our ice-battered citadel, rarely venturing to sally out for exploration or supplies. We feared nothing, of course, but the want of fresh meat, and it was much less important that our neighbours should fear us than that we should secure from them

CHAPTER XXVIII. offices of kindness. They were overbearing sometimes, and needed the instruction of rebuke; but I treated them with carefully-regulated hospitality.

Entertainment of the visitors. When the three visitors came to us near the end of August, I established them in a tent below deck, with a copper lamp, a cooking-basin, and a liberal supply of slush for fuel. I left them under guard when I went to bed at two in the morning, contentedly eating and cooking and eating again without the promise of an intermission. An American or a European would have slept after such a debauch till the recognised hour for hock and seltzer-water. But our guests managed to elude the **Theft.** officer of the deck and escape unsearched. They repaid my liberality by stealing not only the lamp, boiler, and cooking-pot they had used for the feast, but Nannook also, my best dog. If the rest of my team had not been worn down by over-travel, no doubt they would have taken them all. Besides this, we discovered the next morning that they had found the buffalo-robes and India-rubber cloth which M'Gary had left a few days before on the ice-foot near Six-mile Ravine, and had added the whole to the spoils of their visit.

The theft of these articles embarrassed me. I was indisposed to take it as an act of hostility. Their pilferings before this had been conducted with such a superb simplicity, the detection followed by such honest explosions of laughter, that I could not help thinking they had some law of general appropriation, less removed from the Lycurgan than the Mosaic code. But it was plain, at least, that we were now too few to watch our property as we had done, and that our gentleness was to some extent misunderstood.

Pursuit of the thieves. I was puzzled how to inflict punishment, but saw that I must act vigorously, even at a venture. I despatched my two best walkers, Morton and Riley, as soon as I heard of the theft of the stores, with orders to make all speed to Anoatok, and overtake the thieves, who, I thought, would probably halt there to rest. They found young Myouk making himself quite comfortable in the hut, in company with Sievu, the wife of Metek, and Aningna, the wife of Marsinga, and my buffalo-robes already tailored into kapetahs on their backs.

A continued search of the premises recovered the cooking-utensils, and a number of other things of greater or less value that we had not missed from the brig. With the prompt ceremonial which outraged law delights in among the officials of the police everywhere, the women were stripped and tied; and then, laden with their stolen goods and as much walrus-beef besides from their own stores as would pay for their board, they were marched on the instant back to the brig.

The thirty miles was a hard walk for them; but they did not complain, nor did their constabulary guardians, who had marched thirty miles already to apprehend them. It was hardly twenty- four hours since they left the brig with their booty before they were prisoners in the hold, with a dreadful white man for keeper, who never addressed to them a word that had not all the terrors of an unintelligible reproof, and whose scowl, I flatter myself, exhibited a well-arranged variety of menacing and demoniacal expressions.

They had not even the companionship of Myouk. Him I had despatched to Metek, "head-man of Etah, and others," with the message of a melo-dramatic tyrant, to negotiate for their ransom. For five long days the women had to sigh and sing and cry in solitary converse,—their appetite continuing excellent, it should be remarked, though mourning the while a rightfully-impending doom. At last the great Metek arrived. He brought with him Ootuniah, another man of elevated social position, and quite a sledge-load of knives, tin cups, and other stolen goods, refuse of wood and scraps of iron, the sinful prizes of many covetings.

I may pass over our peace conferences and the indirect advantages which I, of course, derived from having the opposing powers represented in my own capital. But the splendours of our Arctic centre of civilization, with its wonders of art and science,—our "fire-death" ordnance included,—could not all of them impress Metek so much as the intimations he had received of our superior physical endowments. Nomads as they are, these people know better than all the world besides what endurance and energy it requires to brave the moving ice and snow-drifts. Metek thought, no doubt, that our strength was gone with the withdrawing party; but the fact, that within ten hours after the loss of our buffalo-skins we had marched to their hut, seized three of their culprits, and marched them back to the brig as prisoners,—such a sixty miles' achievement as this they thoroughly understood. It con-

CHAPTER XXVIII.

firmed them in the faith that the whites are, and of right ought to be everywhere the dominant tribe.

The protocol.

The protocol was arranged without difficulty, though not without the accustomed number of adjournments for festivity and repose. It abounded in protestations of power, fearlessness, and good-will by each of the contracting parties, which meant as much as such protestations usually do on both sides the Arctic circle. I could give a summary of it without invading the privacy of a diplomatic bureau, for I have notes of it that were taken by a subordinate; but I prefer passing at once to the reciprocal engagements in which it resulted.

Promises of the Esquimaux.

On the part of the *Inuit*, the Esquimaux, they were after this fashion :—

"We promise that we will not steal. We promise we will bring you fresh meat. We promise we will sell or lend you dogs. We will keep you company whenever you want us, and show you where to find the game."

On the part of the *Kablunah*, the white men, the stipulation was of this ample equivalent :—

Equivalent promised by the white men.

"We promise that we will not visit you with death or sorcery, nor do you any hurt or mischief whatsoever. We will shoot for you on our hunts. You shall be made welcome aboard ship. We will give you presents of needles, pins, two kinds of knife, a hoop, three bits of hard wood, some fat, an awl, and some sewing-thread; and we will trade with you of these and everything else you want for walrus and seal-meat of the first quality."

The closing formula.

And the closing formula might have read, if the Esquimaux political system had included reading among its qualifications for diplomacy, in this time-consecrated and, in civilized regions, veracious assurance :—

"We, the high contracting parties, pledge ourselves now and for ever brothers and friends."

Ratification of the treaty.

This treaty—which, though I have spoken of it jocosely, was really an affair of much interest to us—was ratified, with Hans and Morton as my accredited representatives, by a full assembly of the people at Etah. All our future intercourse was conducted under it. It was not solemnized by an oath; but it was never broken. We went to and fro between the villages and the brig, paid our visits of courtesy and necessity on both sides, met each other in hunting parties on the floe and the ice-foot, organized a general community of interests, and really, I believe, established some personal attachments deserving of the name. As long as we remained prisoners of the ice, we were indebted to them for invaluable counsel in relation to our hunting expeditions; and in the joint hunt we shared alike, according to their own laws. Our dogs were in one sense common property; and often have they robbed themselves to offer supplies of food to our starving teams. They gave us supplies of meat at critical periods; we were able to do as much for them. They learned to look on us only as benefactors; and, I know, mourned our departure bitterly. The greeting which they gave my brother John, when he came out after me to Etah with the Rescue Expedition, should be of itself

ESQUIMAUX.

enough to satisfy me of this. I should be glad to borrow from his ingenious narrative the story of his meeting with Myouk, and Metek, and Ootuniah, and of the almost affectionate confidence

CHAPTER
XXVIII.
with which the maimed and sick invited his professional succour, as the representative of the elder "Docto Kayen."

Return
from a
walrus
hunt.
"*September* 16, *Saturday.*—Back last night from a walrus-hunt. I brought in the spoil with my dogs, leaving Hans and Ohlsen to follow afoot. This Marston rifle is an admirable substitute for the primitive lance-head. It killed at the first fire. Five nights' camping out in the snow, with hard-working days between, have made me ache a little in the joints; but, strange to say, I feel better than when I left the vessel. This climate exacts heavy feeding, but it invites to muscular energy. M'Gary and Morton are off at Anoatok. From what I gathered on the hunt, they will find the council very willing to ratify our alliance. But they should have been at home before this.

Sunday.
"*September* 17, *Sunday.*—Writing by this miserable flicker of my pork-fat lamp, I can hardly steady pen, paper, or thought. All hands have rested after a heavy week's work, which has advanced us nobly in our arrangements for the winter. The season is by our tables at least three weeks earlier than the last, and everything indicates a severe ordeal ahead of us.

"Just as we were finishing our chapter this morning in the 'Book of Ruth,' M'Gary and Morton came in triumphantly, pretty well worn down by their fifty miles' travel, but with good news, and a flipper of walrus that must weigh some forty pounds. Ohlsen and Hans are in too. They arrived as we were sitting down to celebrate the Anoatok ratification of our treaty of the 6th.

Nomad
life
"It is a strange life we are leading. We are absolutely nomads, so far as there can be anything of pastoral life in this region; and our wild encounter with the elements seems to agree with us all. Our table talk at supper was as merry as a marriage bell. One party was just in from a seventy-four miles' trip with the dogs; another from a foot-journey of a hundred and sixty, with five nights on the floe. Each had his story to tell; and while the story was telling some at least were projecting new expeditions. I have one myself in my mind's eye, that may peradventure cover some lines of my journal before the winter ends.

Visit to
the Esqui-
maux.
"M'Gary and Morton sledged it along the ice-foot completely round the Reach, and made the huts by ten o'clock the night after they left us. They found only three men, Ootuniah, our elfish rogue Myouk, and a stranger who has not been with us that

we know of. It looked at first a little doubtful whether the visit CHAPTER
was not to be misunderstood. Myouk particularly was an awk- XXVIII.
ward party to negotiate with. He had been our prisoner for Myouk.
stealing only a little while before, and at this very moment is an
escaped hostage. He was in pawn to us for a lot of walrus-beef,
as indemnity for our boat. He thought, naturally enough, that the
visit might have something more than a representative bearing on
his interests. Both our men had been his jailers on board the
brig, and he was the first person they met as they came upon the
village.

" But when he found, by M'Gary's expressive pantomime, that
the visit was not specially to him, and that the first appeal was to
his hospitality and his fellows', his entire demeanour underwent a
change. He seemed to take a new character, as if, said Morton, A cordial
he had dropped a mask. He gave them welcome with unmixed welcome.
cordiality, carried them to his hut, cleared away the end furthest
from the opening for their reception, and filled up the fire of moss
and blubber.

" The others joined him, and the attention of the whole settlement was directed at once to the wants of the visitors. Their wet
boots were turned toward the fire, their woollen socks rung out
and placed on a heated stone, dry grass was padded round their
feet, and the choicest cuts of walrus-liver were put into the
cooking-pot. Whatever might be the infirmity of their notions of
honesty, it was plain that we had no lessons to give them in the
virtues of hospitable welcome. Indeed, there was a frankness and
cordiality in the mode of receiving their guests, that explained the
unreserve and conscious security which they showed when they
first visited us.

" I could hardly guess at that time, when we saw them practis- Entering antics and grimaces among the rocks, what was the meaning tainment
of their harlequin gestures, and how they could venture afterward
so fearlessly on board. I have understood the riddle since. It
was a display of their powers of entertainment, intended to solicit
from us a reception; and the invitation once given, all their experience and impulses assured them of safety.

" Everything they had, cooking utensils, snow-melting stone,
scanty weapons of the chase, personal service, pledges of grateful
welcome,--they gave them all. They confirmed all Metek's en-

CHAPTER
XXVIII.

Hunting
with the
Esqui-
maux.

gagements, as if the whole favour was for them; and when our party was coming away they placed on the sledge, seemingly as a matter of course, all the meat that was left.

"*September* 20, *Wednesday.*—The natives are really acting up to contract. They are on board to-day, and I have been off with a party of them on a hunt inland. We had no great luck; the weather was against us, and there are signs of a gale. The thermometer has been 2° below zero for the entire twenty-four hours. This is September with a vengeance!

"*September* 22, *Friday.*—I am off for the walrus-grounds with our wild allies. It will be my sixth trip. I know the country and its landmarks now as well as any of them, and can name every rock, and chasm, and watercourse, in night or fog, just as I could the familiar spots about the dear Old Mills where I passed my childhood.

"The weather does not promise well; but the state of our larder makes the jaunt necessary."

SECTION OF WINTER APARTMENT.

CHAPTER XXIX.

WALRUS-GROUNDS—LOST ON THE ICE—A BREAK UP—IGLOË OF ANOATOK—
ITS GARNITURE—CREATURE COMFORTS—ESQUIMAUX MUSIC—USAGES OF
THE TABLE—NEW LONDON AVENUE—SCANT DIET LIST—BEAR AND CUB—
A HUNT—CLOSE QUARTERS—BEAR FIGHTING—BEAR-HABITS—BEAR'S
LIVER—RATS—THE TERRIER FOX—THE ARCTIC HARE—THE ICE-FOOT
CANOPY—A WOLF—DOGS AND WOLVES—BEAR AND FOX—THE NATIVES
AND OURSELVES—WINTER QUARTERS—MORTON'S RETURN—THE LIGHT.

" *September* 29, *Friday.*—I returned last night from Anoatok, CHAPTER XXIX. after a journey of much risk and exposure, that I should have avoided but for the insuperable obstinacy of our savage friends. A party set out for the walrus grounds.

" I set out for the walrus-grounds at noon, by the track of the 'Wind Point' of Anoatok, known to us as Esquimaux Point. I took the light sledge, and, in addition to the five of my available team, harnessed in two animals belonging to the Esquimaux. Ootuniah, Myouk, and the dark stranger accompanied me, with Morton and Hans.

" Our sledge was overladen; I could not persuade the Esqui- Difficulties maux to reduce its weight; and the consequence was, that we of the journey. failed to reach Force Bay in time for a day-light crossing. To follow the indentations of the land was to make the travel long and dangerous. We trusted to the tracks of our former journeys, and pushed out on the ice. But the darkness came on us rapidly, and the snow began to drift before a heavy north wind.

" At about 10 P.M. we had lost the land ; and, while driving Lost on the dogs rapidly, all of us running alongside of them, we took a the ice. wrong direction, and travelled out toward the floating ice of the Sound. There was no guide to the points of the compass ; our Esquimaux were completely at fault ; and the alarm of the dogs, which became every moment more manifest, extended itself to our party. The instinct of a sledge-dog makes him perfectly aware of unsafe ice, and I know nothing more subduing to a man than the warnings of an unseen peril conveyed by the instinctive fears of the lower animals.

" We had to keep moving, for we could not camp in the gale,

CHAPTER
XXIX.

The sound
of the open
water.

The ice
breaking
up.

Travelling
over the
broken ice.

The ice
storm.

that blew around us so fiercely that we could scarcely hold down the sledge. But we moved with caution, feeling our way with the tent-poles, which I distributed among the party for the purpose. A murmur had reached my ear for some time in the cadences of the storm, steadier and deeper, I thought, than the tone of the wind. On a sudden it struck me that I heard the noise of waves, and that we must be coming close on the open water. I had hardly time for the hurried order, 'Turn the dogs,' before a wreath of wet frost-smoke swept over us, and the sea showed itself, with a great fringe of foam, hardly a quarter of a mile ahead. We could now guess our position and its dangers. The ice was breaking up before the storm, and it was not certain that even a direct retreat in the face of the gale would extricate us. I determined to run to the south for Godsend Island. The floes were heavy in that direction, and less likely to give way in a northerly gale. It was at best a dreary venture.

" The surf-line kept encroaching on us till we could feel the ice undulating under our feet. Very soon it began to give way. Lines of hummocks rose before us, and we had to run the gauntlet between them as they closed. Escaping these, we toiled over the crushed fragments that lay between them and the shore, stumbling over the projecting crags, or sinking in the water that rose among them. It was too dark to see the island which we were steering for ; but the black loom of a lofty cape broke the line of the horizon, and served as a landmark. The dogs, relieved from the burden of carrying us, moved with more spirit. We began to draw near the shore, the ice-storm still raging behind us. But our difficulties were only reaching their climax. We knew as icemen that the access to the land-ice from the floe was, under the most favouring circumstances, both toilsome and dangerous. The rise and fall of the tides always breaks up the ice at the margin of the ice-belt in a tangle of irregular, half-floating masses ; and these were now surging under the energies of the gale. It was pitchy dark. I persuaded Ootuniah, the eldest of the Esquimaux, to have a tent-pole lashed horizontally across his shoulders. I gave him the end of a line, which I had fastened at the other end round my waist. The rest of the party followed him.

" As I moved ahead, feeling round me for a practicable way, Ootuniah followed ; and when a table of ice was found large

enough, the others would urge forward the dogs, pushing the CHAPTER
sledge themselves, or clinging to it, as the moment prompted. XXIX.
We had accidents, of course, some of them menacing for the time, Safe on the
but none to be remembered for their consequences; and at last ice-foot.
one after another succeeded in clambering after me upon the ice-
foot, driving the dogs before them.

" Providence had been our guide. The shore on which we
landed was Anoatok, not four hundred yards from the familiar Anoatok.
Esquimaux homestead. With a shout of joy, each man in his own
dialect, we hastened to the ' wind-loved spot;' and in less than
an hour, our lamps burning cheerfully, we were discussing a famous
stew of walrus-steaks, none the less relished for an unbroken ice-
walk of forty-eight miles and twenty haltless hours.

" When I reached the hut, our stranger Esquimaux, whose Esqui-
name we found to be Awahtok, or ' Seal-bladder float,' was striking maux way
of striking
a fire from two stones—one a plain piece of angular milky quartz, fire.
held in the right hand, the other apparently an oxide of iron. He
struck them together after the true tinder-box fashion, throwing a
scanty supply of sparks on a tinder composed of the silky down
of the willow-catkins (*S. lanata*), which he held on a lump of dried
moss.

" The hut or igloë at Anoatok was a single rude elliptical apart- Descrip-
ment, built not unskilfully of stone, the outside lined with sods. tion of the
igloë.

ESQUIMAUX IGLOË.

At its further end a rude platform, also of stone, was lifted about
a foot above the entering floor. The roof formed something of a

CHAPTER
XXIX.
___
curve. It was composed of flat stones, remarkably large and heavy, arranged so as to overlap each other, but apparently without any intelligent application of the principle of the arch. The height of this cave-like abode barely permitted one to sit upright.

Dimen-
sions.
Its length was eight feet, its breadth seven feet, and an expansion of the tunnelled entrance made an appendage of perhaps two feet more.

Winter
entrance.
"The true winter entrance is called the *tossut*. It is a walled tunnel, ten feet long, and so narrow that a man can hardly crawl along it. It opens outside below the level of the igloë, into which it leads by a gradual ascent.

Dilapida-
tion of the
structure.
"Time had done its work on the igloë of Anoatok, as among the palatial structures of more southern deserts. The entire front of the dome had fallen in, closing up the tossut, and forcing us to enter at the solitary window above it. The breach was large enough to admit a sledge-team; but our Arctic comrades showed no anxiety to close it up. Their clothes saturated with the freezing water of the floes, these iron men gathered themselves round the blubber-fire, and steamed away in apparent comfort. The only departure from their practised routine, which the bleak night and open roof seemed to suggest to them, was that they did not strip themselves naked before coming into the hut, and hang up their vestments in the air to dry, like a votive offering to the god of the sea.

Furniture.
"Their kitchen implements were even more simple than our own. A rude saucer-shaped cup of seal-skin, to gather and hold water in, was the solitary utensil that could be dignified as table-furniture. A flat stone, a fixture of the hut, supported by other stones just above the shoulder-blade of a walrus,—the stone slightly inclined, the cavity of the bone large enough to hold a moss-wick and some blubber; a square block of snow was placed on the stone, and, as the hot smoke circled round it, the seal-skin saucer caught the water that dripped from the edge. They had no vessel for boiling; what they did not eat raw they baked upon a hot stone. A solitary coil of walrus line, fastened to a movable lance-head (noon-ghak), with the well-worn and well-soaked clothes on their backs, completed the inventory of their effects.

"We felt that we were more civilized than our poor cousins, as we fell to work making ourselves comfortable after our own fashion.

The dais was scraped, and its accumulated filth of years removed; a canvas tent was folded double over the dry, frozen stones, our buffalo-bag spread over this, and dry socks and moccasins were drawn from under our wet overclothes. My copper lamp, a true Berzelius Argand, invaluable for short journeys, soon flamed with a cheerful fire. The soup-pot, the walrus-steak, and the hot coffee, were the next things to be thought of; and, while these were getting ready, an India-rubber floor-cloth was fastened over the gaping entrance of the cave.

"During our long march and its series of ice-fights we had taken care to manifest no weariness, and had, indeed, borne both Ootuniah and Myouk at times upon our shoulders. We showed no signs either of cold, so that all this preparation and rich store of appliances could not be attributed by the Esquimaux to effeminacy or inferior power. I could see that they were profoundly impressed with a conviction of our superiority, the last feeling which the egotistical self-conceit of savage life admits.

"I felt sure now that they were our more than sworn friends. The "Amna Ayah." They sang 'Amna Ayah' for us—their rude, monotonous song— till our ears cracked with the discord, and improvised a special eulogistic chant,

Am - na - yah, Am - na - yah, Am - na - yah, Am - na - yah.

which they repeated over and over again with laughable gravity of utterance, subsiding always into the *refrain* of '*Nalegak! nalegak! nalegak-soak!*' 'Captain! captain! great captain!' They nicknamed and adopted all of us as members of their fraternity, with grave and abundant form; reminding me through all their mummery, solemn and ludicrous at once, of the analogous ceremonies of our North American Indians.

"The chant, and the feed, and the ceremony all completed, A night in the igloë Hans, Morton, and myself crawled feet-foremost into our buffalo-bag, and Ootuniah, Awahtok, and Myouk flung themselves outside the skin between us. The last I heard of them or anything else was the renewed chorus of '*Nalegak! nalegak! nalegak-soak!*' mingling itself sleepily in my dreams with school-boy memories of Aristophanes and The Frogs. I slept eleven hours.

"They were up long before us, and had breakfasted on raw meat cut from a large joint, which lay, without regard to cleanliness, among the deposits on the floor of the igloë. Their mode of eating was ingeniously active. They cut the meat in long strips, introduced one end into the mouth, swallowed it as far as the powers of deglutition would allow, and then, cutting off the protruding portion close to the lips, prepared themselves for a second mouthful. It was really a feat of address: those of us who tried it failed awkwardly; and yet I have seen infants in the mother's hood, not two years old, who managed to perform it without accident."

I pass over the story of the hunt that followed. It had nothing to distinguish it from many others, and I find in my journal of a few days later the fresh narrative of Morton, after he had seen one for the first time.

My next extracts show the progress of our winter arrangements.

"*September* 30, *Saturday.*—We have been clearing up on the ice. Our system for the winter has not the dignity of a year ago. We have no Butler Storehouse, no Medary, no Fern Rock, with their appliances. We are ten men in a casemate, with all our energies concentrated against the enemy outside.

"Our beef house is now a pile of barrels holding our water-soaked beef and pork. Flour, beans, and dried apples make a quadrangular blockhouse on the floe; from one corner of it rises our flagstaff, lighting up the dusky grey with its red and white ensign, only on Sunday giving place to the Henry Grinnell flag, of happy memories.

"From this, along an avenue that opens abeam of the brig,—New London Avenue, named after M'Gary's town at home,—are our boats and square cordage. Outside of all these is a magnificent hut of barrel-frames and snow, to accommodate our Esquimaux visitors—the only thing about it exposed to hazard being the tempting woodwork. What remains to complete our camp-plot is the rope barrier that is to mark out our little curtilage around the vessel; this, when finished, is to be the dividing-line between us and the rest of mankind.

"There is something in the simplicity of all this, 'simplex munditiis,' which might commend itself to the most rigorous taste. Nothing is wasted on ornament.

"*October* 4, *Wednesday.*—I sent Hans and Hickey two days

ago out to the hunting-ice, to see if the natives have had any luck
with the walrus. They are back to-night with bad news,—no
meat, no Esquimaux. These strange children of the snow have
made a mysterious flitting. Where or how it is hard to guess, for
they have no sledges. They cannot have travelled very far; and
yet they have such unquiet impulses, that, once on the track, no
civilized man can say where they will bring up.

"Ohlsen had just completed a sledge, fashioned like the Smith
Sound *kommetik*, with an improved curvature of the runners. It
weighs only twenty-four pounds, and, though I think it too short
for light draught, it is just the article our Etah neighbours would
delight in for their land-portages. I intended it for them, as a
great price for a great stock of walrus meat; but the other parties
to the bargain have flown.

"*October* 5, *Thursday.*—We are nearly out of fresh meat again,
one rabbit and three ducks being our sum total. We have been
on short allowance for several days. What vegetables we have—
the dried apples and peaches, and pickled cabbage—have lost
much of their anti-scorbutic virtue by constant use. Our spices
are all gone. Except four small bottles of horse-radish, our carte
is comprised in three lines—bread, beef, pork.

"I must be off after these Esquimaux. They certainly have
meat, and wherever they have gone we can follow. Once upon
their trail, our hungry instincts will not risk being baffled. I will
stay only long enough to complete my latest root-beer brewage.
Its basis is the big crawling willow, the miniature giant of our
Arctic forests, of which we laid in a stock some weeks ago. It is
quite pleasantly bitter, and I hope to get it fermenting in the deck-
house without extra fuel, by heat from below.

"*October* 7, *Saturday.*—Lively sensation, as they say in the
land of olives and champagne. 'Nannook, nannook!'—'A bear,
a bear!'—Hans and Morton in a breath!

"To the scandal of our domestic regulations, the guns were all
impracticable. While the men were loading and capping anew, I
seized my pillow-companion six-shooter, and ran on deck. A
medium-sized bear, with a four months' cub, was in active warfare
with our dogs. They were hanging on her skirts, and she with
wonderful alertness was picking out one victim after another,
snatching him by the nape of the neck, and flinging him many feet,

CHAPTER
XXIX.

or rather yards, by a barely perceptible movement of her head.

The dogs
defeated.

"Tudla, our master dog, was already *hors de combat;* he had been tossed twice. Jenny, just as I emerged from the hatch, was making an extraordinary somerset of some eight fathoms, and alighted senseless. Old Whitey, staunch, but not bear-wise, had been the first in the battle; he was yelping in helplessness on the snow.

"It seemed as if the controversy was adjourned; and Nannook evidently thought so; for she turned off to our beef-barrels, and began in the most unconcerned manner to turn them over and nose out their fatness. She was apparently as devoid of fear as any of the bears in the stories of old Barentz and the Spitzbergen voyagers.

Wonderful
strength of
the bear.

"I lodged a pistol-ball in the side of the cub. At once the mother placed her little one between her hind-legs, and, shoving it along, made her way behind the beef-house. Mr. Ohlsen wounded her as she went with my Webster rifle; but she scarcely noticed it. She tore down by single efforts of her forearms the barrels of frozen beef which made the triple walls of the store-house, mounted the rubbish, and snatching up a half barrel of her-rings, carried it down by her teeth, and was making off. It was time to close, I thought. Going up within half pistol range, I gave her six buckshot. She dropped, but instantly rose, and getting her cub into its former position, moved off once more.

New plan
of bear
fighting.

"This time she would really have escaped but for the admirable tactics of our new recruits from the Esquimaux. The dogs of Smith's Sound are educated more thoroughly than any of their more southern brethren. Next to the walrus, the bear is the staple of diet to the north, and except the fox, supplies the most important element of the wardrobe. Unlike the dogs we had brought with us from Baffin's Bay, these were trained, not to attack, but to embarrass. They ran in circles round the bear, and when pursued would keep ahead with regulated gait, their com-rades effecting a diversion at the critical moment by a nip at her hind-quarters. This was done so systematically and with so little seeming excitement as to strike every one on board. I have seen bear-dogs elsewhere that had been drilled to relieve each other in the *melée* and avoid the direct assault; but here, two dogs without even a demonstration of attack, would put themselves before the CHAPTER XXIX. path of the animal, and retreating right and left, lead him into a profitless pursuit that checked his advance completely.

"The poor animal was still backing out, yet still fighting, The bear's last struggle. carrying along her wounded cub, embarrassed by the dogs, yet gaining distance from the brig, when Hans and myself threw in the odds in the shape of a couple of rifle-balls. She staggered in front of her young one, faced us in death-like defiance, and only sank when pierced by six more bullets.

"We found nine balls in skinning her body. She was of medium size, very lean, and without a particle of food in her stomach. Hunger must have caused her boldness. The net weight of the Size and weight of the bear. cleansed carcass was 300 lbs.; that of the entire animal, 650; her length, but 7 feet 8 inches.

"Bears in this lean condition are much the most palatable food. The impregnation of fatty oil through the cellular tissue makes a well-fed bear nearly uneatable. The flesh of a famished beast, although less nutritious as a fuel diet, is rather sweet and tender than otherwise.

"The little cub is larger than the adjective implies. She was The cub a prisoner. taller than a dog, and weighs 114 lbs. Like Morton's bear in Kennedy's Channel, she sprang upon the corpse of her mother, and raised a woeful lamentation over her wounds. She repelled my efforts to noose her with great ferocity; but at last, completely muzzled with a line fastened by a running knot between her jaws and the back of her head, she moved off to the brig amid the clamour of the dogs. We have her now chained alongside, but snarling and snapping constantly, evidently suffering from her wound.

"Of the eight dogs who took part in this passage of arms, only The dogs after the fight. one—'Sneak,' as the men call him, 'Young Whitey,' as he figures in this journal—lost a flower from his chaplet. But two of the rest escaped without a grip.

"Strange to say, in spite of the powerful flings which they were subjected to in the fight, not a dog suffers seriously. I expected, from my knowledge of the hugging propensity of the plantigrades, that the animal would rear, or at least use her forearm; but she invariably seized the dogs with her teeth, and, after disposing of them for the time, abstained from following up the

CHAPTER XXIX. advantage. The Esquimaux assert that this is the habit of the hunted bear. One of our Smith Sound dogs, 'Jack,' made no struggle when he was seized, but was flung, with all his muscles relaxed, I hardly dare to say how far; the next instant he rose and renewed the attack. The Esquimaux both of Proven and of this country say that the dogs soon learn this 'possum-playing' habit. Jack was an old bear-dog.

"Jack" the old bear-dog.

Bear habits.   "The bear seems to be more ferocious as he increases his latitude, or more probably as he recedes from the hunting-fields.

"At Oominak, last winter (1852), an Esquimaux and his son were nearly killed by a bear that had housed himself in an iceberg. They attacked him with the lance, but he turned on them and worsted them badly before making his escape.

"But the continued pursuit of man seems to have exerted already a modifying influence upon the ursine character in South Greenland; at all events, the bears there never attack, and even in self-defence seldom inflict injury upon the hunter. Many instances have occurred where they have defended themselves, and even charged after being wounded, but in none of them was life lost. I have myself shot as many as a dozen bears near at hand, and never but once received a charge in return.

"I heard another adventure from the Danes as occurring in 1834 :—

An adventure with a bear.   "A stout Esquimaux, an assistant to the cooper of Upernavik, —not a Christian, but a stout, manly savage,—fired at a she-bear, and the animal closed on the instant of receiving the ball. The man flung himself on the ground, putting forward his arm to protect his head, but lying afterward perfectly motionless. The beast was taken in. She gave the arm a bite or two, but finding her enemy did not move, she retired a few paces and sat upon her haunches to watch. But she did not watch as carefully as she should have done, for the hunter adroitly reloaded his rifle and killed her with the second shot.

Bear liver.   "*October* 8, *Sunday*.—When I was out in the *Advance*, with Captain de Haven, I satisfied myself that it was a vulgar prejudice to regard the liver of the bear as poisonous. I ate of it freely myself, and succeeded in making it a favourite dish with the mess. But I find to my cost that it may sometimes be more savoury than safe. The cub's liver was my supper last night,

and to-day I have the symptoms of poison in full measure—
vertigo, diarrhœa, and their concomitants."

I may mention, in connection with the fact which I have given
from my journal, that I repeated the experiment several times
afterward, and sometimes, but not always, with the same result.
I remember once, near the Great Glacier, all our party sickened
after feeding on the liver of a bear that we had killed; and a few
weeks afterward, when we were tempted into a similar indulgence,
we were forced to undergo the same penance. The animal in both
cases was old and fat. The dogs ate to repletion, without injury.

Another article of diet, less inviting at first, but which I found
more innocuous, was the rat. We had failed to exterminate this
animal by our varied and perilous efforts of the year before, and
a well-justified fear forbade our renewing the crusade. It was
marvellous, in a region apparently so unfavourable to reproduction,
what a perfect warren we soon had on board. Their impudence
and address increased with their numbers. It became impossible
to stow anything below decks. Furs, woollens, shoes, specimens
of natural history, everything we disliked to lose, however little
valuable to them, was gnawed into and destroyed. They har-
boured among the men's bedding in the forecastle, and showed
such boldness in fight and such dexterity in dodging missiles, that
they were tolerated at last as inevitable nuisances. Before the
winter ended, I avenged our griefs by decimating them for my
private table. I find in my journal of the 10th of October an
anecdote that illustrates their boldness:—

" We have moved everything movable out upon the ice, and,
besides our dividing moss wall between our sanctum and the forecastle, we have built up a rude barrier of our iron sheathing to
prevent these abominable rats from gnawing through. It is all in
vain. They are everywhere already, under the stove, in the
steward's lockers, in our cushions, about our beds. If I was
asked what, after darkness and cold and scurvy, are the three
besetting curses of our Arctic sojourn, I should say, RATS, RATS,
RATS. A mother-rat bit my finger to the bone last Friday, as I
was intruding my hand into a bear-skin mitten which she had
chosen as a homestead for her little family. I withdrew it of
course with instinctive courtesy; but among them they carried off
the mitten before I could suck the finger.

CHAPTER XXIX.

The dog vanquished by rats.

"Last week I sent down Rhina, the most intelligent dog of our whole pack, to bivouac in their citadel forward : I thought she might at least be able to defend herself against them, for she had distinguished herself in the bear-hunt. She slept very well for a couple of hours on a bed she had chosen for herself on the top of some iron spikes. But the rats could not or would not forego the horny skin about her paws ; and they gnawed her feet and nails so ferociously that we drew her up yelping and vanquished."

Shooting rats.

Before I pass from these intrepid and pertinacious visitors, let me add that on the whole I am personally much their debtor. Through the long winter night, Hans used to beguile his lonely hours of watch by shooting them with the bow and arrow. The repugnance of my associates to share with me the table luxury of "such small deer," gave me the frequent advantage of a fresh-meat soup, which contributed no doubt to my comparative immunity from scurvy. I had only one competitor in the dispensation of this *entremet*, or rather one companion ; for there was an abundance for both. It was a fox. We caught and domesticated him late in the winter ; but the scantiness of our resources, and of course his own, soon instructed him in all the antipathies of a terrier. He had only one fault as a rat-catcher ; he would never catch a second till he had eaten the first.

Terrier fox.

Arctic hares.

At the date of these entries the Arctic hares had not ceased to be numerous about our harbour. They were very beautiful, as white as swans' down, with a crescent of black marking the ear-tips. They feed on the bark and catkins of the willow, and affect the stony sides of the worn down rocks, where they find protection from the wind and snow-drifts. They do not burrow like our hares at home, but squat in crevices or under large stones. Their average weight is about 9 lbs. They would have entered largely into our diet-list but for our Esquimaux dogs, who regarded them with relishing appetite. Parry found the hare at Melville Island, in latitude 75° ; but we have traced it from Littleton Island as far north as 79° 08′, and its range probably extends still further toward the Pole. Its structure and habits enable it to penetrate the snow-crusts, and obtain food where the reindeer and the musk-ox perish in consequence of the glazed covering of their feeding-grounds.

"*October* 11, *Wednesday.*—There is no need of looking at the thermometer and comparing registers, to show how far this season has advanced beyond its fellow of last year. The ice-foot is more easily read, and quite as certain.

THE ICE-FOOT CANOPY.

"The under part of it is covered now with long stalactitic columns of ice, unlike the ordinary icicle in shape, for they have the characteristic bulge of the carbonate-of-lime stalactite. They look like the fantastic columns hanging from the roof of a frozen temple, the dark recess behind them giving all the effect of a grotto. There is one that brings back to me saddened memories of Elephanta and the merry friends that bore me company under its rock-chiselled portico. The fig-trees and the palms, and the gallant major's curries and his old India ale, are wanting in the picture. Sometimes again it is a canopy fringed with gems in the moonlight. Nothing can be purer or more beautiful.

CHAPTER
XXIX.
" The ice has begun to fasten on our brig : I have called a con-
sultation of officers to determine how she may be best secured.

Search for
the Esqui-
maux.
" *October* 13, *Friday.*—The Esquimaux have not been near us,
and it is a puzzle of some interest where they have retreated to.
Wherever they are, there must be our hunting-grounds, for they
certainly have not changed their quarters to a more destitute
region. I have sent Morton and Hans to-day to track them out
if they can. They carry a hand-sledge with them, Ohlsen's last
manufacture, ride with the dog-sledge as far as Anoatok, and
leave the old dogs of our team there. From that point they are
to try a device of my own. We have a couple of dogs that we
got from these same Esquimaux, who are at least as instinctive as
their former masters. One of these they are to let run, holding
the other by a long leash. I feel confident that the free dog will
find the camping-ground, and I think it probable the other will
follow. I thought of tying the two together ; but it would embarrass their movements, and give them something to occupy their
minds besides the leading object of their mission.

A wolf.
" *October* 14, *Saturday.*—Mr. Wilson and Hickey reported last
night a wolf at the meat-house. Now, the meat-house is a thing
of too much worth to be left to casualty, and a wolf might incidentally add some freshness of flavour to its contents. So I went
out in all haste with the Marston rifle, but without my mittens
and with only a single cartridge. The metal burnt my hands, as
metal is apt to do at 50° below the point of freezing ; but I got a
somewhat rapid shot. I hit—— one of our dogs, a truant from
Morton's team ; luckily a flesh-wound only, for he is too good a
beast to lose. I could have sworn he was a wolf."

Similarity
of dogs
and
wolves.
There is so much of identical character between our Arctic dogs
and wolves, that I am inclined to agree with Mr. Broderip, who in
the " Zoological Recreations " assigns to them a family origin. The
oblique position of the wolf's eye is not uncommon among the
dogs of my team. I have a slut, one of the tamest and most
affectionate of the whole of them, who has the long legs and compact body, and drooping tail, and wild, scared expression of the
eye, which some naturalists have supposed to characterize the wolf
alone. When domesticated early—and it is easy to domesticate
him—the wolf follows and loves you like a dog. That they are
fond of a loose foot proves nothing : many of our pack will run

away for weeks into the wilderness of ice ; yet they cannot be persuaded when they come back to inhabit the kennel we have built
for them only a hundred yards off. They crouch around for the
companionship of men. Both animals howl in unison alike : the
bell at the settlements of South Greenland always starts them.
Their footprint is the same, at least in Smith's Sound. Dr.
Richardson's remark to the contrary made me observe the fact,
that our northern dogs leave the same " spread track" of the toes
when running, though not perhaps as well marked as the wolf's.

The old proverb, and the circumstance of the wolf having sometimes carried off an Esquimaux dog, has been alluded to by the
editors of the " Diffusion of Knowledge Library." But this too is
inconclusive, for the proverb is false. It is not quite a month ago
since I found five of our dogs gluttonizing on the carcasses of their
dead companions who had been thrown out on a rubbish-heap ;
and I have seen pups only two months old risk an indigestion by
overfeeding on their twin brethren who had preceded them in a
like imprudence.

Nor is there anything in the supposed difference of strength.
The Esquimaux dog of Smith's Sound encounters the wolf fearlessly and with success. The wolves of Northern America never
venture near the huts ; but it is well known that when they have
been chasing the deer or the moose, the dogs have come up as
rivals in the hunt, beaten them off, and appropriated the prey to
themselves.

" *October* 16, *Monday.*—I have been wearied and vexed for half
a day by a vain chase after some bear-tracks. There was a fox
evidently following them (*C. lagopus*)."

There are fables about the relation between these two animals
which I once thought my observations had confirmed. They are
very often found together : the bear striding on ahead with his
prey ; the fox behind gathering in the crumbs as they fall ;
and I have often seen the parasite licking at the traces of a
wounded seal which his champion had borne off over the snow.
The story is that the two hunt in couples. I doubt this now,
though it is certain that the inferior animal rejoices in his association with the superior, at least for the profits, if not the sympathy it brings to him. I once wounded a bear when I was out
with Morton during our former voyage, and followed him for

CHAPTER
XXIX.
____

Strange
com-
panions.

Morton in
search of
the Esqui-
maux.

Apparatus
for raising
the brig.

twelve miles over the ice. A miserable little fox travelled close behind his patron, and licked up the blood wherever he lay down. The bear at last made the water ; and, as we returned from our fruitless chase, we saw the fox running at full speed along the edge of the thin ice, as if to rejoin him. It is a mistake to suppose he cannot swim : he does, and that boldly.

"*October* 19, *Thursday.*—Our black dog Erebus has come back to the brig. Morton has perhaps released him, but he has more probably broken loose.

"I have no doubt Morton is making the best of his way after the Esquimaux. These trips are valuable to us, even when they fail of their immediate object. They keep the natives in wholesome respect for us. We are careful to impress them with our physical prowess, and avoid showing either fatigue or cold when we are travelling together. I could not help being amused some ten days ago with the complacent manner of Myouk, as he hooked himself to me for support after I had been walking for thirty miles ahead of the sledge. The fellow was worth four of me ; but he let me carry him almost as far as the land-ice.

"We have been completing our arrangements for raising the brig. The heavy masses of ice that adhere to her in the winter make her condition dangerous at seasons of low tide. Her frame could not sustain the pressure of such a weight. Our object, therefore, has been to lift her mechanically above her line of flotation, and let her freeze in on a sort of ice-dock ; so that the ice around her as it sinks may take the bottom and hold her up clear of the danger. We have detached four of the massive beams that were intended to resist the lateral pressure of nips, and have placed them as shores, two on each side of the vessel, opposite the channels. Brooks has rigged a crab or capstan on the floe, and has passed the chain cable under the keel at four bearing-points. As these are hauled in by the crab and the vessel rises, the shores are made to take hold under heavy cleats spiked below the bulwarks, and in this manner to sustain her weight.

"We made our first trial of the apparatus to-day. The chains held perfectly, and had raised the brig nearly three feet, when away went one of our chain-slings, and she fell back of course to her more familiar bearings. We will repeat the experiment to-morrow, using six chains, two at each line of stress.

"*October* 21, *Saturday*.—Hard at it still, slinging chains and planting shores. The thermometer is too near zero for work like this. We swaddle our feet in old cloth, and guard our hands with fur mits; but the cold iron bites through them all.

"6.30 P.M.—Morton and Hans are in, after tracking the Esquimaux to the lower settlement of Etah. I cannot give their report to-night: the poor fellows are completely knocked up by the hardships of their march. Hans, who is always careless of powder and fire-arms,—a trait which I have observed among both the American and the Oriental savages,—exploded his powder-flask while attempting to kindle a tinder-fire. The explosion has risked his hand. I have dressed it, extracting several pieces of foreign matter, and poulticing it in yeast and charcoal. Morton has frostbitten both his heels; I hope not too severely, for the indurated skin of the heel makes it a bad region for suppuration. But they bring us two hundred and seventy pounds of walrus-meat and a couple of foxes. This supply, with what we have remaining of our two bears, must last us till the return of daylight allows us to join the natives in their hunts.

"The light is fast leaving us. The sun has ceased to reach the vessel. The north-eastern headlands or their southern faces up the fiords have still a warm yellow tint, and the pinnacles of the icebergs far out on the floes are lighted up at noonday; but all else is dark shadow."

OUR GREENLAND SLEDGES.

16

CHAPTER XXX.

JOURNEY OF MORTON AND HANS—RECEPTION—THE HUT—THE WALRUS—
WALRUS-HUNT—THE CONTEST—HABITS OF WALRUS—FEROCITY OF THE
WALRUS—THE VICTORY—THE JUBILEE—A SIPAK.

JOURNEY OF MORTON AND HANS.

CHAPTER
XXX.

MORTON reached the huts beyond Anoatok upon the fourth day after leaving the brig.

Esqui-
maux
settle-
ment.

The little settlement is inside the north-eastern islands of Hart-stene Bay, about five miles from Gray's Fiord, and some sixty-five or seventy from our brig. The slope on which it stands fronts the south-west, and is protected from the north and north-east by a rocky island and the hills of the mainland.

There were four huts ; but two of them are in ruins. They were all of them the homes of families only four winters ago. Of the two which are still habitable, Myouk, his father, mother, brother and sister occupied one ; and Awahtok and Ootuniah, with their wives and three young ones, the other. The little community had lost two of its members by death since the spring.

Morton's
reception.

They received Morton and his companion with much kindness, giving them water to drink, rubbing their feet, drying their moc-casins, and the like. The women, who did this with something of the good-wife's air of prerogative, seemed to have toned down much of the rudeness which characterized the bachelor settlement at Anoatok. The lamps were cheerful and smokeless, and the huts much less filthy. Each had its two lamp-fires constantly burning, with a framework of bone hooks and walrus-line above them for drying the wet clothes of the household. Except a few dog-skins, which are used as a support to the small of the back, the dais was destitute of sleeping accommodations altogether : a single walrus-hide was spread out for Morton and Hans. The hut had the usual tossut, at least 12 feet long,—very low, straight, and level, until it reached the inner part of the chamber, when it rose abruptly by a small hole, through which with some squeezing was the entrance into the true apartment. Over this entrance was the rude window,

with its scraped seal-intestine instead of glass, heavily coated with
frost of course ; but a small eye-hole commanding the bay enabled
the indwellers to peep out and speak or call to any who were outside. A smoke-hole passed through the roof.

When all the family, with Morton and Hans, were gathered together, the two lamps in full blaze and the narrow hole of entrance
covered by a flat stone, the heat became insupportable. Outside,
the thermometer stood at 30° below zero ; within, 90° above ; a
difference of 120°.

The vermin were not as troublesome as in the Anoatok dormitory, the natives hanging their clothing over the lamp-frames, and
lying down to sleep perfectly naked, with the exception of a sort
of T bandage, as surgeons call it, of seal-skin, three inches wide,
worn by the women as a badge of their sex, and supported by a
mere strip around the hips.

After sharing the supper of their hosts,—that is to say, after
disposing of six frozen auks apiece,—the visitors stretched themselves out and passed the night in unbroken perspiration and slumber. It was evident from the meagreness of the larder that the
hunters of the family had work to do ; and from some signs, which
did not escape the sagacity of Morton, it was plain that Myouk and
his father had determined to seek their next dinner upon the floes.
They were going upon a walrus-hunt ; and Morton, true to the
mission with which I had charged him, invited himself and Hans
to be of the party.

I have not yet described one of these exciting incidents of Esquimaux life. Morton was full of the one he witnessed ; and his account of it when he came back was so graphic, that I should be glad
to escape from the egotism of personal narrative by giving it in
his own words. Let me first, however, endeavour to describe the
animal.

The specimens in the museums of collectors are imperfect, on
account of the drying of the skin of the face against the skull.
The head of the walrus has not the characteristic oval of the seal ;
on the contrary, the frontal bone is so covered as to present a steep
descent to the eyes and a square, blocked-out aspect to the upper
face. The muzzle is less protruding than the seal's, and the cheeks
and lips are completely masked by the heavy quill-like bristles.
Add to this the tusks as a garniture to the lower face ; and you

have for the walrus a grim, ferocious aspect peculiarly his own. I have seen him with tusks nearly 30 inches long ; his body not less than 18 feet. When of this size he certainly reminds you of the elephant more than any other living monster.

The resemblance of the walrus to man has been greatly overrated. The notion occurs in our systematic treatises, accompanied with the suggestion that this animal may have represented the merman and mermaid. The square, blocked-out head which I have noticed, effectually destroys the resemblance to humanity when distant, and the colossal size does the same when near. Some of the seals deserve the distinction much more : the size of the head, the regularity of the facial oval, the droop of the shoulders, even the movements of this animal, whether singly or in group, remind you strikingly of man.

The party which Morton attended upon their walrus hunt had three sledges. One was to be taken to a cache in the neighbourhood ; the other two dragged at a quick run toward the open water, about ten miles off to the south-west. They had but nine dogs to these two sledges, one man only riding, the others running by turns. As they neared the new ice, and where the black wastes of mingled cloud and water betokened the open sea, they would from time to time remove their hoods and listen intently for the animal's voice.

After a while Myouk became convinced, from signs or sounds, or both,—for they were inappreciable by Morton,—that the walrus were waiting for him in a small space of recently-open water that was glazed over with a few day's growth of ice ; and moving
gently on, they soon heard the characteristic bellow of a bull awuk. The walrus, like some of the higher order of beings to which he has been compared, is fond of his own music, and will lie for hours listening to himself. His vocalization is something between the mooing of a cow and the deepest baying of a mastiff : very round and full, with its barks or detached notes repeated rather quickly seven to nine times in succession.

The party now formed in single file, following in each other's steps ; and, guided by an admirable knowledge of ice-topography, wound behind hummocks and ridges in a serpentine approach toward a group of pond-like discolourations, recently-frozen ice-spots, but surrounded by firmer and older ice.

When within half a mile of these, the line broke, and each man crawled toward a separate pool—Morton on his hands and knees following Myouk. In a few minutes the walrus were in sight. They were five in number, rising at intervals through the ice in a body, and breaking it up with an explosive puff that might have been heard for miles. Two large grim-looking males were conspicuous as the leaders of the group.

Now for the marvel of the craft. When the walrus is above water, the hunter is flat and motionless; as he begins to sink, alert and ready for a spring. The animal's head is hardly below the water-line before every man is in a rapid run; and again, as if by instinct, before the beast returns, all are motionless behind protecting knolls of ice. They seem to know beforehand not only the time he will be absent, but the very spot at which he will re-appear. In this way, hiding and advancing by turns, Myouk, with Morton at his heels, has reached a plate of thin ice, hardly strong enough to bear them, at the very brink of the water-pool the walrus are curvetting in.

Myouk, till now phlegmatic, seems to waken with excitement. His coil of walrus-hide, a well-trimmed line of many fathoms' length, is lying at his side. He fixes one end of it in an iron barb, and fastens this loosely by a socket upon a shaft of unicorn's horn; the other end is already looped, or, as sailors would say, "doubled in a bight." It is the work of a moment. He has grasped the harpoon: the water is in motion. Puffing with pent-up respiration, the walrus is within a couple of fathoms close before him. Myouk rises slowly—his right arm thrown back, the left flat at his side. The walrus looks about him, shaking the water from his crest; Myouk throws up his left arm, and the animal, rising breast-high, fixes one look before he plunges. It has cost him all that curiosity can cost; the harpoon is buried under his left flipper.

Though the awuk is down in a moment, Myouk is running at desperate speed from the scene of his victory, paying off his coil freely, but clutching the end by its loop. He seizes as he runs a small stick of bone, rudely pointed with iron, and by a sudden movement drives it into the ice; to this he secures his line, pressing it down close to the ice-surface with his feet.

Now comes the struggle. The hole is dashed in mad commo-

CHAPTER
XXX.

The
struggle.
tion with the struggles of the wounded beast; the line is drawn tight at one moment, the next relaxed : the hunter has not left his station. There is a crash of the ice; and rearing up through it are two walruses, not many yards from where he stands. One of them, the male, is excited and seemingly terrified; the other, the female, collected and vengeful. Down they go again, after one grim survey of the field ; and on the instant Myouk has changed his position, carrying his coil with him and fixing it anew.

He has hardly fixed it before the pair have again risen, breaking up an area of ten feet diameter about the very spot he left. As they sink once more he again changes his place. And so the conflict goes on between address and force, till the victim, half exhausted, receives a second wound, and is played like a trout by the angler's reel.

Instinct
of the
walrus.
The instinct of attack which charaterizes the walrus is interesting to the naturalist, as it is characteristic also of the land animals, the pachyderms, with which he is classed. When wounded, he rises high out of the water, plunges heavily against the ice, and strives to raise himself with his fore-flippers upon its surface. As it breaks under his weight, his countenance assumes a still more vindictive expression, his bark changes to a roar, and the foam pours out from his jaws till it froths his beard.

Uses of
the tusks.
Even when not excited, he manages his tusks bravely. They are so strong that he uses them to grapple the rocks with, and climbs steeps of ice and land which would be inaccessible to him without their aid. He ascends in this way rocky islands that are sixty and a hundred feet above the level of the sea; and I have myself seen him in these elevated positions basking with his young in the cool sunshine of August and September.

He can strike a fearful blow; but prefers charging with his tusks in a soldierly manner. I do not doubt the old stories of the Spitzbergen fisheries and Cherie Island, where the walrus puts to flight the crowds of European boats. Awuk is the lion of the Danish Esquimaux, and they always speak of him with the highest respect.

I have heard of oomiaks being detained for days at a time at the crossings of straits and passages which he infested. Governor Flaischer told me that, in 1830, a brown walrus, which, according to the Esquimaux, is the fiercest, after being lanced and maimed near Upernavik, routed his numerous assailants, and drove them in fear to seek for help from the settlement. His movements were so violent as to jerk out the harpoons that were stuck into him. The governor slew him with great difficulty after several rifle-shots and lance-wounds from his whaleboat.

CHAPTER XXX.

On another occasion, a young and adventurous Inuit plunged his nalegeit into a brown walrus; but, startled by the savage demeanour of the beast, called for help before using the lance. The older men in vain cautioned him to desist. "It is a brown walrus," said they: "*Aûvek-Kaiok!*" "Hold back!" Finding the caution disregarded, his only brother rowed forward and plunged the second harpoon. Almost in an instant the animal charged upon the kayacker, ripping him up, as the description went, after the fashion of his sylvan brother, the wild boar. The story was told to me with much animation; how the brother remaining rescued the corpse of the brother dead; and how, as they hauled it up on the ice-floes, the ferocious beast plunged in foaming circles, seeking fresh victims in that part of the sea which was discoloured by his blood.

The Inuit and the walrus.

Some idea may be formed of the ferocity of the walrus, from the fact that the battle which Morton witnessed, not without sharing some of its danger, lasted four hours—during which the animal rushed continually at the Esquimaux as they approached, tearing off great tables of ice with his tusks, and showing no indications of fear whatever. He received upward of seventy lance wounds, —Morton counted over sixty; and even then he remained hooked by his tusks to the margin of the ice, unable or unwilling to retire. His female fought in the same manner, but fled on receiving a lance-wound.

Ferocity of the walrus.

The Esquimaux seemed to be fully aware of the danger of venturing too near; for at the first onset of the walrus they jumped back far enough to be clear of the broken ice. Morton described the last three hours as wearing, on both sides, the aspect of an unbroken and seemingly doubtful combat.

The method of landing the beast upon the ice, too, showed a great deal of clever contrivance. They made two pair of incisions in the neck, where the hide is very thick, about six inches apart and parallel to each other, so as to form a couple of bands. A

Method of landing the beast on the ice

CHAPTER
XXX.
line of cut hide, about a quarter of an inch in diameter, was passed under one of these bands and carried up on the ice to a firm stick well secured in the floe, where it went through a loop, and was then taken back to the animal, made to pass under the second band, and led off to the Esquimaux. This formed a sort of "double purchase," the blubber so lubricating the cord as to admit of a free movement. By this contrivance the beast, weighing some seven hundred pounds, was hauled up and butchered at leisure.

A grand
Ice-house.
The two sledges now journeyed homeward, carrying the more valued parts of their prize. The intestines and a large share of the carcass were buried up in the cavities of a berg; Lucullus himself could not have dreamed of a grander icehouse.

As they doubled the little island which stood in front of their settlement, the women ran down the rocks to meet them. A long hail carried the good news; and, as the party alighted on the beach, knives were quickly at work, the allotment of the meat being determined by well-understood hunter laws. The Esqui-

Division of
the game.
maux, however gluttonously they may eat, evidently bear hunger with as little difficulty as excess. None of the morning party had breakfasted; yet it was after ten o'clock at night before they sat down to dinner. "Sat down to dinner!" This is the only expression of our own gastrology which is applicable to an Esquimaux feast. They truly sit down, man, woman, and child, knife in hand, squatting cross-legged around a formidable joint,—say forty pounds,

Glutton
festival at
Etah.
—and, without waiting for the tardy coction of the lamp, falling to like college commoners after grace. I have seen many such feeds. Hans's account, however, of the glutton-festival at Etah is too characteristic to be omitted :—

"Why, Cappen Ken, sir, even the children ate all night; you know the little two-year-old that Awiu carried in her hood—the one that bit you when you tickled it? Yes. Well, Cappen Ken, sir, that baby cut for herself, with a knife made out of an iron hoop, and so heavy that it could barely lift it, and cut and ate, and ate and cut, as long as I looked at it."

"Well, Hans, try now and think; for I want an accurate answer : how much as to weight or quantity would you say that child ate ?" Hans is an exact and truthful man : he pondered a little and said that he could not answer my question. "But I

know this, sir, that it ate a *sipak*"—the Esquimaux name for the
lump which is cut off close to the lips—" as large as its own head;
and three hours afterward, when I went to bed, it was cutting off
another lump and eating still." A sipak, like the Dutch governor's
foot, is, however, a varying unit of weight.

CHAPTER
XXX.

CHAPTER XXXI.

AN AURORA—WOOD-CUTTING—FUEL ESTIMATE—THE STOVE-PIPES—THE
ARCTIC FIRMAMENT—ESQUIMAUX ASTRONOMY—HEATING APPARATUS—
METEORIC SHOWER—A BEAR—HASTY RETREAT—THE CABIN BY NIGHT—
SICKNESS INCREASING—CUTTING INTO THE BRIG—THE NIGHT WATCH.

CHAPTER
XXXI.

The rais-
ing of the
brig

"*October* 24, *Tuesday.*—We are at work that makes us realize
how short-handed we are. The brig was lifted for the third time
to-day, with double chains passed under her at low tide, both
astern and amid-ships. Her bows were already raised three feet
above the water, and nothing seemed wanting to our complete
success, when at the critical moment one of the after-shores parted,
and she fell over about five streaks to starboard. The slings were
hove-to by the crab, and luckily held her from going further, so
that she now stands about three feet above her flotation-line,
drawing four feet forward, but four and a half aft. She has righted
a little with the return of tide, and now awaits the freezing-in of
her winter cradle. She is well out of water ; and, if the chains
only hold, we shall have the spectacle of a brig, high and dry,
spending an Arctic winter over an Arctic ice-bed.

THE BRIG CRADLED.

"We shall be engaged now at the hold and with the housing
on deck. From our lodge-room to the forward timbers everything
is clear already. We have moved the carpenter's bench into our

little dormitorium; everywhere else it is too cold for handling
tools.

"9 P.M.—A true and unbroken auroral arch—the first we have
seen in Smith's Sound. It was colourless, but extremely bright.
There was no pendant from the lower curve of the arc; but
from its outer, an active wavy movement, dissipating itself into
barely-perceptible cirrhus, was broken here and there by rays
nearly perpendicular, with a slight inclination to the east. The
atmosphere was beautifully clear.

"*October* 26, *Thursday.*—The thermometer at 34° below zero,
but fortunately no wind blowing. We go on with the out-door
work. The gangway of ice is finished, and we have passed wooden
steam-tubes through the deck-house, to carry off the vapours of
our cooking-stove and the lighter impurities of the crowded cabin.

"We burn but seventy pounds of fuel a day, most of it in the
galley—the fire being allowed to go out between meals. We go
without fire altogether for four hours of the night; yet such is
the excellence of our moss walls and the air-proof of our tossut,
that the thermometer in-doors never indicates less than 45° above
zero, with the outside air at 30° below. When our housing is
arranged, and the main hatch secured with a proper weather-tight
screen of canvas, we shall be able, I hope, to meet the extreme
cold of February and March without fear.

"Darkness is the worst enemy we have to face; but we will
strive against the scurvy in spite of him, till the light days of sun
and vegetation. The spring-hunt will open in March, though it
will avail us very little till late in April.

"Wilson and Brooks are my principal subjects of anxiety; for
although Morton and Hans are on their backs, making four of our
ten, I can see strength of system in their cheerfulness of heart.
The best prophylactic is a hopeful, sanguine temperament; the
best cure, moral resistance—that spirit of combat against every
trial which is alone true bravery.

"*October* 27, *Friday.*—The work is going on; we are ripping
off the extra planking of our deck for fuel during the winter. The
cold increases fast, verging now upon 40° below zero, and in spite
of all my efforts we will have to burn largely into the brig. I
prepared for this two months ago, and satisfied myself, after a consultation with the carpenter, that we may cut away some seven or

CHAPTER XXXI.

eight tons of fuel without absolutely destroying her sea-worthiness. Ohlsen's report marked out the order in which her timbers should be appropriated to uses of necessity : 1. The monkey-rail; 2. The bulwarks ; 3. The upper ceiling of the deck; 4. Eight extra cross-beams ; 5. The flooring and remaining wood-work of the fore-castle ; 6. The square girders of the forepeak ; 7. The main-top-sail-yard and top-mast ; 8. The outside trebling or oak sheathing.

Fuel estimate.

"We had then but thirty buckets of coal remaining, and had already burnt up the bulkheads. Since then we have made some additional inroads on our stock ; but, unless there is an error in the estimate, we can go on at the rate of seventy pounds a day. Close house-keeping this; but we cannot do better. We must remodel our heating arrangements. The scurvy exacts a comfortable temperature and a drying one. Our mean thus far has been 47°—decidedly too low ; and by the clogging of our worn-out pipe it is now reduced to 42°.

"The ice-belt, sorry chronicler of winter progress, has begun to widen with the rise and fall of the sludgy water.

"*October* 31, *Tuesday.*—We have had a scene on board. We play many parts on this Arctic stage of ours, and can hardly be expected to be at home in all of them.

Cleaning and repairing the stoves.

"To-day was appropriated to the reformation of the stoves, and there was demand, of course, for all our ingenuity both as tinkers and chimney sweeps. Of my company of nine, Hans had the good luck to be out on the hunt, and Brooks, Morton, Wilson, and Goodfellow, were scurvy-ridden in their bunks. The other four and the commanding officer made up the detail of duty. First, we were to give the smoke-tubes of the stove a thorough cleansing, the first they have had for now seventeen months ; next, to reduce our *effete* snow-melter to its elements of imperfect pipes and pans ; and last, to combine the practicable remains of the two into one efficient system for warming and melting.

"Of these, the first has been executed most gallantly. 'Glory enough for one day!' The work with the scrapers on the heated pipes—for the accumulation inside of them was as hard as the iron itself till we melted it down—was decidedly unpleasant to our gentle senses ; and we were glad when it had advanced far enough to authorize a resort to the good old-fashioned country custom of firing. But we had not calculated the quantity of the gases, com-

bustible and incombustible, which this process was to evolve, with CHAPTER
duly scientific reference to the size of their outlet. In a word, XXXI.
they were smothering us, and, in a fit of desperation, we threw Extreme
open our apartment to the atmosphere outside. This made short discom-
work of the smoky flocculi; the dormitory decked itself on the
instant with a frosty forest of feathers, and it now rejoices in a
drapery as grey as a cygnet's breast.

"It was cold work reorganizing the stove for the nonce; but we
have got it going again, as red as a cherry, and my well-worn dog-
skin suit is drying before it. The blackened water is just beginning to drip, drip, drop, from the walls and ceiling, and the bed-
clothes and the table on which I write."

My narrative has reached a period at which everything like Progress
progress was suspended. The increasing cold and brightening night
stars, the labours, and anxieties, and sickness that pressed upon us, closed in.
—these almost engross the pages of my journal. Now and then
I find some marvel of Petersen's about the fox's dexterity as a
hunter; and Hans tells me of domestic life in South Greenland, or
of a seal-hunt and a wrecked kayack; or perhaps M'Gary repeats
his thrice-told tale of humour; but the night has closed down
upon us, and we are hibernating through it.

Yet some of these were topics of interest. The intense beauty Beauty of
of the Arctic firmament can hardly be imagined. It looked close the Arctic
above our heads, with its stars magnified in glory, and the very ment.
planets twinkling so much as to baffle the observations of our astronomer. I am afraid to speak of some of these night-scenes. I have
trodden the deck and the floes, when the life of earth seemed suspended, its movements, its sounds, its colouring, its companion-
ships; and as I looked on the radiant hemisphere, circling above
me as if rendering worship to the unseen Centre of light, I have
ejaculated in humility of spirit, "Lord, what is man that thou art
mindful of him?" And then I have thought of the kindly world
we had left, with its revolving sunshine and shadow, and the other
stars that gladden it in their changes, and the hearts that warmed
to us there, till I lost myself in memories of those who are not
—and they bore me back to the stars again.

The Esquimaux, like other nomads, are careful observers of the
heavenly bodies. An illustration of the confidence with which

CHAPTER XXXI. they avail themselves of this knowledge occurred while Peterson's party were at Tessiusak. I copy it from my journal of November 6.

Esquimaux astronomy. "A number of Esquimaux sought sleeping-quarters in the hut, much to the annoyance of the earlier visitors. The night was clear; and Petersen, anxious to hasten their departure, pointed to the horizon, saying it would soon be daylight. 'No,' said the savage; 'when that star there gets round to that point,' indicating the quarter of the heavens, 'and is no higher than this star,' naming it, 'will be the time to harness up my dogs.' Petersen was astounded; but he went out the next morning and verified the sidereal fact.

"I have been shooting a hare to-day up the ravine pointed out by Ootuniah. It has been quite a pleasant incident. I can hardly say how valuable the advice of our Esquimaux friends has been to us upon our hunts. This desert homestead of theirs is as Esquimaux observation of the seasons and winds thoroughly travelled over as a sheepwalk. Every movement of the ice, or wind, or season is noted; and they predict its influence upon the course of the birds of passage with the same sagacity that has taught them the habits of the resident animals.

"They foretold to me the exact range of the water off Cape Alexander during September, October, November, and December, and anticipated the excessive fall of snow which has taken place this winter, by reference to this mysterious water.

Their inscrutable means of discovering water. "In the darkest weather of October, when everything around is apparently congealed and solid, they discover water by means as inscrutable as the divining-rod. I was once journeying to Anoatok, and completely enveloped in darkness among the rolled-ice off Godsend Island. My dogs were suffering for water. September was half gone, and the water-streams both on shore and on the bergs had been solid for nearly a fortnight. Myouk, my companion, began climbing the dune-like summits of the ice-hills, tapping with his ice-pole and occasionally applying his ear to parts of the surface. He did so to three hills without any result, but at the fourth he called out, 'Water!' I examined the spot by hand and tongue, for it was too dark to see; but I could detect no liquid. Lying down and listening, I first perceived the metallic tinkle of a rivulet. A few minutes' digging brought us down to a scanty infiltration of drinkable water.

"*November 8, Wednesday.*—Still tinkering at our stove and ice-
melter; at last successful. Old iron pipes, and tin kettles, and all
the refuse kitchen-ware of the brig figure now in picturesque association, and rejoice in the title of our heating apparatus. It is
a great result. We have burnt from 6 A.M. to 10 P.M. but seventy-
five pounds, and will finish the twenty-fours with fifteen pounds
more. It has been a mild day, the thermometer keeping some
tenths above 13° below zero; but then we have maintained a temperature inside of 55° above. With our old contrivances we could
never get higher than 47°, and that without any certainty, though
it cost us a hundred and fifty-four pounds a day. A vast increase
of comfort, and still greater saving of fuel. This last is a most
important consideration. Not a stick of wood comes below without my eyes following it through the scales to the wood-stack. I
weigh it to the very ounce.

"The tide-register, with its new wheel-and-axle arrangements,
has given us out-door work for the day. Inside, after rigging the
stove, we have been busy chopping wood. The ice is already
three feet thick at our tide-hole.

"*November 15, Wednesday.*—The last forty-eight hours should
have given us the annual meteoric shower. We were fully prepared to observe it; but it would not come off. It would have
been a godsend variety. In eight hours that I helped to watch,
from nine of last night until five this morning, there were only
fifty-one shooting stars. I have seen as many between the same
hours in December and February of last winter.

"Our traps have been empty for ten days past; but for the
pittance of excitement which the visit to them gives, we might as
well be without them.

"The men are getting nervous and depressed. M'Gary paced
the deck all last Sunday in a fit of home-sickness, without eating
a meal. I do my best to cheer them; but it is hard work to hide
one's own trials for the sake of others who have not as many. I
am glad of my professional drill and its companion influence over
the sick and toil-worn. I could not get along at all unless I combined the offices of physician and commander. You cannot punish
sick men.

"*November 20, Monday.*—I was out to-day looking over the
empty traps with Hans, and when about two miles off the brig—

luckily not more—I heard what I thought was the bellow of a walrus on the floe-ice. 'Hark there, Hans!' The words were scarcely uttered before we had a second roar, altogether unmistakeable. No walrus at all: a bear, a bear! We had jumped to the ice-foot already. The day was just thirty minutes past the hour of noon; but, practised as we all are to see through the darkness, it was impossible to make out an object two hundred yards off. What to do?—we had no arms.

"We were both of us afraid to run, for we knew that the sight of a runner would be the signal for a chase; and, besides, it went to our hearts to lose such a providential accession to our means of life. A second roar, well pitched and abundant in volume, assured us that the game was coming nearer, and that he was large and of no doubt corresponding flavour. 'Run for the brig, Hans,'—he is a noble runner,—'and I will play decoy.' Off went Hans like a deer. Another roar; but he was already out of sight.

"I may confess it to these well-worn pages; there was something not altogether pleasant in the silent communings of the next few minutes; but they were silent ones.

"I had no stimulus to loquacity, and the bear had ceased to be communicative. The floe was about three-quarters of a tide; some ten feet it may be, lower than the ice-foot on which I lay. The bear was of course below my horizon. I began after a while to think over the reality of what I had heard, and to doubt whether it might not be after all a creature of the brain. It was very cold on that ice-foot. I resolved to crawl to the edge of it and peer under my hands into the dark shadow of the hummock-ridges.

"I did so. One look; nothing. A second; no bear after all. A third; what is that long rounded shade! Stained ice? Yes; stained ice. The stained ice gave a gross menagerie roar, and charged on the instant for my position. I had not even a knife, and did not wait to think what would have been appropriate if I had had one. I ran,—ran as I never expect these scurvy-stiffened knees to run again,—throwing off first one mitten and then its fellow to avoid pursuit. I gained the brig, and the bear my mittens. I got back one of them an hour afterward, but the other was carried off as a trophy in spite of all the rifles we could bring to the rescue.

"*November* 24, *Friday.*—The weather still mild. I attempted

to work to-day at charting. I placed a large board on our CHAPTER
XXXI.
stove, and pasted my paper to it. My lamp reposed on the lid
of the coffee-kettle, my instruments in the slush-boiler, my feet
in the ashpan ; and thus I drew the first coast-line of Grinnell
Land. The stove, by close watching and niggard feeding, has
burnt only sixty-five pounds in the last twenty-four hours. Of Division of
labour.
course, working by night I work without fire. In the daytime our
little company take every man his share of duty as he is able.
Poor Wilson, just able to stump about after his late attack of
scurvy, helps to wash the dishes. Morton and Brooks sew at
sledge-clothing, while Riley, M'Gary, and Ohlsen, our only really
able-bodied men, cut the ice and firewood.

"*December* 1, *Friday.*—I am writing at midnight. I have the Writing at
midnight.
watch from eight to two. It is day in the moonlight on deck,
the thermometer getting up again to 36° below zero. As I come
down to the cabin—for so we still call this little moss-lined igloë
of ours—every one is asleep, snoring, gritting his teeth, or talking
in his dreams. This is pathognomonic ; it tells of Arctic winter
and its companion, scurvy. Tom Hickey, our good-humoured,
blundering cabin-boy, decorated since poor Schubert's death with
the dignities of cook, is in that little dirty cot on the starboard
side ; the rest are bedded in rows, Mr. Brooks and myself chock
aft. Our bunks are close against the frozen moss wall, where we
can take in the entire family at a glance. The apartment measures Descrip-
tion of the
igloë on
board.
twenty feet by eighteen ; its height six feet four inches at one
place, but diversified elsewhere by beams crossing at different
distances from the floor. The avenue by which it is approached
is barely to be seen in the moss wall forward ; twenty feet of
air-tight space make misty distance, for the puff of outside-tem-
perature that came in with me has filled our atmosphere with
vesicles of vapour. The avenue—Ben-Djerback is our poetic
name for it—closes on the inside with a door well patched with
flannel, from which, stooping upon all-fours, you back down a
descent of four feet in twelve through a tunnel three feet high and
two feet six inches broad. It would have been a tight squeeze
for a man like Mr. Brooks when he was better fed and fatter.
Arrived at the bottom, you straighten yourself, and a second door
admits you into the dark and sorrowing hold, empty of stores, and
stripped to its naked ceiling for firewood. From this we grope

our way to the main hatch, and mount by a rude stairway of boxes into the open air.

"*December* 2, *Saturday.*—Had to put Mr. M'Gary and Riley under active treatment for scurvy. Gums retracted, ankles swollen, and bad lumbago. Mr. Wilson's case, a still worse one, has been brought under. Morton's is a saddening one; I cannot afford to lose him. He is not only one of my most intelligent men, but he is daring, cool, and everyway trustworthy. His tendon Achilles has been completely perforated, and the surface of the heel-bone exposed. An operation in cold, darkness, and privation, would probably bring on locked-jaw. Brooks grows discouraged: the poor fellow has scurvy in his stump, and his leg is drawn up by the contraction of the flexors at the knee-joint. This is the third case on board—the fourth, if I include my own—of contracted tendons.

"*December* 3, *Sunday.*—I have now on hand twenty-four hundred pounds of chopped wood, a store collected with great difficulty ; and yet, how inadequate a provision for the sickness and accident we must look for through the rest of the dark days ! It requires the most vigorous effort of what we call a healthy man to tear from the oak ribs of our stout little vessel a single day's firewood. We have but three left who can manage even this ; and we cannot spare more than one for the daily duty. Two thousand pounds will barely carry us to the end of January, and the two severest months of the Arctic year, February and March, will still be ahead of us.

"To carry us over these, our days of greatest anticipated trial, we have the outside oak sheathing,—or trebling, as the carpenters call it,—a sort of extra skin to protect the brig against the shocks of the ice. Although nearly three inches thick, it is only spiked to her sides, and carpenter Ohlsen is sure that its removal will not interfere with her sea-worthiness. Cut the trebling only to the water-line, and it will give me at least two and a half tons ; and with this—God willing—I may get through this awful winter, *and save the brig besides!*

"*December* 4, *Monday.*—That stove is smoking so that three of our party are down with acute inflammation of the eyes. I fear I must increase the diameter of our smoke-pipes, for the pitch-pine which we burn, to save up our oak for the greater cold, is redundantly charged with turpentine. Yet we do not want an

increased draught to consume our seventy pounds; the fiat, 'No
more wood' comes soon enough.

"Then for the night-watch. I have generally something on
hand to occupy me, and can volunteer for the hours before my
regular term. Everything is closed tight; I muffle myself in furs,
and write; or, if the cold denies me that pleasure, I read, or at
least think. Thank Heaven, even an Arctic temperature leaves the
mind unchilled. But in truth, though our hourly observations in
the air range between —46° and —30°, we seldom register less
than + 36° below.

"*December 5, Tuesday.*—M'Gary is no better, but happily has
no notion how bad he is. I have to give him a grating of our
treasured potatoes. He and Brooks will doubtless finish the two
I have got out, and then there will be left twelve. They are now
three years old, poor old frozen memorials of the dear land they
grew in. They are worth more than their weight in gold."

KAYACK, OR GREENLANDER'S CANOE.

CHAPTER XXXII.

ESQUIMAUX SLEDGES —BONSALL'S RETURN—RESULTS OF THE HUNT—RETURN
OF WITHDRAWING PARTY—THEIR RECEPTION—THE ESQUIMAUX ESCORT
—CONFERENCE—CONCILIATION — ON FIRE — CASUALTY — CHRISTMAS—
OLE BEN—A JOURNEY AHEAD—SETTING OUT—A DREARY NIGHT—
STRIKING A LIGHT—END OF 1854.

CHAPTER XXXII.

Bonsall and Petersen brought back by Esquimaux.

I WAS asleep in the forenoon of the 7th, after the fatigue of an extra night-watch, when I was called to the deck by the report of "Esquimaux sledges." They came on rapidly, five sledges, with teams of six dogs each, most of the drivers strangers to us; and in a few minutes were at the brig. Their errand was of charity: they were bringing back to us Bonsall and Petersen, two of the party that left us on the 28th of August.

Sad condition of the absent party.

The party had many adventures and much suffering to tell of. They had verified by painful and perilous experience all I had anticipated for them. But the most stirring of their announcements was the condition they had left their associates in, two hundred miles off, divided in their counsels, their energies broken, and their provisions nearly gone. I reserve for another page the history of their wanderings. My first thought was of the means of rescuing and relieving them.

I resolved to despatch the Esquimaux escort at once with such supplies as our miserably-imperfect stores allowed, they giving their pledge to carry them with all speed, and, what I felt to be much less certain, with all honesty. But neither of the gentlemen who had come with them felt himself in condition to repeat the journey. Mr. Bonsall was evidently broken down, and Petersen, never too reliable in emergency, was for postponing the time of setting out. Of our own party—those who had remained with the brig—M'Gary, Hans, and myself, were the only ones able to move, and of these M'Gary was now fairly on the sick list. We could not be absent for a single day without jeoparding the lives of the rest.

"*December* 8, *Friday*.--I am much afraid these provisions will

never reach the wanderers. We were busy every hour since
Bonsall arrived getting them ready. We cleaned and boiled and
packed a hundred pounds of pork, and sewed up smaller packages
of meat-biscuit, bread-dust, and tea; and despatched the whole,
some three hundred and fifty pounds, by the returning convoy.
But I have no faith in an Esquimaux under temptation, and I
almost regret that I did not accompany them myself. It might
have been wiser. But I will set Hans on the track in the morning; and, if I do not hear within four days that the stores are
fairly on their way, *coûte qui coûte*, I will be off to the lower bay
and hold the whole tribe as hostages for the absent party.

"Brooks is wasting with night-sweats; and my iron man,
M'Gary, has been suffering for two days with anomalous cramps
from exposure.

"These Esquimaux have left us some walrus-beef; and poor
little Myouk, who is unabated in his affection for me, made me a
special present of half a liver. These go of course to the hospital.
God knows they are needed there!

"*December 9, Saturday.*—The superabundant life of Northumberland Island has impressed Petersen as much as it did me. I
cannot think of it without recurring to the fortunes of Franklin's
party. Our own sickness I attribute to our civilized diet; had we
plenty of frozen walrus I would laugh at the scurvy. And it was
only because I was looking to other objects—summer researches,
and explorations in the fall with the single view to escape—that I
failed to secure an abundance of fresh food. Even in August I
could have gathered a winter's supply of birds and cochlearia.

"From May to August we lived on seal, twenty-five before the
middle of July, all brought in by one man: a more assiduous and
better organized hunt would have swelled the number without a
limit. A few boat-parties in June would have stocked us with
eider-eggs for winter use, three thousand to the trip; and the
snowdrifts would have kept them fresh for the breakfast-table. I
loaded my boat with ducks in three hours as late as the middle of
July, and not more than thirty-five miles from our anchorage.
And even now, here are these Esquimaux, sleek and oily with
their walrus-blubber, only seventy miles off. It is not a region
for starvation, nor ought it to be for scurvy.

"*December 12, Tuesday.*—Brooks awoke me at three this morning with the cry of 'Esquimaux again!' I dressed hastily, and, groping my way over the pile of boxes that leads up from the hold into the darkness above, made out a group of human figures,

CLIFFS, NORTHUMBERLAND ISLAND.

masked by the hooded jumpers of the natives. They stopped at the gangway, and, as I was about to challenge, one of them sprang forward and grasped my hand. It was Doctor Hayes. A few words, dictated by suffering, certainly not by any anxiety as to his reception, and at his bidding the whole party came upon deck. Poor fellows! I could only grasp their hands and give them a brother's welcome.

The absent party welcomed back.

"The thermometer was at minus 50°; they were covered with rime and snow, and were fainting with hunger. It was necessary to use caution in taking them below; for, after an exposure of such fearful intensity and duration as they had gone through, the

warmth of the cabin would have prostrated them completely.
They had journeyed three hundred and fifty miles ; and their last
run from the bay near Etah, some seventy miles in a right line, was
through the hummocks at this appalling temperature.

"One by one they all came in and were housed. Poor fellows !
as they threw open their Esquimaux garments by the stove, how
they relished the scanty luxuries which we had to offer them !
The coffee and the meat-biscuit soup, and the molasses and the
wheat bread, even the salt pork which our scurvy forbade the
rest of us to touch,—how they relished it all ! For more than
two months they had lived on frozen seal and walrus-meat.

"They are almost all of them in danger of collapse, but I have
no apprehension of life unless from tetanus. Stephenson is prostrate with pericarditis. I resigned my own bunk to Dr. Hayes,
who is much prostrated : he will probably lose two of his toes,
perhaps a third. The rest have no special injury.

"I cannot crowd the details of their journey into my diary. I
have noted some of them from Dr. Hayes's words ; but he has
promised me a written report, and I wait for it. It was providential that they did not stop for Petersen's return, or rely on the engagements which his Esquimaux attendants had made to them as
well as to us. The sledges that carried our relief of provisions
passed through the Etah settlement empty, on some furtive project, we know not what.

"*December* 13, *Wednesday.*—The Esquimaux who accompanied
the returning party are nearly all of them well-known friends.
They were engaged from different settlements, but, as they neared
the brig, volunteers added themselves to the escort till they numbered six drivers and as many as forty-two dogs. Whatever may
have been their motive, their conduct to our poor friends was certainly full of humanity. They drove at flying speed ; every hut
gave its welcome as they halted ; the women were ready without
invitation to dry and chafe their worn-out guests.

"I found, however, that there were other objects connected with
their visit to the brig. Suffering and a sense of necessity had involved some of our foot-worn absentees in a breach of hospitality.
While resting at Kalutunah's hut, they had found opportunity of
appropriating to their own use certain articles of clothing, fox-
skins and the like, under circumstances which admitted of justifi-

CHAPTER
XXXII.

Necessity
for recon-
ciliation.

cation only by the law of the more sagacious and the stronger. It was apparent that our savage friends had their plaint to make, or, it might be, to avenge.

"My first attention, after ministering to the immediate wants of all, was turned to the office of conciliating our Esquimaux benefactors. Though they wore their habitual faces of smiling satisfaction, I could read them too well to be deceived. Policy, as well as moral duty, have made me anxious always to deserve their respect; but I had seen enough of mankind in its varied relations not to know that respect is little else than a tribute to superiority, either real or supposed, and that, among the rude at least, one of its elements is fear.

Conference and
inquiry.

"I therefore called them together in stern and cheerless conference on the deck, as if to inquire into the truth of transactions that I had heard of, leaving it doubtful from my manner which was the party I proposed to implicate. Then, by the intervention of Petersen, I called on Kalutunah for his story, and went through a full train of questionings on both sides. It was not difficult to satisfy them that it was my purpose to do justice all round. The subject of controversy was set out fully, and in such a manner as to convince me that an appeal to kind feeling might have been substituted with all effect for the resort to artifice or force. I therefore, to the immense satisfaction of our stranger guests, assured them of my approval, and pulled their hair all round.

The dormitory.

"They were introduced into the oriental recess of our dormitory,—hitherto an unsolved mystery. There, seated on a red blanket, with four pork-fat lamps throwing an illumination over old worsted damask curtains, hunting-knives, rifles, beer-barrels, galley-stove, and chronometers, I dealt out to each man five needles, a file, and a stick of wood. To Kalutunah and Shunghu I gave knives and other extras; and in conclusion spread out our one remaining buffalo close to the stove, built a roaring fire, cooked a hearty supper, and by noonday they were sleeping away in a state of thorough content. I explained to them further that my people did not steal; that the fox-jumpers, and boots, and sledges were only taken to save their lives; and I thereupon returned them.

"The party took a sound sleep, and a second or rather a continuous feed, and left again on their return through the hummocks with apparent confidence and good humour. Of course they prigged a few knives and forks ;—but that refers itself to a national trait.

"*December* 23, *Saturday.*—This uncalculated accession of num- bers makes our little room too crowded to be wholesome : I have to guard its ventilation with all the severity that would befit a surgical ward of our Blockley Hospital. We are using the Esqui- maux lamp as an accessory to our stove : it helps out. the cooking and water-making, without encroaching upon our rigorously-meted allowance of wood. But the odour of pork-fat, our only oil, we have found to be injurious ; and our lamps are therefore placed outside the *tossut*, in a small room bulkheaded off for their use.

"This new arrangement gave rise yesterday to a nearly fatal disaster. A watch had been stationed in charge of the lamp, with the usual order of ' No uncovered lights.' He deserted his post. Soon afterward Hans found the cooking-room on fire. It was a horrible crisis ; for no less than eight of our party were absolutely nailed to their beds, and there was nothing but a bulkhead be- tween them and the fire. I gave short, but instant orders, station- ing a line between the tide-hole and the main hatch, detailing two men to work with me, and ordering all the rest who could move to their quarters. Dr. Hayes with his maimed foot, Mr. Brooks with his contracted legs, and poor Morton, otherwise among our best men, could do nothing.

"Before we reached the fire the entire bulkhead was in a blaze as well as the dry timbers and skin of the brig. Our moss walls, with their own tinder-like material and their light casing of inflammable wood, were entirely hidden by the flames. For- tunately the furs of the recently-returned party were at hand, and with them I succeeded in smothering the fire. But I was obliged to push through the blaze of our sailcloth bulkhead in order to defend the wall ; and in my anxiety to save time, I had left the cabin without either cap or mittens. I got through somehow or other, and tore down the canvas which hung against that dan- gerous locality. Our rifles were in this corner, and their muzzles pointing in all directions.

" The water now began to pass down ; but with the discharge of the first bucketful the smoke overcame me. As I found myself going I pushed for the hatchway, knowing that the bucket-line would *feel* me. Seeing was impossible; but, striking Ohlsen's legs as I fell, I was passed up to the deck, *minus* beard, eyebrows, and forelock, *plus* two burns on the forehead and one on each palm.

"In about three minutes after making way with the canvas the fire was got under, and in less than half an hour all was safe again. But the transition, for even the shortest time, from the fiery Shadrachian furnace-temperature below, to 46° below zero above, was intolerably trying. Every man suffered, and few escaped without frost-bitten fingers.

"The remembrance of the danger and its horrible results almost miraculously averted shocks us all. Had we lost our brig, not a man could have survived. Without shelter, clothing, or food, the thermometer almost 80° below the freezing point, and a brisk wind stirring, what hope could we have on the open ice field?

"*December* 25, *Christmas, Monday.*—All together again, the

returned and the steadfast, we sat down to our Christmas dinner. There was more love than with the stalled ox of former times; but of herbs none. We forgot our discomforts in the blessings which adhered to us still; and when we thought of the long road ahead of us, we thought of it hopefully. I pledged myself to give them their next Christmas with their homes; and each of us drank his 'absent friends' with ferocious zest over one-eighteenth part of a bottle of sillery,—the last of its hamper, and, alas! no longer *mousseux.*

"But if this solitary relic of festival days had lost its sparkle, we had not. We passed around merrily our turkeys roast and boiled, roast beef, onions, potatoes, and cucumbers, watermelons, and God knows what other cravings of the scurvy-sickened palate, with entire exclusion of the fact that each one of these was variously represented by pork and beans. Lord Peter himself was not more cordial in his dispensation of plum-pudding, mutton, and custard to his unbelieving brothers.

"M'Gary, of course, told us his story. We hear it every day, and laugh at it almost as heartily as he does himself. Cæsar Johnson is the guest of 'Ole Ben,' coloured gentlemen both, who do occasional white-washing. The worthies have dined stanchly on the dish of beans, browned and relished by its surmounting cube of pork. A hospitable pause, and, with a complacent wave of the hand, Ole Ben addresses the lady hostess—'Ole woman, bring on de resarve.' 'Ha'n't got no resarve.' 'Well, den,'—with a placid smile,—'bring on de beans!'

"So much for the Merrie Christmas. What portion of its mirth was genuine with the rest I cannot tell, for we are practised actors some of us; but there was no heart in my share of it. My thoughts were with those far off, who are thinking, I know, of me. I could bear my own troubles as I do my eider-down coverlet, for I can see myself as I am, and feel sustained by the knowledge that I have fought my battle well; but there is no one to tell of this at the home-table. Pertinacity, unwise daring, calamity—any of these may come up unbidden, as my name circles round, to explain why I am still away."

For some days before Christmas I had been meditating a Plan of a sledge journey. sledge journey to our Esquimaux neighbours. The condition of the little party under my charge left me no alternative, uncomfortable and hazardous as I knew that it must be. I failed in the first effort; but there were incidents connected with it which may deserve a place in this volume. I recur to my journal for a succinct record of my motives in setting out :—

"*December* 26, *Tuesday.*—The moon is nearly above the cliffs; the thermometer —57° to —45°, the mean of the past four days. In the midst of this cheering conjunction, I have ahead of me a journey of a hundred miles, to say nothing of the return. Worse than this, I have no landmarks to guide me, and must be my own pioneer.

"But there is a duty in the case. M'Gary and Brooks are To procure fresh meat sinking, and that rapidly. Walrus beef alone can sustain them, and it is to be got from the natives, and nowhere else. It is a merciful change of conditions that I am the strongest now of the whole party, as last winter I was the weakest. The duty of collecting food is on me. I shall go first to the lower Bay Esquimaux, and thence, if the hunt has failed there, to Cape Robertson.

"My misgivings are mostly on account of the dogs; for it is a rugged, hummocked drive of twenty-two hours, even with strong teams and Esquimaux drivers. We have been feeding them on salt meat, for we have had nothing else to give them, and they are out of health; and there are hardly enough of them at best to carry our lightest load. If one of these tetanoids should attack them on the road, it may be *game up* for all of us.

"But it is to be tried at last. Petersen will go with me, and we will club our wits. I do not fear the cold. We are impregnable in our furs while under exercise; though if we should be forced to walk, and give out, it might be a different matter. We shall have, I imagine, a temperature not much above —54°, and I do not see how we are to carry heating apparatus. We have load enough without it. Our only diet will be a stock of meat biscuit, to which I shall add for myself—Petersen's taste is less educated—a few rats, chopped up and frozen into the tallow-balls.

"*December* 28, *Thursday.*—I have fed the dogs the last two days on their dead brethren. Spite of all proverbs, *dog will eat dog* if properly cooked. I have been saving up some who died of fits, intending to use their skins, and these have come in very opportunely. I boil them into a sort of bloody soup, and deal them out twice a day in chunks and solid jelly; for of course they are frozen like quartz rock. These salt meats are absolutely poisonous to the Northern Esquimaux dog. We have now lost fifty odd, and one died yesterday in the very act of eating his reformed diet.

"The moon to-morrow will be for twelve hours above the horizon, and so nearly circumpolar afterward as to justify me in the attempt to reach the Esquimaux hunting-ground above Cape Alexander. Everything is ready, and, God willing, I start to-morrow, and pass the four hours' dog-halt in the untenanted hut of Anoatok. Then we have, as it may be, a fifteen, eighteen, or twenty hours' march, run and drive, before we reach a shelter among the heathen of the bay.

"*January* 2, *Tuesday.*—The dogs began to show signs of that accursed tetanoid spasm of theirs before we passed Ten-mile Ravine. When we reached Basalt Camp, six out of eight were nearly useless. Our thermometer was at —44°, and the wind was blowing sharply out of the gorge from the glacier. Petersen wanted to return, but was persuaded by me to walk on to the huts at Anoatok, in the hope that a halt might restore the animals. We reached them after a thirty miles' march.

"The sinuosities of this bay gave fearful travel: the broken ice clung to the rocks; and we could only advance by climbing up the ice-foot and down again upon the floe, as one or the other CHAPTER XXXII. gave us the chance of passing. It was eleven hours and over before we were at the huts, having made by sledge and foot-tramp forty-five miles. We took to the best hut, filled in its broken front with snow, housed our dogs, and crawled in among them.

"It was too cold to sleep. Next morning we broke down our door and tried the dogs again : they could hardly stand. A gale A gale now set in from the southwest, obscuring the moon and blowing very hard. We were forced back into the hut; but, after corking up all openings with snow and making a fire with our Esquimaux lamp, we got up the temperature to 30° below zero, cooked coffee, and fed the dogs freely. This done, both Petersen and myself, our clothing · frozen stiff, fell asleep through sheer exhaustion; the wind outside blowing death to all that might be exposed to its influence.

"I do not know how long we slept, but my admirable clothing kept me up. I was cold, but far from dangerously so ; and was in a fair way of sleeping out a refreshing night, when Petersen waked me with—'Captain Kane, the lamp's out.' I heard him with a thrill of horror. The gale had increased ; the cold was piercing, the darkness intense; our tinder had become moist, and Cold stormy wind and darkness. was now like an icicle. All our fire-arms were stacked outside, for no Arctic man will trust powder in a condensing temperature. We did not dare to break down our doorway, for that would admit the gale; our only hope of heat was in re-lighting our lamp. Petersen, acting by my directions, made several attempts to obtain fire from a pocket-pistol ; but his only tinder was moss, and our heavily stone-roofed hut or cave would not bear the concussion of a rammed wad.

"By good luck I found a bit of tolerably dry paper in my jumper ; and, becoming apprehensive that Petersen would waste our few percussion-caps with his ineffectual snappings, I determined to take the pistol myself. It was so intensely dark that I had to grope for it, and in doing so touched his hand. At that Striking fire. instant the pistol became distinctly visible. A pale bluish light, slightly tremulous but not broken, covered the metallic parts of it, the barrel, lock, and trigger. The stock too, was clearly discernible as if by the reflected light, and, to the amazement of both of us, the thumb and two fingers with which Petersen was holding it, the creases, wrinkles, and circuit of the nails clearly defined upon the skin. The phosphorescence was not unlike the ineffectual fire of the glow-worm. As I took the pistol my hand became illuminated also, and so did the powder-rubbed paper when I raised it against the muzzle.

"The paper did not ignite at the first trial, but, the light from it continuing, I was able to charge the pistol without difficulty, rolled up my paper into a cone, filled it with moss sprinkled over with powder, and held it in my hand while I fired. This time I succeeded in producing flame, and we saw no more of the phosphorescence. I do not stop for theory or argument to explain this opportune phenomenon; our fur clothing and the state of the atmosphere may refer it plausibly enough to our electrical condition.

"As soon as the wind had partially subsided, we broke out of the hut and tried the dogs toward Refuge Inlet; but the poor broken-down animals could not surmount the hummocks; and as a forced necessity to save their lives and ours, we resolved to push for the brig on foot, driving them before us. We made the walk of forty-four miles in sixteen hours, almost scudding before the gale, and arrived safely at 7 P.M. of Sunday; the temperature —40°."

With this fruitless adventure closed the year 1854.

CHAPTER XXXIII.

MODES OF LIFE—THE INSIDE DOG—PROJECTED JOURNEY—DOG-HABITS—
THE DARKNESS—RAW MEAT—PLANS FOR SLEDGING—THE SOUTH-EAST
WINDS—PLAN OF JOURNEY—A RELISHING LUNCH—ITINERARY—OUTFIT
—CARGO AND CLOTHING—KAPETAH AND NESSAK—FOOT-GEAR—THE FOX
TAIL—CARPET-KNIGHTS—BURNING CABLES.

"*January* 6, 1855, *Saturday.*—If this journal ever gets to be CHAPTER inspected by other eyes, the colour of its pages will tell of the XXXIII. atmosphere it is written in. We have been emulating the Esqui- Smoky lamps. maux for some time in everything else ; and now, last of all, this intolerable temperature and our want of fuel have driven us to rely on our lamps for heat. Counting those which I have added since the wanderers came back, we have twelve constantly going, with the grease and soot everywhere in proportion.

" I can hardly keep my charts and registers in anything like decent trim. Our beds and bedding are absolutely black, and our faces begrimmed with fatty carbon like the Esquimaux of South Greenland. Nearer to us, our Smith's Straits Esquimaux Esquimaux lamps. are much more cleanly in this branch of domestic arrangements. lamps. They attend their lamps with assiduous care, using the long ra- dicles of a spongy moss for wick, and preparing the blubber for its office by breaking up the cells between their teeth. The con- densed blubber, or, more properly, fat, of the walrus, is said to give the best flame.

" Our party, guided by the experience of the natives, use nearly Devices to the same form of wick, but of cotton. Pork fat, boiled to lessen conduct and diffuse its salt, is our substitute for blubber ; and, guided by a suggestion heat. of Professor Olmstead, I mix a portion of resin with the lard to increase its fluidity. Sundry devices in the way of metal rever- berators conduct and diffuse the heat, and so successfully, that a single wick will keep liquid ten ounces of lard with the air around at minus 30°.

" The heat given out by these burners is astonishing. One four-wicked lamp not very well attended gives us six gallons of

CHAPTER XXXIII.

Lamp for cooking.

water in twelve hours from snow and ice of a temperature of minus 40°, raising the heat of the cabin to a corresponding extent, the lamp being entirely open. With a line-wick—another Esquimaux plan—we could bake bread or do other cookery. But the crust of the salt and the deposit from the resin are constantly fouling the flame; and the consequence is, that we have been more than half the time in an atmosphere of smoke.

Effect of smoke on health.

" Fearing the effect of this on the health of every one, crowded as we are, and inhaling so much insoluble foreign matter without intermission, I have to-day reduced the number of lights to four— two of them stationary, and communicating by tin funnels with our chimney, so as to carry away their soot.

" Mr. Wilson has relapsed. I gave him a potash (saleratus) warm bath to-day, and took his place at watch. I have now seven hours' continuous watch at one beat.

Average temperature.

" *January* 12, *Friday.*—In reviewing our temperatures, the monthly and annual means startle me. Whatever views we may have theoretically as to the distribution of heat, it was to have been expected that so large a water area but thirty-five miles to the south-west by west of our position would tell upon our records, and this supposition was strengthened by the increased fall of snow, which was clearly due to the neighbourhood of this water.

The dogs.

" *January* 13, *Saturday.*—I am feeding up my few remaining dogs very carefully; but I have no meat for them except the carcasses of their late companions. These have to be boiled ; for in their frozen state they act as caustics, and, to dogs famishing as ours have been, frozen food often proves fatal, abrading the stomach and œsophagus. One of these poor creatures had been a a child's pet among the Esquimaux. Last night I found her in nearly a dying state at the mouth of our *tossut,* wistfully eyeing the crevices of the door as they emitted their forbidden treasures of light and heat. She could not move, but, completely subdued, licked my hand—the first time I ever had such a civilized greeting from an Esquimaux dog. I carried her in among the glories of the moderate paradise she aspired to, and cooked her a dead puppy soup. She is now slowly gaining strength, but can barely stand.

" I want all my scanty dog-force for another attempt to communicate with the bay settlements. I am confident we will find

Esquimaux there alive, and they *shall* help us. I am not satisfied with Petersen, the companion of my last journey ; he is too
cautious for the emergency. The occasion is one that calls for
every risk short of the final one that man can encounter. My
mind is made up, should wind and ice at all point to its successful accomplishment, to try the thing with Hans. Hans is completely subject to my will, careful and attached to me, and by
temperament daring and adventurous.

" Counting my greatest possible number of dogs, we have but
five at all to be depended on, and these far from being in condition for the journey. Toodla, Jenny—at this moment officiating
as wet-nurse—and Rhina, are the relics of my South Greenland
teams ; little Whitey is the solitary Newfoundlander ; one big
yellow and one feeble little black, all that are left of the powerful
recruits we obtained from our Esquimaux brethren.

" It is a fearful thing to attempt a dog-trot of near one hundred
miles, where your dogs may drop at any moment, and leave you
without protection from 50° below zero. As to riding, I do not
look to it ; we must run alongside of the sledge, as we do on
shorter journeys. Our dogs cannot carry more than our scanty
provisions, our sleeping bags, and guns.

" At home one would fear to encounter such hoopspined, spitting, snarling beasts as the Esquimaux dogs of Peabody Bay. But,
wolves as they are, they are far from dangerous : the slightest appearance of a missile or cudgel subdues them at once. Indispensable to the very life of their masters, they are treated, of course,
with studied care and kindness ; but they are taught from the earliest days of puppy-life a savoury fear that makes them altogether
safe companions even for the children. But they are absolutely
ravenous of everything below the human grade. Old Yellow, who
goes about with arched back, gliding through the darkness more
like a hyena than a dog, made a pounce the other day as I was
feeding Jenny, and, almost before I could turn, had gobbled down
one of her pups. As none of the litter will ever be of sledging use,
I have taken the hint, and refreshed Old Yellow with a daily morning puppy. The two last of the family, who will then, I hope, be
tolerably milk-fed, I shall reserve for my own eating.

" *January* 14, *Sunday.*—Our sick are about the same ; Wilson,
Brooks, Morton, M'Gary, and Riley unserviceable, Dr. Hayes get-

18

CHAPTER
XXXIII.
ting better rapidly. How grateful I ought to be that I, the weak-
ling of a year ago, am a well and helping man !

Twilight. "At noonday, in spite of the mist, I can see the horizon gap of
Charlotte Wood Fiord, between Bessie Mountain and the other
hills to the south-east, growing lighter ; its twilight is decidedly less
doubtful.   In four or five days we will have our noonday sun not
more than 8° below the horizon.   This depression, which was
Parry's lowest, enabled him by turning the paper toward the south
to read diamond type.   We are looking forward to this more pe-
numbral darkness as an era.   It has now been fifty-two days since
we could read such type, even after climbing the dreary hills.   One
hundred and twenty-four days with the sun below the horizon !
One hundred and forty before he reaches the rocky shadowing of
our brig !

"I found an overlooked godsend this morning,—a bear's head,
put away for a specimen, but completely frozen.   There is no in-
considerable quantity of meat adhering to it, and I serve it out
raw to Brooks, Wilson, and Riley.

Raw meat
useful in
scorbutic
disease. "I do not know that my journal anywhere mentions our habitua-
tion to raw meats, nor does it dwell upon their strange adaptation
to scorbutic disease.   Our journeys have taught us the wisdom of
the Esquimaux appetite, and there are few among us who do not
relish a slice of raw blubber or a chunk of frozen walrus-beef.
The liver of a walrus (awuktanuk) eaten with little slices of his fat,
—of a verity it is a delicious morsel.   Fire would ruin the curt,
pithy expression of vitality which belongs to its uncooked juices.
Charles Lamb's roast-pig was nothing to awuktanuk.   I wonder
that raw beef is not eaten at home.   Deprived of extraneous fibre,
it is neither indigestible nor difficult to masticate.   With acids and
condiments, it makes a salad which an educated palate cannot help
relishing ; and as a powerful and condensed heat-making and anti-
scorbutic food it has no rival.

"I make this last broad assertion after carefully testing its truth.
The natives of South Greenland prepare themselves for a long
journey in the cold by a course of frozen seal.   At Upernavik they
do the same with the narwhal, which is thought more heat-making
than the seal ; while the bear, to use their own expression, is
'stronger travel than all.'

"In Smith's sound, where the use of raw meat seems almost

inevitable from the modes of living of the people, walrus holds the
first rank.   Certainly this pachyderm, whose finely-condensed tissue
and delicately-permeating fat—oh ! call it not blubber—assimilate
it to the ox, is beyond all others, and is the very best fuel a man
can swallow.   It became our constant companion whenever we
could get it ; and a frozen liver upon our sledge was valued far
above the same weight of pemmican.   Now as I write, short of all
meat, without an ounce of walrus for sick or sound, my thoughts
recall the frost-tempered junks of this pachydermoid amphibion as
the highest of longed-for luxuries.

" My plans for sledging, simple as I once thought them, and
simple certainly as compared with those of the English parties,
have completely changed.   Give me an eight-pound reindeer-fur
bag to sleep in, an Esquimaux lamp with a lump of moss, a sheet-
iron snow-melter or a copper soup-pot, with a tin cylinder to slip
over it and defend it from the wind, a good *pièce de résistance* of
raw walrus-beef ; and I want nothing more for a long journey, if
the thermometer will keep itself as high as minus 30°.   Give me
a bear-skin bag and coffee to boot ; and with the clothes on my
back I am ready for minus 60°,—but no wind.

" The programme runs after this fashion.   Keep the blood in motion
without loitering on the march ; and for the halt, raise a snow-house ;
or, if the snow lie scant or impracticable, esconce yourself in a
burrow, or under the hospitable lee of an inclined hummock-slab.
The outside fat of your walrus sustains your little moss fire; its
frozen slices give you bread, its frozen blubber gives you butter,
its scrag ends make the soup.   The snow supplies you with water ;
and when you are ambitious of coffee there is a bagful stowed away
in your boot.   Spread out your bear bag, your only heavy move-
able ; stuff your reindeer bag inside, hang your boots up outside,
take a blade of bone, and scrape off all the ice from your furs.   Now
crawl in, the whole party of you, feet foremost ; draw the top of
your dormitory close, heading to leeward.   Fancy yourself in Sy-
baris ; and, if you are only tired enough, you may sleep—like St.
Lawrence on his gridiron, or even a trifle better.

" *January* 16, *Tuesday.*—Again the strange phenomena of the
south-east winds.   The late changes of the barometer ushered them
in, and all hands are astir with their novel influences.   With minus
16° outside, our cabin ceiling distils dirty drops of water, our beds

become doubly damp, and our stove oppressive. We are vastly more comfortable, and therefore more healthy, below hatches, when it is at —60° on deck than when it rises above —30°. The mean heat of our room since the return of the party is, as nearly as can be determined, + 48°.

"The sick generally are about the same; but Wilson has symptoms showing themselves that fill me with distress. The state of things on board begins to press upon me personally ; but by sleeping day-hours I manage well enough. Hans, Ohlsen, and myself are the only three sound men of the organized company.

" *January* 17, *Wednesday.*—There is no evading it any longer ; it has been evident for the past ten days that the 'present state of

things cannot last.' We require meat, and cannot get along without it. Our sick have finished the bear's head, and are now eating the condemned abscessed liver of the animal, including some intestines that were not given to the dogs. We have about three days' allowance ; thin chips of raw frozen meat, not exceeding four ounces in weight for each man per diem. Our poor fellows eat it with zest ; but it is lamentably little.

"Although I was unsuccessful in my last attempt to reach the huts with the dogs, I am far from sure that with a proper equipment it could not be managed by walking. The thought weighs upon me. A foot-travel does not seem to have occurred to my comrades ; and at first sight the idea of making for a point seventy-five miles by the shortest line from our brig, with this awfully cold darkness on, is gloomy enough.

" But I propose walking at first only as far as the broken hut at Anoatok (the 'wind-loved spot '), and giving our poor dogs a chance of refreshing there. After this, Hans and myself will force them forward as far as we can, with nothing but our sleeping gear, and spend the second night wherever they happen to break down. After that, we can manage the rest of the journey without any luggage but our personal clothing.

" It seems hard to sacrifice the dogs, not to speak of the rest of the party ; but the necessity is too palpable and urgent. As we are now, a very few deaths would break us up entirely. Still, the emergency would not move me if I did not feel, after careful, painful thought, that the thing can be accomplished. If, by the blessing of the Great Ruler, it should prove successful, the result will

secure the safety of all hands. No one knows as yet of my inten- CHAPTER
tion except Hans himself. I am quietly preparing a special outfit, XXXIII.
and will leave with the first return of moonlight.

" M'Gary, my relief, calls me; he has foraged out some raw M'Gary's
cabbage and spiced it up with curry-powder, our only remaining lunch.
pepper. This, with a piece of corn-bread,—no bad article either,
—he wants me to share with him. True to my old-times habitude,
I hasten to the cabbage,—cold roast-beef, Worcester sauce, a head
of endive, and a bottle—not one drop less—of Preston ale (I never
drink any other). M'Gary, ' bring on de beans !'

" *January* 18, *Thursday, midnight.*—Wind howling on deck,— Stormy
a number nine gale, a warm south-easter directly from the land. weather.
The mean temperature of this wind is —20°. Warm as this may
seem, our experience has taught us to prefer —40° with a calm to
—10° with a gale in the face.

" If we only had daylight, I should start as soon as the present
wind subsides, counting on a three days' intermission of atmospheric disturbance. But we have no moon, and it is too dark to
go tumbling about over the squeezed ice. I must wait.

" I alluded yesterday to my special equipment. Let me imagine
myself explaining to the tea-table this evening's outfit, promise,
and purposes."

I. *Itinerary.*—From brig *Advance*, Rensselaer Harbour, to the Itinerary.
Esquimaux huts of Etah Bay, following the line of ice-travel close
along the coast :—

	Miles.
1. From brig to Ten-mile Ravine	10
2. From Ten-mile Ravine to Basalt Camp	6
3. From Basalt Camp to Helen River	10
4. Helen's River to Devil's Jaws (off Godsend Island)	9
5. Godsend Island to Anoatok and Hummock Pass	7
6. Hummock Pass to Refuge Inlet	7
7. Refuge Inlet to Cape Hatherton	8
8. Cape Hatherton to Second Hummock Pass	12
9. Across Second Pass to south end of Littleton Island	8
10. South end of Littleton Island to Point Salvation	2
11. Point Salvation to Esquimaux huts	12
Total travel in miles	91

II. *Temperature.*—Mean, about —45°. Range —40° to —60°. Tempera-
III. *Resources.*—Five half-starved dogs ; Hans Cristian, Dr. ture.
Kane, a light sledge, and outfit.

IV. *Outfit.*—To encounter broken ice in the midst of darkness and at a temperature destructive to life, everything depends upon your sledge. Should it break down, you might as well break your own leg; there is no hope for you. Our sledge, then, is made of well-tried oak, dovetailed into a runner shod with iron. No metal is used besides, except the screws and rivets which confine the sledge to its runners. In this intense cold, iron snaps like glass, and no immovable or rigidly-fastened wood-work would stand for a moment the fierce concussions of a drive. Everything is put together with lashings of seal-skin, and the whole fabric is the skeleton framework of a sledge as flexible as a lady's work-basket, and weighing only forty pounds. On this we fasten a sacking-bottom of canvas, tightly stretched, like its namesake of the four-post bedstead, around the margin. We call this ticking the apron and cover; the apron being a flap of sixteen inches high, surrounding the cover, and either hanging loose at its sides like a valance, or laced up down the middle. Into this apron and cover you pack your cargo, the less of it the better; and then lace and lash the whole securely together.

V. *The cargo* may consist of,—1. A blanket-bag of fur, if you can get it; but on our present sleigh-ride, buffalo being too heavy and our reindeer-skins all destroyed by wet, I take an eider-down coverlet, adding—2. A pillow stuffed with straw or shavings, to be placed under the small of the back while sleeping; 3. An extra pair of boots; and 4. A snow saw.

"Superadd to these the ancient soup-pot, our soap-stone, kollopsut, one Esquimaux lamp, one lump of moss, one cup, and a tinder-box,—all these for the kitchen; a roll of frozen meat-biscuit, some frozen lady-fingers of raw hashed fox, a small bag of coffee, and twenty-four pieces of hard tack (ship's bread), for the larder; our fire-arms, and no less essential ice-poles;—all these, no more nor less, and you have the entirety of our outfit,—the means wherewith we are to track this icy labyrinth, under a frozen sky, for an uncertain asylum some ninety-three miles off.

"In general, eight powerful wolf-like dogs will draw such a cargo like the wind: I have but four wretched animals, who can hardly drag themselves.

"The clothing or personal outfit demands the nicest study of experience. Except a spare pair of boots, it is all upon the back, It requires the energies of tyrant custom to discipline a traveller into comfort under these Smith Sound temperatures; and, let him dress as he may, his drill will avail but little unless he has a windless atmosphere without and a heat-creating body within.

"Rightly clad, he is a lump of deformity waddling over the ice, unpicturesque, uncouth, and seemingly helpless. It is only when you meet him covered with rime, his face peering from an icy halo, his beard glued with frozen respiration, that you look with intelligent appreciation on his many-coated panoply against King Death.

"The Smith's Straits fox-skin jumper, or *kapetah*, is a closed shirt, fitting very loosely to the person, but adapted to the head and neck by an almost air-tight hood, *nessak*. The kapetah is put on from below; the arms of the man pass through the arms of the garment, and the head rises through a slit at the top; around this slit comes up the hood. It is passed over the head from behind and made to embrace the face and forehead. Underneath the kapetah is a similar garment, but destitute of the hood, which is put on as we do an inner shirt. It is made of bird-skins chewed in the mouth by the women till they are perfectly soft, and it is worn with this unequalled down next the body. More than five hundred auks have been known to contribute to a garment of this description.

" So far the bust and upper limbs. The lower extremities are guarded by a pair of bear-skin breeches, the *nannooke*,—the characteristic and national vestiture of this strange people. They are literal copies, and in one sense fac-similes, of the courtly knee-buckled ones of our grandfathers, but not rising above the crests of the pelvis, thus leaving exposed those parts which in civilized countries are shielded most carefully.

" I regard these strange and apparently-inconvenient articles of dress as unique. They compressed the muscles, which they affected to cover, in a manner so ungrandisonian that I leave a special description of their structure to my note-book.

" The foot-gear consists of a bird-skin short sock, with a padding of grass nicely distributed over the sole. Outside of this comes a bear-skin leg, sewed with great skill to the natural sole of the plantigrade, and abundantly wadded about the foot with dry non-conducting straw.

CHAPTER XXXIII.

Personal outfit.

Clothing— the "kapetah" and "nessak."

The "nannooke."

The foot gear.

" When this simple wardrobe is fully adjusted to the person, we understand something of the wonderful endurance of these Arctic primates. Wrangell called the Jacuti iron men, because they slept at —50° opposite the fire, with their backs exposed. Now, they of Smith's Sound have always an uncovered space between the waistband of the nannooke and the kapetah. To bend forward exposes the back to partial nudity; and, no matter what the attitude, the entire chest is open to the atmosphere from below. Yet in this well-ventilated costume the man will sleep upon his sledge with the atmosphere 93° below our freezing-point.

" The only additional articles of dress are a fox's tail, held between the teeth to protect the nose in a wind, and mitts of sealskin well wadded with sledge-straw.

" When I saw Kalutunah, who guided the return-party to the brig from Tesseusak, the temperature was below —50°. He was standing in the open air, comfortably scratching his naked skin, ready for a second journey ; which, in effect, he made eight hours afterward.

" We—I mean our party of American hyperboreans—are mere carpet-knights aside of these indomitable savages. Experience has taught us to follow their guidance in matters of Arctic craft ; but we have to add a host of European appendages to their out-door clothing.

" Imagine me, then, externally clad as I have described, but with furs and woollens layer upon layer inside, like the shards of an artichoke, till I am rounded into absolute obesity. Without all this, I cannot keep up my circulation on a sledge ; nor indeed without active exercise, if the thermometer is below —54°, the lowest at which I have taken the floes. I have to run occasionally, or I should succumb to the cold."

So much for my resources of travel, as I have thrown them together from different pages of my journal. The apparent levity with which I have detailed them seems out of keeping with the date under which they stand. In truth, I was in no mirthful humour at any time during the month of January. I had a grave office to perform, and under grave responsibilities ; and I had measured them well. I come back, after this long digression, to my daily record of anxieties :—

" *January* 19 *Friday.*—The declining tides allow the ice

beneath the ship to take the ground at low-water. This occasions, CHAPTER
XXXIII. of course, a good deal of upheaval and some change of position along the ice-tables in which we are cradled. Mr. Ohlsen reports Presence
of the ice a bending of our cross-beams of six inches, showing that the pressure is becoming dangerous. Anything like leakage would be disastrous in the present condition of the party. Our cabin-floor, however, was so elevated by our carpenter's work of last fall, that it could not be flooded more than six inches; and I hope that the under-bottom ice exceeds that height. At any rate we can do nothing, but must await the movements of the floe. March is to be our critical month.

"George Whipple shows swelled legs and other symptoms of the Increasing
illness. enemy; Riley continues better; Brooks weak, but holding his ground; Wilson no better; if anything, worse. I am myself so disabled in the joints as to be entirely unfit to attend to the traps or do any work. I shall try the vapour-bath and sweat, Indian fashion.

"*January* 21, *Sunday.*—We have been using up our tar-laid Turning
cables. hemp hawsers for nearly a week, by way of eking out our firewood, and have reduced our consumption of pitch-pine to thirty-nine pounds a day. But the fine particles of soot throughout the room have affected the lungs of the sick so much that I shall be obliged to give it up. I am now trying the Manilla; but it consumes too rapidly; with care we may make something of it.

"*January* 22, *Monday.*—Busy preparing for my trip to the lower Height of
barometer Esquimaux settlement. The barometer remains at the extraordinary height of 30·85,—a bad prelude to a journey!

"Petersen caught another providential fox. We divided him into nine portions, three for each of our scurvied patients. I am off."

CHAPTER XXXIV.

A BREAK-DOWN—THE HUT IN A STORM—TWO NIGHTS IN THE HUT—FROST
AGAIN — THE BACK TRACK — HEALTH ROLL — MEDICAL TREATMENT —
HEALTH FAILING— UNSUCCESSFUL HUNT—THE LAST BOTTLES.

CHAPTER
XXXIV.

A break-
down.

"*January* 29, *Monday.*—The dogs carried us to the lower curve of the reach before breaking down. I was just beginning to hope for an easy voyage, when Toodla and the Big Yellow gave way nearly together—the latter frightfully contorted by convulsions. There was no remedy for it; the moon went down, and the wretched night was upon us. We groped along the ice-foot, and after fourteen hours' painful walking, reached the old hut.

Darkness
and cold.

"A dark water-sky extended in a wedge from Littleton to a point north of the cape. Everywhere else the firmament was obscured by mist. The height of the barometer continued as we left it at the brig, and our own sensations of warmth convinced us that we were about to have a snow-storm.

Esqui-
maux.

"We hardly expected to meet the Esquimaux here, and were not disappointed. Hans set to work at once to cut out blocks of snow to close up the entrance to the hut. I carried in our blubber-lamp, food, and bedding, unharnessed the dogs, and took them into the same shelter. We were barely housed before the storm broke upon us.

The hut in
a storm.

"Here, completely excluded from the knowledge of things without, we spent many miserable hours. We could keep no note of time, and, except by the whirring of the drift against the roof of our kennel, had no information of the state of the weather. We slept, and cooked coffee, and drank coffee, and slept, and cooked coffee, and drank again ; and when by our tired instincts we thought that twelve hours must have passed, we treated ourselves to a meal,—that is to say, we divided impartial bites out of the raw hind-leg of a fox, to give zest to our biscuits spread with frozen tallow.

"We then turned in to sleep again, no longer heedful of the storm, for it had now buried us deep in with the snow.

" But, in the mean time, although the storm continued, the tem- CHAPTER
XXXIV.
peratures underwent an extraordinary change. I was awakened
by the dropping of water from the roof above me; and, upon Change of
tempera-
ture.
turning back my sleeping-bag, found it saturated by the melting of
its previously-condensed hoar-frost. My eider-down was like a
wet swab. I found afterward that the phenomenon of the warm
south-east had come unexpectedly upon us. The thermometers at
the brig indicated +26°; and, closer as we were to the water, the
weather was probably above the freezing point.

" When we left the brig—how long before it was we did not
know—the temperature was —44°. It had risen at least 70°. I Its effects
defy the strongest man not to suffer from such a change. A close,
oppressive sensation attacked both Hans and myself. We both
suffered from cardiac symptoms, and are up to this moment under
anxious treatment by our comrades. Mr. Wilson, I find, has had
spasmodic asthma from it here, and Brooks has had a renewal of
his old dyspnœa.

"In the morning—that is to say, when the combined light of
the noonday dawn and the circumpolar moon permitted our escape
—-I found, by comparing the time as indicated by the Great Bear Computa-
with the present increased altitude of the moon, that we had been tion of
time by
pent up nearly two days. Under these circumstances we made the moon
directly for the hummocks, *en route* for the bay. But here was a and stars
disastrous change. The snow had accumulated under the windward sides of the inclined tables to a height so excessive that we
buried sledge, dogs, and drivers, in the effort to work through. It
was all in vain that Hans and I harnessed ourselves to, or lifted,
levered, twisted, and pulled. Utterly exhausted and sick, I was
obliged to give it up. The darkness closed in again, and with
difficulty we regained the igloë.

" The ensuing night brought a return to hard freezing tempera- Frost
tures. Our luxurious and downy coverlet was a stiff, clotted lump again.
of ice. In spite of our double lamp, it was a miserable halt. Our
provisions grew short; the snow kept on falling, and we had still
46 miles between us and the Esquimaux.

" I determined to try the land-ice (ice-foot) by Fog Inlet; and we
worked four hours upon this without a breathing-spell,—utterly in
vain. My poor Esquimaux, Hans, adventurous and buoyant as he
was, began to cry like a child. Sick, worn out, strength gone, dogs

fast and floundering, I am not ashamed to admit that, as I thought of the sick men on board, my own equanimity also was at fault.

"We had not been able to get the dogs out, when the big moon appeared above the water-smoke. A familiar hill, 'Old Beacon Knob,' was near. I scrambled to its top and reconnoitred the coast around it. The ridge about Cape Hatherton seemed to jut out of a perfect chaos of broken ice. The water—that inexplicable North Water—was there, a long black wedge, overhung by crapy wreaths of smoke, running to the northward and eastward. Better than all yet,—could I be deceived?—a trough through the hummock-ridges, and level plains of ice stretching to the south!

"Hans heard my halloo, and came up to confirm me. But for our disabled dogs and the waning moonlight, we could easily have made our journey. It was with a rejoiced heart that I made my way back to our miserable little cavern, and re-stuffed its gaping entrance with the snow. We had no blubber, and of course no fire ; but I knew that we could gain the brig, and that, after refreshing the dogs and ourselves, we could now assuredly reach the settlements.

"We took the back track next morning over Bedevilled Reach upon the mid-ice floes, and reached the brig by 4 P.M. on Friday ; since when I have been so stiff and scorbutic, so utterly used up, that to-day gives me a first return to my journal.

"*January* 30, *Tuesday.*—My companions on board felt all my disappointment at bringing back no meat ; but infinite gladness took the place of regret when they heard the great news of a passage through the hummocks. Petersen began at once to busy himself with his wardrobe ; and an eight-day party was organized almost before we turned in, to start as soon as the tempestuous weather subsides and the drifts settle down. It is four days since, but as yet we dare not venture out.

"That there is no time for delay, this health-table will show :—

"Henry Brooks : Unable any longer to go on deck : we carry him with difficulty from his berth to a cushioned locker.

"M'Gary : Less helpless ; but off duty, and saturated with articular scurvy.

Mr. Wilson : In bed. Severe purpuric blotches, and nodes in limbs. Cannot move.

"George Riley : Abed ; limbs less stiff, gums better, unable to do duty.

"Thomas Hickey (our cook) : Cannot keep his legs many days more ; already swelled and blistered.

"William Morton : Down with a frozen heel ; the bone exfoliating.

"Henry Goodfellow : Scurvied gums, but generally well.

"Dr. Hayes is prostrate with his amputated toes ; Sontag just able to hobble. In a word, our effective force is reduced to five, —Mr. Ohlsen, Mr. Bonsall, Petersen, Hans, and the Commander ; and even of these some might, perhaps, be rightfully transferred to the other list. We have the whole burden of the hourly observations and the routine of our domestic life, even to the cooking, which we take in rotation.

" . . . . . Still this remarkable temperature ; the barometer slowly librating between 29·20 and the old 30·40. Snow falling : wind from the south-west, hauling by the west to north : yet the thermometer at —10° and +3°. We long anxiously for weather to enable our meat-party to start. The past two days our sick have been entirely out of meat : the foxes seem to avoid

FOX-TRAPS.

our traps. I gave Wilson one raw meal from the messeter muscle which adhered to another old bear's head I was keeping for a specimen. But otherwise we have had no anti-scorbutic for three days.

"Among other remedies which I oppose to the distemper, I have commenced making sundry salts of iron; among them the citrate and a chlorohydrated tincture. We have but one bottle of brandy left: my applying a half-pint of it to the tincture shows the high value I set upon this noble chalybeate. My nose bled to-day, and I was struck with the fluid brickdusty poverty of the blood. I use iron much among my people: as a single remedy it exceeds all others, except only the specific of raw meat: potash for its own action is well enough to meet some conditions of the disease, and we were in the habit of using freely an extemporaneous citrate prepared from our lime-juice; but, as our cases became more reduced and complicated with hemorrhages, iron was our one great remedy.

"*January* 31, *Wednesday.*—The weather still most extraordinary. The wind has hauled around, and is now blowing from the north and north-east, usually our coldest and clearest quarter. Yet the diffused mist continues, the snow falls, and the thermometer never records below —20°.

"Our sick are worse; for our traps yield nothing, and we are still without fresh food. The absence of raw fox-meat for a single day shows itself in our scurvy. Hemorrhages are becoming common.

My crew,—I have no crew any longer,—the tenants of my bunks cannot bear me to leave them a single watch. Yet I cannot make Petersen try the new path which I discovered and found practicable. Well, the wretched month is over. It is something to be living, able to write. No one has yet made the dark voyage, and January the 31st is upon us.

"*February* 2, *Friday.*—The weather clears, the full moon shows herself, the sledge is packed, and Petersen will start to-morrow.

"*February* 3, *Saturday.*—He is gone with Hans. A bad time with Brooks, in a swoon from exhaustion!

"*February* 4, *Sunday.*—Mr. Ohlsen breaks down: the scurvy is in his knee, and he cannot walk. This day, too, Thomas Hickey, our acting cook, gives way completely. I can hardly realize that among these strong men I alone should be the borne-up man,—the only one, except Mr. Bonsall, on his legs. It sometimes makes me tremble when I think how necessary I am to sustain this state of things. It is a Sunday thought, that it must be for some wise and good end I am thus supported.

"Made an unsuccessful hunt out toward Mary River; but, although the daylight was more than ample, tracked nothing. Our sick have been on short commons for the last five days; and we have given up the traps for want of fresh meat to bait them with. The fiord looked frightfully desolate. Where once was a torrent fighting among ice and rocks, is now a tunnel of drifted snow. Mary Leiper River is a sinuous ravine, swept dry by the gales which issue from the hills, and its rocky bed patched with the frozen relics of its waters.

"I made a dish of freshened codfish-skin for Brooks and Wilson; they were hungry enough to relish it. Besides this, I had kept back six bottles of our Scotch ale to meet emergencies, and I am dealing these out to them by the wine-glass. It is too cold for brewing in our apartment: the water freezes two feet above the floor. I have given up my writing-table arrangements, and my unfortunate study-lamp is now fixed under a barrel to see if it cannot raise a fermenting temperature. I shall turn brewer to-morrow if it succeeds."

CHAPTER XXXV.

THE FIRE-CLOTHED BAG—THE WRAITH—COOKERY—A RESPITE—THE
COMING DAWN — THE TRUST — PROSPECTS — ARGUMENT — COLOURED
SKIES—STOVE-FITTING.

CHAPTER
XXXV.

Return of
Petersen
and Hans.

A slight
Improve-
ment.

"*February 6, Tuesday.*—At ten, last evening, not long after my journal-record, I heard voices outside. Petersen and Hans had returned. I met them silently on deck, and heard from poor Petersen how he had broken down. The snows had been increasing since my own last trial,—his strength had left him ; the scurvy had entered his chest ; in a word, he had failed, and Hans could not do the errand alone. Bad enough !

"But to-day our fortunes are on the mend. It has been beautifully clear ; and for the first time a shade of bronzed yellow has warmed our noonday horizon, with a gentle violet running into rich brown clouds, totally unlike our night skies. Hans and I started for a hunt,—one to explore new grounds, the other to follow tracks in the recent snow. The result was two rabbits, the first-fruits of the coming light, and the promise of more in the numerous feeding-traces among the rocks of Charlotte Wood Fiord. The meat, our first for ten days, was distributed raw. By keeping the rabbits carefully covered up, they reached the ship sufficiently unfrozen to give us about a pint of raw blood. It was a grateful cordial to Brooks, Wilson, and Riley.

Misty
weather
and a gale.

"*February 7, Wednesday.*—The weather was misty when I went out this morning, and the twinkling of the stars confirmed Petersen's prognostic of a warm south-easter before evening. Mist, stars, and Petersen were right. The gale is upon us, darkening the air with snow, and singing ih wild discords through the rigging.

"It is enough to solemnize men of more joyous temperament than ours has been for some months. We are contending at odds with angry forces close around us, without one agent or influence within 1800 miles whose sympathy is on our side.

"My poor fellows, most of them bred in the superstitions of the sea, are full of evil bodings. We have a large old seal-skin bag on deck, that holds our remnant of furs. It hangs from the main-stay, and we have all of us jested in the times of ordinary dark-ness about its grotesque physiognomy. To-night it has worn a new character. One of the crew, crawling outside, saw it swing-ing in the storm with furious energy, and pounding against the mast like a giant boxing-glove. It glowed, too, with supernatural light; and he is sure it spoke some dreadful message, though he was too much perturbed to give it audience. There is no reason-ing with him about it, and his messmates' laugh, as they attempt to ridicule his fear, is like the ghost story merriment of a nursery circle."

It was an ugly and withal an anxious night. Mr. Goodfellow, the youngest of our party, had left the cabin soon after dinner for an inland stroll with his gun, and he had not returned when the scanty twilight closed before its time. The wind blew off the coast, piling the snow in great hills and changing the whole face of the floe. As the darkness wore on we became uneasy, and at last alarmed, at his absence. We burnt bluelights and Roman candles to guide him through the night; but it was six o'clock in the morning before he came in, happily none the worse for his adventure.

Honest Tom Hickey had been on the deck reconnoitring for him while the gale was at its height. He came down to the mess just before the alarm of the thumping fur-bag, declaring he had seen Mr. Goodfellow moving cautiously along the land-ice and jumping down on the field below. He hurried his tea-things to give him a warm supper, but no one came. In the result, though Tom volunteered to make search at the spot where he had seen his messmate, and Riley offered to accompany him, and I myself looked diligently afterward with a lantern for some hundreds of yards around, we found nothing but fresh-drifted snow, without the trace of a human foot. Tom had seen a *wraith ;* he believes it religiously, and associates its mysterious advent with the lumi-nous fur-bag.

"There must be some warm southern area over which this wind comes, some open water, it may be, that is drawing nearer to us, to minister after a time to our escape. But we must go alone. I have given up all hope of rescuing our little vessel. She has been

19

CHAPTER XXXV. safeguard and home for us through many lengthened trials ; but her time has come. She can never float above the waves again.

No hope for the brig. How many of us are to be more fortunate ?

Hans goes to hunt. " *February* 9, *Friday.*—Still no supplies. Three of us have been out all day, without getting a shot. Hans thinks he saw a couple of reindeer at a distance ; and his eyes rarely deceive him. He will try for them to-morrow. I have fitted out for him a tent and a sleeping-bag on the second table-land ; and the thermometer is now so little below zero that he will be able to keep the field for a steady hunt. Our sick are sinking for want of fresh food. It is the only specific : I dislike to use the un-philosophical term ; but in our case it is the true one. In large

Value of fresh meat. quantities it dissipates the disease ; in ordinary rations it prevents its occurrence ; in small doses it checks it while sustaining the patient. We have learned its value too well to waste it; every part of every animal has its use. The skin makes the basis of a soup, and the claws can be boiled to a jelly. Lungs, larynx, stomach, and entrails, all are available. I have not permitted myself to taste more than an occasional entrail of our last half-dozen rabbits. Not that I am free from symptoms of the univer-sal pest. I am conscious of a stiffness in the tendons, and a shortness of breath, and a weariness of the bones, that should naturally attend the eruption which covers my body. But I have

Symptoms of the past. none of the more fearful signs. I can walk with energy after I get warmed up, I have no bleeding of the gums, and, better than all, thank God, I am without that horrible despondency which the disease nourishes and feeds on. I sleep sound and dream pleasantly—generally about successes in the hunt, or a double ration of reindeer or ptarmigan.

A feathery quilt. " It has been a true warm south-easter. The housing-sails have been blown off by the storm, and 'we are buried up in a snow-drift. But one such feathery quilt is worth all the canvas cover-ing in the world.

" My brewing apparatus has worked well, thanks to stove and storm ; and I have on hand now as unsavoury a dose of flax-seed and quinine as was ever honoured by the name of beer.

Three days' re-spite. " *February* 10, *Saturday.*—Three days' respite ! Petersen and myself have made a fruitless hunt ; but Hans comes in with three rabbits. Distribution : the blood to Ohlsen and Thomas ; and to the other eight of the sick men full rations ; consuming a rabbit and a half. I cannot risk the depression that a single death would bring upon the whole party, and have to deal unfairly with those who can still keep about to save the rest from sinking. Brooks and Ohlsen are in a precarious condition : they have lost the entire mucous membrane of the alveoli ; and Mr. Wilson requires special attendance every hour to carry him through.

"The day is beginning to glow with the approaching sun. The south at noon has almost an orange tinge. In ten days his direct rays will reach our hill tops ; and in a week after he will be dispensing his blessed medicine among our sufferers.

"*February* 12, *Monday.*—Hans is off for his hunting-lodge, 'over the hills and far away,' beyond Charlotte Wood Fiord. I have sent Godfrey with him, for I fear the boy has got the taint like the rest of us, and may suffer from the exposure. He thinks he can bring back a deer, and the chances are worth the trial. We can manage the small hunt, Petersen and I, till he comes back, unless we break down too. But I do not like these symptoms of mine, and Petersen is very far from the man he was. We had a tramp to-day, both of us, after an imaginary deer,—a *bennisoak* that has been supposed for the last three days to be hunting the neighbourhood of the waterpools of the big fiord, and have come back jaded and sad. If Hans gives way, God help us ! "

It is hardly worth while to inflict on the reader a succession of journal-records like these. They tell of nothing but the varying symptoms of sick men, dreary, profitless hunts, relieved now and then by the signalized incident of a killed rabbit or a deer seen, and the longed-for advent of the solar light.

We worked on board—those of us who could work at all—at arranging a new gangway with a more gentle slope, to let some of the party crawl up from their hospital into the air. We were six, all told, out of eighteen, who could affect to hunt, cook, or nurse.

Meanwhile we tried to dream of commerce with the Esquimaux, and open water, and home. For myself, my thoughts had occupation enough in the question of our closing labours. I never lost my hope. I looked to the coming spring as full of responsibilities ; but I had bodily strength and moral tone enough to look through them to the end. A trust, based on experience as well as on promises, buoyed me up at the worst of times. Call it fatalism, as you ignorantly may, there is that in the story of every eventful life which teaches the inefficiency of human means and the present control of a Supreme Agency. See how often relief has come at the moment of extremity, in forms strangely unsought, almost at the time unwelcome ; see, still more, how the back has been strengthened to its increasing burden, and the heart cheered by some conscious influence of an unseen Power.

Thinking quietly over our condition, I spread out in my diary the results which it seemed to point to. After reviewing our sick list and remarking how little efficiency there was in the other members of the party, my memorandum went on :—

" We have three months before us of intense cold. We have a large and laborious outfit to arrange,—boats, sledges, provisions, and accoutrements for a journey of alternating ice and water of more than 1300 miles. Our carpenter is among the worst of our invalids. Supposing all our men able to move, four at least of them must be carried by the rest, three in consequence of amputation, and one from frost-wounds ; and our boats must be sledged over some sixty or perhaps ninety miles of terrible ice before launching and loading them. Finally, a part of our force, whatever it may be, must be detailed to guard our property from the Esquimaux while the other detachments are making their successive trips to the open water. So much for the shadow of the picture !

" But it has two sides ; and, whether from constitutional temperament or well reasoned argument, I find our state far from desperate. I cheer my comrades after this fashion :—

" 1. I am convinced, from a careful analysis of our disease, that under its present aspects it is not beyond control. If with the aid of our present hunting resources, or by any providential accession to them, I can keep the cases from rapid depression, next month ought to give us a bear, and in the meantime Hans may find a deer ; and, with a good stock of fresh meat even for a few days, I can venture away from the vessel to draw supplies from the Esquimaux at Etah. I should have been there before this, if I could have been spared for forty-eight hours. We want nothing but meat.

" 2. The coming of the sun will open appliances of moral help CHAPTER XXXV.
to the sick, and give energy to the hygienic resorts which I am
arranging at this moment. Our miserable little kennel, where The coming of the sun.
eighteen are crowded into the space of ten, is thoroughly begrimed
with lampblack from the inevitable smoke of our fuel. The weather has prevented our drying and airing the sleeping-gear. The
floor is damp from the conducted warmth of the sea-water under
us, melting the ice that has condensed everywhere below. Sunshine and dry weather will cure all this. I have window-sash
ready to fix over the roof and southern side of the galley-house ;
and our useless daguerreotype plates, tacked over wooden screens,
make admirable mirrors to transfer the sun-rays into the cabin. I
have manufactured a full-draught pipe for our smoky stove. Chlo-
ride of sodium must do the rest.

" 3. While we live we will stick together ; one fate shall belong Resolution.
to us all, be it what it may.

" There is comfort in this review ; and, please God in his bene- Comfort and hope.
ficent providence to spare us for the work, I will yet give one more
manly tug to search the shores of Kennedy Channel for memorials
of the lost ; and then our duties over here, and the brig still prison-
bound, enter trustingly upon the task of our escape.

" *February* 21, *Wednesday.*—To-day the crests of the north-east Re-appearance of sunshine.
headland were gilded by true sunshine, and all who were able
assembled on deck to greet it. The sun rose above the horizon,
though still screened from our eyes by intervening hills. Although
the powerful refraction of Polar latitudes heralds his direct appearance by brilliant light, this is as far removed from the glorious
tints of day as it is from the mere twilight. Nevertheless, for the
past ten days we have been watching the growing warmth of our
landscape, as it emerged from buried shadow, through all the
stages of distinctness of an India-ink washing, step by step, into
the sharp, bold definition of our desolate harbour scene. We have Coloured skies.
marked every dash of colour which the great Painter in his bene-
volence vouchsafed to us ; and now the empurpled blues, clear,
unmistakeable, the spreading lake, the flickering yellow; peering
at all these, poor wretches ! everything seemed superlative lustre
and unsurpassable glory. We had so grovelled in darkness that we
oversaw the light.

" Mr. Wilson has caught cold and relapsed. Mr. Ohlsen, after a suspicious day, startles me by an attack of partial epilepsy—one of those strange indescribable spells, fits, seizures, whatever name the jargon gives them, which indicate deep disturbance. I conceal his case as far as I can; but it adds to my heavy pack of troubles to anticipate the gloomy scenes of epileptic transport introduced into our one apartment. M'Gary holds his own.

"The work of stove-fitting is completed, and a new era marks its success. The increased draught which the prospective termination of our winter allows me to afford to our fuel brings an un-hoped-for piece of good fortune. We can burn hemp cable and cast-off running-gear. By the aid of a high chimney and a good regulating valve, the smoke passes directly into the open air, and tarred junk is as good as oak itself. This will save our trebling, and, what is more, the labour of cutting it. In truth, very little of it has been used up, scarcely more than a single streak. We have been too weak to cut it off. All our disposable force was inadequate last Saturday to cut enough for a day's fuel in advance.

"The sickness of a single additional man would have left us without fire."

CHAPTER XXXVI.

THE BENNESOAK—A DILEMMA—THE SUN—END OF FEBRUARY—OUR CONDI-
TION—THE WARM SOUTH-EASTER—MOONLIGHT—THE LANDSCAPE.

"*February 22, Thursday.*—Washington's birthday : all our colours CHAPTER
flying in the new sunlight. A day of good omen, even to the XXXVI.
sojourners among the ice. Hans comes in with great news. He Washington's birth-
has had a shot at our bennesoak, a long shot ; but it reached him. day.
The animal made off at a slow run, but we are sure of him now.
This same deer has been hanging round the lake at the fiord through
all the dim returning twilight ; and so many stories were told of
his appearance and movements, that he had almost grown into a
myth. To-morrow we shall desire his better acquaintance.

"The Esquimaux call the deer when he is without antlers a The ben-
bennesoak. The greater number of these animals retain their nesoak.
antlers till the early spring, beginning to drop them about the
return of sunshine ; but some of the strongest lose them before the
winter sets in. They are gregarious in their habits, and fond of
particular localities. Where they have been gathered together
year after year, the accumulation of discarded antlers is immense.
They tell me at Holsteinberg, where more than four thousand reindeer-skins find a market annually, that on the favourite hunting-
grounds these horns are found in vast piles. They bring little or
nothing at Copenhagen, but I suppose would find a ready sale
among the button-workers of England.

"*February 23, Friday.*—Hans was out early this morning on
the trail of the wounded deer. Rhina, the least barbarous of our
sledge-dogs, assisted him. He was back by noon, with the joyful Good
news, 'The tukkuk dead only two miles up big fiord!' The cry news.
found its way through the hatch, and came back in a broken huzza
from the sick men.

"We are so badly off for strong arms that our reindeer threatened
to be as great an embarrassment to us as the auction drawn-ele-
phant was to his lucky master. We had hard work with our dogs
carrying him to the brig, and still harder, worn down as we were,

in getting him over the ship's side. But we succeeded, and were tumbling him down the hold, when we found ourselves in a dilemma, like the Vicar of Wakefield with his family picture. It was impossible to drag the prize into our little moss-lined dormitory; the *fossa* was not half big enough to let him pass, and it was equally impossible to skin him anywhere else without freezing our fingers in the operation. It was a happy escape from the embarrassments of our hungry little council to determine that the animal might be carved before skinning as well as he could be afterward; and in a very few minutes we proved our united wisdom by a feast on his quartered remains.

" It was a glorious meal, such as the compensations of Providence reserve for starving men alone. We ate, forgetful of the past, and almost heedless of the morrow; cleared away the offal wearily : and now, at 10 P.M., all hands have turned in to sleep, leaving to their commanding officer the solitary honour of an eight hours' vigil.

"This deer was among the largest of all the northern specimens I have seen. He measured five feet one inch in girth, and six feet two inches in length, and stood as large as a two years' heifer. We estimated his weight at three hundred pounds gross, or one hundred and eighty net. The head had a more than usually cumbrous character, and a long waving tuft of white hair, that depended from the throat, gave an appearance of excessive weight to the front view.

" The reindeer is in no respect a graceful animal. There is an apparent want of proportion between his cumbrous shoulders and light haunch, which is ungainly even in his rapid movements. But he makes up for all his defects of form when he presents himself as an article of diet.

" *February* 24, Saturday.—A bitter disappointment met us at our evening meal. The flesh of our deer was nearly uneatable from putrefaction; the liver and intestines, from which I had expected so much, utterly so. The rapidity of such a change, in a temperature so low as minus 35°, seems curious; but the Greenlanders say that extreme cold is rather a promoter than otherwise of the putrefactive process. All the graminivorous animals have the same tendency, as is well known to the butchers. Our buffalo-hunters, when they condescend to clean a carcass, do it at once; they have

told me that the musk-ox is sometimes tainted after five minutes' *CHAPTER XXXVI.*
exposure. The Esquimaux, with whom there is no fastidious sen-
sibility of palate, are in the practice at Yotlik and Horses' Head, *Rapidity of putre-*
in latitude 73° 40', even in the severest weather, of withdrawing *faction.*
the viscera immediately after death and filling the cavity with stones.

"*February* 25, *Sunday.*—The day of rest for those to whom rest *Welcome*
can be ; the day of grateful recognition for all! John, our volun- *day of rest.*
teer cook of yesterday, is down : Morton, who could crawl out of
bed to play baker for the party, and stood to it manfully yesterday,
is down too. I have just one man left to help me in caring for
the sick. Hans and Petersen, thank God! have vitality enough
left to bear the toils of the hunt. One is out with his rifle, the
other searching the traps.

"To-day, blessed be the Great Author of. Light ! I have once *The sun appears.*
more looked upon the sun. I was standing on deck, thinking over
our prospects, when a familiar berg, which had long been hid in
shadow, flashed out in sun-birth. I knew this berg right well : it
stood between Charlotte Wood Fiord and Little Willie's Monument.
One year and one day ago I travelled toward it from Fern Rock to
catch the sunshine. Then I had to climb the hills beyond, to get
the luxury of basking in its brightness ; but now, though the sun
was but a single degree above the true horizon, it was so much
elevated by refraction, that the sheen stretched across the trough of
the fiord like a flaming tongue. I could not or would not resist
the influence. It was a Sunday act of worship : I started off at *Running to see the sunshine.*
an even run, and caught him as he rolled slowly along the horizon,
and before he sank. I was again the first of my party to rejoice
and meditate in sunshine. It is the third sun I have seen rise for
a moment above the long night of an Arctic winter.

"*February* 26, *Monday.*—William Godfrey undertook to act as
cook to-day, but fainted before completing the experiment. The
rest of us are little better ; and now it looks as if we were to
lose our best caterer, for Hans too shows signs of giving way to
the scurvy.

"I have been at work for an hour, cutting up the large Manilla
hawser for fuel. I do not know that I have any very remarkable
or valuable quality ; but I do know that, however multiform may
be my virtues, I am a singularly awkward hand in chopping up
frozen cables.

"*February* 28, *Wednesday.*—February closes : thank God for the lapse of its twenty-eight days ! Should the thirty-one of the coming March not drag us further downward, we may hope for a successful close to this dreary drama. By the tenth of April we should have seal ; and when they come, if we remain to welcome them, we can call ourselves saved.

"But a fair review of our prospects tells me that I must look
the lion in the face. The scurvy is steadily gaining on us. I do my best to sustain the more desperate cases ; but as fast as I partially build up one, another is stricken down. The disease is perhaps less malignant than it was, but it is more diffused throughout our party. Except William Morton, who is disabled by a frozen heel, not one of our eighteen is exempt. Of the six workers of our party, as I counted them a month ago, two are unable to do out-door work, and the remaining four divide the duties of the ship among them. Hans musters his remaining energies to conduct the hunt. Petersen is his disheartened, moping assistant.
The other two, Bonsall and myself, have all the daily offices of household and hospital. We chop five large sacks of ice, cut six fathoms of eight-inch hawser into junks of a foot each, serve out the meat when we have it, hack at the molasses, and hew out with crowbar and axe the pork and dried apples, pass up the foul slop and cleansings of our dormitory ; and, in a word, cook, *scullionize*, and attend the sick. Added to this, for five nights running I have kept watch from 8 P.M. to 4 A.M., catching cat-naps as I could in the day without changing my clothes, but carefully waking every hour to note thermometers.

" Such is the condition in which February leaves us, with forty-one days more ahead of just the same character in prospect as the twenty-eight which, thank God ! are numbered now with the past. It is saddening to think how much those twenty-eight days have impaired our capacities of endurance. Yet there are resources—
accidental perhaps, mercifully providential let me rather term them, contingent certainly, so far as our prescience goes—which may avail to save us : another reindeer of sound carcass, a constant succession of small game, supplies of walrus from the fugitive Esquimaux, or that which I most expect and hope for—a bear. We. have already seen some tracks of these animals ; and last March there were many of them off Coffee Gorge and the

Labyrinth. If Hans and myself can only hold on, we may work our way through. All rests upon destiny, or the power which controls it.

"It will yet be many days before the sun overrides the shadow of Bessie Mountain and reaches our brig. The sick pine for him, and I have devised a clever system of mirrors to hasten his visit to their bunks. He will do more for them than all medicine besides.

"That strange phenomenon, the warm south and south-east winds which came upon us in January, did not pass away till the middle of this month. And, even after it had gone, the weather continued for some days to reflect its influence. The thermometer seldom fell below —40°, and stood sometimes as high as —30°. It has been growing colder for the last three days, ranging from —46° to —51°; and the abundant snows of the warm spell are now compacted hard enough to be traversible, or else dissipated by the heavy winds. There is much to be studied in these atmospheric changes. There is a seeming connection between the increasing cold and the increasing moonlight, which has sometimes forced itself on my notice; but I have barely strength enough to carry on our routine observations, and have no time to discuss phenomena.

"Two attempts have been made by my orders, since the month began, to communicate with the Esquimaux at their huts. Both were failures. Petersen, Hans, and Godfrey came back to denounce the journey as impracticable. I know better: the experience of my two attempts in the midst of the darkness satisfies me that at this period of the year the thing can be done; and, if I might venture to leave our sick-bay for a week, I would prove it. But there are dispositions and influences here around me, scarcely latent, yet repressed by my presence, which make it my duty at all hazards to stay where I am.

"*March* 1, *Thursday.*—A grander scene than our bay by moonlight can hardly be conceived. It is more dream-like and supernatural than a combination of earthly features.

"The moon is nearly full, and the dawning sunlight, mingling with hers, invests everything with an atmosphere of ashy grey. It clothes the gnarled hills that make the horizon of our bay, shadows out the terraces in dull definition, grows darker and

CHAPTER
XXXVI.

Intense
moon-
light.

colder as it sinks into the fiords, and broods sad and dreary upon the ridges and measureless plains of ice that make up the rest of our field of view. Rising above all this, and shading down into it in strange combination, is the intense moonlight, glittering on every crag and spire, tracing the outline of the background with contrasted brightness, and printing its fantastic profiles on the snow-field.   It is a landscape such as Milton or Dante might imagine,—inorganic, desolate, mysterious.   I have come down from deck with the feelings of a man who has looked upon a world unfinished by the hand of its Creator."

THE GRAVES BY MOONLIGHT.

CHAPTER XXXVII.

OUR CONDITION—THE RESORTS—THE SICK—THE RAT IN THE INSECT-BOX—
ANTICIPATIONS—HAN'S RETURN—FAMINE AT ETAH—MYOUK ON BOARD
—WALRUS-TACKLE—THE MEAT DIET.

My journal for the beginning of March is little else than a chronicle of sufferings. Our little party was quite broken down. Every man on board was tainted with scurvy, and it was not common to find more than three who could assist in caring for the rest. The greater number were in their bunks, absolutely unable to stir.

CHAPTER XXXVII.

Progress of disease.

The circumstances were well fitted to bring out the character of individuals. Some were intensely grateful for every little act of kindness from their more fortunate messmates ; some querulous ; others desponding; others again wanted only strength to become mutinous. Brooks, my first officer, as stalwart a man-o'-war's man as ever faced an enemy, burst into tears when he first saw himself in the glass. On Sunday, the 4th, our last remnant of fresh meat had been doled out. Our invalids began to sink rapidly. The wounds of our amputated men opened afresh. The region about our harbour ceased to furnish its scanty contingent of game. One of our huntsmen, Petersen, never very reliable in anything, declared himself unfit for further duty. Hans was unsuccessful : he made several wide circuits, and saw deer twice ; but once they were beyond range, and the next time his rifle missed fire.

Characters of the men.

I tried the hunt for a long morning myself, without meeting a single thing of life, and was convinced, by the appearance of things on my return to the brig, that I should peril the *morale*, and with it the only hope, of my command by repeating the experiment.

An unsuccessful hunt.

I laboured, of course, with all the ingenuity of a well-taxed mind, to keep up the spirits of my comrades. I cooked for them all imaginable compounds of our unvaried diet-list, and brewed up flax-seed and lime-juice and quinine and willow-stems into an abomination which was dignified as beer, and which some were

CHAPTER
XXXVII.

Fresh
meat
absolutely
necessary.

persuaded for the time to believe such.   But it was becoming more and more certain every hour, that unless we could renew our supplies of fresh meat, the days of the party were numbered.

I spare myself, as well as the readers of this hastily-compiled volume, when I pass summarily over the details of our condition at this time.

I look back at it with recollections like those of a nightmare. Yet I was borne up wonderfully.   I never doubted for an instant that the same Providence which had guarded us through the long darkness of winter was still watching over us for good, and that it was yet in reserve for us—for some, I dared not hope for all—to bear back the tidings of our rescue to a Christian land.   But how I did not see.

On the 6th of the month I made the desperate venture of sending off my only trusted and effective huntsman on a sledge-journey to find the Esquimaux of Etah.   He took with him our two surviving dogs in our lightest sledge.   The Arctic day had begun to set in ; the ice-track had improved with the advance of the season; and the cold, though still intense, had moderated to about 80° below the freezing-point.   He was to make his first night-halt at Anoatok ; and, if no misadventure thwarted his progress, we hoped that he might reach the settlement before the end of the second night.   In three or at furthest four days more, I counted on his return.   No language can express the anxiety with which our poor suffering crew awaited it.

March 8, Thursday.—Hans must now be at the huts.   If the natives have not gone south, if the walrus and bear have not failed them, and if they do not refuse to send us supplies, we may have fresh food in three days.   God grant it may come in time !

" Stephenson and Riley are dangerously ill.   We have moved Riley from his bunk, which, though lighter than most of the others, was dampened by the accumulations of ice.   He is now upon a dry and heated platform close to the stove.   Dr. Hayes's foot shows some ugly symptoms, which a change of his lodging-place may perhaps mitigate ; and I have determined, therefore, to remove him to the berth Riley has vacated as soon as we can purify and dry it for him.

" In clearing out Riley's bunk, we found that a rat had built his nest in my insect-box, destroying all our specimens. This is a grave loss ; for, besides that they were light of carriage, and might therefore have accompanied us in the retreat which now seems inevitable, they comprised our entire collection, and, though few in numbers, were rich for this stinted region. I had many spiders and bees. He is welcome to the whole of them, however, if I only catch him the fatter for the ration.

" *March 9, Friday.*—Strength going. It was with a feeling almost of dismay that I found how difficult it was to get through the day's labours,—Bonsall and myself the sole workers. After cleansing below, dressing and performing the loathsome duties of a nurse to the sick, cutting ice, cooking and serving messes, we could hardly go further.

" I realize fully the moral effects of an unbroken routine : systematic order once broken in upon, discomfort, despondency, and increase of disease must follow of course. It weighed heavily on my spirit to-day when I found my one comrade and myself were barely able to cut the necessary fuel. The hour of routine-nightfall finds us both stiff and ill at ease. Having to keep the nightwatch until 6 A.M., I have plenty of time to revolve my most uncomfortable thoughts.

" Be it understood by any who may peradventure read of these things in my journal, that I express them nowhere else. What secret thoughts my companions may have are concealed from me and from each other; but none of them can see as I do the alternative future now so close at hand : bright and comforting it may be ; but, if not, black and hopeless altogether.

" Should Hans come back with a good supply of walrus, and himself unsmitten by the enemy, our sick would rise under the genial specific of meat, and our strength probably increase enough to convey our boats to the North Water. The Refuge Inlet Polynia will hardly be more than forty miles from our brig, and, step by step, we can sledge our boats and their cargoes down to it. Once at Cape Alexander, we can support our sick by our guns, and make a regular Capua of the bird-colonies of Northumberland Island. This, in honest truth my yet unswerving and unshaken hope and expectation, is what I preach to my people ; and often in the silent hours of night I chat to some sleepless patient of cochlearia salads and glorious feasts of loons and cider-ducks.

CHAPTER XXXVII.

Fears for the future.
"On the other side, suppose Hans fails: the thought is horrible. The Spitzbergen victims were, at about this date, in better condition than we are: it was not until the middle of April that they began to die off. We have yet forty days to run before we can count upon the renovating blessings of animal life and restoring warmth. Neither Riley nor Wilson can last half that time without a supply of antiscorbutic food. Indeed, there is not a man on board who can hope to linger on till the spring comes unless we have relief.

"I put all this down in no desponding spirit, but as a record to look back upon hereafter, when the immediate danger has passed away, and some new emergency has brought its own array of cares and trials. My mind is hopeful and reliant: there is something even cheering in the constant rally of its energies to meet the calls of the hour.

"*March* 10, *Saturday.*—Hans has not yet returned, so that he must have reached the settlement. His orders were, if no meat be obtained of the Esquimaux, to borrow their dogs and try for bears along the open water. In this resource I have confidence. The days are magnificent.

The return of Hans and his adventures.
". . . . I had hardly written the above, when '*Bim, bim, bim!*' sounded from the deck, mixed with the chorus of our returning dogs. The next minute Hans and myself were shaking hands.

"He had much to tell us; to men in our condition Hans was as a man from cities. We of the wilderness flocked around him to hear the news. Sugar-teats of raw meat are passed around. 'Speak loud, Hans, that they may hear in the bunks.'

Changes for the worse at Etah Bay.
"The 'wind-loved' Anoatok he had reached on the first night after leaving the brig: no Esquimaux there of course; and he slept not warmly at a temperature of 53° below zero. On the evening of the next day he reached Etah Bay, and was hailed with joyous welcome. But a new phase of Esquimaux life had come upon its indolent, happy, blubber-fed denizens. Instead of plump, greasy children, and round-cheeked matrons, Hans saw around him lean figures of misery: the men looked hard and bony, and the children shrivelled in the hoods which cradled them at their mothers' backs. Famine had been among them; and the skin of a young sea-unicorn, lately caught, was all that remained to them of food. It was the old story of improvidence and its

miserable train. They had even eaten their reserve of blubber, CHAPTER XXXVII.
and were seated in darkness and cold, waiting gloomily for the
sun. Even their dogs, their main reliance for the hunt and for Miserable condition of the Esquimaux.
an escape to some more favoured camping-ground, had fallen a
sacrifice to hunger. Only four remained out of thirty : the rest
had been eaten.

"Hans behaved well, and carried out my orders in their full
spirit. He proposed to aid them in the walrus-hunt. They
smiled at first with true Indian contempt ; but when they saw
my Marston rifle, which he had with him, they changed their
tone. When the sea is completely frozen, as it is now, the wal- Mode of hunting walrus.
rus can only be caught by harpooning them at their holes or in
temporary cracks. This mode of hunting them is called *utok*. It
requires great skill to enter the harpoon, and often fails from the
line giving way in the struggles of the animal. They had lost a
harpoon and line in this manner the very day before Hans' arrival.
It required very little argument to persuade them to accept his
offered company and try the effect of his cone-ball on the harpooned animal before he made good his retreat.

"I have not time to detail Hans' adventurous hunt, equally im- Successful hunt.
portant to the scurvied sick of Rensselaer and the starving residents of Etah Bay. Metck (the eider-duck) speared a medium-
sized walrus, and Hans gave him no less than five Marston balls
before he gave up his struggles. The beast was carried back in
triumph, and all hands fed as if they could never know famine
again. It was a regular feast, and the kablunah interest was
exalted to the skies.

"Miserable, yet happy wretches, without one thought for the
future, fighting against care when it comes unbidden, and enjoying to the full their scanty measure of present good ! As a beast,
the Esquimaux is a most sensible beast, worth a thousand Cali-
bans, and certainly ahead of his cousin the Polar bear, from whom
he borrows his pantaloons.

"I had directed Hans to endeavour to engage Myouk, if he Myouk engaged assistant in hunt-ing.
could, to assist him in hunting. A most timely thought : for the
morning's work made them receive the invitation as a great favour.
Hans got his share of the meat, and returned to the brig accompanied by the boy, who is now under my care on board. This
imp—for he is full of the devil—has always had a relishing fancy

for the kicks and cuffs with which I recall the forks and tea-spoons when they get astray; and, to tell the truth, he always takes care to earn them. He is very happy, but so wasted by hunger that the work of fattening him will be a costly one. Poor little fellow! born to toil, and necessity, and peril; stern hunter as he already is, the lines of his face are still soft and childlike. I think we understand one another better than our incongruities would imply. He has fallen asleep in a deer skin at my feet.

"*March* 11, *Sunday.*—The sick are not as bright as this relief ought to make them. The truth is, they are fearfully down. Neither poor Wilson nor Riley could bear the meat, and they both suffered excessive pain with fever from a meal that was very limited in quantity. Even the stoutest could hardly bear their once solicited allowance of raw meat. I dispensed it cautiously, for I knew the hazards; but I am sure it is to be the salvation of all of us. It gives a respite at any rate, and we could not in reason ask for more.

"Hans is making a walrus-harpoon and line; and, as soon as he and Myouk have freshened a little, I shall send them back to Anoatok in search of water-cracks. I am hard worked, getting little rest, yet gratefully employed, for my people seem to thank me. My cookery unfortunately shows itself on the smeared pages of my journal.

"*March* 12, *Monday.*—The new tackle is finished. Myouk had lost his ussuk-line upon the iceberg, but we supplied its place with a light Manilla cord. Hans made the bonework of his naligeit from the reindeer antlers which are abundant about the hills. They both rest to-night, and make an early start in the morning for their working ground.

"The less severe cases on our sick list are beginning to feel the influence of their new diet; but Wilson and Brooks do not react. Their inclination for food, or rather their toleration of it, is so much impaired that they reject meat in its raw state, and when cooked it is much less prompt and efficient in its action. My mode of serving it out is this:—Each man has his saucer of thinly sliced frozen walrus heart, with limejuice or vinegar, before breakfast: at breakfast, blood gravy with wheaten bread; at dinner, steaks slightly stewed or fried, without limit of quantity,

none at tea proper ; but at 8 P.M. a renewed allowance of raw
slices and vinegar.   It shows how broken down the party is, that
under the appetizing stimulations of an Arctic sky all our convalescents and well men together are content with some seven
pounds of meat.   Their prostrate comrades are sustained by
broth."

ESQUIMAUX WATCHING A SEAL.

CHAPTER XXXVIII.

LINE OF OPEN WATER—AWAHTOK—HIS FIRST BORN—INSUBORDINATION—
THE PLOT—THE DEVELOPMENT—THE DESERTION.

CHAPTER XXXVIII.

Departure of Hans and Myouk.

"*March* 13, *Tuesday.*—I walked out with Hans and Myouk to give them God speed. Myouk had made me dress his frosted feet with rabbit-fur swaddled with alternate folds of flannel and warm skins. The little scamp had not been so comfortable since his accident. The dogs were only four in number, for 'Young Whitey' had been used up at Etah ; but the load was light, and Myouk managed to get a fair share of riding. Hans, with the consequential air of 'big Injin,' walked ahead.

"I enjoined on them extreme caution as to their proceedings. They are to stretch over to the Bergy ground, of dismal associations, and to look for ice-cracks in the level channel way. Here, where I so nearly lost my life, they will seek bears and walrus, and, if they fail, work their way downward to the south. They sleep to-night in a snow-burrow, but hope to-morrow to reach Anoatok.

"*March* 15, *Thursday.*—Hans and Myouk returned at eight o'clock last night without game. Their sleep, in a snowdrift about twenty miles to the northward, in a temperature of —54°, was not comfortable, as might be expected. The marvel is how life sustains itself in such circumstances of cold. I have myself slept in an ordinary canvas tent without discomfort, yet without fire, at a temperature of —52°.

Sleep in a snow drift.

"Myouk was very glad to get back to my warm quarters ; but Hans was chopfallen at the dearth of game. They found no open water, but ice, ice, ice, as far to the north and east as the eye could range from an iceberg elevation of eighty feet. It is the same opposite Anoatok ; and, according to the Esquimaux, as far south of Cape Alexander as a point opposite Akotloowick, the first Baffin Bay huts. Beyond this, in spite of the severity of the winter, there is an open sea. It is in the month of March. if at all during the year, that the polynias are frozen up. Those ot Refuge Bay

An open sea beyond the ice.

and Littleton were open during the whole of last winter; and, con- CHAPTER XXXVIII
sidering how very severe the weather is now and has been for
months past, I question very much if such extensive areas as the
so-called North Water ever close completely.

"Hans saw numerous tracks of bears; and I have no doubt now Tracks of bears.
but that we can secure some of these animals before the seal season opens. One large beast passed in the night close by the snow-
burrow in which our would-be hunters were ensconced. They
followed his tracks in the morning; but the dogs were exhausted,
and the cold was excessive, and they wisely returned to the
brig.

". . . . . To-day we have finished burning our last Manilla Want of fuel.
hawser for fuel, the temperature remaining at the extraordinary
mean of —52°. Our next resort must be to the trebling of the
brig: Petersen—what remains of him, for the man's energies are
gone—is now at work cutting it off. It is a hard trial for me.
I have spared neither exertion, thought, nor suffering, to save the
sea-worthiness of our little vessel, but all to no end: she can
never bear us to the sea. Want of provisions alone, if nothing
else, will drive us from her; for this solid case of nine-foot ice
cannot possibly give way until the late changes of fall, nor then
unless a hot summer and a retarded winter afterward allow the
winds to break up its iron casing.

"*March* 16, *Friday.*—We have just a scant two days' allow- Scarcity of food.
ance of meat for the sick. Hans has done his best; but there is
nothing to be found on the hills; and I fear that a long hunting
journey to the south is our only resource.

"Awahtok: I have often mentioned him as a plump, good- Awahtok.
natured fellow. He was one of my attachés; by which I mean
one of the many who stick to me like a plaster, in order to draw
or withdraw a share of the iron nails, hoops, buttons, and other
treasures which I represent. Awahtok always struck me as a
lazy, pleasant sort of fellow, a man who would be glad to bask in
sunshine if he could find any. He has a young wife of eighteen,
and he himself is but twenty-two. His hut is quite cleanly, and
we become his guests there with more satisfaction than at any
other hostel in the village of Etah. Awahtok is evidently happy
with his wife, and, the last time I saw him, was exulting over the
first pledge of their union, a fine little girl. Well, all this about

CHAPTER XXXVIII.

A child buried a'ive.

Awahtok is a prelude to the fact that he has just buried his daughter alive under a pile of stones.

"Myouk, who gave us the news to-day, when delicately questioned as to the cause of this little family arrangement, answered, with all simplicity of phrase, that the child had certain habits, common, I believe, to all the varieties of infancy.

"The month is gliding on, but without any contributions to science, though there are many things about me to suggest investigation.

Preparations for hunting.

"It is as much as I can do to complete the routine of the days, and enable them to roll into each other. What a dreary death in life must be that of a maid or man of all work!

"*March 17, Saturday.*—I have been getting Hans ready for the settlement, with a five-sinnet line of Maury's sounding-twine. The natives to the south have lost nearly all their *allunaks* or walrus-lines by the accidents of December or January, and will be unable to replace them till the return of the seal. A good or even serviceable allunak requires a whole ussuk to cut it from. It is almost the only article whose manufacture seems to be conducted by the Esquimaux with any care and nicety of process. Our sounding-line will be a valuable contribution to them, and may, perchance, like some more ostentatious charities, include the liberal givers among those whom it principally blesses.

Suspicions of two of the men.

"*March 18, Sunday.*—I have a couple of men on board whose former history I would give something to know,—bad fellows both of them, but daring, energetic, and strong. They gave me trouble before we reached the coast of Greenland; and they keep me constantly on the watch at this moment, for it is evident to me that they have some secret object in view, involving probably a desertion and escape to the Esquimaux settlements. They are both feigning sickness this morning; and, from what I have overheard, it is with the view of getting thoroughly rested before a start. Hans' departure with the sledge and dogs would give them a fine chance, if they could only waylay him, of securing all our facilities for travel; and I should not be surprised if they tried to compel him to go along with them. They cannot succeed in this except by force.

Necessary watchfulness.

"I am acting very guardedly with them. I cannot punish till I have the evidence of an overt act. Nor can I trust the matter to other hands. It would not do to depress my sick party by disclosing a scheme which, if it could be carried out fully, might be fatal to the whole of us. All this adds to my other duties those of a detective policeman. I do not find them agreeable.

" *March* 19, *Monday*.—Hans got off at eleven. I have been all right in my suspicions about John and Bill. They were intensely anxious to get together this morning, and I was equally resolved to prevent any communication between them. I did this so ingeniously that they did not suspect my motive, by devising some outside duty for one or the other of them, and keeping his comrade in the plot at work under my own eye. Their impatience, and cunning little resorts, to procure the chance of a word in private, were quite amusing. It might be very far otherwise if they could manage to rob us of our dogs and gain the Netlik settlements.

" I hope the danger is over now. I shall keep the whole thing to myself; for, situated as we are, even the frustration of a mutinous purpose had best be concealed from the party.

" Petersen brought in to-day five ptarmigan, a cheering day's work, promising for the future, and allowing me to give an abundant meal to the sickest, and something to the sick. This is enough to keep up the health-working impression of the fresh meat diet.

" *March* 20, *Tuesday*.—This morning I received information from Stephenson that Bill had declared his intention of leaving the brig to-day at some time unknown. John, being now really lame, could not accompany him. This Stephenson overheard in whispers during the night; and, in faithful execution of his duty, conveyed it to me.

" I kept the news to myself; but there was no time to be lost. William, therefore, was awakened at 6 A.M.—after my own nightwatch—and ordered to cook breakfast. Meantime I watched him. At first he appeared troubled, and had several stealthily-whispered interviews with John : finally his manner became more easy, and he cooked and served our breakfast meal. I now felt convinced that he would meet John outside as soon as he could leave the room, and that one or both would then desert. I therefore threw on my furs and armed myself, made Bonsall and Morton acquainted with my plans, and then, crawling out of our dark passage, concealed myself near its entrance. I had hardly waited half an hour,—pretty cold work too,—when John crawled out, limping and grunting. Once fairly out, he looked furtively round, and then, with a sigh of satisfaction, mounted our rickety steps entirely cured of his lameness. Within ten minutes after he had gained the deck, the door opened again, and William made his appearance, booted for travel and clad in buffalo. As he emerged into the hold, I confronted him. He was ordered at once to the cabin; and Morton was despatched on deck to compel the presence of the third party; while Mr. Bonsall took his station at the door, allowing no one to pass out.

"In a very few minutes John crawled back again, as lame and exhausted as when he was last below, yet growing lamer rapidly as, recovering from the glare of the light, he saw the tableau. I then explained the state of things to the little company, and detailed step by step to the principals in the scene every one of their plans.

"Bill was the first to confess. I had prepared myself for the emergency, and punished him on the spot. As he rose with some difficulty, I detailed from the log-book the offences he had committed, and adduced the proofs.

"The short-handed condition of the brig made me unable to confine him; therefore I deemed it best to remove his handcuffs, to accept his protestations of reform, and put him again to work. He accepted my lenity with abundant thanks, went to duty, and in less than an hour deserted. I was hunting at the time, but the watch reported his having first been discovered on the ice-foot, and out of presenting distance. His intention undoubtedly is to reach Etah Bay, and, robbing Hans of sledge and dogs, proceed south to Netlik.

"Should he succeed, the result will be a heavy loss to us. The dogs are indispensable in the hunt and in transporting us to Anoatok. The step, however, is not likely to be successful. At all events, he is off, and I regret that duty prevents my rejoicing at his departure. John remains with us, closely watched, but apparently sincere in his protestations of absolute reform."

CHAPTER XXXIX.

COLLOQUY IN THE BUNKS—WINTER TRAVEL—PREPARATIONS—REINDEER
FEEDING GROUNDS—TERRACED BEACHES—A WALK—OCCUPATIONS.

"*March* 21, *Wednesday.*—On this day one year ago Mr. Brooks
and his party were frozen up in the hummocks. The habit
of comparing the condition of two periods, of balancing the
thoughts and hopes of one with the realized experience of the
other, seems to me a very unprofitable one. It interferes with
the practical executive spirit of a man, to mix a bright and happy
past with a dim and doubtful present. It's a maudlin piece of
work at best, and I'll none of it.

"But listen to poor Brooks there, talking. He is sitting up,
congratulating himself that he can nearly straighten his worst leg.
'Well, Mr. Ohlsen, I thought we would never get through them
hummocks. You know we unloaded three times; now, I would
not say it then, but seeing I am down I'll tell you. When we
laid down the last pemmican-case, I went behind the ice, and
don't remember nothing till Petersen called me into the tent. I
think I must have strained something, and gone off like in a kind
of fit.'

"Ohlsen, who is as self-absorbed a man as I ever knew, replies
by stating that his boots pinched him; to which poor Brooks,
never dwelling long on his own troubles, says in a quiet, soliloquizing way, 'Yes, and Baker's boots pinched him too; but it wasn't
the boots, but the killing cold outside of them. There was
Pierre,—his boots were moccasins, with deer-skin foot-rags, but
he died of cold for all that; and there's Mr. Wilson and me, both
hanging on in neither one way nor t'other; it's a question which
of us lasts the longest.' M'Gary another bedridden, but convalescent, I hope, here raises himself on his elbows and checks
Brooks for being so down in the mouth ; and Brooks, after a
growling rejoinder, improves his merry reminiscences by turning
to me.

"'Captain Kane, five nights to come one year, you came in

upon four of us down as flat as flounders. I didn't look at your
boots, but I know you wore Esquimaux ones. It was a hard

walk for you, the greatest thing I ever heard tell off; but'—here
he begins to soliloquize—'Baker's dead, Pierre's dead, and Wilson
and I—'. 'Shut up, Brooks, shut up!' I broke in, whisper-
ing across the boards that separated our blankets; 'you will make
the patients uncomfortable.' But no; the old times were strong
upon him; he did not speak loud, but he caught me by both
hands, and said, in his low bass, quiet tones, ' Doctor, you cried
when you saw us, and didn't pull up till we jabbed the stopper
down the whisky-tin and gave you a tot of it.'

" The general tone of the conversation around is like this specimen. I am glad to hear my shipmates talking together again,
for we have of late been silent. The last year's battle commenced
at this time a year ago, and it is natural the men should recall it.
Had I succeeded in pushing my party across the bay, our success
would have been unequalled ; it was the true plan, the best-con-
ceived, and in fact the only one by which, after the death of my
dogs, I could hope to carry on the search. The temperatures were
frightful, —40° to —56°; but my experience of last year on the
rescue-party, where we travelled eighty miles in sixty odd hours,

almost without a halt, yet without a frost-bite, shows that such
temperatures are no obstacle to travel, provided you have the
necessary practical knowledge of the equipment and conduct of
your party. I firmly believe that no natural cold as yet known
can arrest travel. The whole story of this winter illustrates it.
I have both sledged and walked sixty and seventy miles over the
roughest ice, in repeated journeys, at fifty degrees below zero, and
the two parties from the south reached our brig in the dead of
winter, after being exposed for three hundred miles to the same
horrible cold.

" The day has been beautifully clear, and so mild that our mid-
day thermometers gave but 7°. This bears badly upon the desertion of Godfrey, for the probabilities are that he will find Hans's
buffalo-robe at the hut, and thus sleep and be refreshed. In that
case, he can easily reach the Esquimaux of Etah Bay, and may
as easily seize upon the sledge-dogs, rifle, and trading articles.
The consequences of such an act would be very disastrous ; nearly
all my hopes of lifting the sick, and therefore of escaping in boats

to the south, rest upon these dogs. By them only can we hunt
bear and early seal, or rapidly transport ourselves to the tide-holes
(*polynia*) of the spring, where we can add water-fowl to our game
list. I am entirely without a remedy. We cannot pursue him,
nor could we well have prevented his escape; it is the most cul-
pable desertion I ever knew or heard of. Bonsall, Petersen, and
myself are the only men now on board who can work for the rest.
Save the warnings of a secret trouble, the fox gnawing under the
jacket, I do better than the rest; but I bear my fox. Bonsall is
evidently more disabled.

"*March* 22, *Thursday.*—Petersen's ptarmigan are all gone (five
of them), and of the rabbit but two rations of eight ounces each
remain. We three, Bonsall, Petersen, and myself, have made up
our minds to walk up Mary River Ravine until we reach the deer
plains, and there separate and close in upon them. To-day is
therefore a busy one, for we must prepare beforehand the entire
daily requirements of the sick: the ice for melting water must be
cut in blocks and laid near the stove; the wood, of which it
requires one entire day to tear enough out for two days, must be
chopped and piled within arm-reach; the bread must be cooked
and the provisions arranged, before we can leave our comrades.
When we three leave the brig, there will not be a single able man
on board. M'Gary is able to leave his bed and stump about a
little; but this is all. Need the dear home-folks, who may some
day read this, wonder that I am a little careworn, and that I leave
the brig with reluctance? Of we three God-supported men, each
has his own heavy load of scurvy.

"*March* 23, *Friday.*—We started this morning, overworked and
limping, rather as men ending a journey than beginning one. After
four hours of forced walking, we reached the reindeer feeding
grounds, but were too late; the animals had left at least two hours
before our arrival. An extensive rolling country, rather a lacus-
trine plain than a true plateau, was covered with traces of life.
The snow had been turned up in patches of four or five yards in
diameter, by the hoofs of the reindeer, over areas of twenty or fifty
acres. The extensive levels were studded with them; and wherever
we examined the ground surface it was covered with grasses and
destitute of lichens. We scouted it over the protruding syenites,
and found a couple of ptarmigan and three hares; these we secured.

A long
walk.

"Our little party reached the brig in the evening, after a walk over a heavy snow-lined country of thirty miles. Nevertheless, I had a walk full of instructive material. The frozen channel of Mary River abounds in noble sections and scenes of splendid wildness and desolation. I am too tired to epitomize here my note-book's record; but I may say that the opportunity which I had to-day of comparing the terrace and boulder lines of Mary River and Charlotte Wood Fiord enables me to assert positively the interesting fact of a secular elevation of the crust, commencing at some as yet undetermined point north of 76°, and continuing to the Great Glacier and the high northern latitudes of Grinnell Land. This elevation, as connected with the equally well sustained depression of the Greenland coast south of Kingatok, is in interesting keeping with the same undulating alternation on the Scandinavian side. Certainly there seems to be in the localities of these elevated and depressed areas a systematic compensation.

Terraced
beaches.

"I counted to-day forty-one distinct ledges or shelves of terrace embraced between our water-line and the syenitic ridges through which Mary River forces itself. These shelves, though sometimes merged into each other, presented distinct and recognisable embankments or escarps of elevation. Their surfaces were at a nearly uniform inclination of descent of 5°, and their breadth either twelve, twenty-four, thirty-six, or some other multiple of twelve paces. This imposing series of ledges carried you in forty-one gigantic steps to an elevation of 480 feet; and, as the first rudiments of these ancient beaches left the granites which had once formed the barrier sea-coast, you could trace them passing from drift-strewn rocky barricades to cleanly-defined and gracefully-curved shelves of shingle and pebbles. I have studies of these terraced beaches at various points on the northern coast of Greenland. They are more imposing and on a larger scale than those of Wellington Channel, which are now regarded by geologists as indicative of secular uplift of coast. As these strange structures wound in long spirals around the headlands of the fiords, they reminded me of the parallel roads of Glen Roy,—a comparison which I make rather from general resemblance than ascertained analogies of causes.

A large
boulder.

"There is a boulder ten miles from our brig, say seven from the coast,—a mass of rounded syenite —at an altitude of 1100 feet,

esting, entirely isolated, upon coarse sandstone; its cubical con- CHAPTER
ents cannot be less than sixty tons. Tired as I am by this hard XXXIX.
valk, I feel that it has rewarded me well. It was too cold for the
pocket-sextant; but I managed to sketch in such features of the
pposite coast as were not marked in our charts of last August. The inland
had a full view of the inland glacier throughout a linear trend of glacier.
wenty miles. I can measure the profitless non-observing routine
f the past winter by my joy at this first break in upon its drudgery.
Jod knows I had laid down for myself much experimental obser-
ation, and some lines of what I hoped would be valuable travel
nd search; but I am thankful that I am here, able to empty a
lop-bucket or rub a scurvied leg.

" My people had done well during my absence, and welcomed
ne back impressively.

" *March* 24, *Saturday.*—Our yesterday's ptarmigan gave the Ptarmi-
nost sick a raw ration, and to-day we killed a second pair, which gan shot.
vill serve them for to-morrow. To my great joy, they seem on that
imited allowance to hold their ground. I am the only man now
vho scents the fresh meat without tasting it. I actually long for
t, but am obliged to give way to the sick.

" Yesterday's walk makes my scorbutized muscles very stiff. I
vent through my routine of labour, and, as usual in this strange
lisease, worked off my stiffness and my pain.

" Bonsall and Petersen are now woodmen, preparing our daily Chopping
uel. My own pleasant duty consists in chopping from an iceberg wood and ice, &c.
ix half-bushel bagfuls of frozen water, carrying it to the brig and
assing it through the scuttle into our den; in emptying by
hree several jobs some twelve to fifteen bucketfuls from the slop-
arrel; in administering both as nurse and physician to fourteen
ick men; in helping to pick eider-down from its soil as material
or boat-bedding; in writing this wretched daily record, eating my
neals, sleeping my broken sleeps, and feeling that the days pass
vithout congenial occupation or improving pursuit.

" Hans has not returned. I give him two days more before I Fears for
all in with the opinion which some seem to entertain, that God- Hans' safety.
rey has waylaid or seized upon his sledge. This wretched man has
een the very bane of the cruise. My conscience tells me that almost
ny measure against him would be justifiable as a relief to the rest;
ut an instinctive aversion to extreme measures binds my hands."

CHAPTER XL.

CHAPTER XL.

A cheerless Sunday.

"*March 25, Sunday.*—A hard-working, busy Sunday it has been, —a cheerless, scurvy-breeding day; and now by the midnight, which is as it were the evening of its continued light, I read the thermometers unaided except by the crimson fires of the northern horizon. It is, moreover, cold again, —37°, and the enemy has a harder grip on my grasshopper. Bonsall and Kane took the entire home-work on themselves to-day, that Petersen might have a chance of following rabbit-tracks up Mary River. He succeeded in shooting one large hare and a couple of ptarmigan,—thus giving our sick a good allowance for one day more.

Refraction.

"Refraction with all its magic is back upon us; the 'Delectable Mountains' appear again; and, as the sun has now worked his way to the margin of the north-western horizon, we can see the blaze stealing out from the black portals of these uplifted hills, as if there were truly beyond it a celestial gate.

The Delectable Mountains.

"I do not know what preposterous working of brain led me to compare this north-western ridge to Bunyan's Delectable Mountains; but there was a time, only one year ago, when I used to gaze upon them with an eye of real longing. Very often, when they rose phantom-like into the sky, I would plan schemes by which to reach them, work over mentally my hard pilgrimage across the ice, and my escape from Doubting Castle to this scene of triumph and reward. Once upon your coasts, O inaccessible mountains, I would reach the Northern Ocean and gather together the remnants of poor Franklin's company. These would be to me the orchards, and vineyards, and running fountains. The 'Lord of the Hill' would see in me a pilgrim.' 'Leaning upon our staves, as is common with weary pilgrims when they stand to talk with any by the way,' we would look down upon an open Polar Sea, refulgent with northern sunshine.

"I did try to gain these summits; and when I think of poor

Baker's and Pierre's death, of my own almost fatalistic anxiety to cross the frozen sea, and of the terrible physical trial by which we saved our advance party, I cannot help dwelling, as something curious in its likeness, on another scene which Bunyan's explorers witnessed among the Delectable Mountains. 'They hied them first to the top of a hill called Error, which was very steep on the furthest side. So Christian and Hopeful looked down, and saw at the bottom several men dashed all to pieces by a fall which they had from the top.

" ' Then said the shepherds, " More than you see lie dashed to pieces at the bottom of this mountain—and *have continued to this lay unburied*, for an example to others to take heed how they clamber too high, or how they come too near to the brink of this mountain." '

" *March* 31, *Saturday.*—This month, badly as its daily record reads, is upon review a cheering one. We have managed to get enough game to revive the worst of our scurvy patients, and have kept in regular movement the domestic wheel of shipboard. Our troubles have been greater than at any time before; perhaps I ought to say they are greatest as the month closes; but whatever of misery Bonsall, and Petersen, and myself may have endured, it seems nearly certain now that at least four men will soon be able to relieve us. Brooks, M'Gary, Riley, and Thomas have seen the crisis of their malady, and, if secured from relapse, will recover rapidly. Ohlsen also is better, but slow to regain his powers. But the rest of the crew are still down.

" The game season, besides, is drawing nearer; and, once able to shoot seal upon the ice, I have little fears for the recovery of the larger portion of our party. Perhaps I am too sanguine; for it is clear that those of us who have till now sustained the others are beginning to sink. Bonsall can barely walk in the morning, and his legs become stiffer daily; Petersen gives way at the ankles; and I suffer much from the eruption, a tormenting and anomalous symptom, which affects eight of our sick. It has many of the characteristics of exanthemata ; but is singularly persistent, varied in its phases, and possibly in its result dangerous.

" The moral value of this toilsome month to myself has been the lesson of sympathy it has taught me with the labouring man. The fatigue, and disgust, and secret trials of the overworked

CHAPTER XL.
brain are bad enough, but not to me more severe than those which follow the sick and jaded body to a sleepless bed. I have realized the sweat of the brow, and can feel how painful his earnings must be to whom the grasshopper has become a burden.

Re-appearance of the deserter.
" *April 2, Monday.*—At eleven o'clock this morning Mr. Bonsall reported a man about a mile from the brig, apparently lurking on the ice-foot. I thought it was Hans, and we both went forward to meet him. As we drew closer we discovered our sledge and dog-team near where he stood; but the man turned and ran to the south.

His story.
" I pursued him, leaving Mr. Bonsall, who carried a Sharpe rifle, behind; and the man, whom I now recognised to be Godfrey, seeing me advance alone, stopped and met me. He told me that he had been to the south as far as Northumberland Island; that Hans was lying sick at Etah, in consequence of exposure; that he himself had made up his mind to go back and spend the rest of his life with Kalutunah and the Esquimaux; and that neither persuasion nor force should divert him from this purpose.

" Upon my presenting a pistol, I succeeded in forcing him back to the gangway of the brig; but he refused to go further; and being loath to injure him, I left him under the guardianship of His escape. Mr. Bonsall's weapon while I went on board for irons; for both Bonsall and myself were barely able to walk, and utterly incapable of controlling him by manual force, and Petersen was out hunting; the rest, thirteen in all, are down with scurvy. I had just reached the deck when he turned to run. Mr. Bonsall's pistol failed at the cap. I jumped at once to the gun-stand; but my first rifle, affected by the cold, went off in the act of cocking, and a second, aimed in haste at long, but practicable distance, missed the fugitive. He made good his escape before we could lay hold of another weapon.

Anxiety about Hans.
" I am now more anxious than ever about Hans. The past conduct of Godfrey on board, and his mutinous desertion, make me aware that he is capable of daring wrong as well as deception. Hans has been gone more than a fortnight; he has been used to making the same journey in less than a week. His sledge and dogs came back in the possession of the very man whom I suspected of an intention to waylay him; and this man, after being driven

by menaces to the ship's side, perils his life rather than place him- CHAPTER XL.
self in my power on board of her.

"Yet he came back to our neighbourhood voluntarily, with sledge and dogs and walrus-meat! Can it have been that John, his former partner in the plot, was on the look-out for him, and had engaged his aid to consummate their joint desertion?

"One thing is plain. This man at large and his comrade still on board, the safety of the whole company exacts the sternest observance of discipline. I have called all hands, and announced it as a standing order of the ship, and one to be observed inflexibly, that desertion, or the attempt to desert, shall be met at once by the sternest penalty. I have no alternative. By the body of my crew, sick, dependent, unable to move, and with everything to lose by the withdrawal of any portion of our efficient force, this announcement was received as a guarantee of their personal safety. But it was called for by other grave considerations. There is at this time on the part of all, men as well as officers, a warm feeling toward myself, and a strict, stanch fidelity to the expedition. But, for moral reasons which would control me, even if my impulse were different, I am constrained for the time to mingle among them without reserve, to act as a servant to their wants, to encourage colloquial equality and good humour; and, looking only a little way ahead to the juncture when a perfectly-regulated subordination will become essential, I know that my present stand will be of value. Necessity of strict discipline.

"This sledge-load of Godfrey's meat, coming as it does, may well be called a Godsend: one may forgive the man in consideration of the good which it has done us all. We have had a regular feed all round, and exult to think we need no catering for the morrow. It has cheered our downhearted sick men wonderfully. Our brew of beer, too,—the 'Arctic Linseed Mucilage Adaptation,'—turns out excellent. Our grunts and growls are really beginning to have a good-natured twang. Our faces lessen as our shadows promise to increase. I think I see a change which points to the happier future. Value of the supply of fresh meat.

"Our sick, however, are still non-operatives, and our one room is like the convalescent ward of an hospital, with Bonsall and myself for the only nurses." Convalescent ward.

CHAPTER XLI.

ROUTINE—GETTING UP—BREAKFAST—WORK—TURNING IN—HANS STILL
MISSING—THE DETERMINATION.

CHAPTER XLI.

"*April 3, Tuesday.*—To-day I detained Petersen from his hunt, and took a holiday rest myself,—that is to say, went to bed and —sweated : to-morrow I promise as much for Bonsall.

"While here in bed I will give the routine of a day in this spring-time of year :—

Getting up.

"At 7.30 call 'all hands;' which means that one of the well trio wakes the other two. This order is obeyed slowly. The commander confesses for himself that the breakfast is well-nigh upon table before he gets his stiff ankles to the floor. Looking around, he sees the usual mosaic of sleepers as ingeniously dovetailed and crowded together as the campers-out in a buffalo-bag. He winds his way through them, and, as he does so, some stereotyped remarks are interchanged. 'Thomas!'—our ex-cook, now side by side with the first officer of the expedition,—'Thomas, turn out!' 'Eugh-ng, sir.' 'Turn out; get up.' 'Ys-sir;' (sits bolt upright, and rubs his eyes.) 'How d' you feel, Mr. Ohlsen?' 'Better, sir.' 'How've you passed the night, Mr. Brooks?' 'Middlin', sir.' And, after a diversified series of spavined efforts, the mystical number forms its triangle at the table.

Breakfast table.

"It still stands in its simple dignity, an unclothed platform of boards, with a pile of plates in the centre. Near these is a virtuoso collection of cups grouped in a tumulus or cairn, commencing philosophically at the base with heavy stoneware, and ending with battered tin : the absolute pinnacle a debased dredging-box, which makes a bad goblet, being unpleasantly sharp at its rim. At one end of this table, partly hid by the beer-barrel, stands Petersen; at the side, Bonsall ; and a lime-juice cask opposite marks my seat. We are all standing : a momentary hush is made among the sick : and the daily prayer comes with one heart :—'Accept our gratitude, and restore us to our homes.'

"The act of devotion over, we sit down, and look—not at the CHAPTER XLI. breakfast, but at each other.

"It may sound absurd to those who cannot understand the nar- Detail of symptoms of illness. rowing interest which we three availables feel in our continued mutual ability, for me to say that we spend the first five minutes in a detail of symptoms. The state of each man's gums, and shins, and ankles, his elbows, loins, and kidneys, is canvassed minutely and compared with his yesterday's report: the recital might edify a specialist who was anxious to register the Protean indications of scurvy. It is sometimes ludicrous, but always sad.

"Now for the bill of fare. 'Who cooked?' I am describing a gala-day. 'It was Morton: he felt so much better that he got up at six; but he caved in soon after:'—

"First, coffee, great comforter to hard-worked men; one part of Bill of fare the genuine berry to three of navy-beans; next, sugar; what complex memories the word brings back!—the veritable sugar has been long ago defunct; but we have its representative molasses twice a week in our tea. Third, butter; there it is in a mutilated vegetable-dish; my own invention, melted from salt beef and washed in many waters: the unskilled might call it tallow. Fourth, a real delicacy, not to be surpassed in court or camp, for Morton was up to see to it,—a pile of hot rolls of fine Virginia flour. What else? Nothing else: the breakfast resolves itself into bean-coffee, tallow, and hot bread. Yet a cordial meal it is. I am sorry to hurry over it so uncourteously, for I could dwell with Charles Lamb's pensive enthusiasm upon the flesh-pots; but I have been longer in describing the feast than it takes us to dispose of it. I hurry on with the interesting detail. Dinner is breakfast, with the beans converted into soup instead of coffee; and supper boasts of stewed apples.

"Work commences at nine. Petersen is off with his gun, and Work. the two remaining dearly-beloved Rogers arrange their carte: one makes the round of the sick and deals out their daily allowance of raw meat; the other goes to cutting ice. Those who can sit in bed and work, pick eider-down or cotton, for coverlets to our boat-bedding on the escape; others sew canvas bags for the same purpose; and Brooks balls off twine in order to lay up 'small stuff.'

"At times when the sun comes out very brightly, Brooks and Wilson get permission to go on deck. One of us assists them,

and, by the aid of creeping and crawling, these poor cripples manage to sit upon the combings of the hatch and look around in
the glorious daylight. The sight seldom fails to affect them. There are emotions among rude, roughly-nurtured men which vent themselves in true poetry. Brooks has about him sensibilities that shame me.

"The afternoon, save to the cook, is a season of rest; a real lazy, lounging interval, arrested by the call to supper. The coming night-watch obliges me to take an evening cat-nap. I state this by way of implying that I never sleep o' daytimes.

"After supper, we have a better state of things than two weeks ago. Then the few tired outworkers were regaled by the groans and tossings of the sick. There was little conversation, and the physiognomy of our smoke-blackened little den was truly dismal. Now daylight pours in from the scuttle, the tea-kettle sings upon the stove, the convalescents rise up on their elbows and spin merry yarns. We are not yet sufficiently jolly for cards; but we are sufficiently thankful to do without them. At nine, silence almost unbroken prevails throughout our dormitory, and the watch-officer slips on his bear-skin, and, full of thoughts of to-morrow, resigns himself to a round of little routine observances, the most worthless of which is this unbroken record of the changing days.

"*April 6, Friday.*—Our little family is growing more and more uneasy about Hans. William reported him sick at Etah; but we had no faith in this story, and looked on his absence as merely the result of fatigue from exposure. But there really seems ground for serious apprehension now. My own fear is that William may have conveyed to him some false message, or some threat or reproof, using my name, and in this way deterred him from returning. Hans is very faithful; but he is entirely unaware of William's desertion, and he is besides both credulous and sensitive. I am attached to Hans: he has always been a sort of henchman, a body-guard, the companion of my walks. He is a devout Moravian; and when the party withdrew from the brig last fall he refused to accompany them on grounds of religious obligation. The boy has fixed, honourable principles. Petersen thinks that he ought to be sent for, but he has not thought out the question who is to be sent. Bonsall is too lame to travel; Petersen himself is infinitely the best fitted, but he shirks the duty, and to-day he takes to his bed : I alone am left.

" Clearly duty to this poor boy calls me to seek him, and clearly duty to these dependent men calls upon me to stay. Long and uncomfortably have I pondered over these opposing calls, but at last have come to a determination. Hans was faithful to me : the danger to him is imminent; the danger to those left behind only contingent upon my failure to return. With earnest trust in that same supervising Agency which has so often before in graver straits interfered to protect and carry me through, I have resolved to go after Hans.

" The orders are given. In three hours I will be equipped and ready to take advantage of the first practicable moment for the start. It makes me write gravely; for I am far from well, very far from strong, and am obliged to drive our reduced team twice seventy miles. The latter half of the journey I shall have to do entirely on foot, and our lowest night-temperatures are under —40°."

CHAPTER XLII.

JOURNEY AFTER HANS—ESQUIMAUX SLEDGING—HANS FOUND—RECEPTO
AMICO—EXPLANATION—FURTHER SEARCH—MATURING PLANS—CHANCES
OF ESCAPE—FOOD PLENTY—PAULIK—FAMINE AMONG THE ESQUIMAUX—
EXTINCTION—LIGHT HEARTS—DESERTER RECOVERED.

CHAPTER
XLII.

"*April* 10, *Tuesday.*—I left the brig at 10½ A.M., with but five dogs and a load so light as to be hardly felt.

Journey
after Hans.

"It requires some suggestive incident to show us how we have gradually become assimilated in our habits to the necessities of our peculiar life. Such an incident I find in my equipment. Compare it with similar sledge-outfits of last winter, and you will see that we are now more than half Esquimaux. It consists of—

Outfit.

"1. One small sledge, five feet six by two.

"2. An extra jumper and sack-pants for sleeping.

"3. A ball of raw walrus-meat.—This is all.

"The sledge is portable, and adapted to jump over the chasms of the land-ice, and to overturn with impunity, save to the luckless driver. It has two standards, or, as we call them, "upstanders," which spring like elbows from its hinder extremity.

"They serve as handles, by which, running or walking behind, you guide the sledge, lift it over rugged places, or rest yourself and your dogs while in progress together.

"The extra jumper is a bear-skin jacket, or rather shirt, which, after being put on is overlapped at the waist by a large pair of footed trousers. No winter traveller should be without these:—at temperatures below —25° or —30° they are invaluable. Blanket-bags are nearly useless below —30°, in a gale of wind; it riddles through them.

Provi-
sions.

"The ball of raw meat is made by chopping into inch-pieces walrus or other meat, and pouring among it hot tallow, by which the pieces are prevented from freezing too hard, so that you can readily cut out your meal as it is required. A little butter, if you have some, will contribute to soften it : olive-oil perhaps would be better ; but without some such luxurious additions a man in too great a hurry for dinner might be apt to risk his teeth. In the CHAPTER
XLII. present journey, having nothing but tallow, I made my meat-ball like a twist-loaf, and broke it with a stone.

"I have no incidents to record in the shape of disaster. My A rapid dogs were in excellent condition, and the ice good for travel. sledge
journey. The real incident of the journey was its early success. My dogs, in spite of low feeding, carried me sixty-four miles in eleven hours.

"Faithful Hans! Dear good follower and friend! I was out Hans on the floes just beyond the headlands of our old 'Refuge Har- found bour,' when I made out a black speck far in to shoreward. Re- fraction will deceive a novice on the ice; but we have learned to baffle refraction. By sighting the suspected object with your rifle at rest, you soon detect motion. It was a living animal—a man. Shoreward went the sledge; off sprang the dogs ten miles an hour, their driver yelling the familiar provocative to speed, 'Nan- nook! nannook!' 'A bear! a bear!' at the top of his lungs.

"There was no room for mistaking the methodical seal-stalking gait of Hans. He hardly varied from it as we came near; but in about fifteen minutes we were shaking hands and jabbering, in a patois of Esquimaux and English, our mutual news. The poor fellow had been really ill: five days down with severe pains of limbs have left him still a 'little veek;' which means with Hans well used up. I stuck him on the sledge and carried him to Anoatok.

"Fortunately Anoatok for once belied its name: there was no A welcome wind, and the sun broke down upon us with a genial +14°, although tea. the shade gave —25°. I had brought with me, expecting the boy might need it, a small mustard-bottle of our treasured molasses, and a little tea. We keep a camp-kettle at this hut, and both of us wore in our belts the inseparable tin-cup. How the boy enjoyed his hot tea! Metek had given him a few lumps of frozen walrus- liver, the very best provision for cold travel : our appetites were good ; and, the two thus fitly harmonizing, we crunched away right merrily.

"Hans reached Etah with Myouk two days after leaving us, and Hans' at once commenced his hunt. In the course of five days of most story. hazardous ice-range, he killed two fine young animals; his three

CHAPTER
XLII.

Hans
among the
Esqui-
maux.
companions in the hunt killing only three. He had the great advantage of my powerful Marston rifle, but his tackle was very inferior. Our sinnet-laid twine would not stand the powerful struggles of the beast, and on one occasion parted while fast in a large female. Still his success must have acquired for him the good-will of these people, for in the 'flens' or hunting-division of spoil they gained by his companionship.

"In the sickness that followed his long exposure, he tells me he was waited on most carefully at the settlement. A young daughter of Shunghu elected herself his nurse; and her sympathies and smiles have, I fear, made an impression on his heart which a certain damsel near Uppernavik might be sorry to hear of.

"Hans cached part of his meat at Littleton Island, after sending a load by William to the brig. He had no difficulty, I find,
in penetrating this man's designs. He was indeed urged by him to agree that they should drive off together to the south, and so leave us sledgeless. Upon Hans' refusal, he tried to obtain his rifle; but this of course was easily prevented. He consented at last to take up the meat, with a view of making terms with me, and securing probably a companion. Baffled in this, as I have mentioned, he made his escape a second time to Etah. There I might be content to leave him, an unwelcome guest, and dependent upon the Esquimaux. Strong and healthy as he is, our daily work goes on better for his absence, and the ship seems better when purged by his desertion; but the example is disastrous, and, cost what it may, I must have him back.

"*April* 11, *Wednesday.*—Hans started again to bring back the meat from Littleton Island cache. If he feels strengthened, I have given him a commission to which I attach the greatest importance.

"My hopes of again undertaking a spring journey to Kennedy Channel were strong in the early months of the winter; but, as our dogs died away a second time, and the scurvy crept in upon us, I became sad and distrustful as to the chance of our ever living to gain the open water. The return of the withdrawing party absorbed all my thoughts. They brought news of disaster, starvation, and loss of dogs among the natives. Our prospects seemed at the lowest ebb. Still I cherished a secret hope of making another journey, and had determined to undertake it alone, with our poor remnant of four dogs, trusting to my rifle for provision.

In fact, this continuation of my one great duty has been constantly before me, and I now think that I can manage it. Thus :—The Esquimaux have left Northumberland Island, and are now near Cape Alexander, as a better hunting-ground. Kalutunah, the best and most provident man among them, has managed to save seven dogs. I have authorized Hans to negotiate *carte-blanche*, if necessary, for four of these, even as a loan ; promising as a final bait the contingent possession of my whole team when I reach the open water on my return. On this mission I send my '*fides Achates*,' and await his return with anxious hope. CHAPTER XLII.

Expedition in search of dogs.

" I have seen, almost from the first day of our imprisonment by the ice, the probability, if nothing more, that we might never be able to liberate the ship. Elsewhere in this journal I have explained by what construction of my duty I urged the brig to the north, and why I deemed it impossible honourably to abandon her after a single season. The same train of reasoning now leads me to mature and organize everything for an early departure without her, in case she cannot be released. My hopes of this release are very feeble ; and I know that when it does occur, if ever, the season will, like the last, be too far advanced for me to carry my people home. All my experience, carefully reviewed from my note-books, and confirmed by consultation with Petersen, convinces me that I must start early, and govern my boat and sledges by the condition of the ice and hunting-grounds. Prospect of liberating the ship.

" Whatever of executive ability I have picked up during this brain and body-wearying cruise warns me against immature preparation or vacillating purposes. I must have an exact discipline, a rigid routine, and a perfectly-thought-out organization. For the past six weeks I have, in the intervals between my duty to the sick and the ship, arranged the schedule of our future course. Much of it is already under way. My journal shows what I have done, but what there is to do is appalling. Necessity of rigid routine and discipline.

" I state all this to show how much I hazard and possibly sacrifice by my intended journey to the north, and to explain why I have so little time and mood for scientific observation or research. My feelings may be understood when I say that my carpenter and all the working men, save Bonsall, are still on their backs ; and that a month's preliminary labour is needed before I can commence the heavy work of transporting my three boats over the ice to the Continued illness of the men anticipated water. As the moment of my writing this, the water is over eighty miles in a straight line from our brig.

"*April* 12, *Thursday.*—The wind still blowing as yesterday, from the southward and eastward. This is certainly favourable to the advance of open water. The long swell from the open spaces in Baffin's Bay has such a powerful effect upon the ice, that I should not wonder if the floes about Lifeboat Cove, off M'Gary Island, were broken up by the first of May.

"Our sick have been without fresh food since the 5th; but such is the stimulus imparted by our late supply that they as yet show no backward symptoms. M'Gary, and Ohlsen, and Brooks, and Riley, sun themselves daily, and are able to do much useful jobbing. Thomas begins to relieve me in cooking; Riley to take a spell at the slops; Morton cooks breakfast, and, aided by M'Gary and Ohlsen, has already finished one worsted quilted camp-blanket, with which I intend to cover our last remaining buffalo-skins. Wilson comes on slowly; Dr. Hayes' toe begins to heal; Sontag is more cheery. With the exception of Goodfellow, John, and Whipple, I can feel that those of my little household are fast becoming men again.

"*April* 13, *Friday.*—Our sick—which still means all hands, except the cook, which means the captain—entered this morning on their eighth day of fasting from flesh. One or two have been softening about the gums again for some days past, and all feel weak with involuntary abstinence. The evening comes, and 'Bim! bim! bim!' sounds upon the deck: Hans is back with his dogs. Rabbit-stew and walrus-liver!—a supper for a king!

"This life of ours—for we have been living much in this way for nine months past—makes me more charitable than I used to be with our Esquimaux neighbours. The day provides for itself; or, if it does not, we trust in the morrow, and are happy till to-morrow disappoints us. Our smoke-dried cabin is a scene worth looking at : no man with his heart in the right place but would enjoy it. Every man is elbowed up on his platform, with a bowl of rich gravy-soup between his knees, and a stick of frozen liver at his side, gorging himself with the antiscorbutic luxuries, and laughing as if neither ice nor water were before him to traverse.

"Hans has brought Metek with him, and Metek's young nephew, a fine-looking boy of fourteen.

"I do not know whether I have mentioned that, some little time before our treaty of alliance and mutual honesty, Metek stole the gunwale of the *Red Eric*. He has been, of course, in something of uncertainty as to his political and personal relations, and his present visit to the nalegak with a noble sledge-load of walrus-meat is evidently intended as a propitiation for his wrong.

"They are welcome, the meat and Metek, abundantly. He is the chieftain of Etah, and, as such, a vassal of him of Aūnatok, the 'Open Place,' which we have named Rensselaer Harbour. He speaks sadly, and so does Hans, of the fortunes of the winter.

"The Netelik settlement on Northumberland Island was already, when we heard of it last, the refuge of the natives from the further South, even beyond Wolstenholme. It has always been a hunting stronghold; but, as the winter darkness advanced, the pressure of numbers combined with their habitual improvidence to dissipate their supplies.

"It seems that the poor wretches suffered terribly,—even more than our neighbours of Etah Bay. Their laws exact an equal division; and the success of the best hunters was dissipated by the crowds of feeble claimants upon their spoils. At last the broken nature of the ice-margin, and the freezing-up of a large zone of ice, prevented them from seeking walrus. The water was inaccessible, and the last resource pressed itself upon them. They killed their dogs. Fearful as it sounds, when we think how indispensable the services of these animals are to their daily existence, they cannot now number more than twenty in the entire ownership of the tribe. From Glacier South to Glacier North, from Glacier East to the rude ice-bound coast which completes the circuit of their little world, this nation have but twenty dogs. What can they hope for without them?

"I can already count eight settlements, including about one hundred and forty souls. There are more, perhaps, but certainly not many. Out of these I can number five deaths since our arrival; and I am aware of hardships and disasters encountered by the survivors, which, repeated as they must be in the future, cannot fail to involve a larger mortality. Crime combines with disease and exposure to thin their numbers: I know of three murders within the past two years; and one infanticide occurred only a few months ago. These facts, which are open to

CHAPTER
XLII.
———
The Esqui-
maux
tribes
rapidly
dying out. my limited sources of information, cannot, of course, indicate the number of deaths correctly. They confirm, however, a fearful conclusion which these poor wretches have themselves communicated to us,—that they are dying out ; not lingeringly, like the American tribes, but so rapidly as to be able to mark within a generation their progress toward extinction.   Nothing can be more saddening, measured by our own sensibilities, than such a conviction ; but it seems to have no effect upon this remarkable people.   Surrounded by the graves of their dead, by huts untenanted, yet still recent in their memory as homesteads, even by caches of meat which, frozen under the snow by the dead of one year, are eaten by the living of the next, they show neither apprehension nor regret.   Even Kalutunah—a man of fine instincts, and, I think, of heart—will retain his apathy of face as, by the aid of Petersen, our interpreter, I point out to him the certainty of their speedy extinction.   He will smile in his efforts to count the years which must obliterate his nation, and break in Mirth in
misery. with a laugh as his children shout out their 'Amna Ayah,' and dance to the tap of his drum.

" How wonderful is all this !   Rude as are their ideas of numbers, there are those among this merry-hearted people who can reckon up to the fate of their last man.

A melan-
choly mi-
gration. " After Netelik, the receptacle of these half-starved fugitives, had been obliged itself to capitulate with famine, the body corporate determined, as on like occasions it had often done before, to migrate to the seats of the more northern hunt.

" The movements of the walrus, and the condition of the ice, seem to be known to them by a kind of instinct ; so, when the light came, they harnessed in their reserve of dogs, and started for Cape Alexander.

" It could not, one might suppose, have been a very cheerful migration,—women, children, and young babies thrusting themselves into a frozen wilderness at temperatures below —30°, and sometimes verging on —60°.   But Hans, with a laugh that seemed to indicate some exquisite point of concealed appreciation of the ludicrous, said they travelled generally in squads, singing ' Amna Ayah,' and, when they reached any of the halting-huts, ate the blubber and liver of the owners and danced all night.   So at last they came to Utak-soak, the ' great caldron,' which we call

Cape Alexander, and settled down at Petcravik, or the 'Welcome Halt.'

"At first game was scarce here also; but the season came soon when the female walrus is tending her calf on the ice, and then, but for the protracted exposure of the hunt, there was no drawback to its success. They are desperately merry now, and seem to have forgotten that a second winter is ahead of them. Hans said, with one of his quiet laughs, 'One half of them are sick, and cannot hunt: these do nothing but eat, and sing, "Amna Ayah."'

"*April* 18, *Wednesday.*—I am just off a two hundred miles' journey, bringing back my deserter, and, what is perhaps quite as important, a sledge-load of choice walrus-cuts.

"I found from Hans that his negotiation for the dogs had failed, and that unless I could do something by individual persuasion, I must give up my scheme of a closing exploration to the north. I learned, too, that Godfrey was playing the great man at Etah, defying recapture; and I was not willing to trust the influence he might exert on my relations with the tribe. I determined that he should return to the brig.

"I began by stratagem. I placed a pair of foot-cuffs on Metek's sledge, and, after looking carefully to my body-companion six-shooter, invited myself to ride back with him to Etah. His nephew remained on board in charge of Hans, and I disguised myself so well in my nessak that, as we moved off, I could easily have passed for the boy Paulik, whose place I had taken.

"As our eighty miles drew to an end, and that which we call the settlement came close in view, its population streamed out to welcome their chief's return. Among the first and most prominent was the individual whom I desired to meet, waving his hand and shouting 'Tima!' as loudly as the choicest savage of them all. An instant later and I was at his car, with a short phrase of salutation and its appropriate gesture. He yielded unconditionally at once, and, after walking and running, by turns, for some eighty. miles before the sledge, with a short respite at Anoatok, is now a prisoner on board.

"My remaining errand was almost as successful."

CHAPTER XLIII.

HARTSTENE BAY—ESQUIMAUX DWELLINGS—A CROWDED INTERIOR--THE
NIGHT'S LODGING—A MORNING REPAST—MOURNING FOR THE DEAD---
FUNERAL RITES—PENANCE.

CHAPTER
XLIII.
——
Hartstene
Bay.

ETAH is on the north-eastern curve of Hartstene Bay, facing to the south and west. As you stretch over from the south point of Littleton Island to the main, the broken character of the ice subsides into a traversable plain, and the shore-scenery assumes a singular wildness. The bottom series of plutonics rises to grand and mountainous proportions, and in the back-ground, soaring above these, are the escaladed green-stones of the more northern coast. At the very bottom of the bay are two perforations, one a fortress-mantled fiord, the other a sloping ravine: both are occupied by extensions of the same glacier.

Etah

The fiord points to Peteravik, where Kalutunah and his hungry southern corps have now taken up their quarters; the other is the oft-mentioned settlement of Etah. A snow-drift, rising at an angle of forty-five degrees, till it mingles with the steep sides of a mountain, is dotted by two dark blemishes upon its pure white. Coming nearer, you see that the dirt-spots are perforations of the snow: nearer still, you see above each opening a smaller one, and a covered roof connecting them. These are the doors and windows of the settlement; two huts and four families, but for these vent holes, entirely buried in the snow.

Reception
by the
natives.

The inmates of the burrows swarmed around me as I arrived. "Nalegak! nalegak! tima!" was yelled in chorus; never seemed people more anxious to propitiate, or more pleased with an unexpected visit. But they were airily clad, and it blew a north-wester; and they soon crowded back into their ant-hill. Meantime preparations were making for my in-door reception, and after a little while Metek and myself crawled in on our hands and knees, through an extraordinary tossut thirty paces long. As I emerged on the inside, the salute of "nalegak" was repeated with an increase of energy that was anything but pleasant.

There were guests before me,—six sturdy denizens of the CHAPTER XLIII. neighbouring settlement. They had been overtaken by the storm while hunting, and were already crowded upon the central dais of A crowded interior. honour. They united in the yell of welcome, and I soon found myself gasping the ammoniacal steam of some fourteen vigorous, amply-fed, unwashed, unclothed fellow-lodgers. I had come somewhat exhausted by an eighty miles' journey through the atmosphere of the floes : the thermometer inside was at + 90°, and the vault measured fifteen feet by six. Such an amorphous mass of compounded humanity one could see nowhere else : men, women, children, with nothing but their native dirt to cover them, twined and dovetailed together like the worms in a fishing-basket.

No hyperbole could exaggerate that which in serious earnest I give as the truth. The platform measured but seven feet in breadth, by six in depth, the shape being semi-elliptical. Upon this, including children and excluding myself, were bestowed thirteen persons.

The kotluk of each matron was glowing with a flame sixteen An Esquimaux supper and bed. inches long. A flipper-quarter of walrus, which lay frozen on the floor of the netek, was cut into steaks ; and the kolopsuts began to smoke with a burden of ten or fifteen pounds apiece. Metek, with a little amateur aid from some of the sleepers, emptied these without my assistance. I had the most cordial invitation to precede them ; but I had seen enough of the culinary régime to render it impossible. I broke my fast on a handful of frozen liver-nuts that Bill brought me, and, bursting out into a profuse perspiration, I stripped like the rest, threw my well-tired carcase across Mrs. Eider-duck's extremities, put her left-hand baby under my armpit, pillowed my head on Myouk's somewhat warm stomach, and thus, an honoured guest and in the place of honour, fell asleep.

Next morning, the sun nearly at noonday height, I awoke : Mrs. A morning repast. Eider-duck had my breakfast very temptingly ready. It was forked on the end of a curved piece of bone,—a lump of boiled blubber and a choice cut of meat. The preliminary cookery I had not seen : I am an old traveller, and do not care to intrude into the mysteries of the kitchen. My appetite was in its usual blessed redundance, and I was about to grasp the smiling proffer, when I saw the matron, who was manipulating as chief intendant

CHAPTER XLIII.

Esquimaux cookery.

of the other kotluk, performing an operation that arrested me. She had in her hand a counterpart of the curved bone that supported my *déjeuner*,—indeed, it is the universal implement of an Esquimaux cuisine,—and, as I turned my head, I saw her quietly withdrawing it from beneath her dress, and then plunging it into the soup-pot before her, to bring out the counterpart of my own smoking morsel. I learned afterward that the utensil has its two recognised uses ; and that, when not immediately wanted for the purposes of pot or table, it ministers to the "royal luxury" of the Scottish king. I dare not amplify this description.

Dirt or filth in our sense is not a conceived quality with these Esquimaux. Incidentally it may be an annoyance or obstruction ; but their nearest word, "Eberk," expresses no more than this.

It is an ethnological trait of these ultra-northern nomads,—so far as I know, a unique one,—and must be attributed not alone to their predatory diet and peculiar domestic system, but to the extreme cold, which by rapid freezing resists putrefaction, and prevents the joint accumulation of the dogs and the household from being intolerable. Their senses seem to take no cognizance of what all instinct and association make revolting to the sight, and touch, and smell of civilized man.

My note-book proves this by exact and disgusting details, the very mildest of which I cannot transfer to these pages.

I spent some time at Etah in examining the glacier and in making sketches of things about me. I met several old friends.

Meeting with Awahtok.

Among the rest was Awahtok, only now recovering from his severe frost-bite, the effect of his fearful adventure with Myouk among the drifting ice. I gave him a piece of red flannel and powwowed him. He resides with Ootuniah in the second hut, a smaller one than Metek's, with his pretty wife, a sister of Kalutunah's. I could hardly believe the infanticide story which Hans had told me of this young couple ; and, pretending ignorance of the matter, I asked after the child's health. Their manner satisfied me that the story was true ; they turned their hands downward, but without any sign of confusion. They did not even pay its memory the cheap compliment of tears, which among these people are always at hand.

There is a singular custom which I have often noticed here as well as among some of the Asiatics. and which has its analogies

in more cultivated centres. I allude to the regulated formalities
of mourning for the dead. They weep according to system; when
one begins they are all expected to join, and it is the office of
courtesy for the most distinguished of the company to wipe the
eyes of the chief mourner. They often assemble by concert for a
general weeping match; but it happens sometimes that one will
break out into tears, and others courteously follow, without knowing at first what is the particular subject of grief.

It is not, however, the dead alone who are sorrowed for by such
a ceremony. Any other calamity may call for it as well: the
failure of a hunt, the snapping of a walrus-line, or the death of a
dog. Mrs Eider-duck, *née* Small Belly (Egurk), once looked up at
me from her kolupsut and burst into a gentle gush of woe. I was
not informed of her immediate topic of thought, but with remarkable presence of mind I took out my handkerchief,—made by
Morton out of the body of an unused shirt,—and, after wiping
her eyes politely, wept a few tears myself. This little passage
was soon over; Mrs. Eider-duck returned to her kolupsut, and
Nalegak to his note-book.

The ceremonial mourning, however, is attended sometimes, if
not always, by observances of a more serious character. So far as
my information goes, the religious notions of the Esquimaux extend only to the recognition of supernatural agencies, and to certain usages by which they may be conciliated. The angekok of
the tribe—the prophet, as he is called among our Indians of the
West—is the general counsellor. He prescribes or powwows in
sickness and over wounds, directs the policy and movements of
the little state, and, though not the titular chief, is really the
power behind the throne. It is among the prerogatives and duties
of his office to declare the appropriate oblations and penances of
grief. These are sometimes quite oppressive. The bereaved hus-
band may be required even to abstain from the seal or walrus-hunt
for the whole year, from *Okiakut* to *Okiakut*—winter to winter.
More generally he is denied the luxury of some article of food, as
the rabbit or a favourite part of the walrus; or he may be forbidden to throw back his nessak, and forced to go with uncovered
head.

A sister of Kalutunah died suddenly at Peteravik. Her body
was sewed up in skins, not in a sitting posture, like the remains

22

which we found in the graves at the south, but with the limbs extended at full length ; and her husband bore her unattended to her resting-place, and covered her, stone by stone, with a rude monumental cairn. The blubber-lamp was kept burning outside the hut while the solitary funeral was in progress ; and when it was over the mourners came together to weep and howl, while the widower recited his sorrows and her praise. His penance was severe, and combined most of the inflictions which I have described above.

It is almost as difficult to trace back the customs of the Smith's Sound Esquimaux as it is to describe their religious faith. They are a declining—almost an obsolete—people, "*toto orbe divisos,*" and too much engaged with the necessities of the present to cherish memorials of the past. It was otherwise with those whom we met in the more southern settlements. These are now for the most part concentrated about the Danish posts, in very different circumstances, physical as well as moral, from their brethren of the north.

CHAPTER XLIV.

THE ESQUIMAUX OF GREENLAND—CHANGE OF CHARACTER—LABOURS OF
THE MISSIONARIES—NÖLUK—THE OMINAKS—PINGEIAK AND JENS—THE
ANGEKOKS—ISSIUTOK—THE IMNAPOK—THE DECREE.

SOME thirty years ago the small-pox found its way among the CHAPTER
XLIV. natives of the upper coast, and most of those who escaped or sur- vived its ravages sought the protection of the colony.   Others Small-pox
among the followed from the more inland regions; and now there is not an natives Esquimaux, from the Great Glaciers of Melville Bay down to Upernavik, who does not claim fellowship in that community.

We found traces of their former haunts much further north Traces of
deserted than they appear to have been noticed by others; some of such a huts. character as to indicate for them a tolerably recent date.   I have already mentioned the deserted huts which we came upon in Shoal-Water Cove, in lat. 78° 27', and the stone fox-traps upon the rocks near them.   Other huts, evidently of Esquimaux con- struction, but very ancient, were found on the in-shore side of Littleton Island; and among the cairns around them that had served to conceal provisions or that now covered the remains of the dead, were numerous implements of the chase.

The huts which I saw near Refuge Harbour, in lat. 78° 33', were much more perfect, and had been inhabited very recently. From some of the marks which I have referred to in my journal, there was reason to suppose that the inmates might return before the opening of another season.

It was still otherwise with those that we met at Karsuk and elsewhere further to the south.   These, though retaining signs of comparatively modern habitation, were plainly deserted homes. I met at Upernavik an ancient woman, the latest survivor of the The only
survivor of few who escaped from these settlements during the general pestil- a tribe. ence.

The labours of the Lutheran and Moravian missionaries have been so far successful among these people that but few of them are now without the pale of professed Christianity, and its re-

CHAPTER XLIV.

Original state of the natives.

forming influences have affected the moral tone of all. Before the arrival of these self-sacrificing evangelists, murder, incest, burial of the living, and infanticide, were not numbered among crimes. It was unsafe for vessels to touch upon the coast; treachery was as common and as much honoured as among the Polynesians of the Eastern seas. Crantz tells us of a Dutch brig that was seized by the natives at the port of Disco, in 1740, and the whole crew murdered; and two years later the same fate befell the seamen of another vessel that had accidentally stranded.

Change of character.

But for the last hundred years Greenland has been safer for the wrecked mariner than many parts of our own coast. Hospitality is the universal characteristic, enjoined upon the converted as a Christian duty, but everywhere a virtue of savage life. From Upernavik to Cape Farewell, the Esquimaux does not hesitate to devote his own meal to the necessities of a guest.

Benefits of the missionary school.

The benefits of the missionary school are not confined to the Christianized natives; and it is observable that the virtues of truth, self-reliance, and generous bearing, have been inculcated successfully with men who still cherish the wild traditionary superstitions of their fathers. Some of these are persons of strongly-marked character, and are trusted largely by the Danish officials. One of them, the nalegak-soak, or great chief, Nöluk, claims to have been the king or "head-man" of his people.

Traditions and games of the Greenlanders.

But among the native Greenlanders, as among other nomads, there seems to be no recognition of mastership except such as may be claimed by superiority of prowess. They have definite traditions of the organized games and exercises by which this superiority used to be authenticated. Indeed, the custom obtained until within the two last generations, and is traceable still in many of the periodical sports. Wrestling, jumping, tracking by the fingers or with hooked arms, pushing heel to heel in a sitting posture, dealing and receiving alternate blows on the left shoulder, shooting further and with the stronger bow, carrying the heavier stone the greater distance, were among their trials of strength. I have seen some of these stones at Fortuna Bay and Disco Fiord, which remain as they were left at the end of the contest, memorials of the athlete who sustained their weight.

Nöluk is a remarkably powerful man, and as straight and graceful as an Iroquois. He is now a grandfather by his second

wife; but he is still the best hunter of the settlement, and dis- CHAPTER
dains to comply with the usage which would transfer his dog- XLIV.
teams and apparatus of the hunt to his grown-up son.   During Nöluk.
the pestilence of 1820 he resided fifty-six miles north of Upernavik, at Tessiusak, in lat. 73° 36': I have seen the ruins of his
hut there.   When all the families fled from the sick, Nöluk still
drove his sledge homeward and deposited food regularly for his
dying wife.   On his last visit he saw her through the window a
corpse, and his infant son sucking at her frozen breast.   Parental
instinct was mastered by panic: he made his way to the south
without crossing the threshold.

Among the regal perquisites of the nalegak-soak was the Privileges
questionable privilege of having as many wives as he could sup- of the
port.   Besides this, he had little except an imperfectly-defined soak.
claim to certain proceeds of the hunt.   In old times, the subordinate nalegaks, chieftains of minor settlements, held their
office by a similar title of personal might among their immediate
fellows—thus constituting something like a system of feudal
sovereignties without hereditary descent.

It is related, however, much as it is in histories with which we The
are more familiar, that the supremacy of the "Great Master" Master"
sometimes encountered rebuke from his barons.   The Upernavik and his
reindeer-hunters used to ascend the Salmon River, near Svartehuk, barons.
to a point from which by a single day's journey they could reach
Okossisak, a hunting-station of the Ominaks.   It so happened
upon one occasion, when the Ominaks had been more than The Omi-
ordinarily successful in the chase, that a band of Upernaviks, Uperna-
with whom fortune had been less propitious, determined to pay vika.
them a predatory visit, attended by their great chief, the liege
lord of both tribes.   They found the Ominaks with their chief in
company, a short chunky fellow, who proffered the accustomed
hospitalities of his tent in true knightly style.   But, in reply to
the salutation, "Be seated and eat," the Great Upernavik, whose
companions were watching for their cue, gave a scowl, the reverse
of the uniform formula of acceptance, which is simply to sit down
and be filled.   Hereupon old Ominak strung silently a heavy bow,
and, drawing his arrow to the head, buried it in the narrow cleft
of a distant rock, soliloquizing, as it struck, "He who is better
than I am is my master."   I give his words in the original for an

CHAPTER XLIV.

An exercise in phonetics

exercise in phonetics: " Kinajougenerua," who is better, " Ovanöt," than I am; the rest of the sentence—"is my master"—being understood: an elliptical form of expression very common among these people, and often aided by accompanying gestures. Thus euphoniously solicited, the Upernaviks sat down and ate, and, pronouncing the brief acknowledgment, "Thanks," which always end's a stranger's meal, went their way in peace.

The old practice which is found among some of the Asiatic and North American tribes, of carrying off the bride by force, is common among the Esquimaux, and reluctantly abandoned even by the converted. The ceremonial rite follows at the convenience of the

Jens and Pingeiak.

parties. Jens, the son of my old friend Cristiansen at Pröven, came very nigh being left a bachelor by an exercise of this custom. He was not quite ready to perform the gallant function himself toward his lady-love, when a lusty rival, one Pingeiak, carried her off bodily in dead of night. The damsel made good fight, however, and, though the abduction was repeated three times over, she managed to keep her troth. In the result, Jens, as phlegmatic and stupid a half-breed as I ever met with, got the prettiest woman in all North Greenland. Pingeiak was the best hunter and had the largest tent, but Jens was the son of the head man. I believe such things may come about in other parts of the world.

An elopement.

I remember other instances among parties whom I knew. A young aspirant for the favours of an unbaptized daughter of the settlement at Sever-nik got a companion to assist him, and succeeded in carrying her to his sledge. But the ruthless father had the quicker dog-team, and pursued with such ferocious alacrity, that the unlucky devotee of ancient custom had to clamber up a rocky gorge to escape his wrath, leaving the chosen one behind him. The report.—for scandal is not frozen out of Greenland— makes the lady a willing eloper, and more courageous than her runaway lover.

The last angekok.

The mysteries of the angekok, still so marked in their influence further to the north, are not openly recognised near the Danish settlements. The last regular professor of them, Kenguit, was baptized at Pröven in 1844, changing his name to Jonathan Jeremias. But as you recede from the missionary influence the dark art is still practised in all its power.

A fact of psychological interest, as it shows that civilized or savage wonder-workers form a single family, is that the angekoks believe firmly in their own powers. I have known several of them personally, after my skill in powwow had given me a sort of correlative rank among them, and can speak with confidence on this point. I could not detect them in any resort to jugglery or natural magic: their deceptions are simply vocal, a change of voice, and perhaps a limited profession of ventriloquism, made more imposing by the darkness. They have, however, like the members of the learned professions everywhere else, a certain language or jargon of their own, in which they communicate with each other. Lieutenant-Governor Steffenson, who had charge of the Northern District up to 1829, and was an admirable student of everything that regards these people, says that their artificial language is nothing but the ordinary dialect of the country, modified in the pronunciation, with some change in the import of the words and the introduction of a few cabalistic terms.

Besides the angekoks, who are looked up to as the hierophants or dispensers of good, they have the *issiutok*, or evil men, who work injurious spells, enchantments, metamorphoses. Like the witches of both Englands, the Old and the New, these malignants are rarely submitted to trial till they have been subjected to punishment—"castigat auditque." The finder of the Runic stone, old Pelemut, was one of them, and dealt with accordingly. Two others, only as far back as 1828, suffered the penalty of their crime on the same day, one at Karmenak, the other at Upernavik. This last was laudably killed after the "old customs,"—custom being the apology of the rude everywhere for things revolting to modern sense. He was first harpooned, then eviscerated, a flap let down from his forehead "to cover his eyes and prevent his seeing again,"—he had the "evil eye," it might seem; and then small portions of his heart were eaten, so as to make it secure that he could not come back to earth unchanged. All this in accordance with venerated ritual.

The other, the Karmenak case, was that of an old sick man. He was dealt with more succinctly by his neighbour Kamokah, now old Tobias; who, at the instance of the issiutok family, pushed him into the sea after harpooning him, and then gave his flesh to the dogs. I have seen Tobias at Pröven, a Christian-

CHAPTER XLIV.

The angekoks.

The issiutok, or evil men.

Their punishment.

ized man now, of very good repute, and, for aught I know, worthy
of it.

The capital punishment with them, as with us, seems in general
to be reserved for offences of the higher grade. For those of
minor dignity, such as form the staple of our civilized forums,
and even those which might find their way profitably into a court
of honour, the *Imnapok* is the time-honoured tribunal of redress.
The original meaning of this word, I believe, is a native dance or
singsong; but the institution which now bears the name is of
much more dignity, and is found, with only circumstantial
differences, among many other tribes within and beyond the Arctic
circle.

An Esquimaux has inflicted an injury on one of his countrymen: he has cut his seal-lines, or harmed his dogs, or burned his
bladder-float, or perpetrated some enormity equally grievous. A
summons comes to him from the angekok to meet the "country-
side" at an Imnapok. The friends of the parties and the idlers of
many miles around gather about the justice-seat, it may be at
some little cluster of huts, or, if the weather permits, in the open
air. The accuser rises and preludes a few discords with a seal-rib
on a tom-tom or drum. He then passes to the charge, and pours
out in long paragraphic words all the abuse and ridicule to which
his outrageous vernacular can give expression. The accused
meanwhile is silent ; but, as the orator pauses after a signal hit,
or to flourish a cadence on his musical instrument, the whole
audience, friends, neutrals, and opponents, signalize their approval
by outcries as harmonious as those which we sometimes hear in
our town-meetings at home. Stimulated by the applause, and
warming with his own fires, the accuser renews the attack, his
eloquence becoming more and more licentious and vituperative,
until it has exhausted either his strength or his vocabulary of
invective. Now comes the accused, with defence and counter-
charge and retorted abuse; the assembly still listening and
applauding through a lengthened session. The Homeric debate
at a close, the angekoks hold a powwow, and a penalty is de-
nounced against the accused for his guilt, or the accuser for his
unsustained prosecution.

CHAPTER XLV.

WALRUS-HUNTING— ESQUIMAUX HABITS—RETURN FROM ETAH—PREPARING
FOR ESCAPE—MAKING SLEDGES—DR. HAYES.

THE six storm-arrested strangers were off early in the morning: I CHAPTER
sent messages of compliment by them to Kalutunah, inviting him XLV.
to visit the brig; and in the afternoon Myouk and myself followed Departure
them to the floes for a walrus-hunt. of the
strangers.

The walrus supplies the staple food of the Rensselaer Bay
Esquimaux throughout the greater part of the year. To the
south as far as Murchison Channel, the seal, unicorn, and white
whale alternate at their appropriate seasons ; but in Smith's Sound
these last are accidental rather than sustained hunts.

The manner of hunting the walrus depends in a considerable Manner of
degree on the season of the year. In the fall, when the pack is the walrus.
but partially closed, they are found in numbers hanging around
the neutral region of mixed ice and water, and, as this becomes
solid with the advance of winter, following it more and more to
the south.

The Esquimaux approach them then over the young ice, and
assail them in cracks and holes with nalegeit and line. This
fishery, as the season grows colder, darker, and more tempestuous,
is fearfully hazardous; scarcely a year passes without a catastrophe. It was the theme of happy augury last winter, that no
lives had been lost for some months before, and the angekoks
even ventured to prophesy from it that the hunt would be auspicious,—a prophecy, like some others, hazarded after the event, for
the ice had continued open for the walrus till late in December.

With the earliest spring, or, more strictly, about a month after The spring
the re-appearance of the sun, the winter famine is generally fishery.
relieved. January and February are often, in fact, nearly always,
months of privation; but during the latter part of March the
spring fishery commences. Everything is then life and excitement.

The walrus is now taken in two ways. Sometimes he has risen

by the side of an iceberg, where the currents have worn away the floe, or through a tide-crack, and, enjoying the sunshine too long, finds his retreat cut off by the freezing up of the opening; for, like the seal at its attuk, the walrus can only work from below. When thus caught, the Esquimaux, who with keen hunter-craft are scouring the floes, scent him out by their dogs and spear him.

The early spring is the breeding season, and the walrus then are in their glory. My observations show that they tenant the region throughout the entire year; but at this time the female, with her calf, is accompanied by the grim-visaged father, surging

CHILDREN PLAYING BALL.

in loving trios from crack to crack, sporting around the berg-water, or basking in the sun. While thus on their tours, they invite their vigilant enemies to the second method of capture. This is also by the lance and harpoon; but it often becomes a

regular battle, the male gallantly fronting the assault and charging the hunters with furious bravery. Not unfrequently the
entire family—mother, calf, and bull—are killed in one of these
contests.

The huts—those poor, miserable, snow-covered dens—are now
scenes of life and activity. Stacks of jointed meat are piled upon
the ice-foot; the women are stretching the hide for sole-leather,
and the men cutting out a reserve of harpoon-lines for the winter.
Tusky walrus heads stare at you from the snow-bank, where they
are stowed for their ivory; the dogs are tethered to the ice; and
the children, each one armed with the curved rib of some big
amphibion, are playing ball and bat among the drifts.

On the day of my arrival, four walrus were killed at Etah, and
no doubt many more by Kalutak at Peteravik. The quantity of
beef which is thus gained during a season of plenty, one might
suppose, should put them beyond winter want; but there are
other causes besides improvidence which make their supplies
scanty. The poor creatures are not idle; they hunt indomitably,
without the loss of a day. When the storms prevent the use of
the sledge, they still work in stowing away the carcasses of previous hunts. An excavation is made either on the mainland, or,
what is preferred, upon an island inaccessible to foxes, and the
jointed meat is stacked inside and covered with heavy stones.
One such cache, which I met on a small island a short distance
from Etah, contained the flesh of ten walrus, and I know of several
others equally large.

The excessive consumption is the true explanation of the
scarcity. By their ancient laws all share with all; and, as they
migrate in numbers as their necessities prompt, the tax on each
particular settlement is excessive. The quantity which the members of a family consume, exorbitant as it seems to a stranger, is
rather a necessity of their peculiar life and organization than the
result of inconsiderate gluttony. In active exercise and constant
exposure to cold the waste of carbon must be enormous.

When in-doors and at rest, tinkering over their ivory harness-
rings, fowl-nets, or other household gear, they eat as we often do
in more civilized lands—for animal enjoyment and to pass away
time. But when on the hunt they take but one meal a day, and
that after the day's labour is over; they go out upon the ice

CHAPTER XLV.

Esquimaux ration.

without breakfast, and, except the "cold cuts," which I confess are numerous, eat nothing until their return. I would average the Esquimaux ration in a season of plenty—it is of course a mere estimate, but I believe a perfectly fair one—at eight or ten pounds a day, with soup and water to the extent of half a gallon.

At the moment of my visit, when returning plenty had just broken in upon their famine, it was not wonderful that they were hunting with avidity. The settlements of the South seek at this season the hunting-ground above, and, until the seals begin to form their basking-holes, some ten days later, the walrus is the single spoil.

Haunts of the walrus.

I incline to the opinion that these animals frequent the half-broken ice-margin throughout the year; for, after the season has become comparatively open, they are still found in groups, with their young, disporting in the leads and shore-water. They are, of course, secure under such circumstances from the Esquimaux hunters of the Far North, who, not having the kayak of the more southern settlements, can only approach them on the ice.

In the late summer or "ausak," after all ice has melted, the walrus are in the habit of resorting to the rocks. They are then extremely alert and watchful ; but the Esquimaux note their haunts carefully, and, concealing themselves in the clefts, await their approach with patient silence, and secure them by the harpoon and line.

Departure from Etah.

My departure from Etah Bay was hastened by news from the brig. Hans brought me a letter from Dr. Hayes, while I was out walrus-hunting near Life-Boat Cove, which apprised me of the dangerous illness of Mr. M'Gary. I had a load of meat on my sledge, and was therefore unable to make good speed with my four tired dogs; but I rode and ran by turns, and reached the brig, after fifty miles' travel, in seven hours from the time of meeting Hans. I was thoroughly broken down by the effort, but had the satisfaction of finding that my excellent second officer had passed the crisis of his attack.

I left Hans behind me with orders to go to Peteravik and persuade Kalutunah to come to the brig, sending him a capstan-bar as a pledge of future largess,—invaluable for its adaptation to harpoon-shafts.

" *April* 19, *Thursday.*—The open water has not advanced from

the south more than four miles within the past three weeks. It
is still barely within Cape Alexander. It is a subject of serious
anxiety to me. Our experience has taught us that the swell
caused by these winds breaks up the ice rapidly. Now, there can
be no swell to the southward, or these heavy gales would have
done this now. It augurs ill not only for the possible release of
the brig, but for the facility of our boat-voyage if we shall be
obliged to forsake her, as everything seems to say we must do
soon. Last year, on the 10th of May, the water was free around
Littleton Island, and coming up to within two miles of Refuge
Inlet. It is now forty miles further off!

" Petersen and Ohlsen are working by short spells at the boats
and sledges.

" I will not leave the brig until it is absolutely certain that she
cannot thaw out this season; but everything shall be matured for
our instant departure as soon as her fate is decided. Every detail
is arranged ; and, if the sick go on as they have done, I do not
doubt but that we may carry our boats some thirty or forty miles
over the ice before finally deciding whether we must desert the
brig.

" *April* 20, *Friday.*—A relief-watch, of Riley, Morton, and
Bonsall, are preparing to saw out sledge runners from our cross-
beams. It is slow work. They are very weak, and the thermometer sinks at night to —26°. Nearly all our beams have been
used up for fuel ; but I have saved enough to construct two long
sledges of 17 feet 6 inches each. I want a sledge sufficiently long
to bring the weight of the whaleboat and her stowage within the
line of the runner; this will prevent her rocking and pitching
when crossing hummocked ice, and enable us to cradle her firmly
to the sledge.

" They are at this moment breaking out our cabin bulkhead to
extract the beam. Our cabin dormitory is full of cold vapour.
Everything is comfortless : blankets make a sorry substitute for
the moss-padded wall which protected us from —60°.

" *April* 21, *Saturday.*—Morton's heel is nearly closed, and there
is apparently a sound bone underneath. He has been upon his
back since October. I can now set this faithful and valuable man
to active duty very soon.

" The beam was too long to be carried through our hatches ;

CHAPTER
XLV.
——

Sledge
making.

we therefore have sawed it as it stands, and will carry up the slabs separately. These slabs are but one and a half inch wide, and must be strengthened by iron bolts and cross-pieces; still they are all that we have. I made the bolts out of our cabin curtain-rods, long disused. Mr. Petersen aids Ohlsen in grinding his tools. They will complete the job to-morrow,—for we must work on Sunday now,—and by Monday be able to begin at other things. Petersen undertakes to manufacture our cooking and mess-gear. I have a sad-looking assortment of battered rusty tins to offer him; but with stove-pipe much may be done.

"*April 22, Sunday.*—Gave rest for all but the sawyers, who keep manfully at the beam. Some notion of our weakness may be formed from the fact of these five poor fellows averaging among them but one foot per hour.

Dr. Hayes.

"I read our usual prayers; and Dr. Hayes, who feels sadly the loss of his foot, came aft and crawled upon deck to sniff the day-light. He had not seen the sun for five months and three weeks."

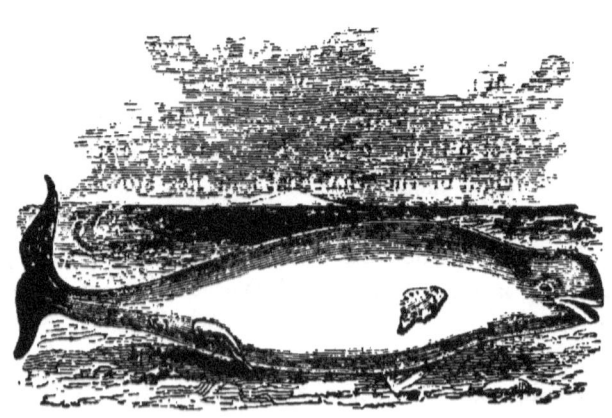

KALUTUNAH—THE HUNTING PARTY—SETTING OUT—MY TALLOW-BALL,—
A WILD CHASE—HUNTING STILL—THE GREAT GLACIER—THE ESCA-
LADED STRUCTURE—FORMATION OF BERGS—THE VISCOUS FLOW—
CREVICES — THE FROZEN WATER-TUNNEL—CAPE FORBES—FACE OF
GLACIER.

WE continued toiling on with our complicated preparations till
the evening of the 24th, when Hans came back well laden with
walrus meat. Three of the Esquimaux accompanied him, each
with his sledge and dog-team fully equipped for a hunt. The
leader of the party, Kalutunah, was a noble savage, greatly superior in everything to the others of his race. He greeted me with
respectful courtesy, yet as one who might rightfully expect an
equal measure of it in return, and, after a short interchange of
salutations, seated himself in the post of honour at my side.

I waited, of course, till the company had fed and slept, for
among savages especially haste is indecorous, and then, after distributing a few presents, opened to them my project of a northern
exploration. Kalutunah received his knife and needles with a
" Kuyanaka," " I thank you :" the first thanks I have heard from
a native of this upper region. He called me his friend,—" Asa-
kaoteet," " I love you well,"—and would be happy, he said, to
join the " nalegak-soak" in a hunt.

The project was one that had engaged my thoughts long before
daylight had renewed the possibility of carrying it out. I felt
that the further shores beyond Kennedy Channel were still to be
searched before our work could be considered finished ; but we
were without dogs, the indispensable means of travel. We had
only four left out of sixty-two. Famine among the Esquimaux
had been as disastrous as disease with us : they had killed all but
thirty, and of these there were now sixteen picketted on the ice
about the brig. The aid and influence of Kalutunah could secure
my closing expedition.

I succeeded in making my arrangements with him, provisionally

CHAPTER
XLVI.

Return of
Hans with
a party of
Esqui-
maux.

Kalutu-
nah.

Project of
a northern
explora-
tion.

CHAPTER XLVI.

Departure of the exploring expedition.

at least, and the morning after we all set out. The party con-sisted of Kalutunah, Shanghu, and Tatterat, with their three sledges. Hans, armed with the Marston rifle, was my only com-

KALUTUNAH PARTY.

Equip-ment.

panion from the ship's company. The natives carried no arms but the long knife and their unicorn-ivory lances. Our whole equipment was by no means cumbersome: except the clothes upon our back and raw walrus-meat, we carried nothing. The walrus, both flesh and blubber, was cut into flat slabs half an inch thick, and about as long and wide as a folio volume. These, when frozen, were laid directly upon the cross-bars of the sledge, and served as a sort of floor. The rifle and the noonghak were placed on top, and the whole was covered by a well-rubbed bear-skin, strapped down by a pliant cord of walrus-hide.

Thus stowed, the sledge is wonderfully adapted to its wild travel. It may roll over and over, for it defies an upset; and its runners of the bones of the whale seem to bear with impunity the fierce shocks of the ice. The meat, as hard as a plank, is the

A strange driving seat.

driver's seat: it is secure from the dogs; and when it is wanted for a cold cut, which is not seldom, the sledge is turned upside-down, and the layers of flesh are hacked away from between the cross-bars.

We started with a wild yell of dogs and men in chorus, Kalu-tunah and myself leading. In about two hours we had reached a high berg about fifteen miles north of the brig Here I recon-noitred the ice ahead. It was not cheering; the outside tide-channel, where I had broken through the fall before, was now full of squeezed ice, and the plain beyond the bergs seemed much distorted. The Esquimaux, nevertheless, acceded to my wish to attempt the passage, and we were soon among the hummocks. We ran beside our sledges, clinging to the upstanders, but making perhaps four miles an hour where, unassisted by the dogs, we could certainly have made but one. Things began to look more auspicious.

We halted about thirty miles north of the brig, after edging along the coast about thirty miles to the eastward. Here Shanghu burrowed into a snow-bank and slept, the thermometer standing at —30°. The rest of us turned in to lunch; the sledge was turned over, and we were cutting away at the raw meat, each man for himself, when I heard an exclamation from Tatterat, an out-landish Esquimaux, who had his name from the Kittywake gull. He had found a tallow-ball, which had been hid away without my knowledge by my comrades for my private use. Instantly his knife entered the prized recesses of my ball, and, as the lumps of liver and cooked muscle came tossing out in delicate succession, Kalutunah yielded to the temptation, and both of them picked the savoury bits as we would the truffles of a "Perigord pâté." Of necessity I joined the group, and took my share; but Hans, poor fellow, too indignant at the liberty taken with my provender, refused to share in the work of demolishing it. My ten-pound ball vanished nevertheless in scarcely as many minutes.

A feast on the tallow-ball.

The journey began again as the feast closed, and we should have accomplished my wishes had it not been for the untoward influence of sundry bears. The tracks of these animals were becoming more and more numerous as we rounded one iceberg after another; and we could see the beds they had worn in the snow while watching for seal. These swayed the dogs from their course: yet we kept edging onward; and when in sight of the northern coast, about thirty miles from the central peak of the "Three Brothers," I saw a deep band of stratus lying over the horizon in the direction of Kennedy Channel. This water-sky

Tracks of bears.

indicated the continued opening of the channel, and made me more deeply anxious to proceed. But at this moment our dogs encountered a large male bear in the act of devouring a seal. The impulse was irresistible: I lost all control over both dogs and drivers. They seemed dead to everything but the passion of pursuit. Off they sped with incredible swiftness, the Esquimaux clinging to their sledges, and cheering their dogs with loud cries of "Nannook!" A mad, wild chase, wilder than German legend, —the dogs, wolves; the drivers, devils. After a furious run, the animal was brought to bay; the lance and the rifle did their work, and we halted for a general feed. The dogs gorged themselves, the drivers did as much, and we buried the remainder of the carcass in the snow. A second bear had been tracked by the party to a large iceberg north of Cape Russell; for we had now travelled to the neighbourhood of the Great Glacier. But the dogs were too much distended by their abundant diet to move: their drivers were scarcely better. Rest was indispensable.

We took a four hours' sleep on the open ice, the most uncomfortable that I remember. Our fatigue had made us dispense with the snow-house; and, though I was heavily clad in a full suit of furs, and squeezed myself in between Kalutunah and Shanghu, I could not bear the intense temperature. I rose in the morning stiff and sore. I mention it as a trait of nobleness on the part of Kalutunah, which I appreciated very sensibly at the time, that, seeing me suffer, he took his kapetah from his back and placed it around my feet.

The next day I tried again to make my friends steer to the northward. But the bears were most numerous upon the Greenland side; and they determined to push on toward the glacier. They were sure, they said, of finding the game among the broken icebergs at the base of it. All my remonstrances and urgent entreaties were unavailing to make them resume their promised route. They said that to cross so high up as we then were was impossible, and I felt the truth of this when I remembered the fate of poor Baker and Schubert at this very passage. Kalutunah added, significantly, that the bear-meat was absolutely necessary for the support of their families, and that Nalegak had no right to prevent him from providing for his household. It was a strong argument, and withal the argument of the strong.

I found now that my projected survey of the northern coast must be abandoned, at least for the time. My next wish was to get back to the brig, and to negotiate with Metck for a purchase or loan of his dogs as my last chance. But even this was not readily gratified. All of Saturday was spent in bear-hunting. The natives, as indomitable as their dogs, made the entire circuit of Dallas Bay, and finally halted again under one of the islands which group themselves between the headlands of Advance Bay and at the base of the glacier.

Anxious as I was to press our return to the brig, I was well paid for my disappointment. I had not realized fully the spectacle of this stupendous monument of frost. I had seen it for some hours hanging over the ice like a white-mist cloud, but now it rose up before me clearly defined and almost precipitous. The whole horizon, so vague and shadowy before, was broken by long lines of icebergs; and as the dogs, cheered by the cries of their wild drivers, went on, losing themselves deeper and deeper in the labyrinth, it seemed like closing around us the walls of an icy world. They stopped at last; and I had time, while my companions rested and fed, to climb one of the highest bergs. The atmosphere favoured me: the blue tops of Washington Land were in full view; and, losing itself in a dark water-cloud, the noble headland of John Barrow.

The trend of this glacier is a few degrees to the west of north. We followed its face afterward, edging in for the Greenland coast, about the rocky archipelago which I have named after the *Advance*. From one of those rugged islets, the nearest to the glacier which could be approached with anything like safety, I could see another island larger and closer in shore, already half covered by the encroaching face of the glacier, and great masses of ice still detaching themselves and splintering as they fell upon that portion which protruded. Repose was not the characteristic of this seemingly solid mass; every feature indicated activity, energy, movement.

The surface seemed to follow that of the basis-country over which it flowed. It was undulating about the horizon, but as it descended toward the sea it represented a broken plain with a general inclination of some nine degrees, still diminishing toward the foreground. Crevices, in the distance mere wrinkles, ex-

CHAPTER XLVI. panded as they came nearer, and were crossed almost at right angles by long continuous lines of fracture parallel with the face of the glacier.

A gigantic stairway. These lines too, scarcely traceable in the far distance, widened as they approached the sea until they formed a gigantic stairway. It seemed as though the ice had lost its support below, and that the mass was let down from above in a series of steps. Such an action, owing to the heat derived from the soil, the excessive surface-drainage, and the constant abrasion of the sea, must in reality take place. My note-book may enable me at some future day to develop its details. I have referred to this as the escaladed structure of the Arctic glacier.

Indication of a great propelling agency The indication of a great propelling agency seemed to be just commencing at the time I was observing it. These split-off lines of ice were evidently in motion, pressed on by those behind, but still widening their fissures, as if the impelling action was more and more energetic nearer the water, till at last they floated away in the form of icebergs. Long files of these detached masses could be traced slowly sailing off into the distance, their separation marked by dark parallel shadows—broad and spacious avenues near the eye, but narrowed in the perspective to mere lines. A more impressive illustration of the forces of nature can hardly be conceived.

Formation of icebergs. Regarded upon a large scale, I am satisfied that the iceberg is not disengaged by *debâcle*, as I once supposed. So far from falling into the sea, broken by its weight from the parent-glacier, it rises from the sea. The process is at once gradual and comparatively quiet. The idea of icebergs being discharged, so universal among systematic writers, and so recently admitted by myself, seems to me now at variance with the regulated and progressive actions of nature. Developed by such a process, the thousands of bergs which throng these seas should keep the air and water in perpetual commotion, one fearful succession of explosive detonations and propagated waves. But it is only the lesser masses falling into deep waters which could justify the popular opinion. The enormous masses of the Great Glacier are propelled, step by step and year by year, until, reaching water capable of supporting them, they are floated off to be lost in the temperatures of other regions.

The frozen masses before me were similar in structure to the

Alpine and Norwegian ice-growths. It would be foreign to the character of this book to enter upon the discussion which the re- mark suggests. I may add, however, that their face presented nearly all the characteristic features of the Swiss Alps. The *overflow*, as I have called the viscous overlapping of the surface, was more clearly marked than upon any Alpine glacier with which I am acquainted. When close to the island-rocks and looking out upon the upper table of the glacier, I was struck with the homely analogy of the batter-cake spreading itself out under the ladle of the housewife, the upper surface less affected by friction, and rolling forward in consequence.

The crevices bore the marks of direct fracture and other more gradual action of surface-drainage. The extensive water-shed be- tween their converging planes gave to the icy surface most of the hydrographic features of a river-system. The ice-born rivers which divided them were margined occasionally with spires of discoloured ice, and generally lost themselves in the central areas of the glacier before reaching its foreground. Occasionally, too, the face of the glacier was cut by vertical lines, which, as in the Alpine growths, were evidently outlets for the surface-drainage. Everything was, of course, bound in solid ice when I looked at it; but the evi- dences of torrent-action were unequivocal, and Mr. Bonsall and Mr. Morton, at their visits of the preceding year, found both cas- cades and water-tunnels in abundance.

The height of this ice-wall at the nearest point was about three hundred feet, measured from the water's edge; and the unbroken right line of its diminishing perspective showed that this might be regarded as its constant measurement. It seemed, in fact, a great icy table-land, abutting with a clean precipice against the sea. This is, indeed, characteristic of all those Arctic glaciers which issue from central reservoirs or *mers de glace* upon the fiords or bays, and is strikingly in contrast with the dependent or hanging glacier of the ravines, where every line and furrow and chasm seems to indicate the movement of descent and the mechanical dis- turbances which have retarded it.

I have named this great glacier after Alexander Von Humboldt, and the cape which flanks it on the Greenland coast after Profes- sor Agassiz.

The point at which this immense body of ice enters the Land

of Washington gives even to a distant view impressive indications
of its plastic or semi-solid character.   No one could resist the im-

pression of fluidity conveyed by its peculiar markings.   I have
named it Cape Forbes, after the eminent crystallogist whose views
it so abundantly confirms.

CAPE FORBES.

As the surface of the glacier receded to the south, its face
seemed broken with piles of earth and rock-stained rubbish, till
far back in the interior it was hidden from me by the slope of a
hill.   Still beyond this, however, the white blink or glare of the
sky above showed its continued extension.

It was more difficult to trace its outline to the northward, on
account of the immense discharges at its base.   The talus of its
descent from the interior, looking far off to the east, ranged from
7° to 15°, so broken by the crevices, however, as to give the effect
of an inclined plane only in the distance.   A few black knobs rose
from the white snow, like islands from the sea.

The general configuration of its surface showed how it adapted
itself to the inequalities of the basis-country beneath.   There was
every modification of hill and valley, just as upon land.   Thus
diversified in its aspect, it stretches to the north till it bounds
upon the new land of Washington, cementing into one the Greenland of the Scandinavian Vikings and the America of Columbus.

CHATER XLVII.

CAPE JAMES KENT—MARSHALL BAY—ICE-RAFTS—STRIATED BOULDERS—
ANTIQUITIES—THE BEAR-CHASE—THE BEAR AT BAY—THE SINGLE
HUNT—TEETH-WOUNDS—THE LAST EFFORT—CLOSE OF THE SEARCH.

WHILE the Esquimaux were hunting about the bergs, I sat with my sketch-book, absorbed in the spectacle before me ; but, seeing them come to a halt above the island, I gained the nearest sledge, and the whole party gathered together a few miles from the face of the glacier. Here Hans and myself crawled with Tatterat and his dogs into an impromptu snow-hut, and, cheered by our aggregated warmth, slept comfortably. Our little dome, or rather burrow, for it was scooped out of a drift, fell down in the night ; but we were so worn out that it did not wake us.

On rising from a sleep in the open air, at a temperature of 12° below zero, the hunt was resumed along the face of the glacier, with just enough of success to wear out the dogs and endanger my chances of return to the brig. In spite of the grandeur of the scenery and the noble displays of force exhibited by the falling bergs, my thoughts wandered back to the party I had left ; and I was really glad when Kalutunah yielded to my renewed persuasion, and turned his team toward the ice-belt of the southeastern shore.

The spot at which we landed I have called Cape James Kent. It was a lofty headland, and the land-ice which hugged its base was covered with rocks from the cliffs above. As I looked over this ice-belt, losing itself in the far distance, and covered with its millions of tons of rubbish, greenstones, limestones, chlorite slates, rounded and angular, massive and ground to powder, its importance as a geological agent in the transportation of drift struck me with great force. Its whole substance was studded with these varied contributions from the shore ; and further to the south, upon the now frozen waters of Marshall Bay, I could recognise raft after raft from the last year's ice-belt, which had

(marginal notes: CHAPTER XLVII. — An impromptu snow-hut. — A sleep in the open air. — Cape James Kent.)

been caught by the winter, each one laden with its heavy freight of foreign material.

ICE-RAFT.

Causes of
the de-
tachment
of masses
of ice from
the ice-
belt.
The water-torrents and thaws of summer unite with the tides in disengaging the ice-belt from the coast; but it is not uncommon for large bergs to drive against it and carry away the growths of many years. I have found masses that had been detached in this way, floating many miles out to sea,—long, symmetrical tables, two hundred feet long by eighty broad, covered with large angular rocks and boulders, and seemingly impregnated through-

RAFT OF SLATES.

out with detrited matter. These rafts in Marshall Bay were so numerous, that, could they have melted as I saw them, the

bottom of the sea would have presented a more curious study
for the geologist than the boulder-covered lines of our middle
latitudes.

One in particular, a sketch of which I attach, had its origin in
a valley where rounded fragments of water-washed greenstone

ROCHE MOUTONNEE, IN ICE-BELT.

had been poured out by the torrents and frozen into the coast-ice
of the belt. The attrition of subsequent matter had truncated

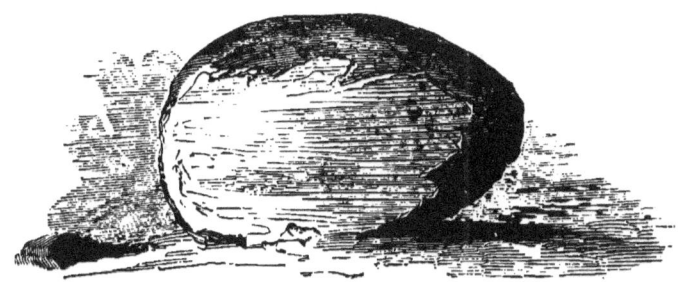

STRIATED BOULDER FROM MARY LEIPER FIORD.

the great egg-shaped rock, and worn its sides into a striated face,
whose scratches still indicated the line of water-flow.

On the south-eastern corner of this bay, where some low
islands at the mouth of the fiord formed a sort of protection

CHAPTER XLVII. against the north wind, was a group of Esquimaux remains,— huts, cairns, and graves. Though evidently long deserted, my drivers seemed to know all about them, for they suspended the hunt around the bergs to take a look at these evidences of a bygone generation of their fathers.

Deserted huts There were five huts, with two stone pedestals for the protection of meat, and one of those strange little kennels which serve as dormitories when the igloë is crowded. The graves were further up the fiord : from them I obtained a knife of bone, but no indications of iron.

These huts stood high up, upon a set of shingle-terraces, similar to those of Rensselaer Bay. The belt-ice at their foot was old and undisturbed, and must have been so for years ; so, too, **Remains round the old homesteads.** was the heavy ice of the bay. Yet around these old homesteads were bones of the seal and walrus, and the vertebræ of a whale similar to that at the igloë of Anoatok. There must have been both open water and a hunting-ground around them, and the huts had in former days been close upon this water-line. " Una suna nuna ? " " What land is this, Kalutunah ? " I did not understand his answer, which was long and emphatic ; but I found from our interpreter that the place was still called " the **Traditions** inhabited spot ; " and that a story was well preserved among them of a time when families were sustained beside its open water and musk-ox inhabited the hills. We followed the belt-ice, crossing only at the headlands of the bays, and arrived at the brig on the afternoon of Wednesday.

Bear-hunts. Our whole journey had been an almost unbroken and scarcely-varied series of bear-hunts. They had lost for me the attractions of novelty ; but, like the contests with the walrus, they were always interesting, because characteristic of this rude people.

Training of the dogs. The dogs are carefully trained not to engage in contest with the bear, but to retard its flight. While one engrosses his attention ahead, a second attacks him in the rear ; and, always alert, and each protecting the other, it rarely happens that they are seriously injured, or that they fail to delay the animal until the hunters come up.

Let us suppose a bear scented out at the base of an iceberg. The Esquimaux examines the track with sagacious care, to determine its age and direction, and the speed with which the animal was moving when he passed along. The dogs are set upon the CHAPTER XLVII. trail, and the hunter courses over the ice at their side in silence. As he turns the angle of the berg his game is in view before him, The game in view. stalking probably along with quiet march, sometimes snuffing the air suspiciously, but making, nevertheless, for a nest of broken hummocks. The dogs spring forward, opening in a wild wolfish yell, the driver shrieking "Nannook! nannook!" and all straining every nerve in pursuit.

The bear rises on his haunches, inspects his pursuers, and starts The chase. off at full speed. The hunter, as he runs, leaning over his sledge, seizes the traces of a couple of his dogs, and liberates them from their burden. It is the work of a minute; for the motion is not checked, and the remaining dogs rush on with apparent ease.

Now, pressed more severely, the bear makes for an iceberg and stands at bay, while his two foremost pursuers halt at a short distance and quietly await the arrival of the hunter. At this moment the whole pack are liberated; the hunter grasps his lance, and, tumbling through the snow and ice, prepares for the encounter.

If there be two hunters, the bear is killed easily; for one makes The encounter. a feint of thrusting a spear at the right side, and, as the animal turns with his arms towards the threatened attack, the left is unprotected and receives the death-wound.

But if there be only one hunter, he does not hesitate. Grasp- The solitary hunter. ing the lance firmly in his hands, he provokes the animal to pursue him by moving rapidly across its path, and then running as if to escape. But hardly is its long, unwieldy body extended for the solicited chase, before with a rapid jump the hunter doubles on his track and runs back toward his first position. The bear is in the act of turning after him again when the lance is plunged into the left side, below the shoulder. So dexterously has this thrust to be made, that an unpractised hunter has often to leave his spear in the side of his prey and run for his life. But even then, if well aided by the dogs, a cool, skilful man seldom fails to kill his adversary.

Many wounds are received by the Etah Bay Esquimaux in Wounds in the chase. these encounters. The bear is looked upon as more fierce in that neighbourhood, and about Anoatok and Rensselaer Bay, than around the broken ice to the south. He uses his teeth much more generally than is supposed by systematic writers. The hugging, pawing, and boxing, which characterize the black and grisly bears, are resorted to by him only under peculiar circumstances. While wandering over his icy fields, he will rear himself upon his hind legs to enlarge his circle of vision ; and I have often seen him in this attitude pawing the air, as if practising for an apprehended conflict. But it is only when absolutely beset, or when the female is defending her cub, that the Polar bear shows fight upon its haunches. Among seven hunters who visited the brig last December, no less than five were scarred by direct teeth-wounds of bears. Two of these had been bit in the calves of the legs while running, and one, our friend Metek, had received a like dishonourable wound somewhat higher. Our dogs were seized by the nape of the neck, and flung violently many paces to one side.

The bear-hunt ranks foremost among the exhibitions of personal prowess. My intelligent friend Kalutunah excelled in it. Shanghu, his principal associate, was also skilful as well as daring.

They both left the brig after a day's rest, fully laden with wood and other presents, and promising to engage Metek, if they could, to come up with his four dogs. They themselves engaged to lend me one dog from each of their teams. It pleased me to find that I had earned character with these people, at first so suspicious and distrustful. They left on board each man his dog, without a shade of doubt as to my good faith, only begging me to watch the poor animals' feet, as the famine had nearly exterminated their stock.

.

The month of May had come. Metek, less confiding because less trustworthy than Kalutunah, did not bring his dogs, and my own exhausted team was in almost daily requisition to bring in supplies of food from Etah. Everything admonished me that the time was at hand when we must leave the brig and trust our fortunes to the floes. Our preparations were well advanced, and the crew so far restored to health that all but three or four could take some part in completing them.

Still, I could not allow myself to pass away from our region of search without a last effort to visit the further shores of the channel. Our communications with the Esquimaux, and some successful hunts of our own, had given us a stock of provisions

for at least a week in advance. I conferred with my officers,
made a full distribution of the work to be performed in my
absence, and set out once more, with Morton for my only companion. We took with us the light sledge, adding the two borrowed dogs to our team, but travelling ourselves on foot. Our
course was to be by the middle ice, and our hope that we might
find it free enough from hummocks to permit us to pass.

My journal, written after our return, gives nothing but a series
of observations going to verify and complete my charts. We
struggled manfully to force our way through,—days and nights of
adventurous exposure and recurring disaster, and at last found
our way back to the brig, Morton broken down anew, and my own
energies just adequate to the duty of supervising our final departure. I had neither time nor strength to expend on my diary.
The operations of the search were closed.

CHAPTER XLVIII

PREPARATIONS FOR ESCAPE — PROVISIONS — BOATS—THE SLEDGES — IN-
STRUMENTS AND ARMS—COOKING APPARATUS—TABLE FURNITURE--
CRADLING THE BOATS—THE SLEDGES MOVING—THE RECREATION.

CHAPTER XLVIII. THE detailed preparations for our escape would have little interest for the general reader ; but they were so arduous and so impor-

Arduous and laborious preparations. tant that I cannot pass them by without a special notice. They had been begun from an early day of the fall, and had not been entirely intermitted during our severest winter-trials. All who could work, even at picking over eider-down, found every moment of leisure fully appropriated. But since our party had begun to develop the stimulus of more liberal diet, our labours were more systematic and diversified.

Manufacture of clothing. The manufacture of clothing had made considerable progress. Canvas moccasins had been made for every one of the party, and three dozen were added as a common stock to meet emergencies. Three pairs of boots were allowed each man. These were generally of carpeting, with soles of walrus and seal hide ; and when the supply of these gave out, the leather from the chafing-gear of the brig for a time supplied their place. A much better substitute was found afterward in the gutta-percha that had formed the speaking-tube. This was softened by warm water, cut into lengths, and so made available to its new uses. Blankets were served out as the material for body-clothing : every man was his own tailor.

Bedding. For bedding, the woollen curtains that had formerly decorated our berths supplied us with a couple of large coverlets, which were abundantly quilted with eider-down. Two buffalo-robes of the same size with the coverlets were arranged so as to button on them, forming sleeping sacks for the occasion, but easily detached for the purpose of drying or airing.

Provision-bags. Our provision-bags were of assorted sizes, to fit under the thwarts of the boats. They were of sail-cloth, made water-tight by tar and pitch, which we kept from penetrating the canvas by first coating it with flour-paste and plaster of Paris. The bread- bags were double, the inner saturated with paste and plaster by boiling in the mixture, and the space between the two filled with pitch. Every bag was, in sailor-phrase, roped and becketed; in ordinary parlance, well secured by cordage.

These different manufactures had all of them being going on through the winter, and more rapidly as the spring advanced. They had given employment to the thoughts of our sick men, and in this way had exerted a wholesome influence on their moral tone and assisted their convalescence. Other preparations had been begun more recently. The provisions for the descent were to be got ready and packed. The ship-bread was powdered by beating it with a capstan-bar, and pressed down into the bags which were to carry it. Pork-fat and tallow were melted down, and poured into other bags to freeze. A stock of concentrated bean- soup was cooked, and secured for carriage like the pork-fat; and the flour and remaining meat-biscuit were to be protected from moisture in double bags. These were the only provisions we were to carry with us. I knew I should be able to subsist the party for some time after their setting out by the food I could bring from the vessel by occasional trips with my dog-team. For the rest we relied upon our guns.

Besides all this, we had our camp-equipage to get in order, and the vitally-important organization of our system of boats and sledges.

Our boats were three in number, all of them well battered by exposure to ice and storm, almost as destructive of their sea-worthiness as the hot sun of other regions. Two of them were cypress whaleboats, twenty-six feet long, with seven feet beam, and three feet deep. These were strengthened with oak bottom-pieces and a long string-piece bolted to the keel. A washboard of light cedar, about six inches high, served to strengthen the gunwale and give increased depth. A neat housing of light canvas was stretched upon a ridge-line sustained fore and aft by stanchions, and hung down over the boat's sides, where it was fastened (stopped) to a jack-stay. My last year's experience on the attempt to reach Beechy Island determined me to carry but one mast to each boat. It was stepped into an oaken thwart, made especially strong, as it was expected to carry sail over ice as well as water; the mast could be readily unshipped, and carried, with the oars, boat-hooks, and ice-poles, alongside the boat. The third boat was my little *Red Eric*. We mounted her on the old sledge, the *Faith*, hardly relying on her for any purposes of navigation, but with the intention of cutting her up for firewood in case our guns should fail to give us a supply of blubber.

Indeed, in spite of all the ingenuity of our carpenter, Mr. Ohlsen, well seconded by the persevering labours of M'Gary and Bonsall, not one of our boats was positively sea-worthy. The *Hope* would not pass even charitable inspection, and we expected to burn her on reaching water. The planking of all of them was so dried up that it could hardly be made tight by calking.

The three boats were mounted on sledges rigged with rueraddies; the provisions stowed snugly under the thwarts; the chronometers, carefully boxed and padded, placed in the sternsheets of the *Hope*, in charge of Mr. Sontag. With them were such of the instruments as we could venture to transport. They consisted of two Gambey sextants, with artificial horizon, our transit-unifilar, and dip-instruments. Our glasses, with a few of the smaller field-instruments, we carried on our persons. Our fine theodolite we were forced to abandon.

Our powder and shot, upon which our lives depended, were carefully distributed in bags and tin canisters. The percussion-caps I took into my own possession, as more precious than gold. Mr. Bonsall had a general charge of the arms and ammunition. Places were arranged for the guns, and hunters appointed for each boat. Mr. Petersen took charge of the most important part of our field-equipage, our cooking gear. Petersen was our best tinker. All the old stove-pipe, now none the better for two winters of Arctic fires, was called into requisition. Each boat was provided with two large iron cylinders, fourteen inches in diameter and eighteen high. Each of them held an iron saucer or lamp, in which we could place our melted pork-fat or blubber, and, with the aid of spun-yarn for a wick, make a roaring fire. I need not say that the fat and oil always froze when not ignited.

Into these cylinders, which were used merely to defend our lamp from the wind and our pots from contact with the cold air, we placed a couple of large tin vessels, suitable either for melting snow or making tea or soup. They were made out of cake-canisters cut down. How many kindly festival associations hung by these now abused soup-cans! one of them had, before the fire rubbed off its bright gilding, the wedding-inscription of a large fruit-cake.

We carried spare tins in case the others should burn out; it was well we did so. So completely had we exhausted our house-hold furniture, that we had neither cups nor plates, except crockery. This, of course, would not stand the travel, and our spare tin had to be saved for protecting the boats from ice. At this juncture we cut plates out of every imaginable and rejected piece of tinware. Borden's meat-biscuit canisters furnished us with a splendid dinner-service; and some rightly-feared tin jars, with ominous labels of Corrosive Sublimate and Arsenic, which once belonged to our department of natural history, were emptied, scoured, and cut down into tea-cups.

Recognising the importance of acting directly upon the men's minds, my first step now was to issue a general order appointing a certain day, the 17th of May, for setting out. Every man had twenty-four hours given him to select and get ready his eight pounds of personal effects. After that, his time was to cease to be his own for any purpose. The long-indulged waywardness of our convalescents made them take this hardly. Some who were at work on articles of apparel that were really important to them threw them down unfinished, in a sick man's pet. I had these in some cases picked up quietly and finished by others. But I showed myself inexorable. It was necessary to brace up and con-centrate every man's thoughts and energies upon the one great com-mon object, our departure from the vessel on the 17th, not to return.

I tried my best also to fix and diffuse impressions that we were going home. But in this I was not always successful; I was displeased, indeed, with the moody indifference with which many went about the tasks to which I put them. The completeness of my preparations I know had its influence; but there were many doubters. Some were convinced that my only object was to move further south, retaining the brig, however, as a home to retreat to. Others whispered that I wanted to transport the sick to the hunt-ing-grounds and other resources of the lower settlements, which I had such difficulty in preventing the mutinous from securing for themselves alone. A few of a more cheerful spirit thought I had

resolved to make for some point of look-out, in the hope of a
rescue by whalers or English expedition-parties which were supposed still to be within the Arctic circle. The number is unfortunately small of those human beings whom calamity elevates.

Cradling
the boats
and mov-
ing them
to the ice-
foot.

There was no sign or affectation of spirit or enthusiasm upon
the memorable day when we first adjusted the boats to their
cradles on the sledges and moved them off to the ice-foot. But the
ice immediately around the vessel was smooth; and, as the boats
had not received their lading, the first labour was an easy one.
As the runners moved, the gloom of several countenances were
perceptibly lightened. The croakers had protested that we could
not stir an inch. These cheering remarks always reach a commander's ears, and I took good care of course to make the outset
contradict them. By the time we reached the end of our little
level, the tone had improved wonderfully, and we were prepared
for the effort of crossing the successive lines of the belt-ice and
forcing a way through the smashed material which interposed
between us and the ice-foot.

This was a work of great difficulty, and sorrowfully exhausting to the poor fellows not yet accustomed to heave together.
But in the end I had the satisfaction, before twenty-four hours
were over, of seeing our little arks of safety hauled upon the

higher plane of the ice-foot, in full trim for ornamental exhibition
from the brig; their neat canvas housing rigged tent-fashion over
the entire length of each; a jaunty little flag, made out of one of
the commander's obsolete linen shirts, decorated in stripes from a
disused article of stationery, the red-ink bottle, and with a very
little of the blue-bag in the star-spangled corner. All hands after
this returned on board; I had ready for them the best supper our
supplies afforded, and they turned in with minds prepared for
their departure next day.

They were nearly all of them invalids, unused to open air and
exercise. It was necessary to train them very gradually. We
made but two miles the first day, and with a single boat; and
indeed for some time after this I took care that they should not
be disheartened by overwork. They came back early to a hearty
supper and warm beds, and I had the satisfaction of marching
them back each recurring morning refreshed and cheerful. The
weather, happily, was superb.

CHAPTER XLIX.

THE PLEDGES—THE ARGUMENT—FAREWELL TO THE BRIG—THE MUSTER—
THE ROUTINE—THE MESSES.

OUR last farewell to the brig was made with more solemnity. CHAPTER
The entire ship's company was collected in our dismantled winter- XLIX.
chamber to take part in the ceremonial. It was Sunday. Our The last
moss walls had been torn down, and the wood that supported Sunday.
them burned. Our beds were off at the boats. The galley was
unfurnished and cold. Everything about the little den of refuge
was desolate.

We read prayers and a chapter of the Bible; and then, all Prayers
standing silently round, I took Sir John Franklin's portrait from ing. read-
its frame and cased it in an India-rubber scroll. I next read the
reports of inspection and survey which had been made by the
several commissions organized for the purpose, all of them testify-
ing to the necessities under which I was about to act. I then Captain
addressed the party: I did not affect to disguise the difficulties Kane's
that were before us; but I assured them that they could all be the men
overcome by energy and subordination to command: and that the
thirteen hundred miles of ice and water that lay between us and
North Greenland could be traversed with safety for most of us,
and hope for all. I added, that as men and messmates, it was the
duty of us all, enjoined by gallantry as well as religion, to post-
pone every consideration of self to the protection of the wounded
and sick; and that this must be regarded by every man and
under all circumstances as a paramount order. In conclusion, I
told them to think over the trials we had all of us gone through,
and to remember each man for himself how often an unseen
Power had rescued him in peril, and I admonished them still to
place reliance on Him who could not change.

I was met with a right spirit. After a short conference, an Effect of
engagement was drawn up by one of the officers, and brought to dress. ad-
me with the signatures of all the company, without an exception.
It read as follows :—·

CHAPTER XLIX.

Voluntary engagement signed by officers and men.

" The undersigned, being convinced of the impossibility of the liberation of the brig, and equally convinced of the impossibility of remaining in the ice a third winter, do fervently concur with the commander in his attempt to reach the south by means of boats.

" Knowing the trials and hardships which are before us, and feeling the necessity of union, harmony, and discipline, we have determined to abide faithfully by the expedition and our sick comrades, and to do all that we can, as true men, to advance the objects in view.

" HENRY BROOKS,	J. WALL WILSON,
JAMES M'GARY,	AMOS BONSALL,
GEORGE RILEY,	I. I. HAYES,
WILLIAM MORTON,	AUGUST SONTAG,
C. OHLSEN,	&c. &c."

Memorial of the reasons for leaving the vessel.

I had prepared a brief memorial of the considerations which justified our abandonment of the vessel, and had read it as part of my address. I now fixed it to a stanchion near the gangway, where it must attract the notice of any who might seek us hereafter, and stand with them as my vindication for the step, in case we should be overtaken by disaster. It closed with these words:—

" I regard the abandonment of the brig as inevitable. We have by actual inspection but thirty-six days' provisions, and a careful survey shows that we cannot cut more firewood without rendering our craft unseaworthy. A third winter would force us, as the only means of escaping starvation, to resort to Esquimaux habits and give up all hope of remaining by the vessel and her resources. It would therefore in no manner advance the search after Sir John Franklin.

" Under any circumstances, to remain longer would be destructive to those of our little party who have already suffered from the extreme severity of the climate and its tendencies to disease. Scurvy has enfeebled more or less every man in the expedition ; and an anomalous spasmodic disorder, allied to tetanus, has cost us· the life of two of our most prized comrades.

" I hope, speaking on the part of my companions and myself,

that we have done all that we ought to do to prove our tenacity of purpose and devotion to the cause which we have undertaken. This attempt to escape by crossing the southern ice on sledges is regarded by me as an imperative duty,—the only means of saving ourselves and preserving the laboriously-earned results of the expedition.

" E. K. KANE,

" Com. Grinnell Expedition.

"ADVANCE, RENSSELAER BAY, *May* 20, 1855."

We then went upon deck: the flags were hoisted and hauled down again, and our party walked once or twice around the brig, looking at her timbers and exchanging comments upon the scars which reminded them of every stage of her dismantling. Our figure-head—the fair Augusta, the little blue girl with pink cheeks, who had lost her breast by an iceberg and her nose by a nip off Bedevilled Reach—was taken from our bows and placed aboard the "Hope." "She is at any rate wood," said the men, when I hesitated about giving them the additional burden; "and if we cannot carry her far we can burn her."

No one thought of the mockery of cheers: we had no festival-liquor to mislead our perception of the real state of things. When all hands were quite ready, we scrambled off over the ice together, much like a gang of stevedores going to work over a quayful of broken cargo.

On reaching the boats, the party were regularly mustered and divided between the two. A rigid inspection was had of every article of personal equipment. Each man had a woollen under-dress and an Esquimaux suit of fur clothing,—kapetah, nessak, and nannooke complete, with boots of our own make; that is to say, one pair of canvass faced with walrus-hide, and another inside made of the cabin Brussels carpet. In addition to this, each carried a rue-raddy adjusted to fit him comfortably, a pair of socks next his skin, and a pair of large goggles for snow-blindness, made Esquimaux fashion by cutting a small slit in a piece of wood. Some of us had gutta percha masks fitting closely to the face, as large as an ordinary domino; but these were still less favourable to personal appearance than the goggles. The provision-bags and other stores were numbered, and each man and officer had his

CHAPTER XLIX.

A last look at the brig.

Removal of the "fair Augusta."

Departure.

The muster and inspection of the party.

CHAPTER
XLIX.
own bag and a place assigned for it, to prevent confusion in rapid stowing and unstowing.

Number of
men able
to work.
Excluding four sick men, who were unable to move, and myself, who had to drive the dog-team and serve as common carrier and courier, we numbered but twelve men,—which would have given six to a sledge, or too few to move it. It was therefore necessary to concentrate our entire force upon one sledge at a time. On the other hand, however, it was important to the efficiency of our organization that matters of cooking, sleeping baggage, and rations, should be regulated by separate messes.

Daily
routine.
The routine I established was the most precise:—Daily prayers both morning and evening, all hands gathering round in a circle and standing uncovered during the short exercise; regulated hours; fixed duties and positions at the track-lines and on the halt ; the cooking to be taken by turns, the captains of the boats alone being excused. The charge of the log was confided to Dr. Hayes, and the running survey to Mr. Sontag. Though little could be expected from either of these gentlemen at this time, I deemed it best to keep up the appearance of ordinary voyaging ; and after we left the first ices of Smith's Straits I was indebted to them for valuable results. The thermometer was observed every three hours.

Organiza-
tion of the
party.
To my faithful friend and first officer, boatswain Brooks, I assigned the command of the boats and sledges. I knew how well he was fitted for it; and when forced, as I was afterward during the descent, to be in constant motion between the sick-station, the Esquimaux settlements, and the deserted brig, I felt safe in the assurance of his tried fidelity and indomitable resolution. The party under him was marshalled at the rue-raddies as a single gang ; but the messes were arranged with reference to the two whale-boats, and when we came afterward to the open water the crews were distributed in the same way :—

To the Faith.	To the Hope.
JAMES M'GARY,	WILLIAM MORTON,
CHRISTIAN OHLSEN,	AUGUST SONTAG,
AMOS BONSALL,	GEORGE RILEY,
CARL J. PETERSEN,	JOHN BLAKE,
THOMAS HICKEY,	WILLIAM GODFREY.

With this organization we set out on our march.

CHAPTER L.

THE SICK HUT—TO FIRST RAVINE—MOVING THE SICK—THE HEALTH-
STATION—CONVALESCENCE

I HAD employed myself and the team from an early day in furnishing out accommodations for the sick at Anoatok. I have already described this station as the halting-place of our winter-journeys. The hut was a low dome of heavy stones, more like a cave than a human habitation. It was perched on the very point of the rocky promontory which I have named after Captain Ingle-field, of the British Navy. Both to the north and south it commanded a view of the ice-expanse of the straits ; and what little sunshine ever broke through the gorges by which it was environed encouraged a perceptible growth of flowering plants and coarse grasses on the level behind it. The ice-belt now beautifully smooth, brought us almost to the edge of this little plain.

CHAPTER L.

Situation of Anoatok.

I had made up my mind from an early period that, in the event of our attempting to escape upon the ice, the " wind-loved spot," as the Esquimaux poetically named it, would be well adapted to the purposes of an entrepôt, and had endeavoured within the last few weeks to fit it up also as a resting-place for our sick during the turmoil of removing from the brig. I had its broken outlet closed by a practicable door, and the roof perforated to receive a stove-pipe. Still more recently the stone platform or dais had been thoroughly cleansed, and covered with shavings which Ohlsen had saved while working at his boats. Over these again were laid my best cushions ; and two blankets, all that we could spare, were employed to tapestry the walls. A small pane of glass, formerly the facing of a daguerreotype, inserted in the door, and a stove, made by combining the copper dog-vane of the galley with some dazzling tin pipes, completed the furniture. It was a gloomy hospital after all for the poor fellows, who, more than sharing all the anxiety of their comrades, could have no relief in the excitement of active toil.

Hut fitted up for the sick.

I made many journeys between the brig and Anoatok while the

arrangements for our setting out were in progress, and after the sledges were under way. All of our invalids were housed there in safety, one or two of them occupying the dog-sledge for the trip.

Most of our provision for the march and voyage of escape had also been stacked in the neighbourhood of the huts: eight hundred pounds out of fifteen hundred were already there. The remaining seven hundred I undertook to carry myself, as I had done most of the rest. It would have been folly to encumber my main body with anything more than their boats and sledges; they were barely able at first to carry even these. Our effort to escape would indeed have resulted in miserable failure, had we been without our little Esquimaux dog-team to move the sick, and forward the intended lading of the boats, and keep up supplies along the line of march. I find by my notes that these six dogs, well worn by previous travel, carried me with a fully-burdened sledge
between seven and eight hundred miles during the first fortnight after leaving the brig—a mean travel of fifty-seven miles a day.

Up to the evening of the 23d, the progress had been a little more than a mile a day for one sledge : on the 24th, both sledges had reached First Ravine, a distance of seven miles, and the dog-sledge had brought on to this station the buffalo bags and other sleeping appliances which we had prepared during the winter. The condition of the party was such that it was essential they should sleep in comfort ; and it was a rule therefore during the whole journey, never departed from unless in extreme emergency, never to begin a new day's labour till the party was refreshed from the exertions of the day before. Our halts were regulated by the condition of the men rather than by arbitrary hours, and sleep was meted out in proportion to the trials of the march. The thermometer still ranged below zero ; but our housed boats, well crowded, and fully stocked with sleeping gear, were hardly uncomfortable to weary men ; besides which, we slept by day when the sun was warmest, and travelled when we could avoid his greatest glare.

Mr. Morton, Ohlsen, and Petersen, during this time performed a double duty. They took their turn at the sledges with the rest, but they were also engaged in preparing the *Red Eric* as a comrade boat. She was mounted on our good old sledge, the *Faith* —a sledge that, like her namesake our most reliable whaleboat, had been our very present help in many times of trouble. I believe every man felt, when he saw her brought out, that stout CHAPTER
L. work was to be done, and under auspices of good.

In the meantime I had carried Mr. Goodfellow to the sick sta- State of the sick. tion with my dog-sledge, and had managed to convey the rest one by one to the same spot. Mr. Wilson, whose stump was still unhealed, and who suffered besides from scurvy ; George Whipple, whose tendons were so contracted that he could not extend his legs, and poor Stephenson, just able to keep the lamps burning and warm up food for the rest, were the other invalids, all incapable of moving without assistance. It is just that I should speak of the manly fortitude with which they bore up during this painful imprisonment. Dr. Hayes, though still disabled from his frozen foot, adhered manfully to the sledges.

I have already expressed my belief that this little refuge hut of Usefulness of the refuge hut at Anoatok. Anoatok was the means of saving the lives of these four men. When they were first transported to it, they were all of them so drawn up with scurvy as to be unable to move. There was but one among them able to melt water for the rest. I attended them, myself during the first week, at every interval that I could snatch from the duty of transporting our provisions. The temperature in which they lived was at first below zero ; but, as the sun rose and the warmth increased, they gradually gained strength, and were able at last to crawl out and breathe in the gladdening air.

Had I attempted to bring them down on our boat-sledges, our progress would have been seriously impeded, and their lives jeoparded. I cannot imagine a worse position for a sick and helpless man than some of those which I have described in our transit from the brig.

On the other hand, to have left them for the time behind us would have made it quite possible that they might not at last be reclaimed. Every day was making the ice travel more difficult and full of hazard till we reached the open water ; and they could not fail to know this as soon as they were able to look out on the floes. My occasional visits as I passed Anoatok on my way to Etah, or as I brought supplies for them on the return, gave them assurances of continued interest in their fortunes, and advices of our progress and of their own hopes and ours.

Besides all this, there is something in the insidious disease which was their most dangerous enemy that is best combated by

CHAPTER
L.

moral excitement. A change of scene, renewed or increased responsibilities, topics of active thought, incitements to physical effort, are among the very best prescriptions for men suffering with the scurvy. I have had reason to feel, while tracing these pages, how reluctantly the system renews its energies under the pressure of a daily unvarying task.

Gradual
improve-
ment in
the health
of the
patients.

The patients at our sick station no doubt suffered much, and for a while I never parted from them without anxiety. But their health.improved under the stimulus of a new mode of life ; and by the time that we called on them to rejoin us their whole tone had undergone a happy change. I congratulate myself, as I write, that all who reached the open water with me are able now to bear a part in society and toil.

CHAPTER LI.

TO THE BRIG AGAIN—WELCOME AT THE HUT—LOG OF THE SLEDGES—
EDUCATED FAITH—GOOD-BYE TO THE BRIG—METEK'S PRAYER.

As I review my notes of the first few days of our ice-journey, I CHAPTER
find them full of incidents, interesting and even momentous ____
when they occurred, but which cannot claim a place in this narrative.   The sledges were advancing slowly, the men often discouraged, and now and then one giving way under the unac-
customed labour ; the sick at Anoatok always dreary in their
solitude, and suffering, perhaps, under an exacerbation of disease, or, like the rest of us, from a penury of appropriate food.
Things looked gloomy enough at times.

The *Red Boat* was completed for service in a few days, and The *Red*
joined the sledge-party on the floes,—an additional burden, but *Boat* com
a necessary one, for our weary rue-raddies; and I set out for
the sick-station with Mr. Goodfellow, our last remaining invalid.
As my team reached the entrance of Force Bay, I saw that Incident
poor Nessark, the Esquimaux, who had carried Mr. Wilson and at the
some stores to Anoatok, finding his sledge-load too heavy, had of Force
thrown out a portion of it upon the ice.   He had naturally Bay.
enough selected the bread for his jettison, an article of diet unknown among the Esquimaux, but precisely that of which our
sick were most in need.   I lost some time in collecting such
parts of his rejected cargo as I could find, and, when I reached
the huts after a twelve hours' drive, the condition of our sick
men made it imperative that I should return at once to the
brig.   The dogs gave out while crossing the reach of Force Bay,
and I was forced to camp out with them on the ice-belt, but Camping
early in the morning I came upon the fires of the sledge-party. out on the
ice-belt.

The men were at prayers when I first saw them ; but, as
they passed to the drag-ropes, I was pained to see how wearily
they moved.   Poor Brooks' legs were so swollen that he could
not brace them in his blanket coverings, and Dr. Hayes could
hardly keep his place.   The men generally showed symptoms

CHAPTER
LI. of increasing scurvy. It was plain that they could not hold their own without an increased allowance, if not of meat, at least of fresh bread and hot tea.

Appear-
at Rens-
selaer Bay. Taking with me Morton, my faithful adjutant always, I hurried on to the brig. It was in the full glare of noon that we entered the familiar curve of Rensselaer Bay. The black spars of our deserted vessel cut sharply against the shores; there was the deeply-marked snow-track that led to Observatory Island and the graves of poor Baker and Schubert, with their cairn and its white-cross beacon: everything looked as when we defiled in funeral procession round the cliffs a year before. But, as we came close upon the brig, and drove our dogs up the gang-way, along which Bonsall and myself had staggered so often with our daily loads of ice, we heard the rustling of wings, Ravens on
board the
brig. and a large raven sailed away in the air past Sylvia Headland. It was old Magog, one of a pair that had cautiously haunted near our brig during the last two years. He had already appropriated our homestead.

We lighted fires in the galley, melted pork, baked a large batch of bread, gathered together a quantity of beans and dried apples, somewhat damaged, but still eatable, and by the time our dogs had fed and rested, we were ready for the return. Distributing our supplies as we passed the squads on the floe, I hastened Return to
Anoatok. to Anoatok. I had taken Godfrey with us from his party, and, as it was painfully evident that the men could not continue to work without more generous food, I sent him on to Etah with the dogs, in the hope of procuring a stock of walrus-meat.

Welcome
at the hut. The little company at the hut welcomed my return. They had exhausted their provisions; their lamp had gone out; the snow-drift had forced its way in at the door, so that they could not close it; it was blowing a north-easter; and the thermometer, which hung against the blanketed walls, stood only sixteen degrees above zero. The poor fellows had all the will to protect themselves, but they were lame, and weak, and hungry, and disheartened. We built a fire for them of tarred rope, dried their bedding, cooked them a porridge of meat-biscuit and pea-soup, fastened up their desolate door-way, hung a dripping slab of pork-fat over their lamp-wick, and, first joining in a prayer

of thankfulness, and then a round of merry gossip, all hands CHAPTER
LI. forgot sickness, and privation, and distance in the contentment of our sleeping-bags. I cannot tell how long we slept, for all our watches ran down before we awoke.

The gale had risen, and it was snowing hard when I replen- A tea-
drinking
frolic. ished the fires of our hearthstone. But we went on burning rope and fat, in a regular tea-drinking frolic, till not an icicle or even a frost-mark was to be seen on the roof. After a time Godfrey rejoined us; Metek came with him; and between their two sledges they brought an ample supply of meat. With part of this I hastened to the sledge-party. They were now off Ten- Journey to
relieve the
sledge
party. mile Ravine, struggling through the accumulated snows, and much exhausted, though not out of heart. In spite of their swollen feet, they had worked fourteen hours a day, passing in that time over some twelve miles of surface, and advancing a mile and a half on their way.

A few extracts from their log-book, as kept by Dr. Hayes, Extracts
from the
logbook of
Dr. Hayes. may show something of our mode of travel, though it conveys but an imperfect idea of its trials.

LOG OF SLEDGE-PARTY.

"*May 23, Wednesday.*—Mr. Bonsall, cook, called at 8 P.M. George Riley suffering from snow-blindness, but able to take a place at the drag-ropes. Read prayers, and got under way at 10¼ P.M.

"Took *Faith* to bluff at head of ravine. Left Dr. Hayes there and returned for *Hope.* Carried her on to *Faith's* camp and halted. All hands very much tired. Sledges haul heavy. Snow in drifts on the ice-foot, requiring a standing haul.

"Captain Kane passed us from Esquimaux hut on his way to brig, at 11 A.M., while we were sleeping. Captain Kane overtook and passed us again, with his dog-sledge and provision-cargo, on way to sick station, at two o'clock, Tuesday, while cooking, taking with him William Godfrey.

"*May 24, Thursday.*—Cook, George Riley, called at 4 P.M. Read prayers, and got under way at eight o'clock. Took *Faith* beyond the headland of yesterday. Melted snow for drink. Left Dr. Hayes here and returned for *Hope.* Carried her back to *Faith* camp by 5 A.M. of Friday, and halted. Hayes about the same;

CHAPTER LI. Riley's eyes better. Mr. Bonsall and M'Gary begin to give in. Slush for burning all gone. Party with *Red Boat* not yet come up.

"*May 25, Friday.*—Mr Sontag, cook, called at 6 P.M. Mr. Ohlsen, with the *Red Boat* and cargo, came up at one o'clock, bringing orders from Captain Kane. Being knocked up, he and his party turned in. After prayers, stowed the spare cargo of the

The *Red Eric* hauled to the Ice-foot.

whaleboats into the *Red Eric*, and all hands, except Mr. Sontag and Dr. Hayes, hauled her down to the ice-foot of the Bedevilled Reach Turn-off station, below Basalt Camp.

A SKETCH.

" Returned, and reached the whaleboats at five o'clock, Saturday morning. All hands tired, turned in. Riley's eyes well.

"*May 26, Saturday.*—Strong wind, with snow, during night.

Arrival of Captain Kane with supplies.

Captain Kane came from south at half-past three o'clock with the dog-deam, bringing a supply of walrus-beef, with Metek and sledge."

Once more leaving the party on the floe, Morton and myself, with Metek and his sledge in company, revisited the brig, and set ourselves to work baking bread. We had both of us ample ex-

perience in this branch of the culinary art, and I could gain some chapter LI.
credit, perhaps, with a portion of my readers, by teaching them
how bread may be raised in three hours without salt, saleratus, or Baking bread.
shortening. But it is not the office of this book to deal in occult
mysteries. The thing can be done, and we did it: *sat verbum*.
The brig was dreary enough, and Metek was glad to bid it good-
bye, with one hundred and fifty pounds on his dog-sledge, consigned to Mr. Brooks. But he carried besides a letter, safely Metek's journey.
trusted to his inspection, which directed that he should be sent
back forthwith for another load. It was something like a breach
of faith, perhaps, but his services were indispensable, and his
dogs still more so. . He returned, of course, for there was no
escaping us ; his village lay in the opposite direction, and he
could not deviate from the track after once setting out. In the
meantime we had cooked about a hundred pounds of flour pud-
ding, and tried out a couple of bagfuls of pork-fat;—a good day's
work,—and we were quite ready, before the subdued brightness
of midnight came, to turn in to our beds. Our beds !—there Singular sleeping place.
was not an article of covering left on board. We ripped open the
old mattresses, and, all three crawling down among the curled
hair, Morton, Metek, and the Nalegak, slept as sound as vagrants
on a haystack.

On Monday, the 28th, we all set out for the boats and Anoatok. Return to Anoatok.
Both Metek and myself had our sledges heavily laden. We carried
the last of our provision-bags, completing now our full complement of fifteen hundred pounds, the limit of capacity of our
otherwise crowded boats.

It caused me a bitter pang to abandon our collection of objects Treasures abandoned.
of Natural History, the cherished fruit of so much exposure and
toil ; and it was hardly easier to leave some other things behind,
—several of my well-tested instruments, for instance, and those
silent friends, my books. They had all been packed up, hoping
for a chance of saving them ; and, to the credit of my comrades,
let me say gratefully that they offered to exclude both clothes and
food in favour of a full freight of these treasures.

But the thing was not to be thought of. I gave a last look at A last look.
the desolate galley-stove, the representative of our long winter's
fireside, at the still bright coppers now full of frozen water, the
theodolite, the chart-box, and poor Wilson's guitar,—one more

CHAPTER at the remnant of the old moss walls, the useless daguerreotypes,
LI. and the skeletons of dog, and deer, and bear, and musk-ox,—
stoppered in the rigging ;—and, that done, whipped up my dogs
so much after the manner of a sentimentalizing Christian, that
our pagan Metek raised a prayer in their behalf.

CHAPTER LII.

NEW STATIONS—THE ICE-MARSHES—POINT SECURITY—OOPEGSOAK—
CATCHING AUKS—ANINGNAII—NESSARK.

I FOUND that Mr. Brooks had succeeded in getting his boat and CHAPTER LII.
sledges as far as the floe off Bedevilled Reach. I stopped only
long enough to point out to him an outside track, where I had Meeting with Mr Brooks.
found the ice quite smooth and free from snow, and pressed
my dogs for the hut. I noticed, to my great joy, too, that the
health of his party seemed to be improving under our raw-meat
specific, and could not find fault with the extravagant use they
were making of it.

The invalids at the sick station were not as well as I could
have wished ; but I had only time to renew their stock of provision and give them a few cheering words. Our walrus-meat
was nearly exhausted.

I had fixed upon two new stations further to the south, as Two new stations.
the depôts to which our stores were now to be transported.
One was upon the old and heavy floes off Navialik, "the big
gull's place,"—a headland opposite Cape Hatherton,—the other
on the level ice-plain near Littleton Island. Having now gathered
our stores at Anoatok, I began with a thankful heart to move
them onward. I sent on Metek to the further station with two
bags of bread-dust, each weighing ninety pounds, and, having
myself secured some three hundred pounds at Navialik, drove
on for Etah Bay.

My long succession of journeys on this route had made me Trying a new route to Etah Bay.
thoroughly weary of the endless waste of ice to seaward, and
I foolishly sought upon this trip to vary the travel by following the ice-belt. But, upon reaching Refuge Harbour, I found
the snow so heavy and the fragments from the cliffs so numerous and threatening, that I was obliged to give it up. A
large chasm stopped my advance and drove me out again upon
the floes.

Getting beyond a table-land known as Kasarsoak, or "the big
25

promontory," I emerged from the broken ice upon a wide plain. Here I first saw with alarm that the ice had changed its character: the snow which covered it had become lead-coloured and sodden by the water from beneath, and ice-fields after ice-fields stretching before me were all covered with stained patches. As I rode along these lonely marshes, for such they were, the increased labour of the dogs admonished me that the floe was no longer to be trusted. It chilled my heart to remember the position of our boats and stores. Nearly nine hundred pounds of food, exclusive of the load now upon my sledge, were still awaiting transportation at Anoatok.

Two hundred more, including our shot and bullet-bags, were at the Cape Hatherton station; and Metek's load was probably by this time lying on the ice opposite M'Gary Island. Like Robinson Crusoe with his powder, the reflection came over me:—"Good God! what will become of us if all this is destroyed?"

Only by men experienced in the rapid changes of Arctic ice can the full force of this reflection be appreciated. A single gale might convert the precarious platform, over which we were travelling, into a tumultuous ice-pack. Had the boats their stores on board even, and could they break through without foundering, there was not the remotest prospect of their being liberated in open water; and I knew well what obstacles a wet, sludgy surface would present to our over-tasked and almost worn-out party.

I determined, therefore, as soon as I could secure the meat, which was my immediate errand, to make a requisition upon the Esquimaux for two of the four dogs which were still at Etah, and by their aid to place the provisions in safety. The north cape of Littleton Island, afterward called Point Security, was selected for the purpose, and I left orders with the invalids at the sick station to be in readiness for instant removal. I pursued my journey alone.

It was quite late in the evening when I drew near Etah. I mean that it was verging on to our midnight, the sun being low in the heavens, and the air breathing that solemn stillness which belongs to the sleeping-time of birds and plants. I had not quite reached the little settlement when loud sounds of laughter came to my ear ; and, turning the cape, I burst suddenly upon an encamp- ment of the inhabitants.

Some thirty men, women, and children, were gathered together upon a little face of offal-stained rock. Except a bank of moss, which broke the wind-draught from the fiord, they were entirely without protection from the weather, though the temperature was 5° below zero. The huts were completely deserted, the snow tossut had fallen in, and the window was as free and open as summer to the purifying air. Every living thing about the settlement was out upon the bare rocks.

Rudest of gypsies, how they squalled, and laughed, and snored, and rolled about! Some were sucking bird-skins, others were boiling incredible numbers of auks in huge soapstone pots, and two youngsters, crying at the top of their voices, "Oopegsoak! Oopegsoak!" were fighting for an owl. It was the only specimen (*Strix nyctea*) that I had seen except on the wing ; but, before I could secure it, they had torn it limb from limb, and were eating its warm flesh and blood, their faces buried among its dishevelled feathers.

The fires were of peat-moss greased with the fat of the birdskins. They were used only for cooking, however, the people depending for comfort on the warmth of close contact. Old Kresut, the blind patriarch of the settlement, was the favoured centre, and around him, as a focus, was a coil of men, women, and children, as perplexing to unravel as a skein of eels. The children alone were toddling about and bringing in stores of moss, their faces smeared with blood, and titbits of raw liver between their teeth.

The scene was redolent of plenty and indolence,—the *dolce far* *niente* of the short-lived Esquimaux summer. Provision for the dark winter was furthest from their thoughts ; for, although the rocks were patched with sun-dried birds, a single hunting-party from Peteravik could have eaten up their entire supplies in a night.

There was enough to make them improvident. The little auks were breeding in the low cones of rubbish under the cliffs in such numbers that it cost them no more to get food than it does a cook to gather vegetables. A boy, ordered to climb the rocks with one of their purse-nets of seal-skin at the end

CHAPTER LII. of a narwhal's tusk, would return in a few minutes with as many as he could carry.

CATCHING AUKS.

The dogs seemed as happy as their masters : they were tethered by seal-skin thongs to prevent robbery, but evidently fed to the full extent of their capacity.

Aningnah the "witch of the caldron." Aningnah, wife of Marsumah, was one of the presiding deities of the soup-pot, or rather first witch of the caldron. She was a tall, well-made woman, and, next to Mrs. Metek, had a larger influence than any female in the settlement.

During one of my visits to the settlement, I had relieved her from much suffering by opening a furuncle, and the kind creature never lost an opportunity of showing how she remembered it. Poor old Kresut was summarily banished from his central seat of honour, and the nalegak installed in his place. She stripped herself of her bird-skin kapetah to make me a coverlet, and gave me her two-year-old baby for a pillow. There was a little commotion in the tangled mass of humanity as I crawled over them to accept these proffered hospitalities; but it was all of a welcoming sort. I had learned by this time to take kindly and condescendingly the privileges of my rank ; and, with my inner man well refreshed with auk-livers, I was soon asleep.

In the morning I left my own tired dogs in charge of Marsumah, quite confident that his wife would feed them faithfully, and took from them their only team in unequal exchange. Such had become our relations with these poor friends of ours, that such an act of authority would have gone unquestioned if it had cost them a much graver sacrifice. They saw the condition of my own travel-broken animals, and were well aware of the sufferings of our party, so long their neighbours and allies. Old Nessark filled my sledge with walrus-meat ; and two of the young men joined me on foot, to assist me through the broken ice between Littleton Island and the mainland.

CHAPTER LII.

A living pillow.

Kindness of the natives.

CHAPTER LIII.

THE GAME OF BALL—MY BROTHER'S LAKE—THE POLAR SEASONS—FATE OF
THE ESQUIMAUX—THE ESQUIMAUX LIMITS—ESQUIMAUX ENDURANCE—
AWAHTOK'S HUNT—HIS ESCAPE—THE GUARDIAN WALRUS.

CHAPTER LIII. BEFORE I left Etah on my return, I took an early stroll with Sip-su, "the handsome boy," to the lake back of my old travelling-route, and directly under the face of the glacier.

A play-ground in the snow He led me first to the play-ground, where all his young friends of the settlement were busy in one of their sports. Each of them had a walrus-rib for a *golph* or *shinny-stick*, and they were contending to drive a *hurley*, made out of the round knob of a flipper-joint, up a bank of frozen snow. Roars of laughter greeted the impatient striker as he missed his blow at the shining ball, and eager cries told how close the match was drawing to an end. They were counting on the fingers of both hands, Eight, eight, eight,— the game is ten.

Strange,—the thought intruded itself, but there was no wisdom in it,—strange that these famine-pinched wanderers of the ice should rejoice in sports and playthings like the children of our own smiling sky, and that parents should fashion for them toy sledges, and harpoons, and nets, miniature emblems of a life of suffering and peril! how strange this joyous merriment under the monitory shadow of these jagged ice-cliffs! My spirit was oppressed as I imagined the possibility of our tarrying longer in these frozen regions; but it was ordinary life with these other children of the same Creator, and they were playing as unconcerned as the birds that circled above our heads. "Fear not, therefore: ye are of more value than many sparrows."

I do not wonder that the scene at the lake impressed my brother when he visited it on his errand of rescue. Lieutenant Hartstene and he were the only white men, except myself, that have ever seen it.

A body of ice, resplendent in the sunshine, was enclosed between the lofty walls of black basalt; and from its base a great archway or tunnel poured out a dashing stream into the lake, disturbing its quiet surface with a horse-shoe of foam. Birds flew about in myriads, and the green sloping banks were chequered with the purple lychnis and Arctic chickweeds.

I have named this lake after my brother, for it was near its shores that, led by Myouk, he stumbled on the summer tents of the natives and obtained the evidence of our departure south. I built a large cairn here, and placed within it a copper penny, on which was scratched the letter K; but, like many other such deposits, it never met the eyes for which it was intended.

The lake abounds in fish, apparently the salmon trout ; but the natives have not the art of fishing. The stream, which tunnels its way out near the glacier foot, is about ten feet in diameter ; and I was assured that it never completely suspends its flow. Although the tunnel closes with ice, and the surface of the lake freezes for many feet below, the water may still be seen and heard beneath, even in midwinter, wearing its way at the base of the glacier.

This fact is of importance, as it bears upon the temperature of deep ice-beds. It shows that with an atmosphere whose mean is below zero throughout the year, and a mean summer heat but 4° above the freezing-point, these great Polar glaciers retain a high interior temperature not far from 32°, which enables them to resume their great functions of movement and discharge readily, when the cold of winter is at an end, and not improbably to temper to some extent the natural rigour of the climate. Even in the heart of the ice nature has her compensations.

The phases of the Polar year so blend and separate that it is dif- ficult to distribute them into seasons. In the Arctic latitudes a thousand miles to the south, travellers speak of winter and summer as if the climate underwent no intermediate changes. But nature impresses no such contrasts upon any portion of her realm ; and, whatever may be the registrations of the meteorologist, the rude Esquimaux of these icy solitudes derives from his own experience and necessities a more accurate and practical system of notation.

He measures his life by winters, as the American Indian does by the summers, and for a like reason. Winter is for him the great dominant period of the year; he calls it " okipok," the season of fast ice.

But when the day has come again, and the first thawing begins

CHAPTER LIII. to show itself in the sunshine, as winter declines before the promise of spring, he tells you that it is "upernasak," the time of

"Upernasak," the time of water-drops. water-drops. It is then the snow-bird comes back and the white ptarmigan takes a few brown feathers. His well-known heath, too, the irsutect (*Andromeda tetragona*), is green again below its dried stems under the snow.

"Upernak," the season of thaws. About the end of May, or a little later, comes "upernak," the season of thaws. It is his true summer. Animal and vegetable life are now back again; the floes break upon the sea and drift in ice-rafts about the coasts; snow is disappearing from the hilltops; and the water-torrents pour down from the long-scaled ravines and valleys.

"Aosak," the interval between thaw and frost. About the middle of August the upernak has passed into the season of no ice, "aosak," the short interval between complete thaw and reconsolidation. It is never really iceless; but the floes have now drifted to the south, and the sea along the coast is more open than at any other period. It ends with the latter weeks of September, and sees the departure of all migratory life.

"Okiakut," the return of winter. The fifth season is a late fall, the "okiakut," when the water-torrents begin to freeze in the fiords, and thawing ceases except at noonday. This terminates when the young ice has formed in a permanent layer on the bays, and winter returns with its long reign of cold and darkness.

It is with a feeling of melancholy that I recall these familiar names. They illustrate the trials and modes of life of a simple-minded people, for whom it seems to be decreed that the year must very soon cease to renew its changes. It pains me when I

Probable destiny of the Esquimaux race. think of their approaching destiny,—in the region of night and winter, where the earth yields no fruit and the waters are locked, —without the resorts of skill or even the rude materials of art, and walled in from the world by barriers of ice without an outlet.

If you point to the east, inland, where the herds of reindeer run over the barren hills unmolested,—for they have no means of capturing them,—they will cry "Sermik," "glacier;" and question them as you may about the range of their nation to the north and south, the answer is still the same, with a shake of the head, "Sermik, sermik-soak," "the great ice-wall;" there is no more beyond.

They have no "kresuk," no wood. The drift-timber which

blesses their more southern brethren never reaches them. The
bow and arrow are therefore unknown; and the kayak, the national
implement of the Greenlander, which, like the palm-tree to the
natives of the tropics, ministers to almost every want, exists
among them only as a legendary word.

CHAPTER LIII.

Want of wood.

The narrow belt subjected to their nomadic range cannot be less
than six hundred miles long; and throughout this extent of country every man knows every man. There is not a marriage, or a
birth, or a death that is not talked over and mentally registered
by all. I have a census, exactly confirmed by three separate infor-
mants, which enables me to count by name about one hundred
and forty souls, scattered along from Kosoak, the Great River at
the base of a glacier near Cape Melville, to the wind-loved hut of
Anoatok.

Census of the na-tives.

Destitute as they are, they exist both in love and community
of resources as a single family. The sites of their huts—for they
are so few in number as not to bear the name of villages—are
arranged with reference to the length of the dog-march and the
seat of the hunt; and thus, when winter has built her highway
and cemented into one the sea, the islands, and the main, they
interchange with each other the sympathies and social communion
of man, and diffuse through the darkness a knowledge of the
resources and condition of all.

Love and sympathy among them.

The main line of travel is then as beaten as a road at home.
The dogs speed from hut to hut, almost unguided by their drivers.
They regulate their time by the stars. Every rock has its name,
every hill its significance; and a cache of meat deposited anywhere in this harsh wilderness can be recovered by the youngest
hunter in the nation.

Their main line of travel.

From Cape York to a settlement at Saunders Island, called
Appah, from the "Appah" or Lumme which colonize here in
almost incredible numbers, the drive has been made in a single
day; and thence to Netelik, on the main of Murchison Sound, in
another. In a third, the long reach has been traversed by Cape
Saumarez to the settlement of Karsioot, on a low tongue near
Cape Robertson; and the fourth day has closed at Etah, or even
Aunatok, the open place, — the resting-place now of our poor
deserted Oomiak-soak. This four days' travel cannot be less than
six hundred miles; and Amaladok, Metek's half-brother, assured

Arrange-ment of resting-places.

me that he had made it in three, — probably changing his teams.

Their powers of resistance to exposure and fatigue are not greater perhaps than those of a well-trained voyager from other regions. But the necessities of their precarious life familiarize them with dangers from which the bravest among us might shrink without dishonour. To exemplify this, I select a single one from a number of adventures that were familiar in their recent history.

During the famine at Etah last winter, when we ourselves were so much distressed for fresh food, two of my friends, Awahtok and Myouk, determined to seek the walrus on the open ice. It was a performance of the greatest danger; but it was better in their eyes than the sacrifice of their dogs, and they both possessed to the fullest extent that apathetic fatalism which belongs to all lowly-cultivated races. They succeeded in killing a large male, and were in the act of returning joyfully to their village, when a north wind broke up the ice, and they found themselves afloat. The impulse of a European would have been to seek the land; but they knew that the drift was always most dangerous on the coast, and urged their dogs toward the nearest iceberg. They reached it after a struggle, and, by great efforts, made good their landing with their dogs and the half-butchered carcass of the walrus.

Poor Myouk, as he told the story to Petersen, made a frightful picture of their sufferings, the more so from the quiet, stoical manner with which he detailed the facts. It was at the close, he said, of the last moonlight of December, and in the midst of the heavy storm which held Petersen and myself prisoners at Anoatok. A complete darkness settled around them. They tied the dogs down to knobs of ice to prevent their losing their foothold, and prostrated themselves to escape being blown off by the violence of the wind. At first the sea broke over them, but they gained a higher level, and built a sort of screen of ice.

On the fifth night afterward, judging as well as they could, Myouk froze one of his feet, and Awahtok lost his great toe by frost-bite. But they kept heart of grace, and ate their walrus-meat as they floated slowly to the south. The berg came twice into collision with floes, and they thought at one time that they had passed the Utlak-soak, the Great Caldron, and had entered the North Water of Baffin's Bay. It was toward the close of the second moonlight, after a month's imprisonment, living as only CHAPTER LIII. these iron men could live, that they found the berg had grounded. They liberated their dogs as soon as the young ice would bear their Their deliverance. weight, and, attaching long lines to them, which they cut from the hide of the dead walrus, they succeeded in hauling themselves through the water-space which always surrounds an iceberg, and reaching safe ice. They returned to their village like men raised from the dead, to meet a welcome, but to meet famine along with it.

I believe the explanation was never given to me in detail, or, if it was, I have forgotten it; but the whole misadventure was referred to an infringement of some canonical ritual in their conduct of the hunt. The walrus, and perhaps the seal also, is under the The guardian walrus protective guardianship of a special representative or prototype, who takes care that he shall have fair play. They all believe that in the recesses of Force Bay, near a conical peak which has often served me as a landmark on my sledge-journeys, a great walrus lives in the hills, and crawls out, when there is no moon, to the edge of a ravine, where he bellows with a voice far more powerful than his fellows out to sea. Ootuniah had often heard this walrus, and once, when I was crossing Bedevilled Reach, he stopped me to listen to his dismal tones. I certainly heard them, and Ootuniah said that a good hunt would come of it. I tried to talk to him about echoes; but as neither of us could understand the other, I listened quietly at last to the Big Walrus, and went my way.

CHAPTER LIV.

THE BAKERY—THE GUITAR GHOST—THE BOAT CAMP—NESSARK'S WIFE—
OUT IN A GALE—CAPE MISERY—THE BURROW—THE RETREAT.

CHAPTER LIV. THE sledge-party under Mr. Brooks had advanced to within
Necessity of returning to the brig. three miles of the hut when I reached them on my return They had found the ice more practicable, and their health was improving. But their desire for food had increased proportionably; and, as it was a well-understood rule of our commissariat not to touch the reserved provision of the boats, it became necessary to draw additional supplies from the brig. The seven hundred pounds of bread-dust, our entire stock, could not be reduced with safety.

But the dogs were wanted to advance the contents of our Anoatok storehouse to the stations further south, and I resolved to take Tom Hickey with me and walk back for another baking exploit. Difficulties of the journey. It was more of an effort than I counted on: we were sixteen hours on the ice, and we had forgotten our gutta-percha eyautick, or slit goggles. The glare of the sun as we entered the curve of our ice-cumbered harbour almost blinded us.

Tom had been a baker at home; but he assures me, with all the authority of an ancient member of the guild, that our achievement the day we came on board might be worthy of praise in the " old Baking in the brig. country;" Tom knows no praise more expanded. We kneaded the dough in a large pickled-cabbage cask, fired sundry volumes of the Penny Cyclopædia of Useful Knowledge, and converted, between duff and loaf, almost a whole barrel of flour into a strong likeness to the staff of life. It was the last of our stock; and " all the better too," said my improvident comrade, who retained some of the genius of blundering as well as the gallantry of his countrymen,—" all the better, sir, since we'll have no more bread to bake."

Godfrey came on with the dogs three days after, to carry back the fruits of our labour; but an abrupt change of the weather gave us a howling gale outside, and we were all of us storm-stayed. It was Sunday, and probably the last time that two or three would be gathered together in our dreary cabin. So I took a Bible from one of the bunks, and we went through the old-times service. It was my closing act of official duty among my shipmates on board the poor little craft. I visited her afterward, but none of them were with me.

Tom and myself set out soon after, though the wind drove heavily from the south, leaving our companion to recover from his fatigue. We brought on our sledge-load safely, and had forgotten our baking achievement, with things of minor note, in that dreamless sleep which rewards physical exhaustion, when Godfrey came in upon us. He had had a hard chase behind the sledge, and was unwilling to confess at first what had brought him after us so soon. He had tried to forget himself among the debris of a mattress on the cabin floor, when he heard a sound from Mr. Wilson's guitar, sad and flowing in all its unearthly harmonies. He was sure he was awake, for he ran for it on the instant, and the proof was, he had left his coat behind him. The harp of Æolus had not been dreamed of in Bill's philosophy.

I was glad, when I reached the sick station, to find things so much better. Everybody was stronger, and, as a consequence, more cheerful. They had learned housekeeping, with its courtesies as well as comforts. Their kotluk would have done credit to Aningnah herself: they had a dish of tea for us, and a lump of walrus; and they bestirred themselves real housewife-fashion to give us the warm place and make us comfortable. I was right sorry to leave them, for the snow outside was drifting with the gale; but after a little while the dogs struck the track of the sledges, and following it with unerring instinct, did not slacken their pace till they had brought us to our companions on the floe.

They had wisely halted on account of the storm; and, with their three little boats drawn up side by side for mutual protection, had been lying to for the past two days, tightly housed, and moored fast by whale-lines to the ice. But the drifts had almost buried the *Hope*, which was the windward boat; and when I saw the burly form of Brooks emerging from the snow-covered roof, I could have fancied it a walrus rising through the ice.

They had found it hard travel, but were doing well. Brooks's provision-report was the old story,—out of meat and nearly out of

Marginal notes: CHAPTER LIV. The last Sunday service in the brig. Godfrey frightened out of the brig. Improvement at the sick station. Halt of the sledge party.

bread — no pleasant news for a tired-out man, who saw in this the necessity of another trip to Etah. I was only too glad, however, to see that their appetites held, for with the animal man, as with

BOAT'S CAMP IN A STORM.

all others, while he feeds he lives. Short allowance for working-men on bread diet was, of course, out of the question. For the past week each man had eaten three pounds of duff a day, and I did not dare to check them, although we had no more flour in reserve to draw upon. But the question how long matters could go on at this rate admitted of a simple arithmetical solution.

Six Esquimaux, three of them women—that ugly beauty, Nessark's wife, at the head of them—had come off to the boats for shelter from the gale. They seemed so entirely deferential, and to recognise with such simple trust our mutual relations of alliance, that I resolved to drive down to Etah with Petersen as interpreter, and formally claim assistance, according to their own laws, on the ground of our established brotherhood. I had thought of this before; but both Marsumah and Metek had been so en-

grossed with their bird-catching that I was loath to take them
from their families.

Our dogs moved slowly, and the discoloured ice admonished me
to make long circuits. As we neared Littleton Island, the wind
blew so freshly from the south-west that I determined to take the
in-shore channel and attempt to make the settlement over land.
But I was hardly under the lee of the island, when there broke
upon us one of the most fearful gales I have ever experienced. It
had the character and the force of a cyclome. The dogs were literally blown from their harness, and it was only by throwing
ourselves on our faces that we saved ourselves from being swept
away; it seemed as if the ice must give way. We availed ourselves of a momentary lull to shoulder the sledge, and, calling the
affrighted dogs around us, made for the rocks of Eider Island, and
after the most exhausting exertions, succeeded in gaining terra
firma.

We were now safe from the danger that had seemed most imminent ; but our condition was not improved. We were out on a
blank cliff, the wind eddying round us so furiously that we could not
keep our feet, and the air so darkened with the snow-wreaths that,
although we were in the full daytime of the Arctic summer, we
could neither see each other nor our dogs. There was not a cleft
or a projecting knob that could give us refuge. I saw that we
must move or die. It was impossible that the ice should continue
to resist such a hurricane, and a bold channel separated us from
the shore. Petersen indeed protested that the channel was already
broken up and driving with the storm. We made the effort, and
crossed.

We struck a headland on the main shore, where a dark horn-
blende rock, perhaps thirty feet high, had formed a barricade, behind which the drifts piled themselves; and into this mound of
snow we had just strength enough left to dig a burrow. We knew
it soon after as Cape Misery.

The dogs and sledge were dragged in, and Petersen and myself,
reclining " spoon-fashion," cowered among them. The snow piled
over us all, and we were very soon so roofed in and quilted round
that the storm seemed to rage far outside of us. We could only
hear the wind droning like a great fly-wheel, except when a surge
of greater malignity would sweep up over our burial-place and sift

CHAPTER
LIV.
___

A vapour
bath.

the snow upon the surface like hail. Our greatest enemy here was warmth. Our fur jumpers had been literally torn off our backs by the wind; but the united respiration of dogs and men melted the snow around us, and we were soon wet to the skin. It was a noisome vapour-bath, and we experienced its effects in an alarming tendency to syncope and loss of power.

Is it possible to imagine a juncture of more comic annoyance than that which now introduced itself among the terrors of our position ? Toodla, our master-dog, was seized with a violent fit; and, as their custom is, his companions indulged in a family con-flict upon the occasion, which was only mediated, after much effort, at the sacrifice of all that remained of Petersen's pantaloons and drawers.

Disturb-
ance
among
the dogs.

We had all the longing for repose that accompanies extreme prostration, and had been fearing every moment that the com-batants would bring the snow down upon us. At last down came our whole canopy, and we were exposed in an instant to the fury of the elements. I do not think, often as I have gone up on deck from a close cabin in a gale at sea, that I was ever more struck with the extreme noise and tumult of a storm.

The roof
falls in.

Snowed
up again.

Once more snowed up—for the drift built its crystal palace rapidly about us—we remained cramped and seething till our appetites reminded us of the necessities of the inner man. To breast the gale was simply impossible ; the alternative was to drive before it to the north and east. Forty miles of floundering travel brought us in twenty hours to the party on the floes.

Reach the
boat camp
once more.

They too had felt the force of the storm, and had drawn up the boats with their prows to the wind, all hands housed, and wonder-ing as much as we did that the ice still held.

CHAPTER LV.

FRESH DOGS—THE SLIDES—ROCKING-STONES—OHLSEN'S ACCIDENT—ICE-
SAILING—MOUNTING THE BELT—THE ICE-MARSHES—PEKIUTLIK—HANS
THE BENEDICK.

PETERSEN and myself gave up the sledge to Morton, who, with *CHAPTER* Marsumah and Nessark, set out at once to negotiate at Etah, while *LV.* I took my place with the sledge-parties.

The ice, though not broken up by the storm, had been so much *Melting* affected by it, as well as by the advancing season, that I felt we *snow.* could not spare ourselves an hour's rest. The snow-fields before us to the south were already saturated with wet. Around the bergs the black water came directly to the surface, and the whole area was spotted with pools. We summoned all our energies on the 5th for this dangerous traverse ; but, although the boats were unladen and everything transported by sledge, it was impossible to prevent accidents. One of the sledges broke through, carrying six men into the water ; and the *Hope* narrowly escaped being lost. Her stern went down, and she was extricated with great difficulty.

The 6th saw the same disheartening work. The ice was almost *The ice* impassable. Both sick and well worked at the drag-ropes alike, *almost im-* and hardly a man but was constantly wet to the skin. Fearing *passable.* for the invalids at the sick station in case we should be cut off from them, I sent for Mr. Goodfellow at once, and gave orders for the rest to be in readiness for removal at a moment's notice.

The next day Morton returned from Etah. The natives had *Generosity* responded to the brotherly appeal of the nalegak ; and they came *of the* down from the settlement, bringing a full supply of meat and *natives.* blubber, and every sound dog that belonged to them. I had now once more a serviceable team. The comfort and security of such a possession to men in our critical position can hardly be realized. It was more than an addition of ten strong men to our party. I set off at once with Metek to glean from the brig her last remnant of slush (tallow), and to bring down the sick men from Anoatok.

As we travelled with our empty sledges along a sort of beaten

26

CHAPTER
LV.

Influence
of the
thaw on
the rocks.

track or road which led close under the cliffs, I realized very
forcibly the influence of the coming summer upon the rocks above
us. They were just released from the frost which had bound
them so long and closely, and were rolling down the slopes of the
debris with the din of a battle-field, and absolutely clogging the
ice-belt at the foot. Here and there, too, a large sheet of rocks
and earth would leave its bed at once, and, gathering mass as it
travelled, move downward like a cataract of ruins. The dogs
were terrified by the clamour, and could hardly be driven on till
it intermitted.

Just beyond Six-mile Ravine my sledge barely escaped de-

THE SLIDE.

struction from one of these land-slides. Happily Metek was
behind, and warned me of the danger just in time to cut loose the
traces and drag away the sledge.

But it is not in the season of thaws only that these wonderful
geological changes take place. Large rocks are projected in the
fall by the water freezing in the crevices, like the Mons Meg
cannon-balls. Our old boat, the *Forlorn Hope*, the veteran of
my Beechy Island attempt, was stove in by one of these while
drawn up under the cliffs of "Ten-mile Gorge."

The rocks which fell in this manner upon the ice-belt were
rapidly imbedded by the action of the sun's heat; and it happened
frequently, of course, that one more recently disengaged would
overlie another that had already sunk below the surface. This,
as the ice-belt subsided in the gradual thaw, had given many
examples of the rocking-stone. They were of all sizes, from tons
to pounds, often strangely dissimilar in material, though grouped
within a narrow area, their diversity depending on the varying
strata from which they came. There were some strange illustra-
tions among them of the transporting forces of the ice-raft, which
I should like to dwell on, if the character of my book and the
haste with which it is approaching its close did not forbid me.

Our visit to the brig was soon over : we had very few stores to
remove. I trod her solitary deck for the last time, and returned
with Metek to his sledge.

I had left the party on the floes with many apprehensions for
their safety, and the result proved they were not without cause.
While crossing a "tide-hole," one of the runners of the *Hope's*
sledge broke through, and, but for the strength and presence of
mind of Ohlsen, the boat would have gone under. He saw the
ice give way, and, by a violent exercise of strength, passed a
capstan-bar under the sledge, and thus bore the load till it was
hauled on to safer ice. He was a very powerful man, and might
have done this without injuring himself; but it would seem his
footing gave way under him, forcing him to make a still more
desperate effort to extricate himself. It cost him his life—he
died three days afterwards.

I was bringing down George Stephenson from the sick station,
and my sledge being heavily laden, I had just crossed, with some
anxiety, near the spot at which the accident occurred. A little
way beyond we met Mr. Ohlsen, seated upon a lump of ice, and
very pale. He pointed to the camp about three miles further on,
and told us, in a faint voice, that he had not detained the party ;

he "had a little cramp in the small of the back," but would soon
be better.

I put him at once in Stephenson's place, and drove him on to
the *Faith*. Here he was placed in the stern-sheets of the boat,
and well muffled up in our best buffalo-robes. During all that
night he was assiduously attended by Dr. Hayes ; but he sank
rapidly. His symptoms had from the first a certain obscure but
fatal resemblance to our winter's tetanus, which filled us with
forebodings.

On Saturday, June 6, after stowing away our disabled comrade
in the *Faith*, we again set all hands at the drag-ropes. The ice
ahead of us bore the same character as the day before—no better;
we were all perceptibly weaker, and much disheartened.

We had been tugging in harness about two hours, when a
breeze set in from the northward, the first that we had felt since
crossing Bedevilled Reach. We got out our long steering-oar as

a boom, and made sail upon the boats. The wind freshened
almost to a gale ; and, heading toward the depot on Littleton
Island, we ran gallantly before it.

It was a new sensation to our foot-sore men, this sailing over
solid ice. Levels which, under the slow labour of the drag-ropes,
would have delayed us for hours, were glided over without a halt.
We thought it dangerous work at first, but the speed of the sledges
made rotten ice nearly as available as sound. The men could see
plainly that they were approaching new landmarks, and leaving

old ones behind. Their spirits rose ; the sick mounted the
thwarts, the well clung to the gunwale ; and, for the first time for
nearly a year, broke out the sailor's chorus, "Storm along, my
hearty boys !"

We must have made a greater distance in this single day than
in the five that preceded it. We encamped at 5 P.M. near a small
berg, which gave us plenty of fresh water, after a progress of at
least eight miles.

As we were halting, I saw two Esquimaux on the ice toward
Life-Boat Cove ; and the well-known "Huk ! huuk !" a sort of
Masonic signal among them, soon brought them to us. They
turned out to be Sip-su and old Nessark. They were the bearers
of good news : my dogs were refreshed and nearly able to travel
again ; and, as they volunteered to do me service, I harnessed

up our united teams, and despatched Nessark to the hut to bring **CHAPTER**
down Mr. Wilson and George Whipple. **LV.**

We expected now to have our whole party together again ; and
the day would have been an active cheering one throughout, but
for the condition of poor Ohlsen, who was growing rapidly
worse.

From this time we went on for some days aided by our sails,
meeting with accidents occasionally—the giving way of a spar or
the falling of some of the party through the spongy ice—and occasionally, when the floe was altogether too infirm, labouring our
way with great difficulty upon the ice-belt. To mount this solid **Difficul-**
highway, or to descend from it, the axes were always in requisition. **ties.**
An inclined plane was to be cut—ten, fifteen, or even thirty feet
long, and along this the sledges were to be pushed and guided by
bars and levers with painful labour. These are light things, as I
refer to them here ; but in our circumstances, at the time I write
of, when the breaking of a stick of timber was an irreparable harm,
and the delay of a day involved the peril of life, they were grave
enough. Even on the floes the axe was often indispensable to **Cutting**
carve our path through the hummocks ; and many a weary and **through
the hum-**
anxious hour have I looked on and toiled while the sledges were **mocks.**
waiting for the way to open. Sometimes too, both on the land-
ice and on the belt, we encountered heavy snowdrifts, which were **Snow-**
to be shovelled away before we could get along ; and within an **drifts.**
hour afterward, or perhaps even at the bottom of the drift, one of
the sledge-runners would cut through to the water.

It was saddening to our poor fellows, when we were forced to
leave the ice-belt and push out into the open field, to look ahead
at the salt ice-marshes, as they called them, studded with black pools, **Ice-**
with only a white lump rising here and there through the lead- **marshes.**
coloured surface, like tussocks of grass or rushes struggling
through a swamp. The labour would have been too much for us,
weary and broken as we were, but for the occasional assistance we
derived from the Esquimaux. I remember once a sledge went so
far under, carrying with it several of the party, that the boat
floated loose. Just then seven of the natives came up to us— **Help from**
five sturdy men, and two almost as sturdy women—and, without **the Esqui-**
waiting to be called on, worked with us most efficiently for more **maux.**
than half a day, asking no reward.

CHAPTER LV.

Open water at Pekiutlik.

Still passing slowly on day after day, I am reluctant to borrow from my journal the details of anxiety and embarrassment with which it abounds throughout this period,—we came at last to the unmistakable neighbourhood of the open water. We were off Pekiutlik, the largest of the Littleton Island group, opposite "Kosoak," the Great River. Here Mr. Wilson and George Whipple rejoined us, under the faithful charge of old Nessark. They had broken through twice on the road, but without any serious inconvenience in consequence. It was with truly thankful hearts we united in our prayers that evening.

Hans missing.

One only was absent of all the party that remained on our rolls. Hans, the kind son and ardent young lover of Fiskernaes, my well-trusted friend, had been missing for nearly two months. I am loath to tell the story as I believe it, for it may not be the true one after all, and I would not intimate an unwarranted doubt of the constancy of boyish love. But I must explain, as far as I can at least, why he was not with us when we first looked at the open water. Just before my departure for my April hunt, Hans came to me with a long face, asking permission to visit Peteravik : " he had no boots, and wanted to lay in a stock of walrus hide for soles ; he did not need the dogs ; he would rather walk." It was a long march, but he was well practised in it, and I consented of course. Both Petersen and myself gave him commissions to execute, and he left us, intending to stop by the way at Etah.

Stories and surmises about Hans.

In our labours of the next month we missed Hans much. He had not yet returned, and the stories of him that came to us from Etah were the theme of much conversation and surmise among us. He had certainly called there as he promised, and given to Nessark's wife an order for a pair of boots, and he had then wended his way across the big headland to Peteravik, where Shang-hu and his pretty daughter had their home. This intimation was given with many an explanatory grin ; for Hans was a favourite with all, the fair especially, and, as a *match*, one of the greatest men in the country. It required all my recollections of his " old love" to make me suspend my judgment ; for the boots came, as if to confirm the scandal. I never failed in my efforts afterward to find his whereabouts, and went out of our way to interrogate this and that settlement ; for, independent of everything like duty, I was very fond of him. But the story was everywhere the same. Hans the faithful—yet, I fear, the faithless—was last seen upon a native sledge, driving south from Peteravik, with a maiden at his side, and professedly bound to a new principality at Uwarrow Suk-suk, high up Murchison's Sound. Alas for Hans, the married man !

CHAPTER LVI.

THE RED BOAT SINKING—THE LIFE-BOAT CACHE—THE OPEN WATER—
OHLSEN'S DEATH—HIS FUNERAL—BARENTZ, OUR PRECURSOR—ACCOMODAH
—THE PRESCRIPTION—CAPE WELCOME—THE RESOLVE.

CHAPTER
LVI.

Insecurity
of the ice.

THOUGH the condition of the ice assured us that we were drawing near the end of our sledge-journeys, it by no means diminished their difficulty or hazards. The part of the field near the open water is always abraded by the currents, while it remains apparently firm on the surface. In some places it was so transparent that we could even see the gurgling eddies below it; while in others it was worn into open holes that were already the resort of wild fowl. But in general it looked hard and plausible, though not more than a foot or even six inches in thickness.

This continued to be its character as long as we pursued the Littleton Island channel, and we were compelled, the whole way through, to sound ahead with the boat-hook or narwhal-horn. We learned this precaution from the Esquimaux, who always move in advance of their sledges when the ice is treacherous, and test its strength before bringing on their teams. Our first warning impressed us with the policy of observing it. We were making wide circuits with the whaleboats to avoid the tide-holes, when signals of distress from men scrambling on the ice announced to

The Red
Eric sinks.

us that the *Red Eric* had disappeared. This unfortunate little craft contained all the dearly-earned documents of the expedition. There was not a man who did not feel that the reputation of the party rested in a great degree upon their preservation. It had cost us many a pang to give up our collections of natural history, to which every one had contributed his quota of labour and interest ; but the destruction of the vouchers of the cruise—the log-books, the meteorological registers, the surveys, and the journals —seemed to strike them all as an irreparable disaster.

When I reached the boat everything was in confusion. Blake with a line passed round his waist, was standing up to his knees in sludge, groping for the document-box, and Mr. Bonsall, drip-

THE BROKEN FLOES.

ping wet, was endeavouring to haul the provision-bags to a place of safety. Happily the boat was our lightest one, and everything was saved. She was gradually lightened until she could bear a man, and her cargo was then passed out by a line and hauled upon the ice. In spite of the wet and the cold and our thoughts of poor Ohlsen, we greeted its safety with three cheers.

It was by great good fortune that no lives were lost. Stephenson was caught as he sank by one of the sledge-runners, and Morton, while in the very act of drifting under the ice, was seized by the hair of the head by Mr. Bonsall and saved.

We were now close upon Life-boat Cove, where nearly two years before we had made provision for just such a contingency as that which was now before us. Buried under the frozen soil, our stores had escaped even the keen scrutiny of our savage allies, and we now turned to them as essential to our relief. Mr. M'Gary was sent to the cache, with orders to bring everything except the salt beef. This had been so long a poison to us, that tainted as we were by scurvy, I was afraid to bring it among those who might be tempted to indulge in it.

On the 12th the boats and sledges came to a halt in the narrow passage between the islands opposite Cape Misery, the scene of our late snow storm. All our cargo had been gathered together at this spot, and the rocks were covered with our stores. Out of the fourteen hundred pounds not an ounce had been sacrificed, Everything was cased in its waterproof covering, and as dry and perfect as when it had left the brig.

The Littleton Island of Captain Inglefield is one of a group of four skiers which flank the north-east headland of Hartstene Bay. They are of the bottom series, coarse gneisses and mica schists. When here before, at this time of the year, they were surrounded by water, and the eider ducks were breeding on their slopes. Now, as if to illustrate the difference of the seasons here, as well as the influence which they exert upon the habits of the migratory wild fowl, they were thoroughly cased in ice, and not a nest was to be seen.

I ascended some eight hundred feet to the summit of Pekiutlik, and, looking out, beheld the open water, so long the goal of our struggles, spread out before me. It extended seemingly to Cape Alexander, and was nearer to the westward than the south of my position by some five or six miles. But the ice in the latter direction led into the curve of the bay, and was thus protected from the wind and swell. My jaded comrades pleaded anxiously in favour of the direct line to the water ; but I knew that this ice would give us both safer and better travel. I determined to adopt the inshore route. Our position at Pekiutlik, as we determined carefully by the mean of several observations, is in latitude 78° 22′ 1″ and longitude 74° 10′. We connected it with Cape Alexander, and other determined stations to the north and west.

The channel between the islands was much choked with up-reared ice ; but our dogs had now come back to us so much refreshed that I was able to call their services again into requisi-tion. We carried one entire load to the main which forms the north-east headland of Hartstene Bay, and, the Esquimaux assist-ing us, deposited it safely on the inner side.

I was with the advance boat, trying to force a way through the channel, when the report came to me from Dr. Hayes that Ohlsen was no more. He had shown, a short half hour before, some signs of revival, and Petersen had gone out to kill a few birds, in the hope of possibly sustaining him by a concentrated soup. But it was in vain : the poor fellow flushed up only to die a few minutes after.

We had no time to mourn the loss of our comrade, a tried and courageous man, who met his death in the gallant discharge of duty. It cast a gloom over the whole party ; but the exigencies of the moment were upon us, and we knew not whose turn would come next, or how soon we might all of us follow him together.

Conceal-
ment of
the death
from the
Esqui-
maux.

I had carefully concealed Mr. Ohlsen's sickness from the Esqui-maux, with everything else that could intimate our weakness ; for, without reflecting at all upon their fidelity, I felt that with them, as with the rest of the world, pity was a less active provocative to good deeds than the deference which is exacted by power. I had therefore represented our abandonment of the brig as merely the absence of a general hunting party to the Far South, and I was willing now to keep up the impression. I leave to moralists the discussion of the question how far I erred ; but I now sent them to their village under pretext of obtaining birds, and lent them our dogs to insure their departure.

The body of Mr. Ohlsen was sewed up, while they were gone,

in his own blankets, and carried in procession to the head of a
little gorge on the east face of Pekiutlik, where by hard labour we
consigned his remains to a sort of trench, and covered them with
rocks to protect them from the fox and bear. Without the knowledge of my comrades, I encroached on our little store of sheet-
lead, which we were husbanding to mend our leaky boats with,
and, cutting on a small tablet his name and age—

CHRISTIAN OHLSEN,
AGED 36 YEARS,

laid it on his manly breast. The cape that looks down on him
bears his name.

As we walked back to our camp upon the ice, the death of
Ohlsen brought to my mind the strange parallel of our story with
that of old William Barentz—a parallel which might verify that
sad truth of history that human adventure repeats itself.

Two hundred and fifty-nine years ago, William Barentz, chief
pilot of the States General of Holland—the United States of that
day—had wintered on the coast of Novaia Zemlia, exploring the
northernmost region of the Old Continent, as we had that of the
New. His men, seventeen in number, broke down during the
trials of the winter, and three died, just as of our eighteen three
had gone. He abandoned his vessel as we had abandoned ours,
took to his boats, and escaped along the Lapland coast to lands of
Norwegian civilization. We had embarked with sledge and boat
to attempt the same thing. We had the longer journey and the
more difficult before us. He lost, as we had done, a cherished
comrade by the wayside ; and, as I thought of this closing resemblance in our fortunes also, my mind left but one part of the
parallel incomplete—*Barentz himself perished.*

We gave two quiet hours to the memory of our dead brother,
and then resumed our toilsome march. We kept up nearly the
same routine as before ; but, as we neared the settlements, the
Esquimaux came in flocks to our assistance. They volunteered to
aid us at the drag ropes. They carried our sick upon hand-sledges.
They relieved us of all care for our supplies of daily food. The
quantity of little auks that they brought us was enormous. They
fed us and our dogs at the rate of eight thousand birds a week,

CHAPTER
LVI. all of them caught in their little hand-nets. All anxiety left us
for the time. The men broke out in their old forecastle songs;

CARRYING THE SICK.

the sledges began to move merrily ahead, and laugh and jest
drove out the old moody silence.

A medical
consulta-
tion. During one of our evening halts, when the congregation of
natives had scattered away to their camp fires, Metek and Nualik
his wife came to me privately on a matter of grave consultation.
They brought with them a fat, curious-looking boy. "Accomodah," said they, "is our youngest son. His sleep at night is bad,
and his *nangah*"—pointing to that protuberance which is supposed to represent aldermanic dignity—"is always round and
hard. He eats ossuk (blubber) and no meat, and bleeds at the
nose. Besides, he does not grow." They wanted me, in my
capacity of angekok soak, to charm or cure him.

The pre-
scription.. I told them, with all the freedom from mystery that distin-
guishes the regulated practitioner from the empiric, what must be
my mode of treatment : that I must dip my hand into the salt
water where the ice cut against the sea, and lay it on the offending
nangah ; and that if they would bring to me their rotund little
companion within three days, at that broad and deep Bethesda, I
would signalize my consideration of the kindness of the tribe by a
trial of my powers.

They went away very thankful, taking a preliminary prescrip-

tion of a lump of brown soap, a silk shirt, and a *taboo* of all further eating of ossuk ; and I had no doubt that their anxiety to
have the boy duly powwowed, would urge forward our sledges and
bring us early to the healing waters. We longed for them at
least as much as Metek, and needed them more than Accomodah.

My little note-book closes for the week with this gratefully ex-
pounded record :—

June 16, Saturday.—Our boats are at the open water. We see
its deep indigo horizon, and hear its roar against the icy beach.
Its scent is in our nostrils and our hearts.

"Our camp is but three-quarters of a mile from the sea ; it is
at the northern curve of the North Baffin polynia. We must
reach it at the southern sweep of Etah Bay, about three miles
from Cape Alexander. A dark headland defines the spot. It is
more marked than the southern entrance of Smith's Straits. How
magnificently the surf beats against its sides ! There are ridges
of squeezed ice between us and it, and a broad zone of floating
sludge is swelling and rolling sluggishly along its margin—formidable barriers to boats and sledges. But we have mastered worse
obstacles, and by God's help we will master these."

CHAPTER LVII.

Preparing the boats.

WE had our boats to prepare now for a long and adventurous navigation. They were so small and heavily laden as hardly to justify much confidence in their buoyancy; but, besides this, they were split with frost and warped by sunshine, and fairly open at the seams. They were to be calked, and swelled, and launched, and stowed, before we could venture to embark in them. A rainy south-wester, too, which had met us on our arrival, was now spreading with its black nimbus over the bay, and it looked as if we were to be storm-stayed on the precarious ice-beach. It was a time of anxiety, but to me personally of comparative rest. I resumed my journal :—

Assemblage of Esquimaux to bid good-bye.

July 18, *Monday.*—The Esquimaux are camped by our side,—the whole settlement of Etah congregated around the 'big caldron' of Cape Alexander, to bid us good-bye. There are Metek, and Nualik his wife, our old acquaintance Mrs Eider-duck, and their five children, commencing with Myouk, my body-guard, and ending with the ventricose little Accomodah. There is Nessark and Anak his wife; and Tellerk the 'Right Arm,' and Amaunalik his wife; and Sip-su, and Marsumah and Aningnah—and who not? I can name them every one, and they know us as well. We have found brothers in a strange land.

Keepsakes given.

"Each one has a knife, or a file, or a saw, or some such treasured keepsake; and the children have a lump of soap, the greatest of all great medicines. The merry little urchins break in upon me even now as I am writing—'Kuyanake, kuyanake, Nalegak-soak!' 'Thank you, thank you, big chief!' while Myouk is crowding fresh presents of raw birds on me as if I could eat for ever, and poor Aningnah is crying beside the tent-curtain, wiping her eyes on a bird skin!

"My heart warms to these poor, dirty, miserable, yet happy beings, so long our neighbours, and of late so staunchly our friends

Theirs is no affectation of regret. There are twenty-two of them around me, all busy in good offices to the Docto Kayens ; and there are only two women and the old blind patriarch Kresuk, 'Drift-wood,' left behind at the settlement.

"But see ! more of them are coming up—boys ten years old pushing forward babies on their sledges. The whole nation is gipsying with us upon the icy meadows.

"We cook for them in our big camp kettle ; they sleep in the *Red Eric ;* a berg close at hand supplies them with water ; and thus, rich in all that they value,—sleep, and food, and drink, and companionship,—with their treasured short-lived summer sun above them, the *beau ideal* and sum of Esquimaux blessings, they seem supremely happy.

"Poor creatures ! It is only six months ago that starvation was among them : many of the faces around me have not yet lost the lines of wasting suspense. The walrus season is again of doubtful productiveness, and they are cut off from their brethren to the south, at Netelik and Appah, until winter rebuilds the avenue of ice. With all this, no thoughts of the future cross them. Babies squall, and women chatter, and the men weave their long yarns with peals of rattling hearty laughter between.

"Ever since we reached Pekiutlik, these friends of ours have considered us their guests. They have given us hand-sledges for our baggage, and taken turn about in watches to carry us 'and it to the water's edge. But for them our dreary journey would have been prolonged at least a fortnight, and we are so late even now that hours may measure our lives. Metek, Myouk, Nessark, Marsumah, Erkee, and the half-grown boys, have been our chief labourers ; but women, children, and dogs are all bearing their part.

"Whatever may have been the faults of these Esquimaux heretofore, stealing was the only grave one. Treachery they may have conceived ; and I have reason to believe that, under superstitious fears of an evil influence from our presence, they would at one time have been glad to destroy us. But the day of all this has passed away. When trouble came to us and to them, and we bent ourselves to their habits,—when we looked to them to procure us fresh meat, and they found at our poor Oomiak-soak shelter and protection during their wild bear-hunts,—then we were so

CHAPTER LVII.

True friendship and gratitude of the natives.

blended in our interests as well as modes of life, that every trace of enmity wore away. God knows that since they professed friendship—albeit the imaginary powers of the angekok-soak and the marvellous six-shooter which attested them may have had their influence—never have friends been more true. Although, since Ohlsen's death, numberless articles of inestimable value to them have been scattered upon the ice unwatched, they have not stolen a nail. It was only yesterday that Metek, upon my alluding to the manner in which property of all sorts was exposed without pilfering, explained through Petersen, in these two short sentences, the argument of their morality :—

"'You have done us good. We are not hungry; we will not take (steal).——You have done us good ; we want to help you ; we are friends.'"

Old Kresuk.

I made my last visit to Etah while we were waiting the issue of the storm. I saw old Kresuk (Drift-wood) the blind man, and listened to his long good-bye talk. I had passed with the Esquimaux as an angekok, in virtue of some simple exploits of natural magic; and it was one of the regular old times entertainments of our visitors at the brig, to see my hand terrible with blazing ether, while it lifted nails with the magnet. I tried now to communicate a portion of my wonder working talent. I made a lens of ice before them, and "drew down the sun," so as to light the moss under their kolupsut. I did not quite understand old Kresuk, and I was not quite sure he understood himself. But I trusted to the others to explain to him what I had done, and burned the back of his hand for a testimony in the most friendly manner. After all which, with a reputation for wisdom which I dare say will live in their short annals, I wended my way to the brig again.

Natural magic.

Last news of Hans.

We renewed our queries about Hans, but could get no further news of him. The last story is, that the poor boy and his better half were seen leaving Peteravik, "the halting-place," in company with Shang-hu and one of his big sons. Lover as he was, and nalegak by the all-hail hereafter, joy go with him, for he was a right good fellow.

Parting gifts.

We had quite a scene, distributing our last presents. My amputating knives, the great gift of all, went to Metek and Nessark ; but every one had something as his special prize. Our dogs went to the community at large, as tenants in common, except Toodla-

BIDDING FAREWELL.

From a Sketch by our own.

mik and Whitey, our representative dogs through very many trials, I could not part with them, the leaders of my team ; I have them still.

But Nualik, the poor mother, had something still to remind me of. She had accompanied us throughout the transit of Etah Bay, with her boy Accomodah, waiting anxiously for the moment when the first salt water would enable me to fulfil my promised exorcisation of the demon in his stomach. There was no alternative now but to fulfil the pledge with faithful ceremony. The boy was taken to the water's edge, and his exorbitant little nangah faithfully embrocated in the presence of both his parents. I could not speak my thanks in their language, but I contributed my scanty stock of silk shirts to the poor little sufferer,—for such he was,— and I blessed them for their humanity to us with a fervour of heart which from a better man might peradventure have carried a blessing along with it.

And now it only remained for us to make our farewell to these desolate and confiding people. I gathered them round me on the ice-beach, and talked to them as brothers for whose kindness I had still a return to make. I told them what I knew of the tribes from which they were separated by the glacier and the sea, of the resources that abounded in those less ungenial regions not very far off to the south, the greater duration of daylight, the less intensity of the cold, the facilities of the hunt, the frequent driftwood, the kayak, and the fishing-net. I tried to explain to them how, under bold and cautious guidance, they might reach there in a few seasons of patient march. I gave them drawings of the coast, with its headlands and hunting-grounds, as far as Cape Shackleton, and its best camping-stations from Red Head to the Danish settlements.

They listened with breathless interest, closing their circle round me ; and, as Petersen described the big ussuk, the white whale, the bear, and the long open water hunts with the kayak and the rifle, they looked at each other with a significance not to be misunderstood. ·They would anxiously have had me promise that I would some day return and carry a load of them down to the settlements ; and I shall not wonder if—guided perhaps by Hans— they hereafter attempt the journey without other aid.

This was our parting. A letter which I addressed, at the

CHAPTER LVII. moment of reaching the settlements, to the Lutheran Missions, the tutelar society of the Esquimaux of Greenland, will attest the sincerity of my professions and my willingness to assist in giving them effect.

It was in the soft subdued light of a Sunday evening, June 17, that, after hauling our boats with much hard labour through the hummocks, we stood beside the open sea-way. Before midnight A launch at midnight. we had launched the *Red Eric*, and given three cheers for Henry Grinnell and " homeward bound," unfurling all our flags.

But we were not yet to embark ; for the gale which had been long brooding now began to dash a heavy *wind-lipper* against the Obliged to retreat inward by a gale. floe, and obliged us to retreat before it, hauling our boats back with each fresh breakage of the ice. It rose more fiercely, and we were obliged to give way before it still more. Our goods, which had been stacked upon the ice, had to be carried further inward. We worked our way back thus, step by step, before the breaking ice, for about two hundred yards. At last it became apparent that the men must sleep and rest, or sink ; and, giving up for the present all thoughts of embarking, I hauled the boats at once nearly a mile from the water's edge, where a large iceberg was frozen tight in the floes.

But here we were still pursued. All the next night it blew fearfully, and at last our berg crashed away through the broken ice, and our asylum was destroyed. Again we fell to hauling back the boats ; until, fearing that the continuance of the gale might induce a ground-swell, which would have been fatal to us, I came to a Halt near an iceberg. halt near the slope of a low iceberg, on which I felt confident that we could haul up in case of the entire disruption of the floes. The entire area was already intersected with long cracks, and the surface began to show a perceptible undulation beneath our feet.

It was well for us I had not gratified the men by taking the outside track ; we should certainly have been rafted off into the storm, and without an apparent possibility of escape.

I climbed to the summit of the berg ; but it was impossible to penetrate the obscurity of mist, and spray, and cloud further than a thousand yards. The sea tore the ice up almost to the very base of the berg, and all around it looked like one vast tumultuous caldron, the ice-tables crashing together in every possible position with deafening clamour.

CHAPTER LVIII.

SUTHERLAND ISLAND—HAKLUYT ISLAND—NORTHUMBERLAND ISLAND—
FITZ-CLARENCE ROCK—DALRYMPLE ROCK—GIVING OUT—BREAK UP OF
THE FLOE—BROKEN DOWN—WEARY MAN'S REST—THE FOURTH—SHORT
COMMONS.

THE gale died away to a calm, and the water became as tranquil as CHAPTER LVIII. if the gale had never been. All hands were called to prepare for embarking. The boats were stowed, and the cargo divided be- A calm. tween them equally; the sledges unlashed and slung outside the gunwales; and on Tuesday the 19th, at 4 P.M., with the bay as smooth as a garden-lake, I put off in the *Faith*. She was followed The boats by the *Red Eric* on our quarter, and the *Hope* astern. In the put to sea *Faith* I had with me Mr. M'Gary, and Petersen, Hickey, Stephenson, and Whipple. Mr. Brooks was in the *Hope*, with Hayes, Sontag, Morton, Goodfellow, and Blake. Bonsall, Riley, and Godfrey made the crew of the *Eric*.

The wind freshened as we doubled the westernmost point of Cape Cape Alexander, and, as we looked out on the expanse of the sound, we Alexander. saw the kittiwakes and the ivory-gulls and jagers dipping their wings in the curling waves. They seemed the very same birds we had left two years before screaming and catching fish in the beautiful water. We tried to make our first rest at Sutherland Island; Sutherbut we found it so barricaded by the precipitous ice-belt that it land Island. was impossible to land. I clambered myself from the boat's mast upon the platform and filled our kettles with snow, and then, after cooking our supper in the boats, we stood away for Hakluyt. It was an ugly crossing: we had a short chopping sea from the southeast; and, after a while, the *Red Boat* swamped. Riley and God- The *Red* frey managed to struggle to the *Faith*, and Bonsall to the *Hope*; Boat swamped but it was impossible to remove the cargo of our little comrade; it was as much as we could do to keep her afloat and let her tow behind us. Just at this time, too, the *Hope* made a signal of distress; and Brooks hailed us to say that she was making water faster than he could free her.

The wind was hauling round to the westward, and we could not take the sea abeam. But, as I made a rapid survey of the area around me, studded already with floating shreds of floe-ice, I saw ahead the low, grey blink of the pack. I remembered well the experience of our Beechy Island trip, and knew that the margin of these large fields is almost always broken by inlets of open water which gave much the same sort of protection as the creeks and rivers of an adverse coast. We were fortunate in finding one of these, and fastening ourselves to an old floe, alongside of which our weary men turned in to sleep without hauling up the boats.

When Petersen and myself returned from an unsuccessful hunt upon the ice, we found them still asleep, in spite of a cold and drizzling rain that might have stimulated wakefulness. I did not disturb them till eight o'clock. We then retreated from our break-water of refuge, generally pulling along by the boat-hooks, but sometimes dragging our boats over the ice; and at last, bending to our oars as the water opened, reached the shore of Hakluyt Island.

It was hardly less repulsive than the ice-cliffs of the day before; but a spit to the southward gave us the opportunity of hauling up as the tide rose, and we finally succeeded in transferring ourselves and all our fortunes to the land-ice, and thence to the rocks beyond. It snowed hard in the night, and the work of calking went on badly, though we expended on it a prodigal share of our remaining white lead. We rigged up, however, a tent for the sick, and re-inforced our bread-dust and tallow supper by a few birds. We had shot a seal in the course of the day, but we lost him by his sinking.

In the morning of the 22d we pushed forward through the snow-storm for Northumberland Island, and succeeded in reaching it a little to the eastward of my former landing-place. Myriads of auks greeted us, and we returned their greeting by the appropriate invitation to our table. A fox also saluted us with an admirable imitation of the "Huk-huk-huk," which among the Esquimaux is the never-unheeded call of distress ; but the rascal, after seducing us a mile and a half out of-our way, escaped our guns.

Our boats entered a little patch of open water that conducted us to the beach, directly below one of the hanging glaciers. The interest with which these impressed me when I was turning back

from my Beechy Island effort was justified very fully by what I
saw of them now.   It seemed as if a caldron of ice inside the
coast-ridge was boiling over, and throwing its crust in huge fragments from the overhanging lip into the sea below.   The glacier
must have been eleven hundred feet high ; but even at its summit
we could see lines of viscous movement.

We crossed Murchison Channel on the 23d, and encamped for
the night on the land-floe at the base of Cape Parry; a hard day's
travel, partly by tracking over ice, partly through tortuous and
zigzag leads.   The next day brought us to the neighbourhood of
Fitz-Clarence Rock, one of the most interesting monuments that
rear themselves along this dreary coast : in a region more familiar
to men, it would be a landmark to the navigator.   It rises from a
field of ice like an Egyptian pyramid surmounted by an obelisk.

I had been anxious to communicate with the Esquimaux of
Netelik, in the hope of gaining some further intelligence of Hans.
Our friends of Etah had given me, in their own style, a complete
itinerary of this region, and we had no difficulty in instructing Unsuccessful at-
tempts to
reach the
Esqui-
maux
settle-
ment.
Godfrey how to trace his way across the neck of land which stood
between us and the settlement.   He made the attempt, but found
the snow-drift impassable; and Petersen, whom I sent on the same
errand to Tessiusak, returned equally unsuccessful.

The next day gave us admirable progress.   The ice opened in
leads before us, somewhat tortuous, but, on the whole, favouring,
and for sixteen hours I never left the helm.   We were all of us
exhausted when the day's work came to a close.   Our allowance
had been small from the first ; but the delays we seemed fated to
encounter had made me reduce them to what I then thought the
minimum quantity, six ounces of bread-dust and a lump of tallow
the size of a walnut : a paste or broth, made of these before setting out in the morning and distributed occasionally through the
day in scanty rations, was our only fare.   We were all of us glad
when, running the boats under the lee of a berg, we were able
to fill our kettles with snow and boil up for our great restorative
tea.   I may remark that, under the circumstances of most privation, I found no comforter so welcome to the party as this.   We
drank immoderately of it, and always with advantage.

While the men slept after their weary labour, M'Gary and myself climbed the berg for a view ahead.   It was a saddening one.

CHAPTER LVIII. We had lost sight of Cary Island; but shoreward, up Wosten-holm Channel, the ice seemed as if it had not yet begun to yield to the influences of summer. Everything showed how intense the last winter had been. We were close upon the 1st of July, and had a right to look for the North Water of the whalers where we now had solid ice or close pack, both of them almost equally un-favourable to our progress. Far off in the distance—how far I Dalrymple could not measure—rose the Dalrymple Rock, projecting from the Rock. lofty precipice of the island ahead; but between us and it the land-ice spread itself from the base of Saunders's Island unbroken to the Far South.

The next day's progress was of course slow and wearisome, pushing through alternate ice and water for the land-belt. We fastened at last to the great floe near the shore, making our har-bour in a crack which opened with the changes of tide.

Effects of insuffi-cient food. The imperfect diet of the party was showing itself more and more in the decline of their muscular power. They seemed scarcely aware of it themselves, and referred the difficulty they found in dragging and pushing to something uncommon about the ice or sludge rather than to their own weakness. But, as we en-deavoured to renew our labours through the morning fog, belted in on all sides by ice-fields so distorted and rugged as to defy our efforts to cross them, the truth seemed to burst upon every one. We had lost the feeling of hunger, and were almost satisfied with our pasty broth and the large draughts of tea which accompanied it. I was anxious to send our small boat, the *Eric*, across to the lumme-hill of Appah, where I knew from the Esquimaux we should find plenty of birds; but the strength of the party was in-sufficient to drag her.

Obliged to wait. We were sorely disheartened, and could only wait for the fog to rise, in the hope of some smoother platform than that which was about us, or some lead that might save us the painful labour of tracking. I had climbed the iceberg; and there was nothing in view except Dalrymple Rock, with its red brassy face towering in the unknown distance. But I hardly got back to my boat, before a gale struck us from the north-west, and a floe, taking upon a tongue of ice about a mile to the north of us, began to swing upon it like a pivot and close slowly in upon our narrow resting-place.

At first our own floe also was driven before the wind; but in a

little while it encountered the stationary ice at the foot of the very
rock itself. On the instant the wildest imaginable ruin rose
around us. The men sprang mechanically each one to his station,
bearing back the boats and stores ; but I gave up for the moment
all hope of our escape. It was not a nip, such as is familiar to
Arctic navigators ; but the whole platform, where we stood and
for hundreds of yards on every side of us, crumbled, and crushed,
and piled, and tossed itself madly under the pressure. I do not
believe that of our little body of men, all of them disciplined in
trials, able to measure danger while combating it,—I do not believe there is one who this day can explain how or why—hardly
when, in fact—we found ourselves afloat. We only know that in
the midst of a clamour utterly indescribable, through which the
braying of a thousand trumpets could no more have been heard
than the voice of a man, we were shaken, and raised, and whirled,
and let down again in a swelling waste of broken hummocks, and,
as the men grasped their boat-hooks in the stillness that followed,
the boats eddied away in a tumultuous skreed of ice, and snow,
and water.

We were borne along in this manner as long as the unbroken
remnant of the in-shore floe continued revolving,—utterly powerless, and catching a glimpse every now and then of the brazen
headland that looked down on us through the snowy sky. At
last the floe brought up against the rocks, the looser fragments
that hung round it began to separate, and we were able by oars
and boat-hooks to force our battered little flotilla clear of them.
To our joyful surprise, we soon found ourselves in a stretch of the
land-water wide enough to give us rowing-room, and with the assured promise of land close ahead.

As we neared it, we saw the same forbidding wall of belt-ice as
at Sutherland and Hakluyt. We pulled along its margin, seeking
in vain either an opening of access or a nook of shelter. The
gale rose, and the ice began to drive again ; but there was nothing
to be done but get a grapnel out to the belt. and hold on for the
rising tide. · The *Hope* stove her bottom and lost part of her
weather-boarding, and all the boats were badly chafed. It was an
awful storm ; and it was not without constant exertion that we
kept afloat, baling out the scud that broke over us, and warding
off the ice with boat-hooks.

At three o'clock the tide was high enough for us to scale the ice-cliff. One by one we pulled up the boats upon a narrow shelf, the whole sixteen of us uniting at each pull. We were too much worn down to unload; but a deep and narrow gorge opened in the cliffs almost at the spot where we clambered up; and, as we pushed the boats into it on an even keel, the rocks seemed to close above our heads, until an abrupt turn in the course of the ravine placed a protecting cliff between us and the gale. We were completely encaved.

Just as we had brought in the last boat, the *Red Eric*, and were shoring her up with blocks of ice, a long-unused, but familiar and unmistakable sound startled and gladdened every ear, and a flock of eiders flecking the sky for a moment passed swiftly in front of us. We knew that we must be at their breeding-grounds; and as we turned in wet and hungry to our long-coveted sleep, it was only to dream of eggs and abundance.

We remained almost three days in our crystal retreat, gathering eggs at the rate of twelve hundred a day. Outside, the storm raged without intermission, and our egg-hunters found it difficult to keep their feet; but a merrier set of gourmands than were gathered within never surfeited in genial diet.

On the 3d of July the wind began to moderate, though the snow still fell heavily; and the next morning, after a patriotic egg-nog, the liquor borrowed grudgingly from our alcohol-flask, and diluted till it was worthy of temperance praise,—we lowered
our boats, and bade a grateful farewell to "Weary Man's Rest." We rowed to the south-east end of Wostenholme Island; but the tide left us there, and we moved to the ice-foot.

For some days after this we kept moving slowly to the south, along the lanes that opened between the belt-ice and the floe. The weather continued dull and unfavourable for observations of any sort, and we were off a large glacier before we were aware
that further progress near the shore was impracticable. Great chains of bergs presented themselves as barriers in our way, the spaces between choked by barricades of hummocks. It was hopeless to bore. We tried for sixteen hours together without finding a possibility of egress. The whole sea was rugged and broken in the extreme.

I climbed one of the bergs to the height of about two hundred

feet, and, looking well to the west, was satisfied that a lead which CHAPTER LVIII. I saw there could be followed in the direction of Conical Rocks, and beyond toward Cape Dudley Digges. But, on conferring with The boats injured by the storm. Brooks and M'Gary, I was startled to find how much the boats had suffered in the rude encounters of the last few days. The *Hope* was in fact altogether unseaworthy : the ice had strained her bottom-timbers, and it required nearly all our wood to repair her ; bit by bit we had already cut up and burned the runners and cross-bars of two sledges ; the third we had to reserve as essential to our ice-crossings.

In the meantime, the birds, which had been so abundant when we left Dalrymple's Island, and which we had counted on for a continuous store, seemed to have been driven off by the storm. We were again reduced to short daily rations of bread-dust, and I Short rations again. was aware that the change of diet could not fail to tell upon the strength and energies of the party. I determined to keep in-shore, in spite of the barricades of ice, in the hope of renewing, to some extent at least, our supplies of game. We were fifty-two hours in forcing this rugged passage : a most painful labour, which but for the disciplined endurance of the men might well have been deemed impracticable.

CHAPTER LIX.

A LOOK-OUT—PROVIDENCE HALT—THE GLACIER—PROVIDENCE DIET.

CHAPTER LIX.

Another glacier in sight.

ONCE through the barrier, the leads began to open again, and on the 11th we found ourselves approaching Cape Dudley Digges, with a light breeze from the north-west. It looked for some hours as if our troubles were over, when a glacier came in sight not laid down on the charts, whose tongue of floe extended still further out to sea than the one we had just passed with so much labour. Our first resolve was to double it at all hazards, for our crews were too much weakened to justify another tracking through the hummocks, and the soft snow which covered the land-floes was an obstacle quite insuperable. Nevertheless, we forced our way into a lead of sludge, mingled with the comminuted ice of the glacier; but the only result was a lesson of gratitude for our escape from it. Our frail and weather-worn boats were quite unequal to the duty.

A look-out from an ice-berg

I again climbed the nearest berg,—for these ice-mountains were to us like the look-out hills of men at home,—and surveyed the ice to the south far on toward Cape York. My eyes never looked on a spectacle more painful. We were in advance of the season: the floes had not broken up. There was no "western water." Here, in a *cul-de-sac*, between two barriers, both impassable to men in our condition, with stores miserably inadequate and strength broken down, we were to wait till the tardy summer should open to us a way.

An inhospitable shore.

I headed for the cliffs. Desolate and frowning as they were, it was better to reach them and halt upon the inhospitable shore than await the fruitless ventures of the sea. A narrow lead, a mere fissure at the edge of the land-ice, ended opposite a low platform; we had traced its whole extent, and it landed us close under the shadow of the precipitous shore.

My sketch, intended to represent this wild locality, gives a very imperfect idea of the scene.

Where the cape lies directly open to the swell of the north-west winds, at the base of a lofty precipice there was left still clinging

to the rock a fragment of the winter ice-belt not more than five CHAPTER
feet wide.   The tides rose over it and the waves washed against it LIX.
continually, but it gave a perfectly safe perch to our little boats. Resting
Above, cliff seemed to pile over cliff, until in the high distance the cliffs.
rocks looked like the overlapping scales of ancient armour.   They
were at least eleven hundred feet high, their summits generally lost
in fog and mist ; and all the way up we seemed to see the birds
whose home is among their clefts.   The nests were thickest on the
shelves some fifty yards above the water ; but both lumme and
tridactyl gulls filled the entire air with glimmering specks, cawing
and screeching with an incessant clamour.

PROVIDENCE HALT.

To soften the scene, a natural bridge opened on our right hand
into a little valley cove, green with mosses, and beyond and above
it, cold and white the glacier.

This glacier was about seven miles across at its " debouche ;"
it sloped gradually upward for some five miles back, and then,
following the irregularities of its rocky sub-structure, suddenly became a steep crevassed hill, ascending in abrupt terraces. Then
came two intervals of less rugged ice, from which the glacier passed
into the great *mer de glace.*

On ascending a high craggy hill to the northward, I had a sub-
lime prospect of this great frozen ocean, which seems to form the
continental axis of Greenland,—a vast undulating plain of purple-
tinted ice, studded with islands, and absolutely gemming the horizon with the varied glitter of sun-tipped crystal.

The discharge of water from the lower surface of the glacier exceeded that of any of the northern glaciers except that of Humboldt and the one near Etah. One torrent on the side nearest me
overran the ice-foot from two to five feet in depth, and spread itself upon the floes for several hundred yards ; and another, finding
its outlet near the summit of the glacier, broke over the rocks, and
poured in cataracts upon the beach below.

The ranunculus, saxifrages, chickweeds, abundant mosses, and
Arctic grasses, flourished near the level of the first talus of the
glacier : the stone crops I found some two hundred feet higher.
The thermometer was at 90° in the sun ; in the shade at 38°.

I have tried to describe the natural features of the scene, but I
have omitted that which was its most valued characteristic. It
abounded in life. The lumme, nearly as large as canvas-backs,
and, as we thought, altogether sweeter and more juicy ; their eggs,
well known as delicacies on the Labrador coast ; the cochlearia,
growing superbly on the guano-coated surface ;—all of them in
endless abundance :—imagine such a combination of charms for
scurvy-broken, hunger-stricken men.

I could not allow the fuel for a fire ; our slush and tallow was
reduced to very little more than a hundred pounds. The more
curious in that art which has dignified the memory of Lucullus,
and may do as much for Soyer, made experiments upon the organic
matters within their reach,—the dried nests of the kittiwake, the
sods of poa, the heavy mosses, and the fatty skins of the birds
around us. But they would none of them burn ; and the most
fastidious consoled himself at last with the doubt whether heat,
though concentrating flavour, might not impair some other excel-

lence. We limited ourselves to an average of a bird a-piece per meal,—of choice, not of necessity,—and renewed the zest of the table with the best salad in the world—raw eggs and cochlearia.

It was one glorious holiday, our week at Providence Halt, so full of refreshment and all-happy thoughts, that I never allowed myself to detract from it by acknowledging that it was other than premeditated. There were only two of the party who had looked out with me on the bleak ice-field ahead, and them I had pledged to silence.

CHAPTER LX.

THE CRIMSON CLIFFS—THE ESQUIMAUX EDEN—DEPRESSION OF THE COAST
—INVENTORY—IMALIK—LOSING OUR WAY—AT THE RUE-RADDIES—THE
OPEN SEA—EFFECTS OF HUNGER—RESCUE OF THE FAITH.

IT was the 18th of July before the aspects of the ice about us gave
me the hope of progress. We had prepared ourselves for the new
encounter with the sea and its trials by laying in a store of lumme;
two hundred and fifty of which had been duly skinned, spread
open, and dried on the rocks, as the *entremets* of our bread-dust
and tallow.

My journal tells of disaster in its record of our setting out. In
launching the *Hope* from the frail and perishing ice-wharf on which
we found our first refuge from the gale, she was precipitated into
the sludge below, carrying away rail and bulwark, losing overboard
our best shot-gun, Bonsall's favourite, and, worst of all, that universal favourite, our kettle,—soup-kettle, paste-kettle, tea-kettle,
water-kettle, in one. I may mention before I pass, that the kettle
found its substitute and successor in the remains of a tin can
which a good aunt of mine had filled with ginger-nuts two years
before, and which had long survived the condiments that once
gave it dignity. "Such are the uses of adversity."

Our descent to the coast followed the margin of the fast ice.
After passing the Crimson Cliffs of Sir John Ross, it wore almost
the dress of a holiday excursion,—a rude one perhaps, yet truly
one in feeling. Our course, except where a protruding glacier
interfered with it, was nearly parallel to the shore. The birds
along it were rejoicing in the young summer, and when we halted
it was upon some green-clothed cape near a stream of water from
the ice-fields above. Our sportsmen would clamber up the cliffs
and come back laden with little auks; great generous fires of turf,
that cost nothing but the toil of gathering, blazed merrily; and
our happy oarsmen, after a long day's work, made easy by the
promise ahead, would stretch themselves in the sunshine and
dream happily away till called to the morning wash and prayers.

We enjoyed it the more, for we all of us knew that it could not
last.

PASSING THE CRIMSON CLIFFS.

This coast must have been a favourite region at one time with The Esqui-
the natives,—a sort of Esquimaux Eden. We seldom encamped maux Eden.
without finding the ruins of their habitations, for the most part
overgrown with lichens, and exhibiting every mark of antiquity.
One of these, in latitude 76° 20′, was once, no doubt, an extensive
village. Cairns for the safe deposit of meat stood in long lines,
six or eight in a group; and the huts, built of large rocks, faced
each other, as if disposed on a street or avenue.

The same reasoning which deduces the subsidence of the coast Depression
from the actual base of the Temple of Serapis, proves that the de- of the coast.
pression of the Greenland coast, which I had detected as far north
as Upernavik, is also going on up here. Some of these huts were
washed by the sea or torn away by the ice that had descended

with the tides. The turf, too, a representative of very ancient growth, was cut off even with the water's edge, giving sections two feet thick. I had not noticed before such unmistakable evidence of the depression of this coast: its converse elevation I had observed to the north of Wostenholme Sound. The axis of oscillation must be somewhere in the neighbourhood of latitude 77°.

We reached Cape York on the 21st, after a tortuous but romantic travel through a misty atmosphere. Here the land-leads ceased, with the exception of some small and scarcely-practicable openings near the shore, which were evidently owing to the wind that prevailed for the time. Everything bore proof of the late development of the season. The red snow was a fortnight behind its time. A fast floe extended with numerous tongues far out to the south and east. The only question was between a new rest, for the shore ices to open, or a desertion of the coast and a trial of the open water to the west.

We sent off a detachment to see whether the Esquimaux might not be passing the summer at Episok, behind the glacier of Cape Imalik, and began an inventory of our stock on hand. I give the result :—

Dried lumme	195 birds.	
Pork-slush	112 pounds.	
Flour	50	"
Indian meal	50	"
Meat-biscuit	80	"
Bread	348	"

Six hundred and forty pounds of provision, all told, exclusive of our dried birds, or some thirty-six pounds a man. Tom Hickey found a turf, something like his native peat, which we thought might help to boil our kettle; and with the aid of this our fuel-account stood thus :—

Turf, for two boilings a day	7 days	
Two sledge-runners	6	"
Spare oars, sledges, and an empty cask	4	"

Seventeen days in all; not counting, however, the *Red Boat* which would add something, and our emptied provision-bags, which might carry on the estimate to about three weeks.

The return of the party from Imalik gave us no reason to hesitate. The Esquimaux had not been there for several years. There were no birds in the neighbourhood.

I climbed the rocks a second time with Mr. M'Gary, and took CHAPTER LX. a careful survey of the ice with my glass. The "fast," as the whalers call the immovable shore-ice, could be seen in a nearly View from the rocks. unbroken sweep, passing by Bushnell's Island, and joining the coast not far from where I stood. The outside floes were large, and had evidently been not long broken; but it cheered my heart to see that there was one well-defined lead which followed the main floe until it lost itself to seaward.

I called my officers together, explained to them the motives Prepara- tions for re-em- barking. which governed me, and prepared to re-embark. The boats were hauled up, examined carefully, and, as far as our means permitted, repaired. The *Red Eric* was stripped of her outfit and cargo, to be broken up for fuel when the occasion should come. A large beacon-cairn was built on an eminence, open to view from the south and west; and a red flannel shirt, spared with some reluctance, was hoisted as a pennant to draw attention to the spot. Here I deposited a succinct record of our condition and purposes, and then directed our course south by west into the ice-fields.

By degrees the ice through which we were moving became more and more impacted; and it sometimes required all our ice-knowledge to determine whether a particular lead was practicable or not. The irregularities of the surface, broken by hummocks, and occasionally by larger masses, made it difficult to see far ahead; besides which, we were often embarrassed by the fogs. I was Losing the way. awakened one evening from a weary sleep in my fox-skins, to discover that we had fairly lost our way. The officer at the helm of the leading boat, misled by the irregular shape of a large iceberg that crossed his track, had lost the main lead some time before, and was steering shoreward far out of the true course. The little canal in which he had locked us was hardly two boats'-lengths across, and lost itself not far off in a feeble zigzag both behind and before us: it was evidently closing, and we could not retreat.

Without apprising the men of our misadventure, I ordered the A camp on the ice. boats hauled up, and, under pretence of drying the clothing and stores, made a camp on the ice. A few hours after, the weather cleared enough for the first time to allow a view of the distance, and M'Gary and myself climbed a berg some three hundred feet high for the purpose. It was truly fearful: we were deep in the

28

CHAPTER
LX.

A fearful
prospect.

The
sledges
again.

Reckoning
supplies

Afloat once
more.

recesses of the bay, surrounded on all sides by stupendous icebergs and tangled floe-pieces. My sturdy second officer, not naturally impressible, and long accustomed to the vicissitudes of whaling life, shed tears at the prospect.

There was but one thing to be done : cost what it might, we must harness our sledges again and retrace our way to the westward. One sledge had been already used for firewood; the *Red Eric*, to which it had belonged, was now cut up, and her light cedar planking laid upon the floor of the other boats ; and we went to work with the rue-raddies as in the olden time. It was not till the third toilsome day was well spent that we reached the berg which had bewildered our helmsman. We hauled over its tongue, and joyously embarked again upon a free lead, with a fine breeze from the north.

Our little squadron was now reduced to two boats. The land to the northward was no longer visible; and whenever I left the margin of the "fast" to avoid its deep sinuosities, I was obliged to trust entirely to the compass. We had at least eight days' allowance of fuel on board ; but our provisions were running very low, and we met few birds, and failed to secure any larger game. We saw several large seals upon the ice, but they were too watchful for us ; and on two occasions we came upon the walrus sleeping, —once within actual lance-thrust ; but the animal charged in the teeth of his assailant and made good his retreat.

On the 28th I instituted a quiet review of the state of things before us. Our draft on the stores we had laid in at Providence Halt had been limited for some days to three raw eggs and two breasts of birds a day ; but we had a small ration of bread-dust besides ; and when we halted, as we did regularly for meals, our fuel allowed us to indulge lavishly in the great panacea of Arctic travel, tea. The men's strength was waning under this restricted diet ; but a careful reckoning up of our remaining supplies proved to me now that even this was more than we could afford ourselves without an undue reliance on the fortunes of the hunt. Our next land was to be Cape Shackleton, one of the most prolific bird-colonies of the coast, which we were all looking to, much as sailors nearing home in their boats after disaster and short allowance at sea. ' But, meting out our stores through the number of days that must elapse before we could expect to share its hospitable welcome,

I found that five ounces of bread-dust, four of tallow, and three of bird-meat, must from this time form our daily ration.

So far we had generally coasted the fast ice : it had given us an occasional resting-place and refuge, and we were able sometimes to re-inforce our stores of provisions by our guns. But it made our progress tediously slow, and our stock of small-shot was so nearly exhausted that I was convinced our safety depended on an increase of speed. I determined to try the more open sea.

For the first two days the experiment was a failure. We were surrounded by heavy fogs ; a south-west wind brought the outside pack upon us and obliged us to haul up on the drifting ice. We were thus carried to the northward, and lost about twenty miles. My party, much overworked, felt despondingly the want of the protection of the land-floes.

Nevertheless, I held to my purpose, steering S.S.W. as nearly as the leads would admit, and looking constantly for the thinning out of the pack that hangs around the western water.

Although the low diet and exposure to wet had again reduced our party, there was no apparent relaxation of energy ; and it was not until some days later that I found their strength seriously giving way.

It is a little curious that the effect of a short allowance of food does not show itself in hunger. The first symptom is a loss of power, often so imperceptibly brought on that it becomes evident only by an accident. I well remember our look of blank amazement as, one day, the order being given to haul the *Hope* over a tongue of ice, we found that she would not budge. At first I thought it was owing to the wetness of the snow-covered surface in which her runners were ; but, as there was a heavy gale blowing outside, and I was extremely anxious to get her on to a larger floe to prevent being drifted off, I lightened her cargo and set both crews upon her. In the land of promise off Crimson Cliffs, such a force would have trundled her like a wheelbarrow : we could almost have borne her upon our backs. Now, with incessant labour and standing-hauls, she moved at a snail's pace.

The *Faith* was left behind, and barely escaped destruction. The outside pressure cleft the floe asunder, and we saw our best boat, with all our stores, drifting rapidly away from us. The sight produced an almost hysterical impression upon our party. Two days of want of bread, I am sure, would have destroyed us ; and we had now left us but eight pounds of shot in all.   To launch the *Hope* again, and rescue her comrade or share her fortunes, would have been the instinct of other circumstances ; but it was out of the question now.   Happily, before we had time to ponder our loss, a flat cake of ice eddied round near the floe we were upon ; M'Gary and myself sprang to it at the moment, and succeeded in floating it across the chasm in time to secure her.   The rest of the crew rejoined her by only scrambling over the crushed ice as we brought her in at the hummock-lines.

CHAPTER LXI.

THE SEAL! THE SEAL!—THE FESTIVAL—TERRA FIRMA—PAUL ZACHARIAS
—THE FRAULEIN FLAISCHER—THE NEWS—AT THE SETTLEMENTS—THE
WELCOME.

THINGS grew worse and worse with us: the old difficulty of breathing came back again, and our feet swelled to such an extent that we were obliged to cut open our canvas boots. But the symptom which gave me most uneasiness was our inability to sleep. A form of low fever which hung by us when at work had been kept down by the thoroughness of our daily rest; all my hopes of escape were in the refreshing influences of the halt. *(margin: CHAPTER LXI. Illness and suffering.)*

It must be remembered that we were now in the open bay, in the full line of the great ice-drift to the Atlantic, and in boats so frail and unseaworthy as to require constant baling to keep them afloat.

It was at this crisis of our fortunes that we saw a large seal floating—as is the custom of these animals—on a small patch of ice, and seemingly asleep. It was an ussuk, and so large that I at first mistook it for a walrus. Signal was made for the *Hope* to follow astern, and, trembling with anxiety, we prepared to crawl down upon him. *(margin: A seal in sight.)*

Petersen, with the large English rifle, was stationed in the bow, and stockings were drawn over the oars as mufflers. As we neared the animal, our excitement became so intense that the men could hardly keep stroke. I had a set of signals for such occasions, which spared us the noise of the voice; and when about three hundred yards off, the oars were taken in, and we moved on in deep silence with a single scull astern. *(margin: Intense excitement.)*

He was not asleep, for he reared his head when we were almost within rifle-shot; and to this day I can remember the hard, careworn, almost despairing expression of the men's thin faces as they saw him move: their lives depended on his capture. *(margin: Life at stake.)*

I depressed my hand nervously, as a signal for Petersen to fire. M'Gary hung upon his oar, and the boat, slowly but noiselessly

CHAPTER
LXI.

Paralysed
by anxiety.

sagging ahead, seemed to me without certain range. Looking at
Petersen, I saw that the poor fellow was paralyzed by his anxiety,
trying vainly to obtain a rest for his gun against the cut-water of
the boat. The seal rose on his four-flippers, gazed at us for a
moment with frightened curiosity, and coiled himself for a plunge.
At that instant, simultaneously with the crack of our rifle, he relaxed his long length on the ice, and, at the very brink of the
water, his head fell helpless to one side.

I would have ordered another shot, but no discipline could have
controlled the men. With a wild yell, each vociferating according
to his own impulse, they urged both boats upon the floes. A
Seizing
the prize.
crowd of hands seized the seal and bore him up to safer ice. The
men seemed half crazy; I had not realized how much we were reduced by absolute famine. They ran over the floe, crying and
laughing, and brandishing their knives. It was not five minutes
before every man was sucking his bloody fingers or mouthing long
strips of raw blubber.

Not an ounce of this seal was lost. The intestines found their
way into the soup-kettles without any observance of the prelimin-
The feast.
ary home-processes. The cartilaginous parts of the fore-flippers were
cut off in the *mêlée*, and passed round to be chewed upon ; and
even the liver, warm and raw as it was, bade fair to be eaten before
it had seen the pot. That night, on the large halting-floe, to
which, in contempt of the dangers of drifting, we happy men had
hauled our boats, two entire planks of the *Red Eric* were devoted
to a grand cooking-fire, and we enjoyed a rare and savage feast.

This was our last experience of the disagreeable effects of
hunger. In the words of George Stephenson, " The charm was
The poor
dogs
saved.
broken, and the dogs were safe." The dogs I have said little
about, for none of us liked to think of them. The poor creatures,
Toodla and Whitey, had been taken with us as last resources
against starvation. They were, as M'Gary worded it, " meat on
the hoof," and " able to carry their own fat over the floes." Once,
near Weary Man's Rest, I had been on the point of killing them ;
but they had been the leaders of our winter's team, and we could
not bear the sacrifice.

I need not detail our journey any further. Within a day or two
we shot another seal, and from that time forward had a full supply of food.

On the 1st of August we sighted the Devil's Thumb, and were
again among the familiar localities of the whalers' battling-ground.
The bay was quite open, and we had been making casting for two
days before.   We were soon among the Duck Islands, and, passing
to the south of Cape Shackleton, prepared to land.

"Terra firma! Terra firma!"   How very pleasant it was to look
upon, and with what a tingle of excited thankfulness we drew near
it!   A little time to seek a cove among the wrinkled hills, a little
time to exchange congratulations, and then our battered boats
were hauled high and dry upon the rocks, and our party, with
hearts full of our deliverance, lay down to rest.

And now, with the apparent certainty of reaching our homes,
came that nervous apprehension which follows upon hope long deferred.   I could not trust myself to take the outside passage, but
timidly sought the quiet-water channels running deep into the
archipelago which forms a sort of labyrinth along the coast.

Thus it was that at one of our sleeping-halts upon the rocks—for
we still adhered to the old routine—Petersen awoke me with a
story.   He had just seen and recognised a native, who, in his frail
kayak, was evidently seeking eider-down among the islands.   The
man had once been an inmate of his family.   "Paul Zacharias,
don't you know me?   I'm Carl Petersen!"   "No," said the man;
"his wife says he's dead;" and, with a stolid expression of wonder,
he stared for a moment at the long beard that loomed at him
through the fog, and paddled away with all the energy of fright.

Two days after this, a mist had settled down upon the islands
which embayed us, and when it lifted we found ourselves rowing,
in lazy time, under the shadow of Karkamoot.   Just then a familiar sound came to us over the water.   We had often listened to
the screeching of the gulls or the bark of the fox, and mistaken it
for the "Huk" of the Esquimaux; but this had about it an inflec-
tion not to be mistaken, for it died away in the familar cadence of
a "halloo."

"Listen, Petersen! oars, men!"   "What is it?"—and he
listened quietly at first, and then, trembling, said, in a half whisper,
"Dannemarkers!"

I remember this, the first tone of Christian voice which had
greeted our return to the world.   How we all stood up and peered
into the distant nooks; and how the cry came to us again, just as

having seen nothing, we were doubting whether the whole was
not a dream; and then how, with long sweeps, the white ash
cracking under the spring of the rowers, we stood for the cape that
the sound proceeded from, and how nervously we scanned the
green spots which our experience, grown now into instinct, told us
would be the likely camping-ground of wayfarers.

By-and-by—for we must have been pulling a good half hour—
the single mast of a small shallop showed itself; and Petersen, who
had been very quiet and grave, burst out into an incoherent fit of
crying, only relieved by broken exclamations of mingled Danish
and English. " 'Tis the Upernavik oil-boat ! The Fraulein Flaischer ! Carlie Mossyn, the assistant cooper, must be on his road to
Kingatok for blubber. The *Mariane* (the one annual ship) has
come, and Carlie Mossyn—" and here he did it all over again,
gulping down his words and wringing his hands.

It was Carlie Mossyn, sure enough. The quiet routine of a
Danish settlement is the same year after year, and Petersen had
hit upon the exact state of things. The *Mariane* was at Proven,
and Carlie Mossyn had come up in the Fraulein Flaischer to get
the year's supply of blubber from Kingatok.

Here we first got our cloudy vague idea of what had passed in
the big world during our absence. The friction of its fierce rotation had not much disturbed this little outpost of civilization, and
we thought it a sort of blunder as he told us that France and England were leagued with the Mussulman against the Greek Church.
He was a good Lutheran, this assistant cooper, and all news with
him had a theological complexion.

"What of America, eh, Petersen?"—and we all looked, waiting
for him to interpret the answer.

"America?" said Carlie; "we don't know much of that country
here, for they have no whalers on the coast; but a steamer and a
barque passed up a fortnight ago, and have gone out into the ice
to seek your party."

How gently all the lore of this man oozed out of him ! he seemed
an oracle, as, with hot-tingling fingers pressed against the gunwale
of the boat, we listened to his words. " Sebastopol ain't taken."
Where and what was Sebastopol?

But " Sir John Franklin?" There we were at home again,—
our own delusive little speciality rose uppermost. Franklin's

party, or traces of the dead which represented it, had been found CHAPTER
nearly a thousand miles to the south of where we had been search- LXI.
ing for them.   He knew it ; for the priest (Pastor Kraag) had a
German newspaper which told all about it.   And so we "out oars"
again, and rowed into the fogs.

Another sleeping-halt has passed, and we have all washed clean Preparing
at the fresh-water basins and furbished up our ragged furs and to land.
woollens.   Kasarsoak, the snow top of Sanderson's Hope, shows
itself above the mists, and we hear the yelling of the dogs.   Petersen had been foreman of the settlement, and he calls my attention,
with a sort of pride, to the tolling of the workmen's bell.   It is
six o'clock.   We are nearing the end of our trials.   Can it be a
dream ?—

We hugged the land by the big harbour, turned the corner by The boats
the old brew-house, and in the midst of a crowd of children, hauled up.
hauled our boats for the last time upon the rocks.

For eighty-four days we had lived in the open air.   Our habits
were hard and weather-worn.   We could not remain within the
four walls of a house without a distressing sense of suffocation.
But we drank coffee that night before many a hospitable threshold,
and listened again and again to the hymn of welcome, which, sung A hymn of
by many voices, greeted our deliverance. welcome.

GREENLANDER'S CANOE.

CONCLUSION.

We received all manner of kindness from the Danes of Upernavik. The residents of this distant settlement are dependent for their supplies on the annual trading-ship of the colonies, and they of course could not minister to our many necessities without much personal inconvenience. But they fitted up a loft for our reception, and shared their stores with us in liberal Christian charity.

They gave us many details of the expeditions in search of Sir John Franklin, and added the painful news that my gallant friend and comrade, Bellot, had perished in a second crusade to save him. We knew each other by many common sympathies: I had divided with him the hazards of mutual rescue among the ice-fields ; and his last letter to me, just before I left New York, promised me the hope that we were to meet again in Baffin's Bay, and that he would unite himself with our party as a volunteer. The French service never lost a more chivalrous spirit.

The Danish vessel was not ready for her homeward journey till the 4th of September ; but the interval was well spent in regaining health and gradually accustoming ourselves to in-door life and habits. It is a fact, which the physiologist will not find it difficult to reconcile with established theories, that we were all more prostrated by the repose and comfort of our new condition than we had been by nearly three months of constant exposure and effort.

On the 6th I left Upernavik, with all our party, in the *Mariane*, a stanch but antiquated little barque, under the command of Captain Ammondson, a fine representative of the true-hearted and skilful seamen of his nation, who promised to drop us at the Shetland Islands. Our little boat, the *Faith*, which was regarded by all of us as a precious relic, took passage along with us. Except the furs on our backs, and the documents that recorded our labours and our trials, it was all we brought back of the *Advance* and her fortunes.

On the 11th we arrived at Godhavn, the inspectorate of North

Greenland, and had a characteristic welcome from my excellent
friend, Mr. Olrik. The *Mariane* had stopped only to discharge a
few stores and receive her papers of clearance; but her departure
was held back to the latest moment, in hopes of receiving news of
Captain Hartstene's squadron, which had not been heard of since
the 21st of July.

We were upon the eve of setting out, however, when the look-
out man at the hill-top announced a steamer in the distance. It
drew near, with a barque in tow, and we soon recognised the stars
and stripes of our own country. The *Faith* was lowered for the
last time into the water, and the little flag which had floated so
near the poles of both hemispheres opened once more to the breeze.
With Brooks at the tiller and Mr. Olrik at my side, followed by
all the boats of the settlement, we went out to meet them.

Not even after the death of the usuk did our men lay to their
oars more heartily. We neared the squadron and the gallant men
that had come out to seek us; we could see the scars which their
own ice-battles had impressed on the vessels; we knew the gold
lace of the officers' cap-bands, and discerned the groups who, glass
in hand, were evidently regarding us.

Presently we were alongside. An officer, whom I shall ever
remember as a cherished friend, Captain Hartstene, hailed a little
man in a ragged flannel shirt, "Is that Dr. Kane?" and with the
"Yes!" that followed, the rigging was manned by our countrymen,
and cheers welcomed us back to the social world of love which
they represented.

THE FAITH,
Now at the store of Messrs. CHILDS & PETERSON, *124 Arch Street, Philadelphia.*

GLOSSARY OF ARCTIC TERMS.

Bay-ice, ice of recent formation, so called because forming most readily in bays and sheltered spots.

Berg (see *Iceberg*).

Beset, so enclosed by floating ice as to be unable to navigate.

Bight, an indentation.

Blasting, breaking the ice by gunpowder introduced in canisters.

Blink (see *Ice-blink*).

Bore, to force through loose or recent ice by sails or steam.

Brash, ice broken up into small fragments.

Calf, detached masses from berg or glacier, rising suddenly to the surface.

Crow's nest, a look-out place attached to the top-gallant-masthead.

Dock, an opening in the ice, artificial or natural, offering protection.

Drift-ice, detached ice in motion.

Field-ice, an extensive surface of floating ice.

Fiord, an abrupt opening in the coast-line, admitting the sea.

Fire-hole, a well dug in the ice as a safeguard in case of fire.

Floe, a detached portion of a field.

Glacier, a mass of ice derived from the atmosphere, sometimes abutting upon the sea.

Hummocks, ridges of broken ice formed by collision of fields.

Ice-anchor, a hook or grapnel adapted to take hold upon ice.

Ice-belt, a continued margin of ice, which in high northern latitudes adheres to the coast above the ordinary level of the sea.

Iceberg, a large floating mass of ice detached from a glacier.

Ice-blink, a peculiar appearance of the atmosphere over distant ice.

Ice-chisel, a long chisel for cutting holes in ice.

Ice-face, the abutting face of the ice-belt.

Ice-foot, the Danish name for the limited ice-belt of the more southern coast.

Ice-hook, a small ice-anchor.

Ice-raft, ice, whether field, floe, or detached belt, transporting foreign matter.

Ice-table, a flat surface of ice.

Land ice, floes or fields adhering to the coast, or included between headlands.
Lane or *lead*, a navigable opening in the ice.

Nip, the condition of a vessel pressed upon by the ice on both sides.

Old ice, ice of more than a season's growth.

Pack, a large area of floating ices driven together more or less closely.
Polynia, a Russian term for an open-water space.

Rue-raddy, a shoulder-belt to drag by.

Tide-hole, a well sunk in the ice for the purpose of observing tides.
Tracking, towing along a margin of ice.

Water-sky, a peculiar appearance of the sky over open water.

Young ice, ice formed before the setting in of winter; recent ice.